# The SERPENT DREAMER

BOOKS BY CECELIA HOLLAND

*The Serpent Dreamer*
*The Witches' Kitchen*
*The Soul Thief*
*The Angel and the Sword*
*Lily Nevada*
*An Ordinary Woman*
*Railroad Schemes*
*Valley of the Kings*
*Jerusalem*
*Pacific Street*
*The Bear Flag*
*The Lords of Vaumartin*
*Pillar of the Sky*
*The Belt of Gold*
*The Sea Beggars*
*Home Ground*
*City of God*
*Two Ravens*
*Floating Worlds*
*Great Maria*
*The Death of Attila*
*The Earl*
*Antichrist*
*Until the Sun Falls*
*The Kings in Winter*
*Rakossy*
*The Firedrake*

FOR CHILDREN

*The King's Road*
*Ghost on the Steppe*

A TOM DOHERTY ASSOCIATES BOOK
*New York*

# The SERPENT DREAMER



CECELIA HOLLAND

This is a work of fiction. All the characters and events portrayed in this novel are either fictitious or are used fictitiously.

THE SERPENT DREAMER



This book is printed on acid-free paper.

Edited by Beth Meacham

A Forge Book
Published by Tom Doherty Associates, LLC
175 Fifth Avenue
New York, NY 10010

www.tor.com



Library of Congress Cataloging-in-Publication Data

Holland, Cecelia, 1943–
The serpent dreamer / Cecelia Holland.— 1st ed.
p. cm.
"A Tom Doherty Associates book."
ISBN-10: 0-765-30557-7
ISBN-13: 978-0-765-30557-2
I. Title.

PS3558.O348S47 2005
813'.54—dc22

2005053043

First Edition: December 2005

Printed in the United States of America

0 9 8 7 6 5 4 3 2 1

For JACOB

*corban redux*

# PROLOGUE

So they're on the Turtle Island. For Mav, whose mad mind has no boundaries, time is just another place, and this place just another time in the seamless flow of what she knows is real. By the Christian calendar, which Corban has lost track of anyway, and which pertains an ocean away, it's the year 993. To Miska, who knows nothing but his time and his place, it is the war season, summer. For his people, the Wolves, the men in their lodges, the women in their gardens, the medicine woman Epashti, and the child Ahanton, it is the time of Miska's being sachem, which began ten summers ago when he drove the white men into the sea.

All the white men but Corban Loosestrife, who is still here. Who is still trying to break his father's curse to find some way to go home.

# Wolf

# CHAPTER ONE

Before he reached the gate into the village Corban could see that the men had come back. His steps slowed. The gate opened through the wall of upright stakes that enclosed the stand of lodges and huts against the riverbank; vines and brambles grew up all over the wall and almost hid the way in, but he could see the man dozing in the shadow. When the men were gone the women didn't even bother putting someone to guard the gate but Miska always kept his sentries out.

Corban shifted the squirrel carcasses from one hand to the other, thinking this over. During the winter there was some kind of truce between him and Miska, but the warm time was different. He could stay back in the forest, out of their way, let them ignore him, until they left again. Very likely they had brought meat back with them and nobody needed what he had. Nonetheless the idea rankled, letting Miska frighten him off, not even by doing anything but simply by being here, and Epashti liked squirrel meat, and he had not seen the boys in a while. He went on to the gate, slipping quietly past the guard, who had propped himself up in the cool of the shadows.

As he went by, the guard opened his eyes, one of the lodge men, sharp-witted and glib-tongued. Corban didn't know his name, and the Wolf watched Corban go by without speaking.

Inside the gate Corban turned at once to the right side of the village, where Mother Eonta had her lodge. Across from Eonta's doorway, against the wall, was a little hut, which had been deserted when Corban came, and which he had taken over in the first winter. As he went that way he looked quickly toward the big lodge just opposite, right by the gate, which was Miska's. The doors were shut and nobody stood around there so he knew Miska was not there.

The village was busy and loud. Looking toward the river, through the space between the women's lodges, he could see people moving all around the big oak tree, where they danced and held their councils. As he went along he could hear the women inside Eonta's lodge, their voices piercing through the bark walls, and the wailings and shoutings and shrieks of the children. When he reached his little hut, Epashti was there, sitting on the ground in front of the door, with the baby in her arms.

Corban hung back a moment, his tongue locked; he had been out in the woods most of the spring and the new language had gotten hard again. It stirred him to see her there, with his child at her breast. Then she raised her eyes and smiled at him. He sat down beside her and laid the squirrels down between them, and made a sign that they were for her. For a long time, before he learned her language, they had spoken almost completely with their hands.

She said, "So you are back, husband, and with good meat. I'm glad to see you." She tipped her face forward, and he leaned toward her and pressed his cheek against hers, as her people did, and then turned his head and kissed her mouth. She laughed at that, surprised as always. The Wolves did not kiss much. He sat back, and put his hand on the baby's head.

"He's bigger." The baby was almost a year old, with a mass of black hair, a short straight nose, long arms and legs.

"He's a strong boy, like his father," she said.

"Let me hold him." He reached in to take the baby, who was asleep. As he did, the back of his hand slid down against her breast, and his body tingled. "Where is Finn?"

"With Kalu, I guess." Kalu was her own son, got before she and Corban were together. She let him take the baby from her; she pulled the front of her dress over the full moon of her breast. Her face settled. She looked away, over his shoulder, toward the center of the village. "Miska is coming."

Corban could hear something going on, over in the center of the village. He kept his back to everything and looked down into the baby's face, the tight little puckered mouth, the eyelids fine as shell. More than anything else his children here comforted him. "Did you name him?"

"No one wants to name him that," she said. She was still staring off toward the center of the village.

"I want it," Corban said. "Aengus. Aengus." Behind him, in the village, he could hear people shouting another name. He turned around, the baby in his arms, to face Miska.

The sachem was just coming up from the river, where he usually spent the mornings when he was in the village. As he walked, there stirred around him the steady ripple of interest that followed him everywhere. Everybody here knew every move that Miska made; whenever he was around they watched him constantly and minutely. He ignored this. The center of everyone's eye, he went around almost naked, only a squirrel fur to protect his tender parts. His black hair hung down like a pelt over his shoulders. Today he had painted his face with black marks like a wolf's mask. As he walked up through the village the voices of his people followed him, speaking his name fondly into the air, kissing sweet, strung with endearments. Corban glanced around at Epashti, standing just behind him, and she came up and took the baby from him.

"Talla-Miska."

"Miska-Tonanda, sha-Miska-ma—"

Thunder-Miska, mighty-Miska, big-stalk-Miska. The women all courted him, in the open and in the shadows. Epashti said, "Maybe you should go."

"I'm not going anywhere," Corban said.

From beneath the oak tree a crowd of the men called out, flirtatious as the women.

"Haka-Miska—"

Fighter-Miska. Killer-Miska.

Miska acknowledged none of it, did not stop beneath the oak tree, but kept walking up through the village, coming straight toward Corban. Corban folded his arms over his chest and set himself. The scar along the side of his face gave an electric twinge into his jaw. In Eonta's great lodge a few steps away the women were laughing and singing back and forth. He smelled the ashy smell of banked fires, the aroma of a toasted bean cake.

Miska walked up past the curve of Eonta's lodge, and the men from the oak tree followed in a crowd on his heels. Corban's fists were clenched; he made himself open them. He knew if he ran or jumped first, he was done. Miska walked up to him so close their chests touched. They stood face to face, Miska a few fingers taller; their eyes met. The other men gathered all around them. Corban held fast, thinking if they attacked him he would leap on Miska, tooth and claw. In the black pits of the sachem's face he saw the will rising to strike, and thought he would die, but take Miska also, at least hurt him, and then Miska's gaze flattened, and his eyelids drooped, as if he wanted to hide something.

He waved his hand, and the other men went off, disappearing like smoke into the air. Miska moved a little, turning aside, and said, "Come with me, rodent."

"Call me by my name and I will," Corban said.

Miska shifted his weight, looking at him over his shoulder. Corban watched him steadily, his back set, and his fists clenched again. Miska sniffed at him down his nose.

"Come, then, Corban. Rodent. Come." He moved off, toward the big lodge, by the gate.

Epashti came up beside Corban, the baby slung against her shoulder. "What are you doing? You're not going there with him."

"He wants something," Corban said. "I'll be back."

"Ah," she said. "You are not a Wolf."

He laughed. He patted her cheek and went away off toward the sachem's lodge, on the far side of the gate.

Miska kept this one house all to himself, although it was one of the biggest longhouses in the village, because no one could go in or out of the village without his knowledge. In the short side that faced toward the gate were two doors, one tall enough that

Miska could walk through without stooping, and one much shorter, that made everybody else crouch down. Corban went in through the short door. When he straightened on the other side the sachem was already standing at the far end of the long dim room, taking something down from the wall.

Corban stood looking around. The long elm-bark walls were laid in sheets over rows of saplings, which bent together overhead to form the roof, and under this expanded arch the space went dimly away from him like a cave. Unlike most longhouses, this one had no sleeping apartments along the sides, no line of hearths down the middle. The floor was pounded flat and swept clean, and there was only one apartment, at the far end, and only one hearth, banked and smokeless. The house was far larger than Corban's but empty and quiet. It smelled like no other longhouse he had ever been in, cold, and still, and bitter.

The walls leaked, and the air moved. From the arched ceiling, in rows and rows, there hung thin banners of white and purple beads, cut and smoothed out of clam shells and strung together in complicated patterns, and they shifted and stirred in the drafts with a sound like whispering. Corban knew these were the pledges of other villages, begging Miska for his protection and promising him certain gifts every year. They reminded him of a Viking fahrman's tally sticks. Every year these banners of beads increased, and every year more gifts streamed in through the gate.

Yet this house was empty. Miska kept nothing that came to him, but gave it all away to his people; Epashti had told Corban that often in the evening the people saw their sachem going to one longhouse or another and begging food from hearth to hearth. He kept this huge bare longhouse to himself, he required that they obey him instantly, he allowed no word of argument from anybody, but in return he gave them everything. Corban took his eyes from the Miska's house, and looked toward Miska himself, who was turning toward him, a pipe in one hand, and a little pouch in the other.

Miska said, "You should come to hunt with me, rodent." He

had seen Corban staring at the bead tallies. He gestured toward his banked hearth with the pipe. "Go bring me a coal."

Corban instead untied the corner of his cloak, and took out his tinderbox. Miska grunted. They sat down by the banked hearth, and Corban made fire in the tinderbox and then lit the pipe. Miska's eyes followed his hands with the tool.

"Maybe," Corban said, putting the tinderbox back in his cloak, "you should hunt with me, Miska."

The sachem grimaced. "What you hunt I have no taste for."

He took a long pull on the pipe. Corban wondered what this peace between them was made of, considered what they had in common, and guessed. Miska held the pipe out to him and he inhaled. The sharp, flavorful herbsmoke made his head whirl.

Miska had the pouch still in his hand, and now he shook something out of it. "What is this?"

Surprised, Corban took the thing, small and cool and smooth in his palm. Even inside, in the shadows, the metal gave off a smooth evil glamor. He turned it over in his fingers, studying the detail. "It's a bauble, see, to hang from a cord around someone's neck." He rubbed his finger over the loop on the top of the thing. The image was fine and subtle, and very strange. Tiny rings hung from the ears and the hair was all gathered up on top like a tree. "It must be a man's head, but I've never seen anybody with a head like that. It's made out of gold."

He knew no word for that in the Wolf-tongue, and so said it in dansker. Then, from a deeper well, he found the word in Irish.

Miska frowned at him, his eyes sharp. He took the little gold head back and studied it again, sniffed it, put his teeth to it.

"Where did you get it?" Corban said.

Miska folded his hand over the little gold head. "Someone brought it to me. From the west." He looked away across the house. His voice went flat and even. "You have not seen a man with a head like that—that big nose, and the eyes like that. But I have. Long ago, it was, and I was a child, but I remember them, and what they did." He jerked his gaze around toward Corban. "I want to see—" His breath ran out. He licked his lips. His voice fell to a reverent hush. "Her."

Corban shrugged. This was what he had guessed in the first place. "Go into the forest and wait, that's all I do."

"She will not come to me." Miska beat his fists once on his thighs. His cheeks sucked hollow; Corban saw how it ate at him that he needed Corban for this, that he could not summon her himself—that the one woman he loved paid no heed to him. His eyes lowered. After a moment, he said, "She comes to you."

"She's my sister," Corban said. "We shared the womb." He said the Wolf-word for twins, which was a curse.

Miska looked at him through the corner of his eye. This was old to him. "We kill such babies."

"I know. My people don't." Corban bared his teeth, amused, enjoying having this edge on him. "I will take you. We should take Ahanton also."

"No. She would be frightened."

"Ahanton is afraid of nothing," Corban said. "She should see her mother. We'll go in the evening, before the moon rises." He got to his feet, looking down at Miska sitting on the floor, his head bowed, his hair across his face. "Until then, Tonanda-Miska." He went out of the lodge.

When he crept out of the lodge again into the sunlight the women were going off toward their fields. They went in streams, in their lineages, singing, their tools on their shoulders and their babies slung on their backs. As they went they called to one another. Mother Eonta's family was dancing by him now, tall women who laughed and bounced their breasts at him, and shouted insults across the way to their main rivals, the women of Mother Anapatha's lodge, just now coming up from the river.

"Late—late—late again—" Eonta's daughters and granddaughters picked up the chant, voice on voice, and boomed on the ground with their feet, going out the gate.

From Anapatha's daughters and granddaughters the answering chant, fainter, a little breathless: "Make hurry—Make trouble—Hurry, hurry, come to trouble—"

His house was empty, Epashti gone with the baby and the little boy Finn off to her garden. Kalu, her older son, disdained garden work and with the men here would trail after them. Corban had given Epashti no girls to help her, only Ahanton, who was a daughter to neither of them.

He went down through the village, past the dancing ground, powdery soft, and the fire pit still smoking off the last heat of a celebration from the night before. He was glad he had not been here. He thought he could still smell the stink of burnt flesh and drying blood. Under the overhanging boughs of the big oak tree there was the stake, a pole driven into the ground, old broken cords hanging from it like shreds of bark. He kept his eyes away from it. What happened there made him sick but he could do nothing to stop it, which made him worse than sick, empty-hearted, mind-dulled.

Even Epashti did this. He wiped his hand over his mouth, struggling not to think of it. He went on down toward the riverbank, watching out for the men, and looking for Ahanton.

Most of the time the men of the village were elsewhere, hunting in the great western bison grounds or the closer deer meadows to the east, fishing in the camps upstream and on the narrow lakes in the north, or following Miska in one of his endless sweeps of the country. Now they were all gathered along the riverbank, enjoying the sun, more than twenty of them. He stayed well wide of them, cutting around the far side of Mother Anapatha's longhouse to do so.

The men clustered together in knots, painting themselves, picking through each other's hair, telling stories, eating and gambling. They kept up a steady rumble of talk. They said the women were the talkers but they jabbered just as much. They ignored Corban as he ignored them. Between him and all of them was nothing as sure even as a feud, a lot of blows and anger, cold now, hot again in a moment, at a look from Miska.

Corban went along the river to where it met the wall, and climbed around the end of the wall into the open. The people inside pitched their garbage over the wall here, and the ground just outside smelled bad, a litter of rotten mats and broken pots, nutshells and bean pods, and just beyond, the ditch where the women came out from the village to shit. He circled wide as he could around this place, out along the riverbank.

Beyond the edge of the village, the forest began, and the bank of the river rose up high over the water, held fast in the roots of a line of old trees. The air was still cold here, the boles of the trees hairy with moss, the sky far off above the green crowns. He went along the rank of the old oaks, walking on the ridges of exposed roots, to a place where a tree had fallen, and let in the sunlight down to the water's edge.

The tree had crashed down years before, dragging down its part of the bank and flopping its head into the river, so that a little sandy spit had formed in its shelter upstream. From the top of the bank, Corban looked down on the child Ahanton, sitting on the sandy spit, her head bent, the back of her neck to him.

She was molding something in the mud. Her head was bowed and he could see only her shoulders and back, the knobbed spine like a string of beads under the skin. As always when he saw her he saw his sister in her and his heart went to her. He thought she knew he was there but she made no sign of it. Finally he went on along the bank, to where long usage had worn a gullet of a path to the river's bed, and went down, and walked along the damp shoal and climbed over the fallen tree trunk to where she sat. The damp sand yielded under his feet. The river sang as it went by and the air was rich and moist.

Ahanton gave him a dark look. "Go away."

She was leggy, thin-boned, her hair wild and curly like Mav's, Mav's eyes in the coppery brown of her face. Miska's jaw. Miska's heavy brows. Corban sat on his heels beside her, watching her shape the mud, her hands long and her fingers deft, a woman's skill already in the little girl.

He frowned. She was making something particular, not just a pile of mud, but a carefully edged square, and on it another, smaller square, and on that another, so that they rose into a stepped hill.

He said, "What are you doing, Ahanton?"

She said, "Go away. I don't like you." Then in a flurry of temper she struck at the hill with her hands, and when that only dented what she had made leaned back and kicked it apart with her feet.

He clasped his hands together, still frowning at the shapeless mud. He said, "We're going into the forest to see your mother, and you should come with us."

She pulled impatiently at her hair, her eyes on him. Her lips thrust out. He knew she wanted to order him away again but the mention of her mother held her. In bad temper she kicked at the heap of mud, splattering it, and when he jerked back out of the way, laughed.

"My mother." She put her long narrow feet down flat on the ground and stood up. "I will go. But stay away from me, Corban. I will walk by myself."

"Your father is going also," he said.

"My father." Her face glowed. She leapt forward, her feet dancing. "I will walk with my father." She ran on ahead of him up the path to the riverbank. There she turned and scowled back at him. "I hate you. Why don't you stay gone?" She scrambled up the bank, back toward the village.

# CHAPTER TWO

In the evening, when the gate was shut, Epashti stood by the fence and watched them go out into the forest. Miska went first, tall and lean as bone, and the child danced along beside him, holding to his hand. Then Corban, solid, his square-set shoulders topped with his wild shaggy hair, following after.

The dark was settling over the forest; the air above the fields and meadows was a deep blue, through which spirits moved, and evil vapors, a time when the Bad Twin walked and ruled. She stood there a long while anyway, watching. She ached to see them go, not knowing why.

Her son Kalu, beside her, said, "I wish I could go."

She said, "Yes, I know, you're a fool." But her eyes were fools also, yearning to follow Corban and the others, walking away through the deep blue gloom.

"Mama." He tugged her hand.

"Shhh."

She knew that Corban made his way happily in the forest, day or night, another of the ways he was not like a real human. It was in the village that he suffered.

She thought about when he had first come here. Miska had brought him back from the edge of the world-water, yet from the first it was obvious to everybody that Miska hated him. Easy to see why. The strange creature seemed little more than a beast, a joke of a man, a mistake. Hair covered him, thick and curly, and his skin was washed out of color like fish meat, as if he had been long underwater. His eyes were strange, with light centers, holes where he should have had eyes, seeming empty of any sense. He spoke only a few words and those were garbled. The women decided he was a lump and ignored him. His name was ugly on the tongue, and as close as it came to any real words meant something like witless. They expected him to die, left to take care of himself.

He did not die. The women noticed this. The men tormented him endlessly, whenever they were in the village, but he did not die of that either. When the men left on their endless roaming and fighting he stayed behind and did very well.

At first he hardly came into the village at all but when winter fell he cleared out an abandoned hut near the fence around the village and fixed its walls and began to live there. That this hut was close by Mother Eonta's longhouse was lucky for him, or very clever, since she tolerated no men fighting or shouting around her. The women noticed this also.

He had powers beyond human. He had a small box he used to make fire, and he had a knife with a magic blade. He made a stone-thrower of thongs, which at first they all derided, but soon came to respect. Anyway he was clearly not witless since he paid close heed to the proper ways of life and began to fit into the village. Soon he was making gifts of meat, such as any man who hunted did. Corban gave meat to the poorest, to old blind Kastia who lived in a corner of Mother Eonta's house, and crippled Lasicka, who had been a warrior once, taken a terrible wound, and not died, the worst fate of a man.

Epashti had come on him during that first summer when Corban stayed away from the village. All the women went into the forest sometimes for herbs and barks and stems to make baskets and here and there caught glimpses of him. He asked nothing of them, and he offered them no harm, and they grew used to him. Then, one day, Epashti went far off down the river, to a place where few others ever wandered. There she found a dead porcupine, and while she was making an offering of twigs to the spirit of the porcupine, so that she could take the quills home with her, Kalu wandered off.

He was just starting to walk. She knew he could not have gone far. She went quickly up and down the marshy wood, in among the empty tree trunks, looking, and then calling frantically for him, and then as she came down the path abruptly the strange wild man led the child by the hand out of the trees in front of her.

She screamed, and grabbed Kalu up in her arms, and Corban went away. The child wiggled in her arms, wanting to follow him. Epashti left the porcupine quills behind and fled back to the village.

That night she dreamt that a great porcupine led her child out of the woods to her. She told this dream to no one.

She came out of her lodge one morning, soon after Corban moved into his hut, and found him sitting with Kalu on his lap, the two of them talking gibberish to each other. Corban put the child up onto his feet, when he saw her, and shooed Kalu toward her, and went into his hut.

Her sister Sheanoy said, "What is he teaching him? He'll turn the child into a white demon. We should get the men to kill him, that's what Miska wants, anyway."

Epashti said, "Why doesn't he do it, then?"

They were sitting in her sister's chamber in Eonta's long-house. The men had all gone off days before on one of Miska's raids and the women had the work of the harvest. Sheanoy said, "I don't know. Maybe because of—"

She fell silent, but her eyes sharpened, and with her fingers she made two legs walking in the air. Epashti leaned forward, intense with fresh interest. "Have you seen her?"

"No." Her sister bent to meet her, her eyes shining, and whispered in her ear. "But I heard that Hasei was out by himself hunting and heard someone singing, a strange, high song, like a woman's voice, only he said just hearing it struck him so cold with fear he could hardly draw breath, and he ran all the way back to the camp."

Epashti said, "Hasei loves to make stories." Hasei was her brother, who should have been taking more interest in her sons than he was doing. She pressed her lips together, looking off. She had heard other stories of the Woman Who Walked in the Forest; several people claimed to have seen her, and some claimed to have seen her with Miska. She said, "You think he has something to do with her. Corban." But she had not come with him, Epashti thought. She came earlier, the Forest Woman.

Her sister nodded at her, solemn. "I see the name comes easily to your lips. I've heard—" Sheanoy glanced away again, her face sleek, stroking her secrets. "In the forest, there are glades now full of flowers that were barren rocks before. And she lies there, and with sweet perfumes and songs she lures the men there, one by one—"

"Be quiet," Epashti said sharply. "You know nothing."

"Miska loves her." Her sister watched her steadily. "And he hates the other. Don't be foolish, Epashti. Something is going on here, more than you know. Don't start caring about the wild man. You should get married again anyway."

Her sister went away. Epashti sat in the compartment, musing over what her sister had said, and thinking of the porcupine dream.

Of course her sister was right; this was more than they knew. Corban was not one of them, but surely he was here for some purpose. She thought of the little box that made fire, the magical knife. Someone had given him these special gifts, to help him to some end. He was on some path of power. Through him, somehow, they could all gain some power, if they only knew how, and being the medicine woman, she should be finding that out.

She watched him sitting in the cold sunlight, making himself new boots with his magical knife that cut so true and well. She had no idea how to approach him. He could hardly speak, his tongue formed mostly gibberish still, and of course she had no kinship with him. But the dream of the porcupine lumbering out of the trees stayed always in the back of her mind.

Miska came back soon after that with all the men in a great uproarious gang, singing and dancing about their victory. They had fought over a village somewhere in the east, and driven the people out, burning their houses and carrying off all their new harvests.

They had taken several prisoners, but two of their own had

died in the fighting. The women of the dead men began to cry out for the prisoners, and Miska gave them over. That night two of the prisoners were bound to the stake to give up their lives for the dead.

In the morning Corban stood before Miska's lodge and shouted at him, nothing anybody understood. The people gathered behind him to see what would happen. Miska came out of the lodge and sneered at him, didn't even bother to explain the ceremony, waved him off with disdain.

Corban shouted some more, and Miska struck him, and Corban immediately reached out and struck him back.

From all sides then the men leapt on him, dragged him down and kicked and beat him with their fists, and finally dragged him up, pounded like a deerskin, in front of Miska. Epashti watched this from the edge of the crowd and thought Miska would kill him finally, and some fierce will rose in her to speak out. She bit her lips together. She reminded herself she was nobody, only an herb-woman, and not very good at that. She remembered the porcupine dream. Maybe she had misunderstood. Tears muddled her vision. She saw Miska draw his knife and raise it and in the swimming glossy vision of her tears she thought he looked over at her.

He said something she could not hear, and struck, hard, slashed down, slicing. The men holding Corban screeched and leapt back, and he flopped down on the ground, but he was not dead. Miska's knife had slashed his face open from the temple to the chin. Corban braced himself on one arm, his head hanging, and the blood sheeting down into the dust.

Miska threw the knife down before him, where he could reach it easily. Everybody fell utterly still, even the babies, watching to see if Corban would fight back now. Corban gave a shiver, and pushed himself up and sat with his knees up and his arms over them and his head hanging, and his back to the knife. With a grunt, Miska went away down toward the river. The blood on the ground soaked dark into the pale dust.

The crowd began to stir, puzzled, the men wondering out loud if they should kill the wild man now. Epashti went out of the women and knelt down by Corban and put her arm around his shoulders, and spoke to him, and got him to rise and go off to his house, quickly, before the men decided to do something.

In his lodge where Eonta's closeness would keep the others away she tended his hurts. He was bloody and banged up but nowhere near dead. He began talking, while she staunched the blood running down his face and pressed the edges of the wound together, and although he spoke only a few real words mixed in with his nonsense she began to pick up some sense from it.

She got his shirt off—it was made of a strange hide that rubbed apart into wisps—and cleaned up a scrape on his back, and he said, in some way, "Miska is bad, I came here to get away from Miska."

Describing Miska he used the word for spoiled meat, and she stretched her mind to understand him, and still was unsure. She said, "Then you went strange-footed, Corban, to come here where he is."

"Men like Miska," he said.

Suddenly, forcefully, he spat across the lodge. The wound on his face opened and she got two fingers of the salve out of its pot and slapped it closed again. He stared stonily away from her, rigid with anger. She pulled the remnants of his shirt around him and went out of his lodge, her hands shaky.

Miska was the sachem; spitting at the sachem was spitting on her. She had tried to help him, to draw close to him, and he had spat at her. Now she half-expected Miska to kill him. For the next several days she and the whole village watched to see what would happen.

Yet Miska did nothing. Corban healed, the great wound closing to a livid scar that slowly disappeared into the tangled black curly hair that covered his face.

Then a few days after this Epashti was coming out of Gallara's lodge, where she had been tending the older women's fall-time aches and pains, and she heard a loud outcry down by the gate. She turned to see, and the Woman Who Walked in the Forest came into the village.

She seemed just a woman, like any of them, except that her skin was as pale and clear as moonlight, her eyes shed light like stars, and her feet walked mostly in the air. As she came into the village everyone stopped and stood still and watched her. Even the children were silent. Some of the women sank down onto their knees on the ground.

She walked up through the village, past Epashti, toward the council tree. In her arms she carried a bundle wrapped in a white deerskin. As she went by the women began to chant the birthing song; they knew right away what she held. Epashti's lips parted also and the song came forth unbidden as the Forest Woman passed. And now before her, under the council tree, there stood Miska.

The Woman of the Forest went straight up to Miska, holding the child in her arms. He stood shining before her. Epashti had never seen such a light in his face as when he looked at her. She opened the white deerskin and showed him the baby, and all the people crowded a little closer, to see that it was a girl child, and all saw that this was his child, and there went up a great sigh from every throat.

But then the Woman stepped back, and turned, and called a name, and they all shuddered, astonished, because it was Corban's name. Now they saw that he had come up through the edge of the crowd toward her. The stunned people all turned to stare at him but he paid no heed to them.

He said something to her, some word no one knew. A great smile broke upon his face, and she went to him with laughter, and he put his arm around her, as if she were a mortal woman.

Then looking at them, they all saw that they had the same face. She was made of wind and starlight, and he of flesh and bone, but they were the same, brother and sister.

She put the child into his arms, and smiled up into his face, and laid her head a moment on his shoulder. Then she turned and walked out of the village, and outside the gate, some said afterward, she rose into the air, and flew away.

Corban took the baby up in his arms, with all of them standing there staring at him, and Miska watching, for once helpless, his hands at his sides useless. The baby began to wail. Then Epashti felt her limbs unlock, and her mind quicken, and she went up and took the baby from Corban, and put her to the breast. Kalu was still nursing a little and so there was milk in Epashti's breast.

Miska came then, and stood leaning over them, saying, "I will call her Ahanton; she is my daughter. Care for her, then, Epashti, and this one too." And he went away, but after that everybody understood why he could not do anything about Corban, and why he hated him.

So Epashti moved into Corban's lodge to nurse the little girl. It was best to stay there, she told everybody, since the Woman had clearly meant the child to be there. They should all come there to find Epashti to help them with their coughs and hurts and birthings. They grumbled but they needed her; they came.

The baby thrived at her breast. Between her and Corban something else throve also. She taught him much speech, and she slept in his blankets. By the spring, she was growing round with a baby of her own.

Eonta summoned her, sat her down in the vast dim messy compartment at the head of the longhouse, thumped her belly, and said, "This baby, now. How has it gotten there?"

Epashti had to laugh, and she covered her mouth with her hand, out of respect for her grandmother. "What happens," she said.

Eonta's eyebrows rose. "Are you married, then? How am I to speak of this child?"

Her face was round like the moon; everybody fed her, everybody told her all their secrets, everybody was hers, in some connection, sister, grandchild, niece or nephew, second cousin on the father's side, wife's brother's son's nephew; Eonta like a spider sat at the heart of the web of the people.

Gazing on the broad, mild face, Epashti felt no fear. She had known this would come, and was ready. She said, "Have you not taken meat from him, Grandmother? And what of Ahanton? Who dares tell me to give her up?"

Her grandmother said, "He is not one of us. How do you know what you bring in among us?"

"I don't," Epashti said. "Nor do you. But Miska himself did not kill him."

Eonta shrugged. "Miska's ways are no clearer to me than yours, my girl. The wild man has brought me meat. And the Woman is of great power, and he is her brother, and she has chosen us to nurture this child. Whatever this means, I don't know, but what she wishes I must bow to." She leaned forward and thumped Epashti's belly again. "Welcome, great-grandson."

Now the baby under the belly Eonta had thumped was thunder-footed Finn of bawling words and endless appetite, and Ahanton was old enough for her green bough ceremony, if she would ever sit still long enough for the preparations, and another baby son tugged and fisted at Epashti's breast.

She still knew nothing of Corban. Sometimes in his sleep, or in his lust, he spoke another name, that she dared not ask him about. She loved him but she did not think he loved her. And what his purpose was among them, she had no more notion of than before.

She lingered at the gate looking out across the fields. Corban and Miska and Ahanton had disappeared into the darkness. The night sealed itself against her eyes like a hand over her face. The cold wind brushed her, sharp-edged, nudging her inside. Kalu was already halfway home. Still she kept her eyes on the dark out there, where they had gone. Far down there, beyond the fields, maybe in the edge of the trees, she saw a white light suddenly shine forth. In a blink it was gone again. She turned and went back through the village to her lodge and her children.

# CHAPTER THREE

Ahanton held tight to her father's hand; the cold made her skin rough. Her father was tall and walked fast and she had to skip to keep up, pulling herself along by his hand; she glanced up at him once and saw him smiling down at her and laughed, happy. He gripped her hand hard. His hand was warm.

They were coming to the edge of the forest, where under the darkness of the trees the fireflies winked. The wind was rising, seething through the upper branches, which rose and fell in the air like waves. Some night bird twittered a warning. Abruptly a bright cool light shone all around her.

She gasped, blinked against the blinding glare, throwing her free hand up before her eyes. Her father stopped, still solid beside her, and said, in a voice she had never heard him use before, "Thank you for coming to me. I needed to see you. Thank you for coming to us."

Ahanton opened her eyes into the pale radiance. It was still dark but now she could see everything around her, the air clear but colorless, except where the shadows deepened to a night blue, as if she saw through water. She clung tight to her father's hand. Before her stood a tall woman, shining white as moonlight, and her eyes were fixed on Ahanton's.

The child gulped. She felt her father's hand leave hers; alone she stood there in the blue radiance. The Woman sank down to sit on her heels before her, took her hands, and looked into her face. She said nothing but Ahanton heard words in her mind, her name, and sounds of love, and a rush of warm feeling came over her.

She stopped being afraid. She looked into the face before her and thought that she herself would never be so beautiful as this.

She closed her hands over the warm hands holding hers. She thought, I want to be like you.

The Woman laughed; her eyes sparkled like a quick stream in the sun. She raised Ahanton's hands and kissed the fingers. The warm feeling swept over the child again; she tingled all over her body, she felt as if she had left the ground, and hovered in the air. Then the Woman gave up her hands, and stood and stepped back.

Ahanton folded her arms over her chest, suddenly lonely. She watched as the Woman reached her hand out to Miska, and with him walked away under the trees. Ahanton sank down on the ground, small and cold.

Corban was there, sitting on the ground. She hated him, her not-father, the stranger, but she had to speak, and he was there. She kept her eyes from him. She said, "I could hear her talking. But she wasn't talking." Her eyes stung, teary. She wished the Woman had said more to her. She could remember no words, only the feeling. She wanted to remember every word but she could only remember the feeling.

Corban said, "Sometimes she still talks to me in a real voice."

"I don't have to tell you what she said," Ahanton said.

"No." He sounded as if he were laughing. She frowned. Reluctantly she glanced toward him, sitting there, his face all wooly and ugly, like a beast's.

She said, "Where did she come from? My mother."

He stirred, a little, sitting there, and turned his gaze away. "There is a great water east of here, larger than any river. We lived on the far side of it." He spoke in a mix of words and sounds, as he always had with her, as if he could drag her across the boundary between them with his stranger words. "She was carried off by wicked people. They hurt her. Somebody told me once that her mind broke, like an egg breaking, and her mind spilled, it ran out everywhere into the world. We came here, and here she healed." He made a little cupping motion with his hand. "But she healed outside the shell."

Ahanton shook her head, the words slipping past her, useless. She looked away from him, exhausted. "What do you mean? I don't understand."

He said, "This place makes people larger. Some people." Then he was standing up, and through the dark Miska was coming toward them, while the shining Woman waited behind, under the trees. Corban said, "Go back, I don't need you," and went away toward her.

Ahanton began to shiver. She longed for that rush of warmth again, that hovering in the air. Her heart ached. Everybody else had a mother. She wanted her mother back. Miska stooped and picked her up in his arms, and carried her away back toward the village.

---

Corban went into the shelter of an oak tree, grown thick around as a house, its branches heavy with leaves towering away into the sky, and its roots running in knobs and veins across the ground. The ground crunched under his feet, giving up a fresh breath of rotten mast. The forest spread away from him, shadowy and impenetrable, full of rustlings and groanings, every leaf stirring. Out in the meadow, some small animal gave a last shrill despairing scream.

Mav followed him under the tree. They said nothing for a while. Corban could not think how to speak to her. He yearned toward her but she had gone utterly beyond him. She was there but she was not there. When he looked at her he sometimes saw right through her, as if in the ease of his presence she forgot to keep up her corporeal disguise. He shared nothing with her anymore, no words would come to him, all he had was the great ravelled fabric of their lives flowing back from this moment, a cloak of memories, insubstantial as the wind.

It had been so with Benna, at the end, when she too had

passed on beyond him. He felt worn to nothing with loss, left behind, unworthy of their flights.

Mav turned to him, smiling, and said in a real voice, "Ahanton is wonderful. I'm glad you brought her, thank you. She seems very quick and apt." She reached out, and took hold of his hand, and her touch was warm and real.

The pressure of her hand freed him from himself. He faced her, meeting her eyes, and words came unbidden from him. "She is, her understanding already runs deep. And she takes orders from no one."

"Certainly not you, mean old uncle," Mav said, and her arm slid around him and hugged him. "Does she dream?"

"If she does she will not tell me, she really does not like me."

Mav's smile widened. "You love her."

"Yes."

"That's all that matters," she said. And when he growled at her, annoyed she was so careless of his caring, she hugged him again, warm and young, his flesh-and-blood sister, all the years melted away back to that long-ago oneness, when they had known each other's minds so well they had spoken with looks and touches. She said, "Should you leave her to Miska? Your wife loves her."

"Epashti loves everybody," he said, and put his hand to his face, thinking of Miska.

She moved in his arms, to look at him. "What's wrong?"

He moved a step away from her, and glanced behind them. He had meant to keep from this, for fear of angering her, but it burst out of him. "Miska. Why do you help him? Why have you made him so great? He's evil, Mav, he leads them to war and blood and evil rites."

She took hold of his hand again. "I have less to do with that than you think. He is who he is." She smiled at him, unconcerned. He thought, I am asking the wrong question. That made him angry, too, because it seemed not a question to him, what Miska did, flat evil, impossible not to hate. He looked into her eyes and saw there for an instant the whirling into the abyss.

She still held him by the hand. She said, "Do you want to go home, Corban?"

"Home!" He twitched, startled. "You mean—to Denmark, or Jorvik, or Ireland again? I am home here. This land—" He bit his words off, looking around. The darkness of the forest lay around him, the immense aliveness of the trees, the cool edge of the wind; when he set about trying to gather his feeling into words the world multiplied away from him in all directions, everywhere he looked more various and new. He gave up trying to say how he felt about the place and went on. "I want to live somewhere the people don't devour each other." His mind slipped on past that. "I want justice. I want to be where I belong."

She watched him with her head tipped to one side, her eyes deep. She said nothing, but put her arms around him and hugged him again.

"I don't know what to do," he said, in her arms.

"You never know what to do, Corban. You do it anyway." She held him, her arms around him; he felt in her an immeasurable inhuman strength, as if she could have lifted him up and up into the vault of the sky and set him on the moon. Her voice spoke in his ear. "Miska needs you to go west. Do that. If you go into the west, you will find what you seek."

She stepped back, her hands on his arms, then rising to his face. Her fingers stroked down the scar along the side of his face and a little blaze of feeling ran from his ear to his lip, a cold thread of fire. She said, "Take my daughter with you. She needs to see the world." She took a single step backward, away from him. Her gaze held his a moment longer. She said, "Corban. What she dreams is true." Before him, under his eyes, she vanished into nothing, into air, into space.

"Mav," he said, expecting no answer. He stood a moment, holding on to seeing her, trying to understand, to pack it into memory. She had put him off about Miska, but she loved Ahanton. And she had said—his heart leapt at what she had said. He would find what he was looking for, somewhere to the west, in the heart of the country. He walked back out of the forest, toward the village, already impatient to go.

# CHAPTER FOUR

Ahanton fell asleep in Miska's arms, and he carried her across the darkened village to Epashti's house, her warm weight delightful in his grasp. The herbwoman met him outside the door, and at once took the child from him, long-legged and drowsy.

"Where is Corban?" she said, looking up at him.

"Do you think I've killed him?" Miska said, with a snort. Epashti understood nothing. He said, "Back in the forest. His sister wants him. He will come in when he's done. Tell him then that I will see him." He laid his hand on Ahanton's wild hair. "She was brave. You raise her well, Epashti, I'm pleased." He went off, not waiting to see how she answered that. It lay like a hot coal in his gut that he could not bring his own child into his lodge.

Corban's little rat nest of a house was close by the fence. Miska could have walked straight up along the fence and come quickly to his lodge by the gate but instead he turned and went the other way, to make a circuit around the whole village. He did this every evening, sometimes more than once. This was the real fence around his village, his walking around it, making it his, making it safe.

He could have gone the whole way with his eyes closed. He knew every stone, every root worn polished under passing feet. Every smell was familiar to him, the midden just the other side of the fence, the cold ash of the big hole where the women cooked their pottery. He understood everything, he heard the soft grunts and clicks on the midden and knew the raccoons were hunting for scraps, he listened to the way the leaves rustled and knew there would be no rain for a while. As he came up to the river the sound of the water running by grew louder, clearer, as if he could hear each drop as it passed.

Behind him now was Eonta's longhouse, where as usual people were arguing, the noisiest people in his village, Eonta's kindred, the biggest troublemakers. He loved them anyway, because he knew them, they could hide nothing from him, his people. They were bad sometimes and stupid often but they were his people, always.

He went on along the bank above the river, as it sloped down toward the flat beach. The moon was rising higher over the trees, frail bad twin of the sun, drowning everything in its baleful light. From here he could see up through the center of the village, in past the longhouses and the lodges, to the big oak tree. The people were all going to sleep, no one else walked on the beach and no one walked the pounded open ground beneath the broad spread of the oak tree. The sharp smell of woodsmoke still clung to the air but the night mist was gathering over the river and the wind was falling calm, and the woodsmoke had the stale taste of banked fires.

He went by Merada's longhouse, the smallest of the dwellings of the women; a baby let out a wail in there, and someone comforted it at once. He stood by the wall of the longhouse and listened to the low sleepy laughter and chatter of people going to their beds. As he went off again, walking, a woman cooed to him from the shadows, low and sweet, but he ignored her. This night the Forest Woman had touched him, even kissed him, and he would go days before he could endure the embrace of someone else.

He went on down along the river, the wind rising now, damp and cold. The course of the water came in close against the bank here, and then turned and crossed the riverbed to the far side, leaving a pale wedge of a beach under the moonlight, the glinting black water sweeping by. Near the top of the beach was the broken-backed hut where Lasicka lived. The cripple was sitting in his doorway still, in the dark, staring away toward the river. Miska went by there, and stopped, and said, "What has you up after sundown, old man?"

Lasicka stirred, his good hand clutching the withered arm, trying to rub life into it. "I was watching the light on the river," he said. "Such are the things old men come to." His voice quickened a little, eager. "Can I help you, Miska-Tonanda?"

Miska looked away, hiding his smile in the dark. "Maybe soon. I will remember." He went away, still smiling, remembering how once Lasicka had despised him.

Still, Lasicka was a Wolf, and so Miska loved him, loved them all, not even in spite of how they had scorned him once—all but a few—but because of it. Because he had been so low here, and now he was so high.

They had risen high with him. The shell belts in his lodge were promises not just to him but to his whole people. In the fat moons of autumn other villages, other lineages and clans brought in their harvests, and from every basket of beans, the gourds and berries and sloes, all the fur and horn and flint, they set aside the best for Miska, and they brought it here to his village, so even Lasicka had all he needed.

The village was safe, and fat, and no one dared come to attack them here, not because of their fence, but because of Miska. Children could walk for days away to pick berries or willow stems, the women ranged everywhere looking for their herbs and seeds and grew their beans only in the most perfect garden places, the men fished up the river as far as the Long Lakes and down the river as far as the salt, and no one would hinder any of them, because of Miska. He gave them back good for their evil to him, and on that his power over them stood like a great tree growing from a rock.

He walked along the top of the beach; two young men coming the other way saw him and stopped, lowering their eyes in respect. As he passed by them, he said their names. "Ayana, Lopi." They wheeled, upright as birches, as eager as Lasicka, but he paid no more heed to them. He would have use for their eagerness soon enough, now that the moon was almost full.

He walked up from the river, past the clutter of boys' huts in the angle of the fence, and cut between the back of Gallara's longhouse and the fence past another of the boys' stick-pile huts; the fleas had driven the boys out of the hut and they were sleeping outside on the ground. He circled around behind one of the two men's lodges, and when he rounded the corner was in sight of the gate.

Corban was coming in.

At the sight of him the old hate swept back. Miska stopped, furious. He remembered how she had come to him, to this brother, this low hairy ugly thing, and leaned on him and whispered to him all loving, as Miska longed for her to do with him, and which she never did anymore. He felt as if Corban coming in through the gate made a hole through Miska's side. The sachem's jaw clenched; he took hold of his knife, and the urge rose to leap on Corban and hack him, take Corban's own magic knife and cut him into pieces with it.

The heat faded. He could not do it. He could taste the blood on his tongue and his belly was hungry for it but he thought of Corban's sister and he quailed. She loved Corban and not him, Miska knew that she hardly cared about him, he wondered often why she still protected him, but she loved Corban. He wanted to tear Corban apart, to tie him to the stake and burn him with hot fire until he died, but the thought of bringing her anger on him turned his will to water.

He let go of his knife. Corban had come inside the gate, and swung it closed behind him. Miska stepped forward, and said the stranger's name, sour in his mouth.

Corban wheeled toward him, abrupt, edgy as he always was; Miska thought his long habit of living alone in the woods had made him jumpy. Corban said, "Where is Ahanton?"

Miska grunted at him, annoyed. "I took her to your lodge. Epashti has her. I have a task for you to do." He wondered if Corban would put his back up at that, doing Miska's will, and he said, "She in the forest has required this."

Corban said, "I know. You want me to go west. To find out where that golden head came from?"

"The Sun people made that head. I want you to find them." Miska began to say more, but something moved in the corner of his eye.

It was Epashti, who must have been watching, Miska realized, the whole time—who might have seen him nearly leap on Corban; she came up toward them, looking from one to the other. She said, "What has happened? What is this, husband, where are you going?"

Corban turned to her, his shaggy, ugly head bent toward her. "My sister told me to go to the west. Miska—" He glanced at Miska, and said, with a sting in his tongue, "Haka-Miska needs to know something there."

Epashti looked from him to Miska, and said, "I will go too."

Miska folded his arms over his chest. He wanted to get rid of Corban but Epashti belonged here. "You are the herbwoman of us, we people need you."

Corban said, "He's right, Epashti, you should stay here."

Miska raised his head an inch, wondering why Corban did not want her with him. Epashti laid her hand on the wild man's arm, and turned to the sachem. "A war band going out of the country always takes the herbwoman with them. I went with you last year, remember, when you went to the Long Lakes, and that time to the salt. There is Ehia, now, she has been going around with me for over a year, she can watch over everybody here."

Miska jerked his head up, angry. "He is not a war band. He is not a Wolf." He turned and glared at Corban, standing there with his head down, looking from under his eyebrows at Epashti.

Reluctantly, Corban said, "She wants me to take Ahanton, too."

"No!" Miska took a step toward him, crowding him. "She's a child. She stays here. She's my child."

He bit his teeth together, annoyed with himself for saying so much. Corban never moved; he stood so close Miska felt the heat of his body, and said, with a shrug, "My sister said she should go. It could be a hard journey, I don't wish for either of them to come." He stared up at Miska, daring him to refuse what the Woman had required.

She required it. Miska took hold of his anger, and turned away, walking off a little, thinking this over. She had required it for some reason. He faced the wild man again. "Did she say why?"

Corban shook his head. "I told you, I don't want her to go either."

Epashti said, swiftly, "But if Ahanton goes then I must as well."

Miska lowered his eyes. "Very well," he said. "Take her."

His anger rose again at being overruled. He thought of the Forest Woman, but his belly boiled. If he looked at Corban again, he knew, he would attack him. He said, "Take them both, Ahanton and Epashti."

Epashti saw his temper, and reached out her hand to Corban again. "Come along, husband, it's cold, come along."

Corban saw it also. He gave a low laugh, and said nothing, only stood a moment, watching Miska, and only then went along after the woman. Miska stood there, breathing hard, as if he had fought a great battle, and been ruined.

Epashti was dividing up her medicine pouch; she laid down a bundle of dried mint in the flat basket to her right, for Ehia, and the other into her carrying pouch, to take with her. Ehia knelt down on her left hand, watching, and saying nothing, but every now and then she cast a black look at Corban.

The whole village was angry Epashti was leaving and blamed him for taking her. Corban, watching Epashti through the side of his eye, wondered again how such a quiet little woman could push her way into this against the will of everybody.

"My sister will nurse the baby," she said.

"Aengus," Corban said. "What about Finn, and Kalu?"

"My brothers should be watching over them more anyway. And Mother Eonta will keep an eye on them."

Corban lowered his eyes; he knew none of the men save Miska, certainly not her brothers. He had laid his gear out on his red and blue cloak, his knives and slings, the tinderbox and a piece of flint, his extra boots, a strip of hide stitched with his fish hooks, a leather box for bait, a coil of string. He pushed away a little stab at the thought of leaving his children to these people; the urge to be on the way was as strong as an itch.

Epashti felt like a weight on him, something holding him here even while she went with him. Ahanton, he knew, would make it even worse. He wondered why his sister had wanted them to go along. He wondered what part they could have in what he was searching for.

Ehia packed her basket and went out, with one last scowl in Corban's direction, and the flap over the door fell closed. Epashti spoke, and her voice was like a nettle drawn over his skin. "Where are we going? What did your sister say to you? Why do we go into the west?"

The baby was sleeping in his bundleboard, hanging from the centerpost; they were alone in the hut. All along the walls, on strings, bundles of herbs dried in rows, and there were still two leaves of smoking herb spread across the frame of the hut in the back, so the air was rich with smells. He began to put his belongings into his shoulder sack, picking them up one by one from his red and blue cloak.

"I am to find some people, called the Sun people."

She gasped. He looked up at her, seeing her face pale suddenly, even in the dusk. "Does that change your mind about going?"

She said, "No." She sat there, her hands on her thighs, staring at him.

"Who are these Sun people?"

She hunched her shoulders up. "Very bad. Very hard." Her wide eyes studied him. "You don't know this?"

"No—tell me."

"You know that we came here from the west, we Wolves."

"I know that," he said, thinking it was almost the first thing he had known about the Wolves, that they were interlopers, running from something.

"We used to live near a great water. I was a baby. Maybe I wasn't all the way born yet. I don't remember but we remember." She wiped her eyes with her fingers. "The Sun people came. First there were a few of them, with gifts. Then there were many, and they gave us orders. When we said no to their orders they came on a day when the thunder rolled. They crashed down on our village like thunder and they killed us like lightning. Some of us ran away. Eonta and her husband, who is dead now. Gallara and her husband, who is dead now, and Burns-His-Feet, who is dead now, and old Murula, who is dead now, and Anapatha, and Merada. Most of us died but those few ran away, and we came here. Now let no one ever come against us again." She made a sign with her hand. Tears slicked her cheeks.

"Where was Miska?" he asked.

"Miska was a baby. His grandmother was Murula. She took him by the hand and led him out of the fire of the village. No one else of her lodge remained, none of her daughters, none of her granddaughters. When she died, her lineage died with her." She rubbed her hand over her cheeks, and faced him. "If they are coming we have to find out. And warn everybody. And make ready. You see that." She turned back to her herbs. "So it's even more important that I go."

Corban shut his mouth; he saw she knew nothing but what she had said. I don't remember but we remember. His mind quested after them, out there somewhere in the west, the Sun people, who made fine things of gold, brought gifts and gave orders, and struck like thunder and lightning; what else did they do, he wondered, who were they? She said they were evil, but she was a Wolf; what did she know about evil? He closed up the top of his sack over his belongings and picked up his red and blue cloak, longing to get out the gate.

---

Since she could remember Ahanton had dreamt of her father, that he grew like a huge oak tree out of the midst of the other people, and stood over them all, and was great over them. His arms spread over them, protecting them; he hid them in his shadow, and they grew to be very many. They spread away across the world, and her father was the father of them all, a tree towering to the top of the sky, and spreading its broad leafy arms over all of them.

They ate of him, they gathered nuts from his branches, and nibbled on his bark, and he gave them freely of all of it. Then Mother Eonta came, and she made a hole in his side, the way that sometimes people made holes in trees, to collect the sap, and the sap ran from her father and the people came and drank of it. Ahanton saw all this happen in her dream, but she told nobody.

When she dreamt of Corban, he was always standing off on the side of things, watching, and his head was the head of a wild beast.

# CHAPTER FIVE

Corban left, with Epashti following a step behind him, her herb-woman's pouch over her shoulder, and Ahanton dashing on ahead. When they were out of sight, Miska went around the village, gathering the men.

He said nothing to them, only went among them, touching one or another on the shoulder, and they rose up and followed him. As they proceeded on through the village their voices rose, tremulous, excited, so that ahead of them people knew they were coming, and when they came to another group of men they were already stirring and ready and Miska had only to move through them and they followed him.

He led them at last to the oak tree, where they milled around, the older men, who all lived together in the two lodges, flexing their arms and looking each other deep in the eyes, the boys howling and laughing and embracing, until he raised his hand, and then they all hushed. They came up around him, the eight men of the lodges in front, and sat down at his feet, and he looked calmly from one to the other, letting each one know that he was in Miska's eye.

Hasei was there, who always had a mouthful of words, often annoying. Miska nodded to him. "Hasei, take all these—" He pointed around the band, saying the names of the older men, who had followed him the longest. "There is a village of the Bear people, down by the Broad River. Go there and tell their headman I am coming."

Hasei stood up, frowning. Short and square, he always tried to find some way to escape from Miska's will. He said, "The Bear people. They don't even like us, Haka-Miska, what am I supposed to say to them?"

"I told you," Miska said. "Say that I will be coming there, and they should get ready." He smiled at Hasei, pleased to make him uncomfortable. The other men were already on their feet, shuffling around, ready to follow when Hasei was ready to lead them. Miska said, "Go, get your war bundles, and do as I tell you." He turned away, showing the side of his face to Hasei, and with a shrug the other man went off, and with him the other seven, reliable and steady, as long as nothing unusual happened.

Miska turned toward the rest, the untopped boys and young men, his green sticks, more of them than the men of the lodges, almost twice as many. He let his gaze drift over them, as if he were mulling over what to do, although he had already decided. When his gaze finally lit on Lopi, the young man snapped upright like a sapling, his face shining.

"Haka-Miska! Give me an order!"

Miska laughed at him. "Go for a long walk, and then do nothing," he said, and Lopi's face slumped. Miska laughed again. "But you can all do this together." With a gesture he gathered them in toward him. "Lopi leads. Go away to the east, to the hills beyond the Broad River. There is a pass through them. You will know it by the blasted oak tree on the top, like a tree of feathers."

Lopi was nodding at him; Lopi had been there. Miska went on, "Find the pass but don't go into it, make a camp there, at the western foot of the way into it, and wait for me."

Lopi was rigid with excitement, his face flaming. "Haka-Miska-ka, how do I—"

"You will find out," Miska said. "Just do as I say, Lopi." He nodded, and the young men bounded up, gathering around Lopi in a sudden bubbling of excited talk, arms around each other's shoulders. One threw back his head and howled to the sky out of sheer exhuberance. It would take them a long while even to leave the village, Miska guessed. He left them to sort it all out and went to his own lodge.

His war bundle, wrapped in a wolf skin, hung from the lodge

pole, and his club beside it. He had made the club himself, the haft of ashwood as long as his arm, the killing end a fist-sized stone, bound into the split of the ash with rawhide. At the other end of the haft he had sunk a smaller stone, to give it a better feel in his hand.

It seemed alive to him. Whenever he picked it up he felt its joy, its eagerness for the hunt. He held it in his hands a moment, enjoying its weight and balance, feeling it awaken. With it something deep and hot within him wakened also. He gathered himself; then he slung the bundle over his shoulder and went out of the village and away to the east.

He followed an old trail of the woods bison. The great beasts had mostly left this country now but their paths remained, pounded knee-deep into the ground, thick with powdery dust and overhung with trees. The lower leaves of the brush on either side were gray with the dust. As he went along he ate what he came on, mushrooms and berries, leaves and grubs. He thought little, his mind open to the forest as he went through it. His feet knew the ground under them, his nose knew the smell and sound of the wind, his ears knew the birds shrilling at him and calling warning to one another. He moved fast. Twice in the first day he spooked deer, coming quickly on them from upwind.

At night he found shelter under the overhang of a creek bank, and there he woke in the dark, and then miserable thoughts crowded into his mind. He saw himself small and lost and unnoticed, a little nut between earth and sky, that the indifferent world would crush at its whim, and then he consoled himself thinking of the Forest Woman, who had raised him up and made him sachem, and chosen him to father her daughter.

After a few days he left the bison trail and cut through the forest and hills, moving steadily eastward. In the low ground he crossed stretches of burnt-out ground, with the grass springing up through the black ruin. He avoided the villages of the Bear people who lived here, who had burnt the ground to bring the grass to lure the deer. He saw much sign of them, the burnouts, trails, and traps set, and once or twice through the trees he caught a glimpse of a hut, but they never knew he was there, he passed through their midst like a shadow.

He came to the Broad River, flowing brown and deep in its southward course. On the bank he found a big old dry limb fallen from an oak tree and he lugged it into the water, and with one arm around it and his feet kicking let it carry him down the current and across to the other side.

He picked up a deer trace that took him on east, and a few days later he came down a little creek and into sight of the pass where he had told Lopi to make his camp. The pass was a notch in the craggy old hills, with a big chunk of rock overhanging it; at the foot of this rock, in the hump of the pass, the broken fire-blackened crown of an oak tree stuck out like a burnt hand over thickets of brush and green vines. From the meadow at the hills' foot a narrow path snaked up toward the blasted tree.

There was no sign of Lopi in the meadow, which did not surprise him; the boys would be slow getting here, needing to hunt food, to find a way to cross the river. Miska walked back and forth across the meadow, noticing who had come by, and watching the heights for signs the pass was guarded, but he didn't expect that and saw no evidence of it.

Yet he did not cross through the hills by the low and gentle way. Instead he climbed up the steep side of the hill south of the pass, moving up through young oak trees and dense patches of brush, insects swarming thick in the still green light. The summer was coming and the day grew warm around him, smelling of leaves. Crossing over the rocky summit he went on down the far side, moving carefully now, slow and cautious, watching ahead of him, his ears up, sniffing the air.

For two years now this pass had marked the eastern edge of his power. East of this place the people gave their respect to another sachem, the Turtle chief, Tisconum. Tisconum had once been a greater chief than he was now, for which he blamed Miska, which Miska accepted as an honor, although he knew that the rodent, Corban, had a lot also to do with Tisconum's downfall.

Tisconum hated the Wolves, and he hated Miska above any other Wolf. For two years Miska had been pretending he didn't care about Tisconum. This year he meant to make it unnecessary to care about Tisconum ever again.

These hills were the margin between them. He had been scouting them for over a year, finding out how to move around them, learning where everything was. In the course of that scouting he had noted that some of Tisconum's people kept a hunting camp at the foot of the eastern slope of this hill, where also they could watch the pass; but mostly it was a hunting camp.

He drifted that way, easing slowly through the forest, his ears stretched open and his eyes looking everywhere, as the day grew hot and the wind died. Around noon he stopped, his nose picking up the faint tang of woodsmoke from up ahead of him.

He stayed where he was through the heat of the day, listening, and noticing the way the animals in the forest were acting. He knew where the camp was, off to his left by a little spring; he could tell that people were moving up and down between it and the large meadow away on his right. A jay was keeping up a racket in a tall tree ahead of him. A few breaths later he heard the quail in the meadow piping out their alarms. After a while, back in the camp, someone was singing.

Two men and a woman, he thought. As the sun sank down, and the air cooled a little, he left his pack behind and moved in through the woods, from one tree to the next, the club in his hand.

He circled the camp once, noting the paths in and out. The sun was rolling over the edge of the sky, the wind was moving in fitful little swirls through the leafy masses of the trees. He could hear the men coming up from the meadow, carrying something heavy. From the thick cover on the slope above the spring he looked down and watched the woman laying sticks on her fire. The spits were ready for the meat the men were bringing. In nearby baskets she had other food, berries and acorn meal cakes. Their gear hung on the tree branches and lay tumbled on the ground of the camp, beds of pine boughs, heaps of firewood.

He moved slowly down the slope, moving one foot and then the other, to avoid giving her any warning. He edged his way down to where the path from the meadow came up to the camp, and there the men were just approaching, one after the other, with a deer slung between them on a pole.

He leapt straight at them. With one blow of his club he crushed the first man's head in, and he went down like a rock, the deer going down with him. The other man yelled, half-pinned under the falling load, and before he could get free Miska killed him too.

He wheeled around, back toward the camp, where the woman had sprung up to her feet, ready to run, her face wild with fear. He fixed her with his eyes. She stood fast, she could not run. He held her with his look, and walked to her, and she did not move. He took her by the hair and pushed her up against a tree, hauled her skirt up around her waist and used her until her knees gave way and she sagged down against the tree, her face slobbered with tears. He let her go. He thought of killing her but she would bring Tisconum quickly and so he let her go. He went to the nearer of the two dead men; he wanted some proof he had killed them, these Turtles, and the best was the long lock of hair they wore above their ears. With his knife he cut the scalp quickly in a circle around the first man's lock, and yanked the hair off.

He heard a whimper, behind him, and looked around, but the woman was running. She darted past him and down the path and disappeared into the green brush. The urge came over him to chase her, bring her down again, but he stayed where he was, listening to the sounds she made fading into the usual sounds of the forest.

He tore the lock of hair off the other body, and fixed both of the long bloody trophies to the haft of his war club.

Night was falling. He went back and found his bundle, and returning cut out the tongue of the deer; in the camp, over the woman's fire, he roasted the tongue and ate of the cakes and the berries. In the deep night, with the trees stirring in the wind, and the owls gliding soundlessly under the branches, he went up the pass a little, crawled under an outcrop of stone, and slept.

Hasei squatted down on his hams and rubbed his hands together, staring up at the Bear village. The people here had rebuilt it since he had seen it last; then it had been some way closer to the Broad River, but now it stood on the crown of a rocky little hill, its wood fence tracing around the rim of the hill, and the way up winding along the side.

These people, he remembered, had sent gifts to Miska of their own will, courting him, in spite of how much the two clans disliked each other. Now he thought they had done so to keep Miska away until they could build themselves this fort.

Yoto, his brother, hunkered down next to him. The rest of the men were sprawled idly under the trees. Yoto said, "What does Miska want us to do here?"

Hasei shrugged. He had been mulling over Miska's orders since they left their own village and he still didn't understand. He said, "He said he would come."

Yoto grunted, looking around at the woods. Here the forest yielded softly through a borderland of high brush and young trees to a broad flat meadow that sloped down toward the distant stream. Strips of fields crisscrossed the meadow, women's wealth, stands of beans, clumps of green lit up with the little yellow suns of melon blossoms. "Should we wait?" Yoto said.

"No," Hasei said. Tell them to get ready, Miska had said. Tell them I am coming. He said, "Who is their headman? Is he a sachem?"

"Ekkatsay, his name is. I don't know where he stands in the Bear council." Yoto was still looking around. "In any case, Hasei, they don't like us, we should wait for him to get here."

Whatever Miska wanted, Hasei was sure it wasn't for them to do nothing. He straightened to his feet, his gaze on the village. "Go up there and tell them that we are here. We have to have a gift for him—who brought a pipe?"

Yoto got up, his forehead crumpled. "Basha has a pipe." He bobbed his head up at the village. "They aren't going to like this, Hasei, and there aren't very many of us."

"Do it," Hasei said.

A little while into the day, Yoto came back, trotting down the path beaten through the meadow, and behind him, Hasei could see people crowding on down out of the city. He went back to the trees, where the other men were lolling around half-asleep, and roused them. He got the pipe from Basha and collected all the smokeherb the men had, and with him going first they moved out onto the path to greet the Bears.

Yoto jogged up to him. "All their men are here, they just finished some ceremony, even the outliers are here, there are a lot more of them than us."

"We're Wolves," Hasei said. Up ahead, the crowd of the Bears had stopped, at the foot of the path up to their village, and he straightened himself up and strode forward down the path to meet them, the other men on his heels.

They got up close enough to see the eyes of the waiting Bears, and then one in front of the crowd threw his hand out, palm out, and said, "Stop! What are you here for?"

Hasei glanced from this man to the broad-shouldered man

behind him, who wore a great breastplate of shell and horn, and a shock of feathers in the knot of hair on top of his head. Hasei said, looking at this man, "I bring the greetings of Miska of the Wolves to his brother Ekkatsay."

Ekkatsay was looking through the pack of men behind Hasei, and as he did the harsh planes of his face eased, relieved. Hasei knew he had seen that Miska was not with them. Ekkatsay turned back to him, fierce.

"What are you doing here? We have sent the year's gifts to your village. We need give you nothing else."

Hasei said, "Haka-Miska-ka sent me here to tell you he would come, and you should be ready." His face burned. Ekkatsay's voice had a rough jeering edge that made Hasei want to plunge his knife into the other man's chest. He had the pipe still in his hand but this was going in the opposite direction than sharing smoke.

"But Miska isn't here," Ekkatsay said. "Just go away. There is nowhere for you to stay here. Nor do we have any food for you."

At that Hasei stiffened. He turned and put the pipe into the hands of the man nearest him, who was Yoto, standing there with his eyes blazing, glaring at the Bears. Hasei swung back toward Ekkatsay. "We are blood with you. Are you not Miska's brother? We have the right of guests with you."

Ekkatsay sneered at him. "There are less of you than us. Don't try to threaten me." From the dense mob of people packing the ground behind him came a general murmur of supportive amusement.

Hasei stared this big man up and down. Behind him were seven Wolves, and around him, as Ekkatsay said, a good number of Bear men, but there were women and children also, and the Bears did not fight much. He thought if they fought much they would not need such a fort to live in. He wondered again what Miska expected of him—certainly not to accept insult, to give in.

He stared at Ekkatsay, trying to look him into obedience, as

Miska did, but Ekkatsay only stared back, and folded his arms across his chest.

Then from the crowd behind Hasei, standing higher on the hill, a gasp went up. They were pointing out over the heads of the men in front, at something down the path, and they were calling out and more and more were moving up the path to look. Hasei wheeled. Behind him, the Wolves were jumping out of the way, and down this open path Miska walked.

He had painted himself with black and red clay on his face and his chest. He wore his wolf skin robe, with the wolf's mask set over his forehead. He carried his war club in his hand, and from its haft swung two fresh swags of long black hair. Hasei's heart thudded at the sight of them, his muscles tightened, his belly stirred, hungry. In the whole great crowd watching, nobody spoke, their eyes followed him, the Wolves turned to watch him go by. Hasei stepped back away from Ekkatsay. It occurred to him suddenly that, whatever it was, he had done what Miska wanted.

Miska walked straight up to Ekkatsay and stood chest to chest with him. He thundered words into Ekkatsay's face.

"I greet my brother Ekkatsay." His voice rang loud in the stark silence. "And thank him for coming down here to greet me from his high place."

"You are nothing but trouble, Miska," Ekkatsay said. They were almost the same height and he did not have to look up at Miska the way other men did. His face was set hard and stiff. Hasei saw his eyes flick toward the woods in the distance, and knew he was wondering how many other Wolves lurked under the trees. The people crowded together onto the path behind him were watching keenly, leaning on each other's shoulders and craning their necks.

Miska said, "I'm sorry to hear you say that, my brother. Yet I have only come here to help you." He moved a step closer to Ekkatsay, his wolf paint almost touching Ekkatsay's fancy breastplate.

"To help us," Ekkatsay said. He held his ground, although he swayed slightly on his feet. He gestured at Miska's war club, with the two long swags of bloody hair dangling from it. "You will bring Tisconum down on us."

"Hai," the people in the crowd murmured, agreeing. "Hai, hai." But at the back of the crowd Hasei could see people sneaking away up the path to the safety of the village on its height above them.

"Bring Tisconum on you," Miska said, looking puzzled. "Should Tisconum not worry that you will come at him? Surely my brother will not stand and see his hunting grounds stolen."

Ekkatsay suddenly took a step backward, getting space between them. "You make trouble, Miska!" His voice had a high nasty whine to it.

"Hai," someone called, but another voice rose in the packed crowd. "Which hunting grounds have they stolen, those hard-backed fish eaters?"

Miska raised his war club over his head, the bloody hair swinging. "These came from your deer meadows, from Bear deer meadows east of the Broad River, from the heads of men hunting on those meadows." He turned back to Ekkatsay, and took another step toward him, so that they were almost nose to nose again. "Are you afraid of Tisconum, my brother?"

Ekkatsay bellowed, "I am afraid of nobody! Not of Tisconum, nor of you, Miska!"

"Hai," somebody called, but not loudly.

Miska smiled. "Then welcome me and the rest of us into your high place, there"—he jerked his head toward the village—"and give us food and shelter for the night. My brother."

Ekkatsay shot another glance toward the distant trees. His eyes narrowed.

"Just you," he said. "And these others here."

Miska gave a harumph of a laugh. "Just us, Ekkatsay."

Ekkatsay's gaze licked over them all again. Hasei thought if they went into his village they might not come out again. But it amused him the way Miska said "high place," as if it were a joke. Whatever happened, Miska would get them through it.

"Very well," Ekkatsay said, now, his voice smooth, hiding thoughts. "Come in, then, Brother, and we shall talk all this over."

"Good," said Miska, and even gave him a little nudge, to lead them up the path.

# CHAPTER SIX

Ekkatsay had moved his home village from a fine flat meadow by the river, with plenty of water and good fields close by, up here on this stony hilltop where everything had to be hauled up from below, all to keep Miska out, and now here was Miska sitting in the center of it, eating Ekkatsay's own meat.

The Bear headman's gaze went to the war club, which never lay far from Miska's hand. The round black stone head was crusted with something, hair, maybe, stuck on with blood. Ekkatsay's belly churned. He wanted to pick that club up and strike with it and feel the crunch of bone under it.

Miska's bone. He straightened, pulling his eyes away. Two of the women were bringing up flat baskets with bean cakes, ground cherries, wedges of gourd roasted soft and brown, whose nutty aroma made his mouth water. He glanced at Miska, who was not eating.

"My brother disdains our food." Ekkatsay reached for a piece of the gourd.

"My brother's people eat well, and they have fed me well," Miska said. "I cannot eat mouthful and mouthful with a Bear, I admit that, brother."

Ekkatsay grunted, wondering if he should take that for an insult. He fell to thinking again that he could seize Miska, that he had far more men here than Miska, that he could take him prisoner and kill him.

When he thought that, part of him went off to one side, and looked back, and said, "He is your brother, eating your food at your fire."

Another part of him, in his head still, said, "He would fight, he would fight, they would all fight." He found himself staring at the war club again, lying beside Miska's thigh. He had heard how Miska did battle, always in the middle, always striking furious blows; they said he had never taken a wound, that some power protected him, no living man could even pierce his skin.

The other Wolves were sitting beside Miska, and many more of Ekkatsay's men were sitting on the other side of the fire. The women brought more food but nobody was eating. Then one of the Wolves held out a pipe, and another offered a little pouch, and the smoke went from hand to hand.

Ekkatsay took the pipe, when it came to him, but he did not smoke it. He passed it on. Miska saw this and said, "What troubles you, my brother, that you are not friends with me?"

Ekkatsay turned his head to one side, sorting through his mind for words, but then someone on the other side of the fire called out, "What about these deer meadows? All the ground east of the Broad River to the Lightning Tree belongs to us, by ancient right."

Ekkatsay knew that voice, Taksa, his troublemaking nephew. He clenched his teeth together. Taksa did not know his place, talking out, not waiting for Ekkatsay to choose words. Miska was already answering, as if any Bear could speak to him, any Bear at all.

"Tisconum will take everything he can. I will drive him back, if you will help me—" He turned his face toward Ekkatsay, his eyes wide and solemn, and said, "If you will not lead them, my brother, let your fighters come with me, and we will regain your rights."

Ekkatsay burst out, "I will lead my people!" His face felt hot, he glared across the fire at Taksa who had betrayed him, and who would feel it, and thrust out his hand at Miska to hold him back. "If Tisconum is hunting on my grounds, then I will deal with him, and if my people need to fight, I will lead them."

Miska sat back, smiling, his face bland behind the stripes of paint. "Good, then," he said. "We should leave early, in the first morning. I shall wait for you."

There was a sharp gasp among the people watching. Miska reached out for the pipe, which the Wolf beside him had just packed again.

Ekkatsay said, "The morning is too soon."

"Noon will be too late," Miska said. Another of his Wolves had fished a coal from the fire, and was lighting the pipe for him. Miska inhaled the smoke deeply, and let it out in a gust.

He said, "In my village there lives one who keeps fire in a little box. The smoke tastes different when he lights it." He was smiling. All around, the fire shone on faces, the people creeping closer to see, to hear, and every shining eye was fixed on him. Ekkatsay knew of Miska's stranger, everybody did, a sorcerer of some kind, with much magic, people said, part of the web of power that surrounded Miska.

He wondered what Miska was threatening him with. He wondered if Miska and Taksa knew each other already.

The pipe came to him, with its fragrance, its promises. He took it. Miska was watching him; everybody was watching him. He put the pipe to his lips and inhaled the smoke.

"All right," he said. "At first morning. But I go first."

"As you wish, my brother," Miska said.

---

Ekkatsay's people had spent the spring by the salt, fishing and digging for clams, and they were soft and lazy from it. They were Bears anyway, Miska thought, lazy and strong and fat and slow. The day was well along before the men were even ready to leave their hilltop village; they had to travel well south of the village to ford the Broad River and Miska drove them hard, wanting to get to the camp below the blasted tree before Lopi had been there long enough to get into trouble. He wanted also to see how Ekkatsay's men went, who was capable and who was stupid, and who might be of use to him.

Ekkatsay kept no order over his people. The Bears complained and lagged back and stopped and strayed and by afternoon it was constant work to keep them moving. Miska gave up, sent the other Wolves out to hunt, and pushed the Bears into making a camp where they were. Since neither of the bands had brought any women with them the work fell on the men, who groaned and tried to sneak away and did a bad job of everything when they did do it, even the Wolves.

They were at the edge of the broad grassy meadows between the river and the hills, which were the deer grounds Miska had told them Tisconum was poaching on, and he wanted them across the place before it occurred to them that there were no signs of any Turtles anywhere here. The haze of summer hung in the sky. By the spring where they were camping a few tall trees grew, casting a deep shade on the fading grass; under the widespreading boughs the Bears were gathering up the wood for their fires. Miska went away toward the open meadow, looking east across the bending grass, the land flowing away from him in waves. He walked along the edge of a great trampled swath where some deer had lain. Their droppings lay everywhere like black pebbles. The sun lay soft on his arms and he stretched them up into the light and shut his eyes.

The Forest Woman came into his mind; he knew she was everywhere, and he promised to be worthy of her. He felt the gentle warmth of the land around him as her kindness toward him. The wind and sun like her arms around him. Then he heard footsteps behind him.

He wheeled, annoyed at having his thoughts broken into. A tall Bear was coming toward him across the grass, and seeing Miska face him now he stopped, lowered his head, and turned his hands up at his sides.

"Come," Miska said. He disliked these empty-hearted ritual shows; most of the Wolves had cleverly noticed this, so he was unused to it.

The Bear glanced around, back toward the camp, and approached him. He was young, thin, with sharp eyes and a smooth, womanish smile. Miska had marked him already, noticed all day how most of the other young Bears followed him, and how openly he disdained Ekkatsay.

"Haka-Miska-ka, let me apologize for the way my uncle Ekkatsay greeted you."

"Apologize," Miska said. He noted the tattoos like snakeskin mottling the man's arms and the elaborate beadwork necklace hanging on his chest and wondered if he were Ekkatsay's heir; he remembered the challenge shouted out of the crowd at Ekkatsay, the day before, and thought it was the same man.

"There are those here who know how to greet the greatest of sachems," said the young man in front of him, and made a little gesture with his hand. "Who would have met you with celebrations and given you gifts and honor, instead of ugly words and a harsh face."

Miska smiled at him. "Taksa," he said, "from some men ugly words and a harsh face are signs of honor. But thank you, anyway."

The youth straightened bolt upright, his eyes shining. "You know my name. Let me say then only that I am at your order, whatever you wish—only speak and I will obey you."

Miska nodded to him. "Thank you, I will remember that."

Taksa waited a moment, but Miska only stared at him, and finally the young man backed away, murmuring ridiculous words. Miska rubbed his hands together, thinking this funny. Bear ways sometimes looked different from Wolf ways but underneath they were all the same. Looking back into the trees, where the men were raising shelters, he tried to pick Ekkatsay out in the crowd.

"Haka-Miska!"

The shout came from out on the grass, and he shaded his eyes and saw Hasei coming, with his brother, a deer slung on a pole between them. He waited for them to catch up to him and went along beside them.

"How is the hunting?"

Yoto laughed. Hasei said, "These are fat meadowlands, the deer are everywhere." Slyly: "Nobody's been hunting them very much, O Haka-Miska-ka-ba-ta-ta."

"Don't say so to the Bears," Miska said. He cuffed Hasei on the shoulder, a little rough, letting him know he didn't like the gibe. Hasei quailed down, his hands up like a woman, but he was laughing, and Yoto laughed. They strode off with their pole, headed for the camp, and Miska followed, slower, thinking how to use what he knew about Ekkatsay and Taksa.

Ekkatsay waited until after dark, and then got his nephew alone, on the other side of the trees from the camp. Taksa saw him coming and tried to get out of the way but Ekkatsay got him and slapped him.

"You worthless featherhead." He whacked Taksa again, hard on the side of the head. "Who are you to talk over me to Miska? To a Wolf!"

Taksa shuddered off the blows. He said, between his teeth, "I did nothing. Accuse me before the others, if I did anything."

"You dirt-eating woman's man." Ekkatsay struck at him again.

Taksa eeled back out of the way, out of his uncle's grip. His gaze flickered toward the camp, and Ekkatsay lunged for him. Taksa bounded away.

"You are old," he said, under his breath, his eyes burning. "You are old and stupid, we will lose everything, with you."

Ekkatsay roared, and rushed at him, got him by the shoulders, and flung him down, but the young man came up furious, his arms milling. Then abruptly he broke it off, stepped back, and looked away, toward the camp: someone was coming.

The headman's chest was heaving, his breath burning in his throat. He fought down the will to leap on his nephew and kick his skull in. But here through the trees was one of Miska's Wolves, the short, broad-faced man Ekkatsay had spoken to first, Hasei.

This man gave him a casual wave of his hand, and made no proper greeting, no effort to avert his eyes in respect, but stared boldly at him and Taksa, and went on by past the edge of the trees.

"Wolves have no propriety," Ekkatsay said. "They have no idea of order."

Taksa laughed, startled, and then was moving off, taking the moment to vanish quickly into the dark. Ekkatsay waited a moment, settling himself. He wished he had used a knife on Taksa but that would have been hard to explain. He wondered how much the Wolf had seen. Grimly he went back into the camp.

In the morning the Bears were slow and late again to get ready. Hasei wanted to move on, to get into the cool of the forest before the sun got much higher, but Miska held him up, would not let any of them leave, until finally the Bears had gotten themselves together.

Then Miska with a great show, in front of everybody, sent Ekkatsay's sister-son Taksa out to take the lead. Hasei was amazed; he saw how Ekkatsay stiffened and jerked his head up, and under his breath he muttered, "This is not good, Miska."

Behind him, Yoto said, "What's he doing? Taksa's barely got his feathers yet." He was eating a piece of meat from the night before; his mouth was full and he chewed as he talked.

"Shhh." Hasei shook his head at his brother. Miska was coming toward them, as Taksa loudly and with wavings of his arms got his followers together and started away across the meadow. Miska caught Hasei's attention with a look.

"Go with them, Hasei," he said. "Keep them out of trouble."

"I'll go too," Yoto said. He swallowed first, before he spoke to Miska.

Miska's lips stretched into a smile; his eyes glittered. "No, you stay with me. Keep me out of trouble."

Yoto gave a derisive yelp. He tossed the last of the meat over his shoulder. Hasei left him strutting around and went off after Taksa. He knew what trouble Miska had been talking about; there were a lot more Bears than Wolves, even with Taksa's band gone on ahead.

The land rolled on to the east, in deep meadows between stands of old oaks. The Bear people burned off the meadows every now and then, so the grass grew deep and lush. The dew was heavy on the flowering stems; with every step Hasei sent a shower of water in front of him. He went along just after Taksa's band and a little to one side, out of their tracks. There were ten of them, all young, green boys, and they were Bears, they lumbered along as if anything they met would run away from them, they grumbled to each other, dragging their spears and bows along behind them, they stopped often, to pick at berries, to talk and argue.

Toward the end of the morning they came into the broken, heavily wooded hills, and there Hasei caught up with Taksa.

"Are you going to send somebody out ahead?" Hasei said. The Bears had stopped again, this time by a stream, where they were jostling each other for space to drink. Tall maple trees grew up here, and the wind got them to swaying suddenly, as if they were waving their arms.

Taksa snorted at him. He had a spear, with a thin long tip of earth's blood, and he leaned on it as he stood there, like some wise old man propping himself on the earth. "There are so many of us—who would attack us?"

Hasei didn't bother to explain. He drifted off by himself. The Bears followed the stream backward up the crease between the folded hills, but Hasei climbed to the ridgeline, and went along the rise of the hill, watching around him.

The wind had died, and the heat of the day thickened in the dusty air under the trees. The oaks and maples gave way to pines, the crunchy leaves and mast to mats of needles under his feet. He found some good mushrooms, what the women called baby's thumbs, and the men woods pricks, and gathered them up in his hand. A little while later he came out on the brow of the hill, looking out over the narrow valley to the east, and sat down and ate the mushrooms.

The hill was higher than anything around. Sitting on its brim he looked down eastward over a sweep of trees stretching toward the next hills. Somewhat to the south a pond glistened in among the trees; nearer, more easterly, the dark green flow of the forest opened out into two narrow stretches of meadow, one alongside the other. The second meadow lay at the foot of a distant hill, rising steep through green trees to a gray rocky crag. Just below the bare rock, the lightning-blasted tree like a big wooden feather poked up from the brush. The air above the meadow and the tree looked smoky. Everywhere else the sky was clear.

Hasei sat comfortably in the sun, watching the valley. From the rock where he was sitting, littered with owl pellets and broken twigs and bones, he could see out over the top of the forest. The wind tossed everything into constant motion. Above the seething heads of the trees three little sparrows were chasing a raven as big as a hawk. Off in the nearer of the two meadows a doe and a fawn grazed. He could tell where Taksa was by the way the birds veered and boiled up above them, screeching. The great stirring and swaying of the forest held his eyes. He tried to find words to describe it, not merely to say what he saw, but words that would sound like the forest churning in the wind. He did this often, and had many little strings of words, which in his mind felt like the belts of power that hung in Miska's lodge. He never told anybody any of his words; he was afraid of what the other men would say if they knew what he did.

He watched the big raven dodge and dive, trying to escape from the furious sparrows, its black feathers splayed. Ragged winged raven, he thought, and waited for more words to come. He was still waiting when in the nearer meadow the mother deer abruptly lifted her head and stared away into the trees.

He put the word belt away in his mind; he watched carefully where the doe was looking. After a moment, far off in the trees, he saw something moving, and although he caught only a glimpse and far away, he saw that it ran upright and knew it was a human being. Someone was going along through the forest on a path that matched Taksa's, slightly somewhat off to the north. Not many people, he thought, only one, perhaps, but somebody was watching them.

He thought he knew who this was, but he wasn't sure, and so he went with some urgency down the slope and off through the woods to catch up with Taksa again.

He found the Bears again at the foot of the ridge, working their way along the creek through dense woods. Ahead of them beyond the dark lacing of the trees lay the first of the bright green sunlit meadows, and even through the trees Hasei could hear the chattering of birds up there. He went to Taksa, who was walking along at the front of everybody.

"You should send someone out ahead," Hasei said. "Don't you hear those birds? Something's bothering them out there."

"They're birds," Taksa said, irritated. "Birds are like women, they are always chattering. Haka-Miska gave me this to lead, and I will lead, not you."

Hasei shrugged; but he let all the rest of the Bears go ahead of him into the meadow.

They walked out onto the lush bending grass. The birds had stopped their uproar entirely. Under the clear blue sky the meadow stretched away toward the trees at the far edge. Beyond them the pale rocks of the hilltop lifted up into the sky. Hasei looked widely all around him, and trotted up to Taksa again.

"You should get your weapons ready, we are walking into an ambush."

Taksa barked out a startled laugh, his eyes wide. He swung his hand out toward the meadow. "What are you talking about? We can see everything around us, who can ambush us here?"

Hasei gave him a single hard look. The other Bears were looking around them, and one or two muttered, "Get him out of here. Who is he to tell Bears what to do?" Hasei cleared his throat. He turned, and went out past Taksa, into the grass, shouting.

"Come up, come up, I can see you, get up."

For a moment his voice rang hollow in the silence, and he felt a sudden horrible doubt. Then up out of the grass the Wolves stood, the untopped boys, all around the Bears, some only a few steps away, their bows and spears and war clubs in their hands.

A great yell went up from all the Bears. They bunched up, putting their backs to each other, their spears bristling. "What is this?" Their voices rose in shouts. "Stay back—there's more of us than you—"

Lopi was directly in front of Hasei. He gave the older man a glare, and came up stiff-legged toward Taksa, fumbling for something to say. "Unh—We greet you, unh—" He shot another angry look at Hasei.

Taksa was backing away from him, his spear gripped in both hands. "Get back! Who are you? Stand where you are or I'll gut you like a fish!"

Hasei gritted his teeth together. This was getting out of hand fast. He kept his eye on Taksa's spear, with its sleek black tip of earth's blood; if it came to a fight, he wanted that spear. Then, off behind them on the meadow, someone shouted.

He stepped back, looking out across the trampled grass, and his voice went slippery with relief. "Here comes Miska, and Ekkatsay, too."

Lopi and Taksa were still staring at each other, Taksa with his spear before him, and Lopi gripping his war club. Hasei went up to the younger Wolf and grabbed him by the arm and shook him, backing him away from the other man. Into his ear, he said, "This is Taksa, the sister-son of the Bear headman. Miska has already made something of him."

Lopi cast him off. "I was just—Haka-Miska!" He swung toward the men coming up through their midst, and his face shone.

Miska and Ekkatsay walked up among them, with the rest of the band coming along behind them. Ekkatsay said, loud, "What is this, now?" He strode up to Taksa and bellowed at him, and Hasei could see he wanted to hit him. "This is how you lead fighters?"

Miska moved up past him, the other Wolves pressing after. Lopi went up to him, bubbling like a brook with words.

"Haka-Miska-ka! I have been here now many days, waiting. Up in the pass, someone is there. I have kept watch. You must let us go fight them."

"Who were you fighting here?" Miska said, and shoved him in the chest. "Many days. You lie, boy, you have been here one day. Now you embarrass me in front of this other great headman. Take us to your camp, which had better be ready for us." He shoved Lopi again, but Hasei could see he was pleased. Lopi's face fell, not understanding.

The other boys were already running back across the meadow; some of them were dancing as they went, making up a loud song about hunting bears. Hasei looked all around him, at the other men, Ekkatsay's people amassed behind him, and the Wolves scattered around the edge. He thought altogether they still were fewer than the Bears but he liked the look of it anyway, if they got the jump, especially after what had just happened.

Miska was walking right in front of him, side by side with Ekkatsay. The war club swung from his hand, trailing the two swaths of hair. Hasei's gaze kept straying back to that hair. He had thought at first they would be going after the Bears. Then it had been Turtles. Now, from what Lopi had babbled out, they were likely going to fight both Turtles and Bears. His brother Yoto stood just beyond the sachem; behind Miska's back, he caught Hasei's eye and made a face, puffing up his cheeks and sticking his tongue out, and Hasei nodded. Then Miska set off again, and he moved to keep close to Miska, following Lopi's band back to their camp.

# CHAPTER SEVEN

"It was just a game," Lopi said. "We wouldn't have hurt them."

"You sound like a baby," Miska said. "Why threaten somebody unless you mean to hurt them? You made a good camp here, though." Lopi had put his camp by the creek at the edge of the meadow, where he could watch the pass and the approach to it at once, and no one could sneak up on him easily. Most of the other men were settling around the little blackened circle of the fire, although it was still daylight. The hunters had not come in yet and so there was nothing to eat. Because even the topped Wolves had fallen into the habit of wearing their hair down and long, like Miska, it was easy to pick them out, scattered in among the Bears with their topknots. Miska looked up at the pass, a dent in the hill below the upjerk of the rock, where the sun's light still blazed. "How many people are up there now?"

Hasei and Yoto drifted toward him and Lopi. The boy cast a white-rimmed look at them and cleared his throat, suddenly even more nervous. "I'm not sure, Haka-Miska—I think two handfuls maybe." His voice squeaked.

Hasei, coming up to them, elbowed the boy in the side. "Why aren't you sure? Did you go up yourself to look?"

Lopi twitched his head around. "I did. But—"

"But he can't count," Yoto said. As usual, he was eating something. "Haka-Miska, let me scout the camp."

Miska folded his arms over his chest. "Lopi's already done that. What I need to know is how Tisconum is watching us."

"Unh," Hasei and Yoto said, together.

"I want you and Yoto and the rest of the two lodges all to go out and get between him and this camp. Go up on the way toward the pass, spread out, and make sure nobody from up there ever gets close to us. Lopi, where is their camp up there?"

Lopi said, "At the foot of the broken tree. There's a spring, I think."

"I think there is. Good. The turtle doesn't leave its shell but still he's clever and he may have put some scouts out, make his shell bigger that way." He nodded at the two older Wolves. "Don't use any Bears. Get the rest of the lodges up with you, and go up onto the slope below the pass and if he has put anybody around there to watch us, drive them back toward his camp. Go carefully, I think he has more than Lopi counted, maybe. Wait until you see Lopi and the boys coming to attack the camp."

Hasei said, "I don't like fighting at night," and Yoto spoke with him. "You said the last time—"

"I think you won't have to fight until day comes," Miska said. "And I know what I said the last time but every time is different. Go do as I say. Take bows. Hasei—"

Hasei looked up. Miska saw the fear in him and nudged him with his arm, impatient, crowding him into shape. "You think too much sometimes. Just listen to me. Keep watch on everybody. In the morning, see if you can get above the pass, somehow."

Hasei grunted at him, out of words for once. He went away after Yoto, back to get the two lodges of Wolves; as he walked along Miska saw his head turn, aiming his gaze not toward the pass but into the trees across the creek, which would cover him. Miska swung around toward the camp again, where there were many more Bears now than Wolves, and they were already jostling each other.

Lopi said, "I did scout the pass."

Miska laid his hand on the boy's shoulder. "I believe you. Now come on. Let's get them doing something other than killing each other." He pushed the younger Wolf on ahead of him, into the camp.

Wolves and Bears, the boys were dancing, not to mean anything or make anything happen but just to dance, their bodies flowing darkly shining in circles around the fire. Ekkatsay glanced at Miska, sitting beside him on the ground, wondering what was going on here.

They had crossed the deer meadows in two days and seen no sign of any Turtles. Yet now the men in both bands, especially the young men, were excited and ready to fight anything. He thought of Taksa and his heart chilled. He could see Miska favored Taksa, believed his fat tongue and his sleek look, and, maybe, wanted someone else to lead Ekkatsay's village, someone who had not defied him.

The dancers sang and stamped their feet and two of the boys pounded on a log with sticks and the steady throb flooded over him, lifting him up on its swell; his heart beat with their hearts, he wanted to fight also, whoever that was in the pass.

He shook himself, fighting off Miska's spell. He had to be careful, he thought Miska was only waiting for the chance to kill him and put Taksa in his place.

He wondered briefly if he might kill Miska instead, leap on him now and strike him down with his own club.

The sachem moved suddenly, and Ekkatsay jerked, half-rising, and then falling down on his hams again, tense as a cocked arm. But Miska only glanced up at him, had not seen into his thoughts. The paint had worn off Miska's face and he looked younger, like an untopped boy, easy to think since he wore his hair long and shaggy in the ugly fashion of the Wolves.

Ekkatsay said, stiffly, "What do you intend to do tomorrow?"

Miska said nothing. He held a little pouch in his hands, and looked down at it. Ekkatsay felt the unanswered question hanging between them, and stiffened up with insult. He thought what Miska had in his hands was a pouch of smoking herb, but then Miska held something out to him, not smoke.

"Look at this."

Ekkatsay made a sound in his chest, surprised. He took the small cool stone from Miska's palm. Too smooth even for stone. He held it in the light of the fire. The glisten reminded him of sunlight on water. At first he didn't even recognize the object itself, but then he saw it was supposed to look like a head, a man's head, very strange and not real, with a long arched nose and a drooping mouth, and the hair all drawn up in a huge topknot.

"That's a Bear knot," he said, and put his free hand up to his own head. "I don't think this is Bear work, though. That's some kind of demon."

He let Miska take it from him, although he wanted it. The cool smooth touch lingered on his fingertips long after Miska had taken it back.

"No," Miska said. "This comes from far away to the west." His voice was soft, barely audible under the pounding and stamping and the shouts of the men, and Ekkatsay tipped closer to him. Miska's fist closed over the little head. "It's not a demon. It's a man, there are men who look like this."

Ekkatsay was awkwardly tilted toward him; the sachem's soft voice gripped him, and when it stopped, he looked into Miska's face and saw him shut his eyes and lower his head. Something rushed into his mind, then, some hope, he saw Miska smaller, weaker, only a man, after all. Then the sachem opened his eyes, and stared at him, and said, "I have sent someone to bring me word of them, where they are now, how close they are. If I can strike at them, I mean to. When I decide, I will call, and you will come, with all your fighters."

Ekkatsay straightened up, away from him, annoyed. He reminded himself that Miska had not beaten the Bears, as he had other villages, and now the Bear village on the bluff was a stronghold against him. But Ekkatsay was not in his village now, was out here in the forest, and the thunderous drumming kept him from thinking well. He grunted something not yes or no, and turned his face toward the dancers.

It came to him that Miska would not be telling him this if he planned to kill him. At once he thought Miska might speak so to lull him, before he killed him. His mind twisted and lurched, unsteady. His fingertips still held the cool smooth luster of the little head. He stared into the fire, afraid to sleep.

From the dark behind him, up toward the pass, there came the long quavering howl of a wolf.

Hasei was afraid of the night; he had heard enough stories of the Bad Twin to be wary of the moon and the darkness, and he knew that the night air was poisonous. The steady croaking of frogs sounded everywhere, a deafening clatter. He curled back deeper into the space under the uprooted tree, angry at Miska for sending them out here.

Miska had given them enough daylight that Hasei had been able to get far up onto the slope below the pass, where he could watch the way down and see anybody creeping on the camp. As soon as the sun had set he found this shelter, a downed tree at the edge of a little clearing, just below the approach to the pass. Now he crawled in out of the way of the rising moon. He was already used to the yelling of the frogs, and he wanted to sleep, but his body was too wakeful, and being angry at Miska he thought of what he might say to him. Then he realized that the frogs' voices were dying away, not everywhere, but up above him on the slope. Down from the height, someone was coming toward him in the dark.

He lifted his head, his ears straining, catching the small crunch of leaves, the startled warning call of an owl almost over his head. He got quietly out from under the log, leaving his bow and war club behind, and crouched in the shadowy moonlight by the uprooted end. Feeling along the ground around him, he found a rock, which he pried out of the mossy dirt.

Out there the other man was creeping along again, circling the clearing. The glare of the moon washed everything into black and white shapes. Hasei, crouched down behind the cover of the wild tangle of roots, saw the stooped figure sidle along the edge of the open ground, and cocking his arm back he threw the rock.

He missed his aim, the rock crashing into the brush, but the other man bounded into the air like a spooked deer and plunged away into the trees. Hasei dashed after him, trying to follow his course through the dark, zigzagging through the first spindling birches at the edge of the woods.

In the deep darkness of the forest he stopped, one hand on the rough bark of a maple trunk. The other man had stopped running, or at least was making no noise doing it; there was no sound anywhere but the drift of the wind in the branches overhead, and farther off the jugging of the frogs. Hasei leaned against the maple, feeling the darkness pack itself tighter around him, muffling and smothering; he fought off his sense of panic. Then, somewhere very close, he heard a twig snap.

He went stiff, his breath stopped. He thought he smelled sweat. His skin tingled all over. He leaned his whole body against the tree trunk, letting it protect him, and then almost within reach he saw the other man, stooped, cautious, making his way back toward the clearing.

Hasei leapt on him. The other man went down under his weight, twisting under him. Hasei flailed away at the writhing body, trying to pin it down, to strike a good blow, but the other man was slithering away from him. He saw the vague shape leap upright, and he grabbed around him for some weapon, a branch, a stone, but then the other man was running again, this time going uphill, and stopping for nothing, careless of how much noise he made.

Hasei stayed where he was. He thought that man would not

come back this way again, not before daybreak anyway. The dark closed in around him again, tangible as fog, filling his eyes and nostrils and mouth. His skin was shrinking from the cold and the dark and he wanted to get in somewhere safe.

Off to his left and downhill a little, there rose the wobbling yell of a wolf. He stopped, put his hands to his mouth, and howled back, to tell the others where he was, and went quickly back to his shelter and his weapons, to wait until the sun rose.

Ekkatsay lay still, but not asleep, wondering how he had lost control of this. Taksa had never been more than an annoyance before Miska showed up; among the Bears the older people of course paid no heed to anything a boy said or did. Now half the village was following him.

That wasn't it, Ekkatsay knew. He thought he had never had any control over what was happening, that moving the village up onto the hill had made him think he was safe, and so he had not been careful. And Miska like the wind blowing had found the chink in his wall. Bear and Wolf, man and boy, they were all following Miska.

Lying on the ground with the stars over him, wondering where that wind would blow him in the fight to come, he shivered in a strange eagerness, to have it happen, to get it done. To see what happened.

If they failed, anyway, it would be Miska's fault. If Miska failed, Taksa would come creeping to his uncle's feet to beg forgiveness. If Taksa even survived. If Ekkatsay survived. He had not fought in years, since he was a boy, like Taksa, chafing under his uncle's hand. The thing went around and around in his head like the eddy in a stream, never stopping, going nowhere. Ekkatsay shut his eyes, trying to sleep.

## CHAPTER EIGHT

Ekkatsay slept fitfully, and in the morning he jolted awake. For an instant he was merely glad to find himself still alive. The sky was pale but the sun had not risen. He got up from the ground and went around arousing the other Bears, made them take their weapons up, and got his spear. He wanted to be ready to move, when Miska called him.

Miska was already awake, he saw, getting his own fighters up, drawing them close around the dead campfires. Ekkatsay took his people there also, and Taksa, so they were all standing there together when the first long fingers of the sun reached up over the hill to the east.

Miska went around them all, speaking names, nodding to others, even Bears—Taksa he spoke to, and Taksa smiled sleekly under the stroke of Miska's voice.

Then Miska came to Ekkatsay. Paint streaked his face like the mask of a wolf and the Bear headman could make out nothing of his expression.

"We will go first, but not straight. We go around. Follow me, I know the way." He spoke loudly enough that all the others could hear him, even over their low talk. "Lopi will stay here with his band, and make noise, and dance, until the height of the sun." He turned his head, looking around, to see Lopi. The Bears, Ekkatsay saw, were still chattering, like birds or women, Taksa on the strut among them pretending to give orders, but the Wolves stood utterly quiet, watching Miska. "Then Lopi will bring his band up into the pass and start the fight."

"Ahhh," Lopi cried, and leapt into the air, his knees flexing. All the men gave up a huge shout.

Miska turned and started off, with no more talking than that.

Ekkatsay followed, determined not to fall behind him—to keep Miska always under his eyes. They went across the clearing—not directly up toward the pass, but in another direction, as if they were leaving. As soon as they got under the cover of the trees, Miska turned hard to his left, and they began to climb.

Ekkatsay followed close behind him. Miska was following a narrow little trail that wound up through stands of maple and oak, where rocks poked up through mats and drifts of old leaves. Ekkatsay's spear was awkward to carry, got in his way, snagged in the close dense forest. He glanced back once to see where Taksa was, and saw the other Bears all filing after him and Miska, a snake of men winding back down the brushy slope. He faced forward again, his stomach rolling. Every step he took now was harder, going uphill, going into trouble. He pushed on after Miska, itching to get on with it.

Before the dawn even broke Hasei left his shelter and climbed on up the hillside, not following the easy way to the pass, which the fighters up there could keep under their eyes, but struggling up through the rocks and broken ground on the flank of the hill. Just below the crest of the ridge, where the ground broke into a long narrow ledge, Yoto his brother joined him, and then the other six men, scratched and bloody from fighting their way through the brush.

Nobody said anything. Everybody had brought some cold meat from the day before and they ate it and passed a gourd of water around. Birch trees grew thick on the sheltered ledge and the night air still clung here and there in little fogs on the ground. Hasei stood looking up at the ridge of the hill, which seemed to arch up over him; behind the brushy summit the sky was turning blue. Off well to the right, beyond clumps of pine trees, the broken rock jutted up into the sky, so he knew the pass was just below it, about even with this ledge.

He glanced at the other men; he was remembering what Miska had said, that they should try to get above the pass. His gaze rose to the broken rocky slope before them, rising straight up, tangled in poison bushes and brambles. Maybe they could find a way up there. He waved to the others to follow him, and started off.

Miska was quick and sure-footed and the way was hard, through thickets where the only path was a narrow track like a tunnel through dense twigs, the branches whipping and slapping their faces as they passed, the ground rocky underfoot. Ekkatsay rushed over the rocks and crashed through the brush, Miska always just disappearing ahead of him.

They climbed up and up. The path itself disappeared and they were fighting through chest-high brush, poisonbush and vines. They came to the foot of a sheer wall of stone, the seamed cracked face of the hill. At once Miska began to scale it, climbing four-footed up a vertical crease in the cracked jumbled cliff. Ekkatsay held back a moment, looking up at the climb, while the other men gathered panting and sweating around him; then he cut a thong from his shirt, and hung his spear on his back, and began to scramble up after Miska—he would die, he thought, before he let Miska do more than he did.

The other men came after him. He rose from rock to rock, moving fast, watching Miska's feet above him. His breath began to burn and his arms hurt, his fingertips sore and raw from the stone. He hauled himself out on a ledge of the rock face, up into the open air. Ahead, Miska was jogging off across a narrow rocky flat toward a thick stand of trees, dark green against the blazing blue sky.

Ekkatsay flung himself after him. The trees were thinner here, older, shrouding the hillside, trunks erupting up out of the rocky ground like tongues of the earth; a hare darted suddenly out of the way, Ekkatsay catching just a flash of gray-brown flank and white tail, the suspended leap like an instant's flight, before he was deep into the trees.

There was no path, the ground beneath the heavy boughs of leaves was broken under the crust of tree droppings. Picking his way along Ekkatsay lost sight of Miska and rushed on past the last of the big maples and out onto a sudden treeless ridge of rock, and Miska directly in front of him was waving wildly at him to get down.

He sank onto his hams. Crouching over, the Wolf sachem slipped back past him, back toward the men coming after them. Ekkatsay shuffled forward toward the peak of the ridge, staying down out of the sky, until sheltering by a rocky spur he could look out.

Astonished, he saw that they had come out on top of the great rocky crag that stood above the pass. The steep brushy ridge on the other side faced him; between, he could see the whole of the enemy camp. Below him, at the foot of the rock, the stumped lightning-blackened branches of the tree spread like a bad web, a litter of camp gear visible on the ground beneath. Out farther on the flat ground, in the hollow of the pass, a lot of people were moving around, rushing here and there, and then as he watched they all reached where they were rushing to, the sides of the pass, and disappeared into the rocks.

Ekkatsay didn't have to look into the sky to tell where the sun was; he could see his own shadow, huddled as close under him as it could get. From somewhere below the pass, now, he heard the first faint breath of a yell. Lopi and the boy Wolves were rushing up into the pass, and down there, the Turtles were ready for them.

He took his spear off his back, and tested the blade with his thumb; his belly rolled, he felt sick to his stomach. A quick look at the rock behind him showed him men appearing out of the trees, where Miska was gathering them—most of the Bears were still coming up the hill, the last of them would not be here for a while yet. Miska brought the handful who had kept up with him and Ekkatsay, led them on hands and knees up to the edge of the rock.

Miska crawled up next to Ekkatsay, said nothing, laid his hand on the Bear headman's shoulder, and pointed off to the right. Ekkatsay blinked, wondering what he was looking at. He saw no place to go. Along the face of the rock there ran a narrow steep sloping ledge, but it was certainly no trail for people. The thin high yelling of the attacking boys grew louder. Ekkatsay could see them now, the leaders anyway, running headlong up the wide much-used path into the broad cleft of the pass. Among the rocks, the men lurking in ambush raised their bows, with arrows set. For a moment, stiff under Miska's hand, Ekkatsay thought, He has led us into a slaughter. We shall see them all dead in a moment. He clutched his spear; but he could hit nothing from this distance.

Lopi, first of all the boys, ran screaming into the saddle of the pass. The archers in the rocks stood up, their bows drawn. Ekkatsay held his breath, he thought to see the wild Wolf-boys die, and then, above them all on the sheer slope on the far side of the pass, up where nobody could possibly be, eight other bowmen suddenly popped up out of the brush.

As the archers in the pass below them flexed their bows to mow down the onrushing boys, these on the height drew their own bows, and shot a volley down into the ambushers. At the same time, Miska bounded suddenly to his feet, and waved his arm, and grabbing Ekkatsay by the arm, he plunged over the rim of the ridge and down the long precipitous ledge.

As he ran he let out a howl that brought every hair on Ekkatsay's body up on end. Helpless in Miska's tow he rushed down the tiny ledge for a few desperate steps, and then bounded free, jumping like the hare into moments of flight above the slippery rock, Miska just ahead of him, going straight down. Their passage broke loose a stream of small rocks that clattered down along with them onto the gentler slope at the foot of the hill. Hurtling after Miska, Ekkatsay raised his own roar into the air, a Bear's deep-lunged bellow. Across the pass, the ambush had broken, the men scurrying and crouching away from the arrows pelting down on them. Lopi and the screeching young Wolves streamed into the pass, and Ekkatsay and Miska and the Bears were rushing down from the height, and in the flat of the pass the Turtles were jerking around, open-mouthed, confused, trapped inside a suddenly closing fist.

Ekkatsay shrieked, triumphant, seeing now how well this all had worked. He forgot to think of Miska or Taksa, he saw only that after days of gnawing fret now he could strike out, and with the spear in his hands stabbing and slicing he cut his way into the fighting.

---

Taksa went down the slope in the midst of the charging Bears, but he did not look for Turtles to kill; he looked for his uncle.

He knew this would be the greatest day of his life, the day of his triumph over Ekkatsay. Today he would become headman of his village, and Miska's trusted friend, and he had already built in his mind a great story of all that would mean.

Now he had to find his chance. He wormed his way through the running pack of screeching men, searching the crowded pass with his eyes. Half the Bears around him veered suddenly off, whooping, to chase the fleeing Turtles. Taksa clutched his spear tight; up there he saw his uncle, fighting with another man, clubbing and stabbing at each other with their spears.

That was an opening, he knew, and started there, to kill Ekkatsay while his back was turned. But before he reached him Ekkatsay drove his spear through the other man's chest.

Taksa stopped still. He reminded himself Ekkatsay was a stupid old fool, not some hero, even though now a man sprawled dead before him. Ekkatsay put one foot on the body and pulled his spear loose. Taksa felt the prickle of warning along his arms and back, and drew aside, watching and waiting.

Ekkatsay stormed on up the pass. Everybody else was moving the other way, going east, chasing the last of the Turtles. Taksa followed his uncle at a distance. He thought Ekkatsay was really a coward, going where there were no enemies, but then Ekkatsay rushed suddenly at a clump of white rocks, and a man hidden there leapt up and they struggled together for an instant, and then the Turtle was bounding away.

Ekkatsay did not chase him. His arms were bloody and he was limping. He turned and went ponderously on, and now Taksa saw where he was going. In the height of the pass, at the foot of the Lightning Tree, was a circle of little stones, sitting stones, and a fire bed. Ekkatsay was going after the Turtles' camp. Taksa moved quietly closer.

Hasei dropped his bow, out of arrows. Below him the fighting filled the pass. Lopi and the boys were hacking hand to hand with Turtles all across the flat ground, and on the far side of the pass from Hasei, Ekkatsay's Bears were pouring like a waterfall down the sheer drop below the rock. Down there, seeing their chances, the Turtles were already starting to run.

Hasei gripped his war club and rushed down the steep slope, struggling through the dense brush, his feet sliding out from under him, and the air thick with dust. The open trampled ground of the pass was clogged with men, some screaming and fighting and some down and others running. Through the haze of dust in the air he could make out no one. Two men came rushing at him and he saw their long Turtle earlocks and jumped to stop them. One dodged by him but he tripped the other down, and swung his club around to strike. The man leapt up and they faced each other a moment, snarling. Hasei crouched down, looking for an opening, while the other man danced from side to side. Then from behind something struck Hasei on the head.

He went down hard, his senses flying; for maybe a long time he hung in some endless dark space. He came to on his hands and knees, his stomach rolling. He leapt up, but the other man, and whoever had struck him, were gone.

His club lay on the ground near him. He snatched it up and went running across the pass. There were still people fighting. Lopi and some of the other young Wolves ran past him, whooping, blood streaked on their faces. He swerved to keep from stepping on a body lying face up on the ground. Then ahead of him, where the path through the pass dipped down to the east, he saw his brother Yoto and two of the other Wolves, still fighting.

He ran to help them. They had several men backed up against a boulder at the side of the pass. Just as he reached them the knot of bodies burst apart and the Wolves staggered back under a flurry of blows. Two Turtles rushed by them, and a third, a tall man with feathers in his hair, struck Yoto down.

The other two Turtles were running off but the tall man swung around, his spear in his hands, to stab Yoto as he sprawled on the ground.

Hasei yelled; he rushed in toward his brother, swinging his club at knee height, and knocked the down-thrusting spear aside. His counterstroke swished past the tall man's belly. For an instant they glowered at each other, ready to strike, and Hasei saw the dark eyes of the other man small with hatred and a ripple of fear went through him and he lunged forward, to smash him down, this man who hated him so much. But the tall man wheeled suddenly, dodged his strike, ran off down the hill to the east.

As he ran, he raised his voice in a high rippling yell, and at that sound the last of the Turtles left fighting in the pass turned and ran too.

Hasei knelt by Yoto, who was trying to sit up. The side of his head was swelling and bloody. Hasei took his arm and helped him rise. As he did, Yoto looked up, and their eyes met; Hasei tightened his hand on his brother's arm, thinking of the spear descending, how Yoto might now be dead, dead forever, and then Yoto was on his feet beside him, alive, smelling of sweat and blood, and both of them looked away, speechless in a rush of feeling.

Hasei drew a deep breath, looking around the pass. Nobody was fighting anymore. Lopi was leaping and shouting at the very height of it; a lot of the men had run down the east side of the pass after the fleeing Turtles but they were starting to come back up the path. "We are done here," he said. He let go of his brother's arm. "Let's go find Miska."

Yoto wiped his hand over his face, smearing blood across his cheek. "Let's go find some water first." He hung his arm around Hasei's neck, and they went along together toward the captured camp.

Even before the fighting started, Ekkatsay had noticed where the Turtles' camp was, in under the dead tree. He looked quickly around it. The fire was cold ash, and the bones scattered all around were gnawed clean, but by the foot of the tree he saw what he really wanted: two big pots full of water. He laid his spear down and dipped his hand into the pot and drank.

From here he could see almost all the way down the pass to the east. They were still fighting down there but most of the Turtles were already gone, and half the Bears and Wolves after them. He wiped his hand over his face. There had been many more of the Turtles than of Bears and Wolves, but he thought he would run too, if he found himself surrounded like that. He bent over the pot of water to drink from it directly, and heard something behind him.

He wheeled. Taksa stepped in from the sunlight, into the thin striped shadow of the tree. He held his spear low in his hand, and a tilted smile crept across his face. Ekkatsay stiffened; he saw his nephew intended to kill him. His own spear impossibly far away at his feet.

"You don't dare," he said, his voice rasping.

Taksa said, "Do I not? Ask him." He nodded past Ekkatsay, toward the sunlight, and the Bear headman jerked his head around to look.

Miska came up toward them. He was naked, shining with sweat, all his Wolf paint streaked across his body, his war club in his hand. Ekkatsay's back tingled up with fear. He took a step sideways, trying to get out from between Miska and Taksa. His nephew was staring at him, his arms tensed, ready to spring; he would wait for Miska's signal, Ekkatsay thought. Ekkatsay licked his lips, looking from one to the other, thinking he would fight them both, knowing with a stony heart that they would kill him. Miska walked up to him and Taksa, and Ekkatsay's foul nephew swooped his hand out in a broad groveling gesture.

"I greet you, great sachem, who has given us victory." He straightened, and his eyes went to Ekkatsay. "Let me present you with a victory of my own, Haka-Miska-ka."

Miska glanced at Ekkatsay, and said, "I need no victories from you, snake tongue." He raised his club and smashed Taksa across the head.

Ekkatsay let out a bellow. His nephew went to his knees and then flat on his face, spraying the thick red mess of his brain across the ground. Ekkatsay raised his eyes, startled, to look at Miska.

Miska said, "Why do you look so surprised, Ekkatsay?" He stepped forward, turning, so that he stood astride Taksa's body, facing Ekkatsay; his body was splattered with Taksa's blood. His voice was easy, almost gentle, but his eyes were hard and hot and bright. "Did you think I would let this slippery boy kill you? We are brothers, remember. I would not do such a thing."

Ekkatsay stammered, "I never—I didn't think—"

"Don't lie to me," Miska said. "We are brothers, we can trust each other. But, Ekkatsay, heed this, you are my younger brother. Give me my rights as your older brother, and all will go well between us." He lifted the war club and touched Ekkatsay's chest with the blood-soaked stone. "Do you understand me?"

Ekkatsay licked his lips. “Yes, Haka-Miska.”

“Make me a belt of power to signify this, and send it to my village, so that I know you understand.”

“Yes, Haka-Miska.”

Miska smiled at him, and the smile went all the way to his eyes. “Good. You are a good fighter, Ekkatsay, I saw how you fought and I liked it.”

Down the pass suddenly a quavering yell went up, distant, fading. Miska nodded. “He’s running. Let’s go and see who is still alive.”

“I have to take up my nephew’s body,” Ekkatsay said.

Miska nodded. “Whatever you wish.” He went away down toward the hollow of the pass, where a knot of Wolves and Bears were screaming and cheering and waving their arms.

Ekkatsay lowered his eyes to Taksa. A surge of hate filled him and he put one foot on Taksa and stood on him. The women of his village would wail, they had loved him, pretty-tongued evil little man. Ekkatsay began to laugh; he thought of Taksa leering at him, ready to kill him, and now he was lying under Ekkatsay’s foot. The laughter shook him, so for a while he could not bend to pick the body up. He would follow Miska anywhere, he thought, anywhere. Slowly he gathered up his nephew’s body and took it away.

# CHAPTER NINE

They all gathered in the Turtle camp and looked over their hurts. Altogether, four of the Bears had been killed, and two of the Wolves, and nearly everybody had wounds and bruises. There was very little food, but Miska had it all given out equally and they sat around together and finished it. The sun was lowering down into the massed trees on the western side of the world. Miska showed no signs of wanting to move on; the pass anyway was as good a place to camp as any, although the spring under the rock was too slow to water so many people.

When they had eaten all the food, they built the fire up, found some logs and rocks to drum on, and began to dance. They danced their fighting, each of them in his fearsome strength killing hundreds, each almost dying many times, over and over, saving himself by desperate courage. Miska, who never danced, sat under the Lightning Tree with Ekkatsay, and called to Hasei to find him a pipe.

Yoto had a pipe with him. Hasei's head hurt and he had no wish to dance; he and his brother went over to sit by the sachem. Some of Ekkatsay's followers joined them, and Lopi came up too, stooping and bowing with a great air of humility, until Miska pointed to him to sit down with them and be quiet. Lopi sank down beside Hasei, his face glowing. Hasei nudged him.

"What are you here for, boy? Are you the water bringer?"

Lopi muttered, dropping his gaze. On his far side, Faskata, his uncle, patted his head like a child. Miska ignored them. He was packing herb into the pipe. Ekkatsay, on his far side, stretched his arms up expansively, and a wide smile crossed his face.

"So, Miska, I suppose now the Turtles will leave our hunting grounds alone?"

Miska said, "This is the only time I wish for Corban the rodent. Who has fire?"

Lopi bounded up and ran for a coal. Ekkatsay was still chuckling. Hasei had never seen him so jovial and friendly; he thought victory was a good medicine. Of course Taksa was dead, too, which likely helped.

Miska gave the Bear headman a sideways look, perhaps finding him too happy. He said, "He won't let this be. Tisconum. He will want revenge."

The Bear headman shrugged his burly shoulders. He had stuck feathers into his hair. A long hank of Turtle hair hung from the sleeve of his shirt. He said, "Today we killed many of them."

"There are many more," Miska said.

Ekkatsay shuffled that off with a gesture. "What of these prisoners?" They had taken six captives; one was badly wounded and would die anyway and they would probably leave him.

Lopi came back with a hot stick and Miska lit the pipe. He sucked on it, exhaling puffs of smoke, until the herb in the bowl was glowing red. He took the pipe in his hand, and looked around the circle of men. Hasei could smell the sweet smoke; he leaned forward, his arms on his knees. His head ached and he was tired. Then Miska was holding the pipe out to him, first of them all.

He straightened, warm all over with pride. He said, "Lopi led the charge."

Miska said, "Lopi was glad to see you there too." He waved the pipe at Hasei, who took it, feeling all their eyes watching him, put the stem to his lips, and drew in the hot sacred smoke. At once his head stopped hurting and he wasn't tired anymore. He took the pipe in his hand, looked around at the men watching him, and turned and gave the pipe to Lopi.

"He didn't know we were there and he still ran straight into their teeth."

Lopi swelled, his head rising, his face shining. He took the pipe, nodding, first at Hasei, and then at Miska, and then at everybody, nodding and smiling, as if at any moment he might say something very momentous, but he never did. He took a long pull on the pipe and exploded in coughs and doubled up, hacking, while the other men laughed.

Faskata his uncle pounded him on the back. "Next time, don't take in so much. Remember, you're still just a little boy."

Lopi straightened, still choking. He had the pipe still; he fought for enough control to pass it on, and held it out to Ekkatsay, but he could not talk.

Ekkatsay took the pipe and smoked it. He said, "There are many warriors here," and passed the pipe along.

When they had all smoked, Miska said, "More of you died than we did, so you can have most of the prisoners. But I need two, because two Wolves died."

Ekkatsay shrugged. "You are the sachem."

Miska laughed. One of the Bears had produced a little pouch of smoke and was packing the pipe again. Hasei could feel the pounding of the drums in the ground under him. Yoto nudged him and he grinned and wrapped his arm around his brother's neck, sharing the glory.

The pipe was going around again. More of the men were joining them. Abruptly Miska got up and went off across the height of the pass, and stood there, looking out toward the east, where Tisconum had gone. He was already thinking about what to do next. Hasei was glad he didn't have to think; all he had to do was follow Miska. The pipe came around to him again and he smoked, tired again, very content.

The two Wolves who had died were both boys, sons of women in Anapatha's lodge. Miska carried them back to the village. The two prisoners came along with them—one fought and argued and tried twice to escape, although they soothed him and told him how lucky he was, since now he might become a Wolf. The other captive, an older man, only walked along quietly and said nothing.

The women came out to meet them, moaned and cried and wept over the bodies of the two boys, and led them all back into the village, where they had a big feast waiting. The bodies of the two dead boys lay by the river, covered with branches, until the morning, when they would be buried in the ground. All through the evening their mothers and sisters and the other people went and sat there and wept and called their names and made promises to them of memory and duty.

Later, when the moon rose, their mothers, daughters of Anapatha, went to Miska and demanded the prisoners.

The one who had argued and fought and tried to escape, as Miska had thought, was a weakling, moaned even while he was being bound to the stake, and wept for mercy when he saw the women approaching him with their hot sticks and knives. Miska moved away from him, sick with his weakness. But the older man sat with his back to the stake and his arms folded, and stared straight ahead and began to sing his death song.

Anapatha's daughters went to him with their knives and he sang of his boyhood and what he had learned from his elders, and the women put coals on the bottoms of his feet and the palms of his hands and he sang of his manhood ceremonies and how he had slain a woods bison by himself. They cut off his fingers and sliced his scalp and cheeks and he sang of fighting and winning and washing in the gore of his enemies.

They slashed his arms and chest until the blood streamed from him and he sang of a great battle, in which he and Tisconum and his brothers had fought against the Wolves, who had come on them all unprovoked, but the Turtles had driven them back into the forest. At this, with his face hacked in pieces and his arms half cut from his body, he turned to Miska and smiled, and sang triumphantly of the death of the Wolf sachem Burns-His-Feet and the humiliation of his people.

Miska sat by this brave man and listened to his song. He could feel the man's life gathering at his lips, ready to flow away, but the

Turtle warrior's great heart fought to hold on. The other prisoner died, and his body was hauled off; he would not be taken into the Wolves, he had failed the test, no Wolf would eat such meat. The women piled hot fire around the remaining captive and the smell of his own body roasting rose around him and the man struggled to keep his voice steady and strong and sang of his deeds in the battle just past and Miska knew he was giving way and yet he faced death strongly and he held his life within him, it begging to escape, yet he held tight to it, Miska could almost see it, a glow around him, the power streaming around him. He leaned closer, even into the heat of the fire, to share that power with the dying man, to carry him on in his struggle toward death. The women stuck their knives in to the hilt and the Turtle warrior gave up his life in a great bellow and was dead.

Miska sank down, exhausted and satisfied. He took the honor and power of the dead man as a gift, a Wolf 's heart. The daughters of Anapatha divided the body up for the cooking pots, to accept this man into the clan, to make him one of them. Miska sat slumped there, sweat covering him, his whole body aching. The dying man had taken him far, had taken him to the edge of death, to the leap between worlds.

He thought of Corban, even now, in this moment of connection and power, he thought of Corban, who somehow had leapt between worlds without dying.

# The City of the Just

# CHAPTER TEN

Green where the sun reached it, brown in the shadows, the river roared along broad between banks clogged with the leavings of the spring flood, clumps of grass wound high into the branches of the willow trees, twigs and leaves rammed into the spaces between them, everything covered with an inch of brown dust patterned with bird tracks. Corban worked his way down to the water, hearing ahead of him the plop of creatures leaving as he approached.

He reached the lip of the bank where it curled over a pool of deep quiet water, sheltered from the race of the river by a fallen oak tree. Six feet below the top of the bank, at the edge of the pool, was a tiny shelving beach, and he dropped down onto it. In such a sheltered place the heat was unbearable. Having no need here to hide the color of his skin, he put his line and the gourd down on the beach, peeled his shirt off and tossed it up onto the bank above his head.

He splayed his hand over his chest, where the skin was fish-white. This whiteness, which he had never noticed until he came here, was bad, one of the reasons Miska hated him. For the whole summer after he joined Epashti's people he had gone around naked in the forest, trying to get his skin to turn as brown as theirs, but he had never gone so dark, and so around them he always wore all the clothes he could. When his little boy Finn was born he was pale and Corban had fretted until he saw that as the child grew he was darkening to his mother's coppery color. He rubbed his hand over his chest, struggling with the problem why this was so important.

Here it was not, here, days, even weeks away from the Wolves. The willows leaned over the water and insects floated in the air above it. Nobody noticed he was white. He picked up the line and the gourd with his bait, and he worked the top of the gourd carefully off and shook the contents into his hand. A clutter of insects fell into his palm, most of them dead. He took the liveliest, a little green grasshopper, and tied it to the hook with a strand of Epashti's hair. With the line looped in his hand so that it would spin freely out he tossed the hook lightly up into the air above the pool, to settle down on the still water by the log.

Nothing happened. The grasshopper wriggled uselessly on the surface. After a moment Corban brought the line in, shook the water off, and did it again, aiming for the grasshopper to settle down onto the surface just inside the curving barrier of the fallen tree, where the water would be deepest.

As he did he heard something moving above him in the tree. He knew who this was. Since she would be eating whatever he caught, he wondered why she worked so hard to prevent him from catching it. He gathered in the line again, thinking of changing the bait.

Bits of leaf and bark and broken twigs began to shower down on him. The branch over his head bucked violently up and down. Nothing would rise now, no matter what the bait. He looked up into the green masses of the willow.

"Ahanton! Get down."

She laughed at him. He could barely see her through the massy green leaves. She had crept out along a branch that snaked far over the water; a thicket of new shoots sprouted up from it, which bent and cracked as she passed. "There's a nest," she said.

He waded out into the shallow water, watching her; she was crawling far out over the river, the branch bending under her weight in a great shaking and sweeping of leaves.

"Ahanton, get back here."

"I can feed myself," she said, out there, and the branch suddenly snapped with a loud crack and pitched down into the river.

"Ahanton!"

He crashed through the water toward the fallen branch, clawing swathes of leaves and sticks out of his way. The branch was half-sunk into the river, and the current was lashing through it, dragging the long sidestems out madly flapping. He could not see Ahanton. She was trapped in the branches, under the water. He thrashed around in the great streaming net of the willow branches, looking for her, and then he heard her yell.

The sound jerked his head up. Not in the tree. She had fallen clear of it, or leapt away into it, and now she was sweeping away down the river, only her head showing, already rushing away from him down the river.

He shouted, wordless; as he watched, she flung one arm up, struggling, and went entirely under the water.

He scrambled across the fallen branch and dove into the river and swam, keeping his head above the surface, his eyes on the place she had gone under. The river hurled him along like a leaf in its grip, banging and yanking at him, splashing dirty water into his mouth and nose. He would never find her. He would never find her. Then some way down from where he was watching she popped up again, thrashing, bleating.

He was nearer, he was catching up; he shouted wordlessly to her, to give her hope. His arms milling at the water, his legs churning, he went wildly along, bundled in the current. Her head swung toward him, he saw the wild shine of terror in her eyes, and then she went under again.

He dove down, his arms sweeping out ahead of him. Beneath the sunlit surface she twisted in the murky green water, her hair streaming around her, and he kicked hard down toward her. His outstretched hand caught her arm and he turned upward, pushing her ahead of him, toward the air.

They broke the water in the middle of the rushing river; the roar of its coursing burst deafening into his ears, the hot air struck his face. He gulped for air, and the child, choking and coughing, flung her arms around his neck like an anchor and drove them both under again.

His legs milled the water. He held her tight, pressed to his chest, and struggled back up to the surface. "Ahanton! Be still—I have you—" Still she was strangling him with her desperate grip. He sobbed for breath. By force he tore her arms from around his neck, swung her backward against his chest, and grappled her against him with one arm.

Quickly he looked around. The current was hurrying them down into a great bend of the river, where on the inside of the curve the land shoaled out to a point. The child clutched his arm around her; he could feel her body bucking as she coughed and gasped. He swam along with the current, angling across it, toward the shoal. They would be a long way from their camp. Epashti would know something had happened. His feet struck the ground and he walked up the shelf of the point, holding Ahanton tight against him.

She was limp in his arms, vomiting water. He turned her upside down and held her by the ankles and shook, and water ran out of her. She screeched; she writhed around in his grip, and he knew she was recovered.

At that his temper went hot against her. He swung her around again, gripped her by the arms and held her up in front of him and shouted at her. "You see what you do! You could have died—brat! Fool! I should beat you bloody!" Half of it was in languages she did not speak, and she twisted in his grip, half-drowned, streaming dirty water through her hair and down her face, her eyes brimming with rage, and roared back at him.

"I hate you!" She tore herself from his grasp and scrambled up the shoal toward the riverbank. From the top she turned and volleyed fury at him. "I never want to see you again! I'm going to run away and live in the woods and never come back!" She wheeled and disappeared into the green thickets.

He waded to the riverbank and leaned against it, still standing ankle-deep in the slapping water, and coughed. He had water in his belly and his chest somewhere. He put one hand to his belt; his knife was still there, fastened with a thong, but he had lost his fishing line, his hook and the gourd. He thought it was a good thing Ahanton had run away before he did kill her. After a while he hauled himself up onto the bank and walked back along the river to find his shirt.

Epashti cleared old leaves and dirt from under an overhanging rock and spread out Corban's red and blue robe, and built a hearth of stones at the opening of this little cave; every day when they broke camp she brought a stone from that hearth to make the new one, so it was not entirely cold. Corban had left his firebox in the camp, but she did not put the wood to flame, because the day still hung warm around her.

There was still much daylight left, and she had seen some interesting plants down by the river. Yet she lingered in the new camp. She was glad to be by herself. All the while now, with only the three of them, she was set between Ahanton and Corban, and she felt worn to a sliver from it.

For a moment she sat there by the unlit fire, listening to the rustle and clatter of the forest. The sticky overheated air was busy with insects. She kept watch for the little whining biters and for big slow bugs Corban might use for bait. She listened also for some sign of Ahanton. After a moment she took up her bag and got out an awl to mend her shoes, which were always falling apart now.

She wondered what she had thought would come of this, travelling along with him on this quest. They were much together now and yet Corban was still as strange to her as before. He moved through the forest as quickly and surely as a deer, and yet it seemed to her he only saw half of it. He only saw the parts of it he wanted. He made no offerings when he killed, although the forest gave bountifully to him. He crossed streams and rivers without ceremony; he stepped across the fire, just like the wild man they had all believed him at first.

Sometimes though she saw him sitting alone, at night, staring into the stars, and this gave her hope. He was hurt, she thought, he had lost his way, but he still felt the call of his home place.

She finished her shoes and worked on some of Ahanton's. She had her own reasons for being glad they weren't in the village. Under her belt, she was beginning to think, there was a baby growing, and out here, she didn't have to think about what that meant.

This was the baby nobody wanted, the baby who would never have a name. She knew without having to count that it would be born in the Hunger Moon, when there was hardly enough food for the hunters, and everybody starved. As she grew bigger with it, the other women would pretend not to notice. When she came to bear it, no one would help her. If she lived through the labor, and the baby lived, she would have to take it to the midden and leave it there.

She poked the needle into the hide of the shoe. Here, she didn't have to see the knowledge surface on her sisters' faces, the fear, the turning away. She didn't have to think how quickest and easiest to kill a newborn baby so it wouldn't suffer long. She pushed it out of her mind again. She worked steadily on Ahanton's shoes.

Toward the end of the day, Corban came back, very gloomy, and with nothing to put on the fire. When she asked him where Ahanton was he grunted at her. He sat down with his back to the edge of the rock; he was covered in a fine film of dust, and his hair was wet. A little while later Ahanton came back, naked, also filthy with dust, and sat down and would not let Epashti touch her. She kept her back to Corban, and stuck out her lower lip.

Epashti got her food basket, and took out acorn cakes, and some dried meat; it was still too hot for the fire. She laid the food out where they could reach it. Neither of them moved, nor looked at each other or her. Finally, and sitting in the wide space between them, she began to tell a story.

"In the beginning, you know, there was no world. All the people lived on an island that floated in the sky, and beneath was only water. On the sky island there was peace and plenty, and so the people were happy there.

"In a lodge on the sky island lived Sky Woman and her husband. They lived on opposite sides of the lodge. Every day Sky Woman went around the fire to her husband, and combed his hair, but they had no other relations. Still, by some miracle, she became pregnant.

"When her husband found out she was pregnant he was furious. This being angry made him seem sick, so sick he was near to death, and all the people were very worried, and came and begged him to get better."

Now Ahanton at least was eating, her little hand reaching out to the acorn cakes. Corban's head was turned toward her, listening. She went on.

"Sky Woman's husband told all the people that he would not be well or happy until a big tree that grew on the sky island was dug up, and so everybody went to the tree and dug the tree up. This made a big hole in the island, and all the people gathered around to look down. Sky Woman also stood at the edge of the hole looking down, and her husband came up behind her then and he pushed her into the hole."

Ahanton gasped, her wide pale eyes fixed on Epashti's face; the woman looked at her, and waited a moment, but the child said nothing and Epashti went on.

"Sky Woman fell and fell through the air. Some birds saw her, and they flew right away to the Great Turtle, who lived in the water below, and warned her that Sky Woman was falling. The Great Turtle summoned up all the creatures of the water, and asked each one to dive down to the bottom and bring up some dirt, to make a place for Sky Woman to live on, when she reached them.

"They all dove down through the sea, but none of them could reach the bottom. Finally the little toad dove all the way down and brought up a mouthful of mud, and then died from it. But the Great Turtle spread the mud on her back, and so the whole world grew on the Turtle's back, and was ready for Sky Woman when she fell. And this is the world we live in now and that's why we call it the Turtle Island."

Ahanton said, "What about her baby?"

"That's another story," Epashti said. She glanced at Corban, who was watching her from the side of his face.

He said, "What happened to the bad husband?"

Epashti snorted at him. "I don't know. He doesn't matter anymore." She wondered why he paid attention to the wrong things. She had hoped talking about the sky island would remind him of something, but he was looking at her with a half-angry, half-smiling face, as if at some joke, and in a rush of anger she thought he had understood nothing.

He said, "They used to tell us that we lost heaven—the sky island—because of a tree. Maybe there's a tree at the middle of everything."

She blinked at him, astonished, trying to gather in what he had said. It came to her that he did understand, somehow, but crooked, broken, like something seen through water. Ahanton was tugging on her arm.

"What about the baby?"

Epashti reached out and smoothed the child's filthy hair back from her face. "That's another story. Tomorrow." She turned to Corban, who had finally begun to eat. "What do you remember of the tree?"

He shrugged. The anger had run out of him, he was tired, and he sat breaking off pieces of the dried meat to chew. He said, "There are two stories. One—"

He stopped, chewing, staring away. The light was fading into evening; sideways to her, his pale eyes seemed to shine like water.

Finally he said, slowly, feeling the words out, "There was a sky spirit, who made the world, and he made the first people also. They lived in a wonderful place, where they had all they wanted, but they disobeyed the sky spirit, who had told them not to eat some fruit from a certain tree, and he drove them out into the outside world. Now we all have to struggle just to stay alive."

"Ah," she said, excited; she saw that he did remember, in his crooked way, that once he had lived in the world above. But now he turned and faced her, and his voice had a harsh edge to it.

"So that is one tree. There is another story, that the world began with frost, and giants, and there is a great ash tree in the middle, whose branches are the world of spirits, and giants, and whose trunk is the world of men, and whose roots are a place called Hel, the underworld, where the dead go. And a rat gnaws at the taproot of the tree, a serpent girdles its trunk, the leaves are turning yellow, and soon the tree will die, and with it, the whole world."

Her skin prickled up, as if the wind turned cold; beside her Ahanton murmured, and slid her hand into Epashti's. The woman saw that he meant this fear, that he was fighting her with this story. She held the child's hand tight, and faced him.

"Which of them do you believe?"

Even in the growing dark she could see the glint of his pale eyes. Then abruptly he turned away. Somehow she had found the right words. In another voice, he said, "I don't believe either of them. I don't believe anything." She licked her lips, wondering what this meant, how she should speak now, and then he said, "I believe in justice." He got up and went away, off around the fire into the dark trees.

Epashti sagged, baffled. Ahanton was leaning against her now, suddenly half-asleep, and she turned and busied herself getting the child down onto the robe. What he had said ran through her mind over and over. She wondered what "justice" meant, if it meant anything, some word he had made up, part of the gibberish that still underlay the slow-gathered store of his words. He had intended the terrible story as a weapon against her, somehow, but she had turned it aside. She knew he would not be back for a while; probably he had gone out to stare up at the stars again.

Ahanton was asleep now. Epashti stretched herself out next to her on the red and blue robe, put her head on her arm, and shut her eyes. The story of the tree still unsettled her, like something she had heard before and not understood. She had never heard it before.

She was still awake when he came quietly in and lay down beside her. After a moment, his arm slid around her waist, and his breath warmed the back of her neck. She sighed, glad in spite of herself, and slept.

Ahanton dreamed of a great tree, so dense with leaves and branches she could move all around it by her hands and feet.

She saw, through a gap in the leaves, a white mountain, sharp-topped, blazing in the sun. She saw, off across some branches, a huge lodge. She saw, beyond a curling sideshoot, a clearing full of people, fighting or dancing. None of these places was in the tree, but the tree led to them.

She crawled down along the branch until she came to the great trunk, with bark seamed in ridges her fingers fit into, and branches sprouting out in all directions, some thick as her whole body and covered with leaves, and some small and bare. Drawing herself in between the branches she crept down along the trunk, which widened and spread under her until it seemed no longer round, the branches dense and leafy as a forest, chattering with birds. The webs of spiders hung in the little twigs; a coiled snake hissed at her and dragged its glistening red and yellow length off across the trunk.

She stepped down finally onto the ground. There the tree burst down into the rock and dirt, and the tops of its roots bulged like knobby fingers clawing into the earth, and in between two roots she found a hole. She crawled in through the hole into a vast dim underworld, with the roots of the tree all dangling down through it, and everywhere, the place stirring with ghosts.

Like luminous smokes, like mists, they hovered in the air among the roots. Some were alone, some together, some were talking, some going at some work, and some just sitting quietly, but as she went by them they began to notice her. She saw faces turning toward her, a mouth falling open, a finger pointing. She scurried down along the root, trying not to see them.

Through the mass of roots there gleamed, for an instant, a face half-living and half-dead, a woman, one eye bright, one cheek warm and flushed under the fine pale skin, half the lips lush and moist. The other half a skull, bare teeth, the eye a hole in the bone. Ahanton for an instant met this gaze and her head felt pierced, as if a sheet of light went through her.

She kept on climbing down, afraid to stop, afraid to look around, picking her way down the tangled roots. Now there were fewer ghosts, and the roots were thinner also. She could hold two and three strands of the roots at once, then ten or twelve. Something below her was like sunrise, brightening, yellow-white. The roots were disappearing out of her hands. She looked down past her feet and saw the last strand of the tree stretching down away from her, on down into the hazy glowing center of everything. Looking around, now, and up, she saw other threads dangling into the indefinite light, like an upside-down forest of roots into the earth.

She began to worry she would not find her way back, and she looked up, and saw above her the whole world, all spread above her at the end of the strings of roots, like a cloud island in the sky. She thought she might find her father there, and began to climb up, and then she woke.

Dawn was still breaking. She was lying on the ground under

an overhang of rock, with Epashti's arm around her. Up past the edge of rock, through the still patterned leaves, she could see the sky like milk. Epashti was sleeping deeply behind her, keeping her warm and safe, and she felt too good to get up. She thought of the dream, wishing she had gone on down to the bottom of the root, to see what was there. Then Corban was coming toward her, his great shaggy head bobbing through the trees, and she saw he had caught fish, and she got quickly up, ready to be fed.

# CHAPTER ELEVEN

Corban was glad now that Epashti had come. She slowed him less than he had expected—Ahanton held them up far more—and she helped him find food and she took care of the little girl, who liked Epashti better than him.

She was good company, too, with her stories, her notions, her constant camp work. He did not think of her as his wife. Whenever that idea came to him, even for an instant, there rose between him and Epashti the memory of his real wife, Benna, buried on the island, back at the ocean's edge.

He missed Benna like part of the world gone, the ears that had listened and understood him, the eyes that had known who he really was. Whatever lay between him and Epashti, it was not understanding.

They had left their village in the waxing of the Buck Moon, and now that moon had grown and gone. For a while, after they left the Wolf country, they saw no other people. They walked westward along the paths of the forest, following the river backward as it trickled and dwindled down its valley. Near the top of the valley they came on five or six men gathered to hunt woods bison.

Corban hung back, wary, and the men stood up at once and faced them, weapons in their hands. But without hesitating Epashti went forward, stretching her arm out and her open palm toward them, and called to them in greeting, and used Miska's name, heavily ornamented.

At once the men put down their weapons, and beckoned her in. Corban went slowly on toward them; Ahanton came out of the woods. The men poked at him with their eyes, and at first kept away from him, even when he was sitting down by their fire, but soon they were reaching out slyly behind his back to touch his hair, or the red and blue cloak, and he heard bursts of their laughter behind him, and went hot all over, and wished he was still in the forest.

Epashti paid no heed to this. She got out her basket of herbs and potions and the men gathered around her. She put salve on their cuts and bruises, her touch alone soothing them. Ahanton hung close by, still for once, watching everything. Corban sat with his face to the fire, and two of the hunters came up and sat down by him, the oldest of them, their hair braided with feathers, their ears hung with curved bones and cords.

They had smoke, and passed him the pipe. It was old, and of clever workmanship, with woodpecker scalps along the stem, and bits of shell laid into the wood, and he looked it over before he drew on it. They aimed the pipe here and there before they smoked it, but he did not; it reminded him unsettlingly of crossing himself.

One of the men said, "You are Haka-ta-Miska's—" and said some word Corban had never heard before.

"Miska sent me here," Corban said. He didn't like the idea he was Miska's anything.

The other said, "Haka-Miska is the greatest man under the sun. We long to join his war band. What does he wish of us? Why has he sent you here?"

Corban said, "He sent me to find some people who live west of here." He paused, collecting himself. He had thought out how to speak this and it was still hard. "They are newcomers, big fighters, big talkers. They wear a lot of fancy decoration, and they keep their hair knotted up, like this—" He pulled his own hair up on the top of his head with his hands. "They have long broad noses." He paused, watching the faces before him; another of the hunters had come up to join the first two. He saw no recognition in their looks. He said, "They fight when the thunder booms. They are very strong, big men. Maybe they have a big village." He was running out of words. He had no way to say that these people made things of gold, that possibly they had many more things than these forest hunters knew of. He said, "Sometimes they're called the Sun people."

The three men before him stared back a moment, and then turned to look at each other, and one by one shook their heads. Their leader spoke. "I have never heard of any of these things. The hair, of course, many people knot their hair." His eyes glinted in the firelight; he wore his hair bound at the nape of his neck and hanging down his back. He looked pointedly at Corban's hair, long and tangled over his shoulders and into his beard. "Even the people of Haka-ta-Miska sometimes knot their hair."

Corban said, "Anybody who wants to knot Miska's hair may try."

The hunter's face settled, and he stretched his head up, as if he wanted to be taller. He said, "All honor to Haka-Miska-ka!"

Corban laughed, looking away, toward the fire. "We will go on, then. We have a long way ahead."

"You must stay here and share our meat. We want Haka-Miska to know how well we honor him. So share our meat and we will give up our whole shelter to you and your woman and the child." He waved his hand at the lean-to, half-full of gear. "You must tell Haka-Miska this."

"I will," Corban said. "He'll know it all, when I see him again." The words were acid on his tongue, outright lies; he was hoping never to see Miska more. Whatever he found, out there to the west, it would be better than Miska.

In the dawn they went off again, now following along the foot of an endless ridge like a great dark fence to their right; there was good water and hunting all the way. Epashti found patches of some kind of mint she valued, and a purple flower she called wolf-weed. They came on more people, who again knew Miska, and at the mention of his name brought the wanderers into their camp and fed them and gave them honors, but knew nothing of the Sun chief.

After many days of walking westward, someone came to them, having somehow heard of Epashti that she was a healer, and asked for her help: a child had fallen into the fire. Corban went with Epashti to a village of three little round huts, made of straw mats, on a bench above a creek. Long before they reached it he could hear the child's hoarse, agonized, exhausted cries. Ahanton went white as ash at the sound, and turned and went back into the forest.

In the little village the women were sitting there on the ground weeping. The child, only a baby, lay facedown on her mother's knees, her skin red and blistered over all her back and legs, charred black on her shoulders, oozing horrible matter. Corban stood back, horrified, shrinking away.

Epashti went straight to the mother and sat beside her, and lifted the child gently, trying to touch only what wasn't burned. She laid the baby facedown on her own lap, with its head turned a little. At Epashti's touch the child's cries lessened, her eyelids fluttered and closed. Her mouth opened round as if she would suckle at an unseen breast.

The mother clung to Epashti's arm, her face aslime with tears. "Thank you. Thank you."

Epashti said, "Don't thank me. I have done nothing. She will die. I'm sorry."

The mother wept, and her sisters came on either side of her and held her in their arms, and one said, "But she doesn't hurt anymore."

"That's all I can do," Epashti said. "Corban." She glanced around toward him. "Bring me my pouch and some water."

Corban obeyed her. She told him what to do, what to get from her pouch, and how to mix it. She soaked knitbone leaves in salve, and settled them gently on the baby's burns. The little girl whimpered now and then, and Epashti stroked her head and murmured to her.

Corban sat with her and brought her what she needed. He

thought somehow she would save the baby, that she could not struggle so hard and not triumph, no matter what she had said. He brought her food, and slept there beside her, and she ate but did not sleep, she watched over the child all the rest of the day and that whole night, and in the morning the little girl died.

The women all wept together. Epashti got up and went straight away, out of the village, her face like a piece of wood, her eyes vacant. She walked away into the forest, and Corban gathered up the pouch and followed her. As he stretched his legs to catch up with her, ahead of him among the stands of upright birches Epashti suddenly slumped down onto the ground.

He dropped the pouch and went and gathered her up. "Epashti. Epashti." Her eyes fluttered at him, her cheeks sunken with exhaustion.

"She was a baby, just a baby. Why can I do nothing?"

Corban lifted her up, cradled in his arms, and carried her off into the forest; she was asleep in his arms before he put her down on the grass under a big oak tree. Ahanton came immediately out of the trees and stood there.

"What's the matter with her?"

"The child died," Corban said. He touched Epashti's face, amazed at her, who had always known the child would die, and yet fought so hard anyway. "Go back to that camp and find something for us to eat. I'm too tired to hunt. They'll give it to you for Epashti's sake."

Ahanton's narrow little face darkened with temper. "They will give it to me for my father's sake," she said, and left.

She came back soon, with meat and acorn cakes and berries, and with one of the villagers, a man who sat beside Corban and thanked him as if he and not Epashti had done the work, and as if something good had come of it. Corban talked with him a while. The villager knew Miska's name only, and shrugged at it, but he recognized the description of the Sun people, and then his face stilled and his lips pressed together. He would say nothing much about them, except that they were somewhere to the west, but he was obviously afraid of them. He gave Corban good directions to travel, and when Epashti woke up, they went on.

Miska went into the forest at night, or maybe he dreamed it.

The Forest Woman came to him, walking toward him down through the trees, her skin shining like rain and her hair tangled with starlight. She stood before him; he could not speak, he could barely stand against the streaming radiance of her look, running him through and through.

She said, "Soon Corban is going to find what he's looking for. You have to go quickly, to be there when he calls you."

"Calls me," he said, annoyed. "But I sent him there."

"Come with me," she said, and she put out her hand to him, and suddenly she grew up into the sky, with him so small he stood on the palm of her hand, and she rose up high above the trees, her face against the moon, the night whirling her hair into winds and clouds, and she lifted him up high to see. He stood on her fingertip and looked out across the dark land and could see it all clearly as daylight and as far as his eyes could reach.

He saw the land rippling away in great still waves under the heavy cover of the trees, he saw the big rivers rushing glossy into the south, he saw the wide plain beyond, going on to forever. Far down there, in the sprawled forest, he saw the red and blue hide that Corban wore, moving along.

Beyond, where the hills rolled down to meet the river, the treeless creases and slopes of the land swarmed with men, coming toward him like crawling ants.

His spine tingled up. Coming toward him. He saw their topknots, their long noses. He smelled the smoke of burning villages. More in his memory than his eyes now, he saw their hands grabbing for everything, killing everything, leaving burnt rubble behind them.

His heart clenched, not from fear, but because if he could get there he could strike at them.

She said, "Be wise, Miska. Be patient. They have far more warriors than you. When Corban calls you, only then, you can win."

He said, "I will." His belly stiffening as if he swallowed ice, he watched the hateful swarm creep closer. His blood sang in his veins. "I will."

Then they were descending, she lowered him down to the ground, and stood beside him again, face to face with him. He reached out for her.

"Lie down with me. Lie with me again. Please."

She laughed. He saw the laughter sparkling in the air between them like fireflies. She put her fingertips against his face and his body quickened all over.

She said, "I will. But then, after, I am going on. We shall not see each other again, not as we are."

Miska brushed that off, not caring, just wanting her, and she slipped into his embrace, and they lay down together, and he coiled himself around her and into her. But when he was spent, lying still beside her with her hair across him, he said, "Why are you going? I need you."

She kissed him, her lips unbearably sweet and tender. "You never needed me, you just wanted me. Pay attention to Ahanton, she will give you good advice someday."

"Please," he said. "Please stay."

But she only laughed. She rose, leaving him there, and walked away. He watched her until his eyes hurt, until he could see nothing except the air she had blessed with her passage, all the while the ache growing in his chest, that she did not love him, she had never loved him, if she could leave him like this. Tears lay on his cheeks and he struck at his eyes, furious, that he wept like a child.

The ache quieted slowly to a ruthless appetite. After a while he found himself on his feet, and back in his village he sent messengers around to all the villages that paid him tribute, to summon every warrior to him.

---

"What happened to the baby?" Ahanton asked, again. "When Sky Woman fell."

Epashti glanced at Corban; she had been reluctant to tell this story, for his sake, and yet it was one of her favorites. She turned back toward the fire, and began.

"When Sky Woman fell to earth, which the animals had all made for her on the back of the Turtle, she was with child with two babies. The babies were one good boy and one bad boy, and they fought together even in the womb. The bad child, whose name was Malsum, determined to get out into the world, and he burrowed out through his mother's armpit. But the Good Twin, Kooska, was born the right way.

"As soon as her boys were born, Sky Woman died. The Twins used her body to build the world. But they worked in opposite ways. Kooska, the Good Twin, took her hair and her blood and made rivers and meadows full of grass and trees. Malsum, the Bad Twin, stirred the blood into waterfalls and whirlpools, so that the rivers were treacherous, and he piled up rocky crags where nothing grew. Kooska made deer and bison and fish, and Malsum made poisonous mushrooms and rattlesnakes."

"Did they make people?" Ahanton asked. Beside her, Corban sat silent, watching.

"I'm coming to that. When they had filled up the world with trees and animals, Kooska wanted to make people, to enjoy everything, and be his family. So he took his bow and he fired arrows into the ash tree, and the bark of the tree split and out came the first people, just as we are now.

"But Malsum saw this and he hated the people Kooska made. He hated everything about Kooska, and he decided to kill him."

Ahanton gasped. Corban started to say something, but then was still, and at the point of their rapt attention Epashti went on.

"Now, the Twins had been made so that only one thing could kill Kooska, and only one thing could kill Malsum. Malsum knew this, and he began to nag and worry his brother to find out what the thing was that could kill him. And eventually Kooska, who was good-hearted and could not lie, told him that he could only be killed by the feather of an owl.

"Then Malsum went and got an owl feather, and made a dart of it, and he cast it at Kooska, and Kooska died."

Ahanton cried out, her hands to her face. Epashti sat a moment, watching them, Corban's gaze fixed on her, Ahanton's eyes wide above her hands; she enjoyed making them wait.

She said, "But the goodness in Kooska would not die. Sky Woman his mother would not let him die. She plucked out the owl feather and took him into her body, and there healed him, and the animals all came and brought herbs to heal him. And soon Kooska was alive again, and going around the world making good things, and helping his people.

"But he knew that Malsum would not give up. So he knew he had to kill Malsum."

Corban now let out a spate of gibberish, like words but not. He was frowning, indignant, as if the story were going wrong somehow. Ahanton gave him a swift, piercing glance. "Go on," he said. "Go on." Ahanton turned to face Epashti again, her face blazing.

Epashti thought a moment, startled, about Corban's reaction. Nobody else had ever seemed to object to Kooska killing Malsum, which seemed so obvious and right. The thought rushed over her that he really was the Evil Twin, that he was Malsum, and wanted not to die again. She pushed this away. The story carried her on.

"Now Kooska knew that Malsum could be killed only by the

root of a certain fern, which grew along a stream. He went down by the stream, and stood there, talking loudly about how he himself could be killed, this time, forever, by a white flower that grew nearby. Malsum heard, and crept up, determined to pick the flower and kill Kooska again. But when he came near Kooska threw the fern at him, and the root struck him, and he fell down dead."

Ahanton gave a huge whoop, flung her arms up over her head, and turned to Corban and stuck out her tongue at him. He was still frowning, he ignored Ahanton utterly, and said, "Is that all? There's more, isn't there?"

Epashti said nothing a moment, staring at him, startled. "Yes, of course. Malsum could not die forever either, because evil does not die. Sky Woman made him live again. But she forces him always to stay in dark places, in shadows and in the forest, in caves and at night, and he goes around making trouble then, which is why we people don't like to go around at night, and why we always clear away the forest where we live so the sun reaches down."

Corban rubbed his hands together, one over the other, his shoulders hunched. His face was gripped with some thought. He said, "We have—the people where I was born had a story of two brothers who fought, but the bad brother killed the good one."

She said, "Well, you see, they were wrong. Because they are far away, perhaps." She ran her tongue over her lips. She had thought, if he remembered more of who he really was, that it would be a good thing. More and more she was wondering differently.

He was still watching her keenly, hunched, and his hands churning together. He said, "They have also a story about someone too good to die, and that's their big story. They make—"

Now his hands moved, trying to shape something in the air. He straightened, and his voice was surer. "He came and went away a long time ago, but they keep him at the middle of everything, to remind them how to live. All important things are done in his name and every day they make offerings and ask him for help in everything."

"Is he still there, then?" Epashti said.

"No. He's in the sky. But they have special ways of summoning him among them, a great"—he used some strange sound—"and they have special water, and stuff like cakes, and they say these things become him, and—"

His jaw fell open. He blinked at her, his whole face slack, as if something had just bitten him between the eyes. He said, in a strange, strangled voice, "And they eat him."

Her breath left her in a startled gasp. He turned his head, looking away, the frown deeper on his brows. Ahanton was looking from him to Epashti and back, bewildered.

Presently, when Corban said nothing, Epashti said, "What does this mean?"

He jerked. His mind had led him somewhere else, far off, and she had brought him back. He glanced at her as if he hardly saw her. He said, "I don't know. I'm sick of meaning anyway. I have to find us something to eat, I'm very tired of acorn cakes." He looked hard at Ahanton. "Don't stray off. And stay away from where I'm fishing." He took his gear and went away down toward the river.

Ahanton turned to her. "That's why he's mean."

Epashti swelled up, furious, all the pent feeling of the problems with Corban welling up in her, and reached out and gripped the child by the chin. "You foolish, selfish brat, how can you talk? There is no meanness in him, and he loves you. Go find me firewood. Now." She pinched Ahanton's chin and let her go. Ahanton glared at her, and then plunged away into the forest. Alone, Epashti finally let herself relax.

The story explained everything, Ahanton thought. Her father and Kooska were alike, even their names sounded alike, so her father was the Good Twin. And Corban then was the Bad Twin, so

Epashti herself thought, Ahanton had seen that in the way her foster mother looked at him while she told the story.

She went away into the woods, out of Corban's reach. Day after day Corban and Epashti followed a path that wound along beside the river, but Ahanton hated the river. During the days she saw them seldom, but wandered along as she willed.

They were travelling through high steep hills, the place very strange to her, and yet she felt no fear. The great trees that loomed around her were different from the trees of her village, but when she laid her hand against them she felt through her palm the same thrill of their attention. They bent over her, their leaves rustling, and they played with her; a stand of trees opened its boughs up, luring her in, and then when she went running through, the leafy arms swung closed behind her, and she had to find another way back. Sometimes she got so lost she had to sit down and listen and smell the air until she knew which way to go. Always the trees stood around her like big sisters, swaying and whispering.

She wore their leaves in her hair, she curled up in their roots, she gorged herself on the big meaty mushrooms growing in ledges from their north-facing bolls.

The river frightened her. She remembered how it had chuckled, dragging her down into its cold darkness, wrapping her around and around in its arms, smothering her with its wet kiss. Whenever she went near it now it called to her again, jeering, promising her it would have what it wanted of her, and she felt the cold wet arms around her again and her breath stopped in her throat and she ran. Now she could not cross any water, not even a little stream, the rippling water no deeper than her shoes, and she stood there and wept and could not move.

Corban carried her across. She clutched handfuls of his mossy hair and sobbed, slung over his shoulder, until he put her down again on the far side. Her father would have done it better. She told him that. But she remembered what Epashti said. He was mean and evil but she could make him do what she wanted because he loved her.

The valley narrowed, as they walked westward, the steep walls pinching together ahead of them, and she could not go along on her own course or avoid the river anymore. From hill to hill it filled the valley. She walked behind Corban, behind Epashti, picking their way along the foot of the southern ridge, the sound of the river plunging along over rocks growing louder in their ears.

"There," he said, and led them through spindling trees toward the river. The ground was wet long before they came to the bank and she began to shiver. They came to the bank and the heavy dark green water was rushing by, its surface breaking into leaps and chops, and all the while laughing, laughing to see her so close.

She clung to Epashti. "No—I won't go—I won't go—"

Corban picked her up then, and set her on his shoulders. She coiled her fingers in his hair. He walked into the river and she felt him shudder as the water struck him, and she lifted her feet up and screamed at the water.

Here great rocks littered the river, the water plunging and foaming around them, and Corban walked upstream of them, the water climbing to his waist. She felt him lean against the current. The water burbled and laughed at her, calling her, mocking; then he went down deeper, to his chest, and the cold wet reached for her.

She lifted herself all up onto his shoulders, gripping his hair tight, screaming, and he staggered and she swayed, unbalanced, feeling herself fall. He caught her arm and held her. He pushed on, each step separate, shouting at her something she could not understand. One foot at a time he came up out of the water, to his waist, to his knees. She sank down onto his back, slack with relief, half-crying. She turned to look back to jeer at the river and saw Epashti there, halfway across, not moving, the water high and swift around her, shoving her sideways.

"Epashti," she said. "See there, Epashti!"

"Here." He put her down on the bank and went back down into the water, to bring Epashti; she saw how he pushed upstream against the river, and it yielded and broke around him.

Ahanton thought, my father would do this better. But when he came up out of the river, his arm around Epashti, and the water streaming from him, she took hold of the end of the red and blue hide he wore, and followed him away to the west.

# CHAPTER TWELVE

Beyond the gap in the mountains, the river led them steadily southwestward. The craggy mountains flattened into hills, drowned in forests of oak and hickory, where the racket of the birds in the canopy sometimes made Epashti put her hands over her ears, and the wide-spaced trees opened now and then into sun-blasted meadows of grass and dense brush. They ate as they walked along, picking nuts and berries and mushrooms almost without pausing. At night they camped with the sound of the rushing water in their ears. Day after day, the river braided itself into other rivers, streams big and small running in from either side, until it made the greatest stream Corban had ever seen, a tremendous sprawl of water, copper-brown, coiling back and forth but always pushing steadily toward the southwest.

Corban had never been so far from the ocean. He had always thought, in the back of his mind, that he had come ashore into this country in some hinterland, at the very edge of some greater realm or other. Every day as they moved westward he looked for signs of it—for roads or watchtowers, bridges or castles.

There was nothing. One day when Epashti wanted to camp early, he climbed up a sheer crag that jutted out toward the river, and from the narrow point looked across the rolling heads of an oak forest riotous with birds, the infinite leaves tossing and fluttering in the wind stretching as far as he could see, until on all sides the rising hills carried it beyond the reach of his eyes. Only the river broke it, ranging in its broad coils along the west-running valley. The sky was clear as heaven.

He sat there a while, staring toward the sinking sun, which was cupped in clouds like an old man wrapped in his nightclothes. He knew why Epashti had wanted to stop early; she had been sick earlier, she was with child again, she needed to rest. He felt the baby in her belly like a part of him she held to ransom.

He drew his mind from that, from the attending worry of what he would do with her and Ahanton, when he found what he was looking for. They could find their way home, he thought. They knew the way as well as he did. He fixed his mind firmly on what his sister had said, that he would find what he was looking for, somewhere to the west.

Somewhere out there, he imagined, there would be a city, like Jorvik or Hedeby, but better, a place of justice, a place—

He tried, as he had tried so many times before, to form into words what this was, but every frame of words failed him. In his mind he saw the cluttered wooden streets of Hedeby, the high spire that stood over Jorvik. But he thought of other cities, too, places he had never seen, white-walled Rome, and Miklagard the Great, shining with gold, halfway between heaven and earth, and Jerusalem itself, at the center of the world, with its seven-ringed ladder up to heaven.

He could imagine spires and streets. It was when he thought of the people in this city, his mind stuck, baffled. He could think of all that a just people was not; he could think of the evil, but he could not imagine the good. All he knew was that they would not be like any of the people he had met so far.

Justice, he thought. He would know when he saw it.

They walked down through the folded land, the hills like loops up and down, bending the river this way and that between them. Where another river poured in from the north he took them across again, struggling upstream two days to a ford across the big river, and then swimming first Epashti and then the screaming kicking Ahanton over the swift-charging water coming down from the north. On the far side, they went along the big river again. The hills were milder here, broken at their feet into seeps and bogs slicked over with an eerie rainbow touch, and the river's western edge spread out in a broad rolling plain. Trees grew along the riverbank but the plain was open rolling grassland. Every once in a while clumps of salt broke up out of the lower ground, and around these sinks, and all over the curly browning grass, were scattered bison beyond counting.

They walked along through the loose scattering of the beasts, picking the way carefully among them, Epashti murmuring charms, and Corban always watching for some place to go if the bison turned on them and charged.

The smell of the bison hung over the land, deep and musky, like all the world's wildness gathered up into one stink. The beasts all moved steadily, step by step, toward the west, only a little slower than the people. In spite of the summer heat the bison still carried patches of wool clinging to their massive humps. Their heads were enormous. Their slender, smooth-coated hindquarters seemed to belong to another, much smaller animal. In their wake they left the ground trampled to dust, strewn with shed hair and enormous excrement. Wherever the river's banks ran low, the shore was trampled down into a mucky swamp. Where the salt broke out they clustered in mobs, fought and groaned and pawed up the ground into clouds of dust.

After days of walking Corban could still see no end to the herd. Most were cows with their calves. This year's young were well grown now, light brown and still humpless, and they dashed around and butted each other and gamboled, which made Ahanton laugh, and gambol too. She ran fearlessly around the cows, and they snorted at her, and tossed the shaggy horned blocks of their heads, but none ever charged her, and Corban gave up trying to keep her away from them. She played games with the calves, running up to slap their rumps and then wheeling away as the babies bucked and swung their heads. The cows ignored her, munching along.

Corban always camped by trees, often walking well into the

night to find trees to camp by. Wolves howled all around them in the dark. During the day, buzzards followed the herds, circling over the broad sky, and bones littered the bison trail, old ones and new. They passed a rippling mass of sleek black feathers, only at one end a little tail showing of whatever lay underneath. Once heedlessly they came up close to an old bull, which marched at them, snorting, and shaking its head, and pawing the ground, until they had edged away far enough.

On the river, one day, Corban saw a boat, long and slim, gliding into sight around a bend; he crouched down in the shelter of a tree and watched it pass. It was much like the boats Epashti's people used sometimes, double-ended, narrow as a fish; one man in the stern paddled it along past Corban and around the next curve.

Corban watched it go out of sight. His heart was beating hard. Ahead, up there somewhere, there were more people. The man in the boat had looked like one of Epashti's kind, dark, his hair bound back. He wondered how they would take him, Corban, when they saw him.

He wondered how he would talk to them—if he would even be able to talk to them. He waited a long while by the river, watching, but no more boats appeared, and finally he went off again, running to catch up with Epashti, out on the bison-strewn plain.

Epashti wanted to go back to the forest; the open plain oppressed her. The sun was hot, and the day grew steadily heavier on her, every day, until in the afternoons suddenly the sky would blossom with clouds, and the clouds banged together and the thunder rolled.

Then the bison stirred and gathered, snorting, and Corban pushed Epashti and Ahanton along up toward the hills to the west, dragging them by the arms when they lagged; she did not understand this, wanting the shelter, the sinks down out of the sudden rushing wind, until she saw how the water gushed down and flooded all the low ground.

They crept in under a fallen tree, with Corban's red and blue blanket around them, and looked out across the streaming plain. The rain turned the air dark. The thunder sounded like stones rolling around in the sky and the rain fell in sheets that blew back and forth in the wind. Epashti told the story of the flood, how Michabo, hunting with his wolves, saw them run down into the magic lake and disappear, and then the whole world vanished under the water.

Corban listened, but he said nothing, although when she spoke of the raven that Michabo sent out to find land, he gave a sudden laugh, and looked down. He told no other story, but soon after she had finished, the sun came out again, and they walked on.

Two days after, coming along the riverbank, they came on some people.

Corban had been walking ahead of her; he stopped where he was, the river on his left hand, and the bison on his right, and Epashti went quickly past him. The river's bank was overgrown with brush but she could see a boat drawn up on the shore.

Out there before them, five or six men were standing around a bison carcass they were breaking up. They all had knives in their hands, blood covered them, and as they swung out to face Epashti, she saw Corban through the corner of her eye, moving forward a step, ready to defend her, and she put out her hand to stop him.

The hunters were staring at them, open-mouthed, wiry, brown men, like Wolves, their hair braided, wearing only loincloths. She walked toward them, her voice high and firm, her hand stretched out, palm forward, in the sign of peace, and said Miska's name. The men made no sign of recognition. But one of them suddenly thrust his hand out, pointing at Corban.

She stiffened, looked back, saw Corban there with his hand on his knife, and Ahanton, behind him, wide-eyed. But then the men were backing away.

She turned around toward them, startled. They had not known Miska, but Corban they knew. They were backing away from their kill, bending their bodies in deep respect, waving their arms at him, offering him their meat. "Ixewe," they called him, in several voices, a name she did not know, and words she did, white bison, and sky messenger.

She turned her gaze to Corban, standing there at the center of everybody's looks, and saw him differently. A shiver went down her back. With his great shaggy head, his hair and beard, he did look like a bison. She wondered how she had missed this, all along.

And he knew what to do. He went straight up toward the bison, and drew his knife. The hunters had just gutted the huge beast, which lay in a great pile of green intestines, its gaping belly already buzzing with flies. He reached into the slippery mess, up under its arched side, and pulled out the beast's heart, a great dripping mass in his hand. He backed away, and with his free hand he beckoned to the hunters to take their kill back.

They came eagerly forward, all the while bending and spreading their hands and speaking words of honor to him, the white bison. Corban turned to Epashti, calm as if this happened to him always, and said, "Let's go make a fire and eat this."

---

Ahanton sat with her knees drawn up to her chest, her arms around them. Although the night was still far off, Corban had taken them to camp by the riverbank, in some trees. Epashti stooped over her fire, turning the spitted slices of the bison heart. Over there, out on the open plain, the strangers worked steadily at the bison carcass, peeling off the hide and cutting the meat into pieces they could carry.

Epashti said, "Are you this Ixewe they speak of?" Her voice quavered with uncertainty.

Corban said, "So long as they believe it." He sat down on his heels beneath the nearest of the trees.

Epashti licked her lips, and aimed her eyes elsewhere. Ahanton could tell she was worried. She said, "They have no women with them."

"They are just boys. Here come some of them."

Two of the hunters were walking up toward the camp, bobbing like feeding quail as they came. Ahanton drew herself tighter into her knot. It shook her to see Corban so honored. She glared at the young men, trying to send them away with her looks, but they never noticed her, their gazes fixed on Corban.

He bade them sit down, which they did. Ahanton shut her eyes, pretending she was sleeping, and watched them steadily through the slits between her eyelids. The boys had feathers braided into their hair, and one's cheek was deeply scarred, two ruts in a row, like claw marks. Epashti took the meat from the fire, and laid out strips of it for Corban, and Corban gave of the meat to the boys.

They were amazed, she saw, none of this happening as they expected. They sat staring wide-eyed at him, while Corban calmly ate his own meat, and then he waved at them again, impatient.

"Eat. What did you kill it for, except to eat it?"

The boys fumbled and stammered and reached for the pieces of bison heart. Ahanton, watching Corban, saw how keenly he studied them and knew he wanted to ask them his puzzles, but he said nothing. He would let the boys speak first, and in fact when he was done eating, the claw-faced boy licked his fingers, and bobbed his head, and said, "We have heard of your coming, Ixewe, but I didn't believe it until I saw you."

The boy chuckled, as if this were some huge joke. His eyes moved constantly, taking in Corban's whole looks. Corban sat back, his hands loose before him, and said, "I saw your boat on the river a few days ago. Where are your people?"

The boy shrugged, nodded toward the north, indifferent to that. His hand moved slightly toward Corban, finger and thumb pinching. "I would touch your fur, Ixewe."

"No," Corban said sharply, and at that the other boy reached out and gripped the first one's arm and shook him and growled at him, and they both bent over and lowered their heads to him.

"We are sorry. We are sorry. We eat dirt before you."

"Sit up," Corban said. "Stop talking foolishness and tell me who you are."

The boys straightened. The claw-faced boy spoke briskly. "We are Shawuno, the People, and my clan is the Fox and my lineage is the western river. We have always been the keepers of the White Bison. When we heard you were coming, other people didn't know who you were, but we knew." He nodded, pleased, and turned to his friend, who smiled and nodded, his eyes watching Corban.

Corban said, "I have not come to you, to the Shawuno."

The boys both nodded, adamant, and the claw-faced one spoke with many gestures of respect. "We know that, Ixewe, we are blessed that you have passed among us at all. We honor you, the White Bison, come in man form, although your messages are not for us."

Ahanton started; Epashti had come up beside her, and sat down, and put her arm around her. When Epashti touched her she realized she was sitting clenched tight as a fist. Epashti's arm settled around her and Ahanton thought, Epashti is afraid too, and wondered what they were afraid of.

"You know where I am going," Corban said. He sat calm and motionless, like a rock, but Ahanton could see he was clenched tight too.

The boy leaned toward him, intent. "We have heard you go to find the Itzen. The people of the Sun."

"The Itzen," Corban said, his voice drawn out like a sigh. His eyes glinted. "You have seen these people?"

"I haven't," the boy said, and glanced at his friend beside him, who shook his head also. "They are far down the river here, where it meets the Water Father."

Corban leaned forward a little, his voice taut with excitement, and he said a word she had never heard before. "Do they have a city there?" The boy gaped at him, puzzled, and Corban said, "A village? A big village."

"Cibala," the boys said, together. "Yes, Cibala." The claw-faced boy with a dark look at the other went on, "The sacred mountain is there. Where maz comes from."

"At the end of this river," Corban said, his voice crackling.

The claw-faced boy said, "They are coming this way now, though, so you won't have to go that far."

"Hunh," Corban said. "Coming where? Up this river, toward us?"

The boy nodded. "My people have already gone on into the north. We're just getting meat, we will go join them when we are done here. The people down the river"—he nodded downstream—"they're the ones in trouble." He smiled, not particularly anxious for the sake of these others.

"Who are they?" Corban asked.

"Kisko people." The boy made signs with his hands. "They have maz growing, they have to stay there to pick it."

"What is maz?" Corban asked.

The boy shrugged. "Maz is good."

Corban said nothing more, his brows pulling together, but ate of the meat, and drank water Epashti brought him. The boys left, with many bobs and murmured words and wavings of their hands. Ahanton thought they might move on, although the day was old and ready for the night to come, because he often made them walk on in the late day. But he sat there only, staring into the fire, and Epashti laid the camp around him, and they slept.

Ahanton dreamt.

She stood in a mist, on a field of flat stones, the stones fit together perfectly, smooth under her bare feet. The day was coming. The rising sun filled the mist with light, and the mist dissolved, and through it something large began to appear, as if it solidified from the gloom before her, stone out of fog.

First she saw a huge corner, two smooth sides coming together exactly, so smooth that her hands ached to touch it. Higher than her head, heavy as the whole world. The day brightened, and she saw the corner's steep edge, rising away from her, marking where two of the four sides met of a great hill that tilted up away from her into the sky. The mist vanished. Now she could see the whole stone hill, all the way up to the four-sided fence at the very top. The long courses that ran up the center of each face to the top were still slick with dew; she knew that another such way went up each of the other two sides of the hill.

She stood on the flat stone field and thought, People made this, and even in the dream she was amazed. Nothing the Wolves made was anything like this; not even the Sky people, in stories, made such things.

Corban had known. Corban had even called this by some name. She shuddered. She thought somehow Corban's word had spun this dream for her.

Now that, in the dream, the sun was rising, she looked around her and saw other people. She started. She realized these were the people Corban was asking about, people with sloping heads, long noses and thick lips, their hair bound up behind.

Malsum's people. A surge of fear went through her.

She was standing in the middle of the broad flat field, all the stones fit together tight, and she saw nowhere to hide. Carefully she went on through the dream, through the people, hoping if she went softly but quickly no one would see her.

Nobody paid any attention to her. She grew bolder. She stood and watched a line of men and women dance by her, some shaking gourds, and others blowing on reeds and banging things, from all this making a fine sound, like singing. After these came a line of people dressed in feathers, dancing each with his hands on the shoulders of the one in front, going back and forth like a snake.

The procession went off through the crowd that filled the stone plain. All the people around her wore skirts, like Epashti's, and the skirt Ahanton herself was supposed to wear. She did not recognize the skin the skirts were made of. She looked down at herself and saw she was not wearing anything, naked, as usual, her body flat like a reed.

This made her unhappy, and she went looking for a skirt. Turning her back on the stone hill she went down along a path, very straight and broad and even, made of big stones like the field she had just left. On either side stood stone tree trunks in rows, and in between, stone monsters, with long gaping toothy jaws, and stubby legs. Here also were people, walking up and down, and others sitting on the ground, with all their goods around them.

On the round stone tree trunks there were patterns of colors. She went to look, and gradually she saw that the colors made pictures, streams of pictures climbing around and around each of the trees.

She stared at a picture of the night sky, with the stars and the moon, and across it two men paddling a boat.

In the next picture the same two men were making a house for a star. She stared at them and stared at them, trying to see some difference between them, but she could not. They were the same, in picture after picture, although sometimes one of them had animal hair, or an animal head.

She went along the column, looking backward, going downward; she saw them playing with a ball, she saw them cooking a rat over a fire, she saw them playing in a tree, and she saw them being born, and they were born together.

They were twins. But they were not enemies.

She opened her eyes, awake now. She tried to remember the word Corban had said, that she had thought again in the dream, but what clung to her mind was the memory of the two twins who did not fight.

The sun was rising, washing the whole plain with its ruddy glow. She pushed herself up on her arms. Still sleeping, Corban lay there, Epashti beside him, his arm around her. She thought, maybe the story is wrong, or we are hearing it wrong. Maybe he is not Malsum, or maybe Malsum is not bad. Or maybe there has to be both Kooska and Malsum. In her mind she saw Corban and Miska, paddling a boat across the stars. This felt good to her, and she got up and went to stand in the sun, to get warm.

# CHAPTER THIRTEEN

In the morning the boy with the claw marks on his cheek came to say good-bye to them; he brought a basket woven of straw, which he laid down reverently at Corban's feet. Off behind him, at the edge of the plain, his friends were packing up the meat and hide of the bison they had killed, getting ready to move on. A crowd of buzzards waited patiently in the nearby trees, the upper branches bowed under their weight.

The boy lingered, his eyes sharp, and pointed to the south. "You are going on along the river, Ixewe, aren't you?"

Corban nodded. He stooped to pick up the basket; inside it were some flat meal cakes, like acorn cakes. He handed the basket to Epashti. "I want to find the Itzen."

"You will, going as you are. But the Kisko people, south of here, they are probably not friendly." The boy smiled, leaning toward him, sharing some joke, and his voice dropped almost to a whisper. "This is the time when their maz is ripe, and people come to steal it, see." He laughed again, and Corban knew he was one of the thieves; he wondered again what maz was, that they all wanted it so much. "Probably they are stupid, since they are Kisko," the boy said, "and they won't know the White Bison."

"How far south are they?" Corban asked.

"Two, three days hard walking." The boy bobbed up and down a few more times, his hands pressed together. "We are honored, Ixewe. You have blessed us."

"We'll see about that," Corban said. He started away down the riverbank, Epashti and Ahanton coming after him.

When they had gone a little way down the riverbank, so they were away from the hunters, Corban flung his head back and laughed.

Epashti walked along behind him. She thought she knew why he laughed.

She said, "You let them call you by that name. Ixewe. You did not deny it."

Corban was still smiling. He did not look at her, speaking, but his eyes searched along ahead of them, eager. "So what? We'll never see them again."

She said, "But—"

"Leave me alone, Epashti."

Epashti fell still, insulted. She glanced at him as they walked along. He seemed different somehow; his temper was odd, fit to this new Corban, who walked in the disguise of somebody else. Who was burning to get somewhere, somewhere he believed could be just out of sight over the rim of the land, somewhere his feet could not get him to quickly enough.

Up in the distance ahead of them, the hills pressed down high and close along the bank of the river, pinching off the plain, and the bison were turning steadily westward, drifting off through the gaps between the rounded hills. In the distance thunder growled all afternoon, and when the rain struck, they burrowed in under a tree and spread the red and blue cloak over their heads.

Epashti had been carrying the hunters' straw basket with her other gear, and she put it on her lap and opened it. "Is this food?"

"Acorn cakes," Corban said.

Inside the basket was a stack of flat soft cakes. She pulled off a corner of the top one. Ahanton was watching her open-mouthed.

"You're going to eat it?"

Epashti said, "Do you have anything else?" She put the piece of food into her mouth and chewed.

A sweet nutty taste flooded her mouth, so delicious she stopped chewing abruptly, savoring it on her tongue. Corban and

Ahanton saw this, and both reached out for the basket at once. Corban took a whole cake, and folded it and bit into it.

He gave a startled cry. "Bread. This is bread."

Ahanton was stuffing her mouth with her cake; she paid no heed. Epashti gave him a sharp look. Once again she suspected his gibberish was supposed to make sense. "Do you know this stuff?"

"Not this. But it is like, very like something else." There were several more cakes in the basket. "This is good," he said, and his eyes glinted; she saw he was hearing a memory. "This is maz, isn't it?"

"I don't know," she said, eating. "But it is very good."

"I want more," Ahanton said.

"Here," Epashti said, and gave her the basket. Corban was already peering away to the southwest, impatient to get going, but he reached for another cake. They ate all the rest of the cakes in the basket, until they were stuffed full, and when the rain stopped they went on.

Twice in the next day Corban thought he smelled smoke, and on the far side of the river stands of dead trees showed like bare bones in the woods; he thought there were people around here. By early afternoon they were walking into the narrow end of the river valley, where the hills came down and choked the river into a narrows, and Epashti wanted to stop. Reluctantly Corban agreed; he went down to the river, looking for a good place to fish.

The river had shrunk down from its flood, leaving a dry rim of its bed along the foot of the bank. The bank stood up high over his head, tendrils of roots dangling down through it from the trees above. He climbed over a huge spiky clump of branches and brush wedged against the bank, and on the other side saw something wrapped in some dead twigs.

He poked at it, a web of fibers, and saw it was a fish net.

He stood up, looking around him, remembering what the claw-faced boy had said: these people would be unfriendly. The river's channel was along the foot of the far bank, deep and green; on this side the water rippled past him only knee-deep, curling through a line of rocks. Where it broke around the rocks it heaped up into pale green curves, beautiful in the late sunlight.

He went on along the foot of the bank, watching the far shore. The river leaned into a broad curve; just beyond the top of the curve, on the far shore, the bank was broken down and a deep trail made, down to the water, here and there using tree roots to form steps. He climbed up the steep bank on his side, to the top, and from that height he saw across the river.

He was expecting a village but he saw only the flat meadow in the elbow of the river bend, spotted with green growth. Something moved on it, and he stretched his eyes and was patient and soon made out the people there, going back and forth through the green patches.

Back and forth they went, back and forth, and he realized they were harvesting something.

Maz, he thought, unsure. He thought to himself, If you were really a God you would know what's going on.

Thinking that didn't help. He stood up, looking around; he had come up the bank into a stand of massive-bodied trees, the ground under their spreading crowns littered with crunchy bits of shells. The wide spaces between them lulled him, churchlike, safe. He was walking out of the deep shade, going back to Epashti, when something hit him hard from behind.

A faint sound warned him, just before the body slammed into him, and he was already crouching, going down, his hands rising. He went down flat on his face but with his hands out, and he was flipping over even as he hit, kicking out, throwing off the man on top of him.

He bounded to his feet. Just beyond the rolling body of the man he had cast off, in the trees, another man stood, half-naked, a bow in his hands.

That man's eyes were as big as eggs. His mouth hung open. The arrow was locked halfway to the nocking point in his hand. The other man was staggering up, already to one knee.

"Shoot! Shoot!"

Corban rushed them; he hit the rising man first, got him in the chin with his knee, and then kicked him in the chest going down. He dodged as he leapt. The arrow hissed in the air. He felt a sharp rap on his side, but no hurt, and with a yell he charged the bowman.

The man with the bow scrambled away, drawing another arrow, and Corban, lunging after him, got hold of the bow and tore it out of his grasp. The other man shrieked. He had the arrow still in his hand and he threw it at Corban like a dart and crouched down into the underbrush, his arms over his head.

Corban thought of the first man, behind him; he wheeled around, and caught that man just rising dazedly up again, and whacked him over the head with the bow. Whirling, he faced the bow's owner.

He was gone. Corban saw only the flash of motion through the dim shade under the trees, flying away toward the river. A quavering yell carried back to him. He looked around; the first man to attack him was lying flat on the ground, groaning. Corban stepped over him and went off toward his camp. After a few steps, he began to run.

The ground here was rolling, and he ran along the foot of a hill and along the edge of the trees that lined the river, headed for the low ground where his camp was. When he rounded the hill he jerked to an abrupt halt.

He was too late. Down there on the dry grass under the tree where he had left them stood Epashti and Ahanton, their arms around each other, surrounded by strange men with bows and spears.

He stood a moment, watching, his back prickling up, and his guts wound into a knot. They had seen him, down there. Someone pointed. He tensed to run. But there was nothing to do, he could not leave his family there alone, and finally he walked out toward the camp.

He squared his shoulders up. He held his head high. He called out, "You down there, let no harm come to those people, if you know what's good for you."

Among the crowd of men, two or three bows went up, flexed taut, ready to shoot. The crowded men were pointing and talking. He walked steadily toward them, his eyes on them. Something was banging his side, and he looked down, and saw an arrow stuck in his red and blue cloak. He reached down and pulled the arrow out of the cloak, and threw it down.

From the crowded men a low cry of amazement went up. He walked on toward them, his mouth dry, fumbling out what to say, and went in among them, as if he were not afraid of them, as if they could not hurt him. He went straight up to Epashti and Ahanton, in their midst.

"I am Ixewe," he said, looking around at the men, "If you hurt my family I will take bad words of you to Cibala!"

The men closed in around him, babbling to each other. "White," he heard, over and over, "white." He felt them touching him from behind, tugging at his hair. Epashti and Ahanton stood before him, their faces rigid with fear, their eyes fixed on him. He reached out to them and put his hands on their shoulders. He felt the men around them, their murmuring and poking that could turn any moment into jabs and blows. He drew the two women toward him, into the shelter of his body.

"Come," he said to Epashti. "Come now, let's go." Something prodded slyly at his side, where the arrow had struck his cloak, and then a hand plucked the knife out of its sheath on his belt.

He spun around with a yell, stepping away from Epashti and Ahanton. A boy with feathers in his hair stood there, turning the knife in his hands. Corban had been carrying it for years and the blade was worn white from the hone, a thin tongue of steel in a mended haft. The boy touched the edge with his finger, and it cut him.

With a cry he dropped the knife into the dirt and sprang away. Suddenly the space around Corban and the women was clear, the other men stepping back, staring at him, at the knife. He stooped, and picked up the knife and put it away on his belt, and swung a broad look over them all.

"All I want with you is peace. You attack me. You take my family."

"We want peace." An older man came up to the front of the crowd; his face was painted with streaks of red clay and he had a fancy bead collar around his neck. He leaned on a stick. "Are you then Ixewe, as the Shawuno say?"

"I am," Corban said, "and I am going to see the Sun chief, and if you hinder me I'll tell him. So let my family free, now."

The old man held to his stick with both hands. "Yet you look weary and hungry, Ixewe. Come to our village, across the water. We will honor you and feast with you."

Corban said, "I am going on."

The old man's eyes hardened, his face tightened, and he tilted forward on his stick. "Yet we want you to honor us, Ixewe. We must do you honor."

Corban knew then what he intended, and smiled. He said, "The Sun people are coming, are they not? If I do not go on, if they come here before I reach them, how can I carry good word to them of you?"

From the men behind the elder came a low murmur. The old man turned his head a fraction of the way toward them, and the mutter silenced at once. Corban said, "I am going, with my family, and you will not stop me, because it is your one chance." He reached out to Epashti. "Come."

She walked forward at once, reaching for his hand, and leading Ahanton along. Still her face was thin with fear, and her eyes wide. No one spoke. Corban took her hand and turned and walked away, up the sloping way he had come, going southwest again. Behind them was only silence. None of them turned to look back.

When they went up over the top of the hill, Corban felt his back muscles ease, and his whole mind turn forward again, back to where they were going, and away from what might be coming after. He let out his breath in a rush. He said, "Let's go that way," and pointed away from the river; from the top of the next hill, he thought, he would see how the river went.

They followed him along, leaving the grassy meadows behind, following a narrow trace between two hills. Deep in the woods, and in the low ground, the night was coming, and they made a camp in the lee of a craggy hill.

Epashti had not spoken since they had walked away from the river people. She laid out the fire, while he dragged some branches around to shelter the camp. The sky was still pale up beyond the tops of the trees but the camp was in darkness. When he came in and sat down to light the fire, she said, "You have taken the name. You have said you are this person."

"What?" he said. "Now you complain, when that's how we got away from them. Didn't you hear that old man? He wanted to hold onto us."

She said, stubbornly, "You don't even know what this name means and you have taken it on."

He wheeled on her, angry. "Leave me alone. Would you rather they sneered at me, like your people?"

Even in the dark he saw her recoil. He had the tinderbox in his hands, and he sparked up the flame, and bent down to light the fire.

She said, "See, you are already different."

"Epashti," he said, between his teeth, "leave me alone." Then, as he stretched out his hands with the little blossom of fire, his ears picked up something in the distance that made his skin prickle up.

He sat back, the tinderbox forgotten. Epashti had heard it too, rigid in the dark, her head lifted. Ahanton crept in between them.

"What is that? Is that thunder?"

"Shhh."

It was like thunder, but steady, rhythmic, like walking, boom boom boom at the very edge of his hearing, like a giant walking toward him. Then abruptly it stopped.

He drew in the sweet cool night air, realizing he had not breathed for moments. Beside him, Epashti's voice burst out, ragged with fear. "It's them. It's them."

Corban stood up. "You stay here."

"No—" She leapt up, grabbing for him. "You can't go. Corban—" She gripped his shirt in both hands. "Please, I'm afraid. It's like the stories. Please don't go."

He let her drag him down, although his heart was thundering now, like a drum, and did not slow. Ahanton sat still there. He took the tinderbox and lit the fire, and Epashti crept close against him, putting on bits of kindling, all the while whispering charms under her breath. They had only a few mushrooms and nuts to eat, what little they had found on the way. They lay down in the shelter of the camp to sleep.

Corban did not shut his eyes. He lay listening to Ahanton fall at once into a deep sleep, and to Epashti struggling to stay awake, her breathing ragged, her body shifting on the ground; but they had walked all day, and at last she too drifted into sleep.

Then he got up, quietly and carefully. He felt his knife in its sheath, the tinderbox tied into the corner of the cloak. Then he took the cloak and laid it down over them, to cover them, to keep them safe. He thought, I will be back before they wake up. He knew he was lying. He crept off into the woods, and started west, toward the sound of the drums.

Ahanton wanted to dream of the two brothers, and the stone village with its painted trees, but instead she dreamt of a forest, dark as night, and her wandering in it. And something was chasing her. A snake was chasing her. She stirred herself, trying to wake, and got out of the dream, and went back for the dream of the brothers, paddling their boat through the stars. But she came always to the night forest, and the snake, a snake made of people, with hundreds of legs, a snake with wings, that lunged out of the darkness to devour her.

# CHAPTER FOURTEEN

Corban followed a little creek through the darkness of the forest, going upstream until he could scramble up through brush and saplings to the peak of a ridge. From this height he looked out through the clear dark air. The moon was just rising over his left shoulder, a cat's eye, with the greatest of the wandering stars close over its brow. The wind rose into his face, damp from combing through the trees on the hillside.

He tasted smoke in the wind, bitter under the earth smell. Low in the southwest, beyond the next hill, the sky blurred down into haze, underlit with a faint yellow glow.

His body felt like a suit of lead, dragging him down; he had to sleep. Yet it lay there, surely, just before him, if not his golden city, the way to it, and he began down the hillside, going toward the light.

As he went down the slope the darkness swelled up around him, the forest deepened, and he had to walk one step at a time, groping forward. Now that he had somewhere to go he could not follow the natural course of the land; he fought through dense brush, and climbed up and down a steep rocky slope, blind in the dark, his hands stretched forward. His body ached for sleep but he went on, steadily, one foot at a time, until, at last, he began to be able to see: the dawn was coming.

He was climbing another ridge, now able to see the shapes of trees and rocks, the line up there of the edge of the sky, and when he reached the sunlight at the top, suddenly a swarm of men in topknots surrounded him.

"Stand where you are!"

He raised his hands up, too tired to be afraid. "I'm not armed," he said—nobody ever noticed the sling wrapped around his belt. He looked around into their faces, expecting to see the golden face.

Disappointed, he let his hands sag to his sides. These men around him were plain brown forest hunters like all the others he had seen coming here.

One of them was shouting at him, and a spear jabbed at his chest. "Who are you? Who are you?" But another man pushed up beside the first, out of the ring of them surrounding Corban, and reached out and gripped Corban's beard in his fist.

Corban jerked back, angry, and reached up and grabbed hold of the man's forearm. "Let go of me!"

At that they all lunged at him. He shouted, striking out with his fists as they clutched at him, tore at his shirt, pulled his hair and beard; when they bore him down on the ground he kicked out and thrashed around to turn over, and they ripped his shirt half off. Then suddenly they were jerking him up onto his feet again, and backing off, leaving him there panting and angry and exhausted, his shirt around his waist.

"White," one said. "Look how white it is."

"See the fur," somebody else said. "It's on its body, too."

Their language had a strange accent but he understood it well enough. They were no different than Epashti's people. His belly turned over; they would kill him, he would never find the Itzen, he would die without seeing his city.

But then he saw they wore armor, close-fitting leather breastplates over their chests. They carried long spears with tips that looked like earth's blood, which he knew to be sharp as his own knife. These weren't hunters, these were soldiers, and he said, with a little hope, "Who are you?"

The man before him reached out and banged him with the haft of his spear. "Don't try to run! I'll kill you!"

"No—" Another pushed up eagerly. "Temuscah, take him to the Great House. You know how they like odd creatures, they'll give us anything we want. We can go home!"

Corban jerked his head up, his excitement rising even through his exhaustion. "Yes, take me to the Great House!"

Temuscah glowered at him. "Be quiet, thing." He shoved the other man. "I'll decide who—"

Very close, suddenly, there was a rolling patter of sound, like thunder, like thunder underground, and all the leather men stiffened and twitched around toward it. Temuscah reached out and gripped Corban by the arm. "I'll take him. You hear that, we have to go back, they're getting ready to march. Come on! All of you, move! You, come with me." With his men all rushing along with them, he dragged Corban along after him, on down the hill through the rising sun, toward the steady pounding of the drums.

Epashti lifted her head, wakened by a soft trembling in the earth she lay on, a muttering against her ear. She sat up. The dawn was just breaking. Corban was gone. Ahanton lay curled beside her on the red and blue cloak, still asleep. Epashti got carefully up and went to the spring and washed her hands and face in the water. The soft, soft sound went on, but far away, and maybe thunder.

The water was sweet and cool, and she felt the goodness here, and sat a moment asking whatever being was here to help her, to tell her what to do.

The warmth of the rising sun filtered in through the trees. She went back to where they had slept and gathered up her pack, thinking what she might find to eat. Then, with a rush, the thrumming in the distance was suddenly louder.

She got to her feet. The sound was even, pounding, deep-throated, not thunder, not an animal. More like the pounding the men made on logs when they danced.

The hair on the back of her neck prickled up. She thought, They are not dancing. They are hunting.

She went quickly back to Ahanton, who had sat up, wiping

her long hair back from her eyes, looking around. She reached down and wrapped the ends of the red and blue cloak around her, and tipped her face up toward Epashti's. "What should we do?" She reached out and took Epashti's hands and pulled herself onto her feet, the cloak around her. "Where is Corban?" She clung to Epashti's hands. "What's that noise?"

Epashti gripped her hands. The sound was steadily closer, and it seemed to come from all around her, out of the trees, from the ground itself. Her skin fluttered. Her heart banged along with the thunder. She said, "We have to wait for Corban." She clapped her hands over her ears, trying to keep out the oncoming sound.

"No," Ahanton cried. Her eyes were huge and dark, her cheeks sunken, her hair wild. "Run—this way—" Jerking free of Epashti, she ran away into the woods.

"Ahanton!" Epashti slung the pack over her shoulder and rushed after her, following the bright patch of color through the deep green of the forest, calling after her. The drums were coming louder and louder, everywhere but in front of her, a wild pounding in her ears, and suddenly her mind emptied. A fire of panic filled her. Dropping her pack, she fled away down a beaten little path, crossed a stream, followed the path uphill.

Everything else in the forest was running too. A big deer lunged and crashed through the underbrush off on her right, birds flashed and fluttered up through the branches. A raccoon went right down the path ahead of her for a while. She stopped, panting for breath, her sides knifed with pain, and something small pattered over her toes. In her belly the baby rolled furiously, as if it ran with her, as if it still ran. She put her hand over it; the drums were so loud, surely the tiny thing heard the drums also. She blundered on, her arms ahead of her fending off the swinging branches. Then suddenly she was among other people.

She stopped, dazed, at the sight of faces watching her, strangers, women with babies, two or three men, all standing in a clearing. She let out a cry of relief, and put her hands out. No one moved to greet her. Even the children were silent, staring at her, as if she brought news of death. Then, behind them, she saw the men standing around them, and their spears.

The pounding of the drums made it hard to think. She turned, wondering where she was. The other people around her stood motionless, their arms along their sides, their mouths turned down. She watched two more desperate panting women stagger down the path into their midst, one pregnant, one carrying a child in her arms. Behind them all, the drums, like something beating on the sky.

She turned her head again, looking at the ring of spears that surrounded them. The men who carried them looked no different than the men among those they had captured, except they wore leather covers over their bodies, and had their hair tied up. None of them moved, and yet they held these people in their midst like a net.

She covered her ears with her hands, looking around, thinking she would escape from here. They had known she would come here, somehow—because of the path—she would leave the path. She sidled slowly toward the edge of the crowd, where she could slip into the green trees and the shade of the forest. Then a man rushed into sight on the path, heading toward them.

He was naked, covered with dust, his hair wild. He saw them there and slid to a stop. His eyes bulged. He wheeled to run, and from either side the leather-covered men with their spears bounded forward, caught him, and flung him facedown in the dust.

Epashti's heart hammered. Now, she thought, and looked around her. While they are fighting with him, run. But there were still leather men between her and the trees. The scuffling drew her eyes again. The newcomer had struggled up, and the two leather men caught him by the arms, and dragged him toward the other captives.

Now the spear carriers between her and the trees moved a little, their eyes on the struggle, and she thought, They will go help, and she was ready to run when they did. She turned around again to watch, and saw the newly captured man suddenly strike one of the guards down, and lunge back up the path.

The leather men gave one hoarse yell, and surged forward, all around the captives, and cast their spears, all at once. Epashti shrank down; the spears shushed in the air, like horrible birds flying by. She glanced behind her again, toward the forest. Then, in an icy fear, she looked up toward the man who had tried to escape.

He lay dead on the ground with spears jutting up out of him like swamp reeds, the blood spreading thick on the ground around him. She shut her eyes. Her belly turned over. She laid her hand on the swelling of the new baby, and even the baby was quiet.

A harsh voice sounded, one of the leather men. "Don't try to escape. You see what will happen. Don't be afraid. We will not harm you if you obey us. We will feed you soon. If you have children you can keep them with you."

Someone close by Epashti gave a choked sob, and she opened her eyes, and looked, and saw a girl standing there with her finger in her teeth, and her eyes brimming. Epashti moved closer, and put her arm around her, unsure if she wanted to be comforted. Thinking she might push her off.

The girl stiffened under her touch, lowered her arm, and was still. Epashti turned her gaze again at these people now huddling together inside the circle of spears, looked for Ahanton and did not expect to see her and did not. She thought of Corban and her throat closed into a choking lump. She wanted Corban, she thought, with a desperate surge of longing, she wanted Corban. She stood closer to the unresisting, unresponding girl, drawing her nearer under her arm.

Ahanton ran, the red and blue cloak around her like a warm wing. She willed her ears not to hear the drums, and when that noise faded, she began to hear other sounds.

A gurgling voice called to her, and answering it she came to a stream, winding through the forest. Follow me, the stream chuckled at her.

She hung back. "You tried to hurt me once."

Not this time, the water laughed, and she went along with it, sometimes running on the bank, sometimes in the shallows, and from stone to stone. The course took her toward the drum sounds but the stream called to her happily now and again and she followed it.

Then the wind came in through the trees, and breathed into her ear, They are coming.

She stopped, her skin cold, the cloak tight around her. The wind nudged her forward, and she went on a few steps, to her ankles in the cool rushing water.

A willow tree swayed its long limbs toward her, half-drowned in the stream, and sighed, Hide here. Come inside and hide.

She crept in under the branches, to where the tree sprouted out of a bank high as her head. The vast trunk bent out over the stream, its branches like green walls around her. She waded through the shallows to a tiny damp curve of beach deep in the shade of the willow. She sat there and wrapped the cloak around her, her toes in the water. In the shallow water she had just waded through, the stirred silt of her passage slowly cleared away.

Two little bumps appeared on the surface of the water, the eyes of a frog, looking at her. She put her finger to her lips. The drums were coming closer and closer and she could no longer keep them out of her ears. The eyes of the frog watched her steadily, and then suddenly vanished under the water again, and the drums were on her.

They crashed almost over her head. The stream bank behind her shuddered. The shallow water trembled and rippled. Under the deafening thunder she felt the tramping feet passing by, in lines as straight and even as the booming drumbeats. Voices called, and the forest and the stream murmured and protested, buried under the heavy monotonous ear-numbing pound of the drums.

The feet went by. The voices. The drums drew farther away. The frog's eyes popped up above the surface of the water, and she climbed up the riverbank, and walked along through the trees. She thought of all the days she had walked to come here, all the days between her and her home.

The forest had been trampled, branches broken, all the brush flattened to the ground. She went along searching for something to eat, found mushrooms under a battered log, and some grubs; she drank from the stream. The drums had stopped, or gone away. In spite of the heat she kept Corban's red and blue cloak wrapped around her. She saw no people, anywhere, except once, from far off, she saw a body lying on the ground beneath a tree, and smelled the blood, and went wide around it.

Night came. A pine tree sang to her, Sleep here, sleep here, and she climbed from limb to limb, up into the bending, swaying top, going high above the forest, almost touching the starry sky. There she tied the ends of the cloak around the tree, curled herself into the great loose belly of the cloth, and slept.

The wind rose, and the tree began to sway, and the child cradled in the tree swayed side to side with it, sweeping back and forth through the currents of the night air, through the stream of the moonlight and the starlight, and she dreamed.

She was a frog, the one real thing, and her coat was made of many lights. The serpent was coming, was becoming, forming out of thunder and darkness; she saw him only when he moved. His seven coils twined, his jaws yawning wide. Down his throat she looked into eons. She leapt away, just as he struck, and as she sprang she gave birth to the round world like an egg, and he swallowed that down instead of her.

She leapt away, free. His head swung, following.

Over and over, through the night, he came for her, as she sat there bright as the sun; each time, as he struck, she leapt away, and left behind another world.

She woke in the gray dawn, the memory of brilliant color still in her eyes. Someone was saying her name. She looked down from the top of the tree and there, far below, looking back up at her through the branches, was her father.

She cried out, as if she gave up all her fears in a single wail. Like a bird descending she dropped from branch to branch, trailing the red and blue cloak, and fell down into Miska's arms.

Miska sat on his heels on the peak of the hill, looking southeast. Before him lay something he had never seen before, and he could not imagine how to attack it.

Months before, he had left his home village, bringing every warrior who would follow him, more than he had ever led anywhere, away through the forest. At first he only followed the river west, but after a few days he had begun to see, ahead of him, a red and blue ghost, like the lights of the rainbow seen through the trees, travelling along just at the limit of his vision.

He had followed it as fast as he could drive his fighters on, day after day through the forest, through mountains and over the great river, until he came to this place, and here stopped, because of what lay before him now. But he had seen the red and blue beyond it, and leaving the others behind he had gone alone in the night to find it.

Expecting to find Corban. Expecting to learn some secrets about this, how to strike something so large and so strong as this. Instead what he found was Ahanton, alone and frightened, wrapped in the red and blue cloak. And she knew nothing.

He had brought her back here, where he had left his war band, in a crease of the hills. The steep short slopes gave him some protection and also let him climb up high to see along the river plain. Now he sat on the shoulder of the hill, looking southeast, his chin on his fists.

His men were scattered on the sloping ground in the hill's lee;

Ahanton lay sleeping by the fire at the very bottom. Miska lifted his voice. "Hasei, come here."

Hasei came up the hill, longest-sighted of the men of the Lodges; Miska beckoned him around toward him, away from the skyline. Hasei crouched down beside him, and Miska watched him look out over the river plain, and saw his face tighten. Then he himself turned to look again.

The horde of his enemies filled the whole wide open ground from the river to the foot of the hills just south of this one, laid out in line after line, like ribs, rows of people, rows of fires, on and on, until the distance swallowed them. The place churned with people moving around, stooping and rising, like some vast single beast twitching and sprawling in the sun. He said to Hasei, squatting beside him, "How many do you think there are?"

Hasei shrugged, voiceless. His eyes looked blank, like a blind man's.

Now again suddenly the drums began to beat; Hasei started, beside him, and Miska gripped his arm to keep him where he was. He had already noticed some of the drums, round tubs like women's gathering baskets, standing in a little clump along this front edge of the camp. Now that they were beating again, the rise and fall of the drummers' arms marked them out, and he saw them all across the camp, and especially a great number of them, in a curved row, down near the middle of the camp.

In this same place there also were several big huts, much bigger than his longhouse at home, set in the lines of a square. People swarmed around there. There were other things happening, what he could not make out. He tightened his grip on Hasei's arm.

"There. That. What's that?"

Something huge and awkward moved along through the camp toward the square of huts.

Hasei fixed his gaze on it a while, frowning, and finally shook his head. "I'm not sure. A lot of people carrying something."

"What are they burning? There are no trees."

Hasei sniffed the wind, and shrugged. "It all just smells like bison here to me. What are we going to do now, Miska?"

"I don't know," Miska said. He wished the red and blue ghosts were out there somewhere, to give him some guidance, but the cloak was in his camp now, wrapped around a stick of a girl. He sank down on his hams, staring at the horde in front of him, unsure. Then, suddenly, he saw that the crawling and twitching had changed; when the drums started to beat, most of the people had stopped moving, were even sitting down in their rows, and many of the rest were gathering at the edge of the camp nearest him.

This pack of men was coming toward him, and he didn't need Hasei's eyes to see they carried spears.

"They've seen us," he said. "Let's get out of here." He turned and bolted back over the hill, Hasei on his heels.

# CHAPTER FIFTEEN

Epashti's mind felt clogged; she could not think. One among many she only went along and did what the others did. The leather men gave them food, as they had promised, and they ate; then they led them away, and all the people followed.

All day they walked through the forest, and at last they came out of the trees onto the edge of the open plain along the river. Here they were herded together with a much larger crowd, and the leather men made them sit down in lines. Leather men walked up and down past them, with their spears, calling to them, words like a terrible prayer.

"Don't be afraid. No one will harm you. We will feed you and take you to shelter. Families will stay together. If you have children you won't be separated from them. We are going to take care of you. Sit down and stay calm. Listen for instructions. Don't be afraid—"

They let the people go to the creek to drink, and brought baskets of food among them. There was plenty of food. The thin girl sat beside Epashti and cried. Epashti put some of the food before her, even took her hand, and put a piece of maz cake into it, but the girl only cried. Finally Epashti took her hand and held it and said nothing.

The girl's weeping dragged at her. Everything around her pulled her down. As far as she looked, which was not far, since she was sitting on the ground, the lines of people stretched away. The baby paddled its feet against the inside of her belly and she put her hand there. In her memory there rose the sound of the spears flying, the sight of the spears sticking up in a thicket. She felt the spears slicing through her into the baby.

She thought, These people have enough to eat. Maybe if I stay with them, I can keep the baby. She caught her breath, ashamed she even thought of this horrible bargain. She sobbed, her fingers tight around the girl's hand.

The girl turned to her. "Don't cry," she said, wiping her eyes. "Please don't cry too."

Epashti straightened herself, lifting her head up, but something in her gaped open and words poured out. "I've lost my husband. I can't find my daughter."

The girl leaned against her shoulder. "I left my baby with my mother, in the village." She gave another great sob. "They say nothing is left of the village, they burned it all." Epashti put her arm around her. The guard was walking past, his spear on his shoulder. The land under her was pounded dust, without even a blade of grass. The trees around them had been stripped of branches. She felt no power in this ground, nothing she could ask for help.

Still, as long as she kept hold of the thin girl she felt better, and she could think. She began to wonder what would happen to them next. In any case, these leather men were feeding them, and she would tell them the thin girl was her sister and they could stay together. She drew the girl closer to her, looking around her at the other women, wondering which others she could talk to, where they had been captured, what their names were.

The thin girl was named Leilee.

It was late afternoon; there was thunder in the west, and clouds billowed up across the sky, gray as boulders underneath. Before the sun went down, they were given three more cakes, and jugs of water passed along the lines. Leilee said little, slept with her head in Epashti's lap, wakened to sit slumped listlessly with her head down. The heat of the day lingered well into the evening, the air thick and close, and along the horizon lightning flickered constantly like ghost hands reaching down. Epashti wished for her pack, her herbs, her comb; she thought of Ahanton, alone, probably afraid, probably hungry, and put her hand over her mouth and squeezed her eyes shut.

Corban, she thought. Where are you?

She slept fitfully, lying on the ground, unable to get comfortable around the growing baby. At dawn, the drums woke her, beating slowly and steadily. The leather men came around again with more cakes.

"You see how Tok Pakal loves you," they said. "All night long the thunder gods roamed around the sky but he protected you from them."

Epashti thought she should save some of her cake, but looking around she saw nothing else to eat; the whole land was barren here, it seemed, and even the sky looked dusty. She could not help herself, she stuffed all the cake into her mouth, she saved nothing.

A leather man shouted, and they all stood, and the guards led them forward, in their files, past a heap of sacks. All across the valley, she saw, looking, other files like hers walked past other heaps of sacks; her skin prickled up, she felt an intolerable pressure in the back of her head. She clenched her fists, bit her teeth together, afraid of what they would do to her for screaming. My name is Epashti, she thought. My name is Epashti.

Leilee clung to her. "Don't say anything. Do what they say. Epashti, please."

Epashti remembered pleading like this with Corban, which had done no good. The girl turned forward again, trudging along ahead of her. As each of the captives went by the heap, the guards put one of the sacks on her shoulders. Epashti stooped under the weight, and trudged away, in her file, after the stooped burdened back of Leilee, ahead of her.

Halfway through the day the sky turned black and the thunder banged overhead, and rain drenched them. Afterward, the leather men came by, saying, "You must be very wicked, for see how Tok Pakal has punished you."

When they caught him on the hillside, Corban's captors tied his hands together, and led him along with them by a rope. They went to no city, no camp, only walked along after the drums. Fortunately they had been standing sentry all night and were tired also, and stopped as often as possible to rest, and he slept whenever they did.

When they marched they went along through a forest still swaying and groaning from some enormous passage. Even on the steep hillsides the brush was ripped up and smashed flat, young trees broken off near the ground, the grown trees scraped, bark gashed and branches snapped, the ground itself torn in deep ruts.

As they moved along he noticed that other people marched with them, visible on all sides through the stripped forest, many toiling along with bundles on their backs. Once, through the scattered trees, he saw up ahead of him something high and square, much taller than a man, lurching along like a weird ship.

He didn't try to talk to the men guarding him. Halfway through the afternoon they stopped, and they gave Corban some of their food and it was maz. The drums beat on and on ahead of them, like giant footsteps. Toward evening, so exhausted he could barely see, he stumbled after them into a camp at the edge of the river plain, and dropped down where they put him and slept.

In the morning in the gloom of dawn he woke and lay there pretending to be still asleep and looked around as much as he could without moving. The leather men were still sprawled out around their dead campfire. Beyond, he saw another camp, the people there beginning to stir. When he raised his head a little and looked, in all directions, he saw only other camps, other fires and other people.

The leather men at his camp woke, and the one named Temuscah came over to Corban and nudged him with his foot.

"Wake up. We are taking you to the Itzen." He held out some thin cakes of maz.

Corban stood up, reaching for the food. They had taken his knife, when they caught him, and now Temuscah wore it sheathed on a cord around his neck, like an amulet. Chewing maz, he followed the leather man out of their camp, out onto the plain.

Only a few days ago the bison had covered this place. Now they were gone. The broad plain was filled instead with clumps and straggles of people. All that remained of the bison herd were their dried droppings, which he noticed these people were using for their fires.

They walked past a row of strange kettles, covered with skins, that he guessed were the drums. The men around them wore rough pelts cast over one shoulder, like a badge. Corban slowed, watching them, but Temuscah pushed him on.

He walked along looking at all the people in the camp. Many were leather men, togged out in their breastplates, leaning on their long spears. Many others were unarmed, men and women and even children, sitting in little groups, some still sleeping. They clung together, avoiding the leather men, who seemed to tilt over them.

His belly clenched. He lifted his head, looking up before him, where Temuscah was taking him.

He was deep within the camp now, and there ahead of him, in the middle of it all, was a cluster of tents, set in a square, all thronged around with people. The tents were high-peaked at the centers and spread wide on four sides, and as they came closer he saw they were made of leather strung up on poles.

Mostly leather. Here and there, he saw, startled, the tent wall was of something finer than leather, softer, that fluttered in the gentle air. Cloth, he thought, and broke away from Temuscah to see.

The leather man shouted, and leapt after him. Corban stood, resisting the tug on his arm, within reach of the side of a tent, looking at woven cloth, old, very old maybe, but some light woven cloth, finer than wadmal, even finer than linen.

Temuscah yanked him back off his feet, so that he fell sideways into the dirt. The leather man roared over him. "Come! Don't you dare disobey me!" He kicked at Corban, who dodged him, on all fours, scrambling away. Then someone strode up behind Temuscah, someone who stood head and shoulders over him.

"What is this?"

Corban stopped scrambling and looked up, and his mouth fell open. He was looking at a living copy of the golden head. The high topknot was wound around with braided stuff. Rings hung from the broad shapely ears. As he gaped up, the big man frowned down at him, ignoring Temuscah and his friends who babbled and bobbed up and down all around him and made gestures of respect.

Corban stared back. This man was taller by far than even Miska, who was tall; and he was heavyset, too, with stocky arms and long well-muscled legs and a chest like a tree trunk. His face was golden skinned, his nose long and hooked, his eyes wide inside painted curlicues that covered his temples and forehead. His mouth curved in a sneer of contempt. He said, "What is that?" and pointed at Corban.

Corban started up, and then Temuscah and the others leapt on him. He let out a furious yell, fought and kicked and butted at them, to no use. They pinned him down and yanked his shirt off, and then hauled him up bodily before the golden man.

"See?" Temuscah cried. "He's got fur all over him—and he has no skin!"

The big man grunted at him. He reached out to tug Corban's beard; Corban struggled, snarling, humiliated. Another huge golden man walked up beside the first. This one had a ring through his nose as well as his ears, and heavy bands of beadwork around his upper arms; he was older. They spoke, in a language Corban had never heard before, and all the while prodded him and pulled his hair, and laughed. He set his teeth together, waiting. It occurred to him he should be joyful, because these were surely the Itzen.

The big man who had noticed him first now nodded to Temuscah. "Yes, go in and take him to Tok Pakal. Wait." He reached out and took hold of the sheathed knife hanging around the leather man's neck. "What's this?"

Temuscah's hand fluttered up, reaching after the knife in the big man's grasp. "It's mine, Qikab Chan, please."

Corban said, "It's mine."

The two Itzen swung toward him, their large dark eyes wide. The second man tapped the first on the shoulder and said something, his gaze resting on Corban. The first still gripped the sheathed knife in his fist; he jerked hard, and the cord around Temuscah's neck snapped. Temuscah yelped, his hand flying up to the nape of his neck. Then the big man, Qikab Chan, Temuscah had called him, gave Temuscah a shove in the chest.

"He's going with us. There will be something for you, at the proper time. Go." He reached out and gripped Corban by the upper arm; before he muscled him off, Corban looked over and saw Temuscah, behind their backs now, his cheeks quivering with pure rage. Then the big men were hustling him off toward the tents.

Qikab Chan, Corban thought, letting the big man haul him along; he wondered if that were a name or a title. The big man's strength impressed him; he could barely keep up with the long strides, his weight half off the ground in the solid enormous grip.

They went through a gap between two tents, into the wide square space in the middle. This area was crowded with people, swarming everywhere and all talking at once. Corban, looking around, saw to his surprise that even here most of them were ordinary, local men, like Temuscah; there were only a few of the Itzen.

All those were like these two, strapping big men, wearing decorated skirts and face paint, heavy loops of horn or bone in their ears and noses. Corban caught mere glimpses of them, because Qikab Chan was dragging him on toward the biggest of the tents.

In front of this pavilion was a strange monstrous frame, a boxy shape of wood and leather twice as tall as even these men, and Corban realized he had seen it during the march, or something like it, moving ahead of him like a kind of ship. He leaned against Qikab Chan's towing hand, staring at it, and the big man yanked him on again. Even so, he saw that the great contraption, which looked like a giant half-enclosed throne, was made mostly of leather, like the tents, but also of some older stuff. Fragments of feathers, and shells, and cloth, here and there, like relics. Or maybe the leather was a kind of patch, had grown, slowly, like moss, over something older.

The giant chair was behind him. Qikab Chan was hauling him through the wide entry into the tent, where people went in and out in a steady pushing, weaving stream, the wings of the tent pulled back on either side. Inside was so full of people even Qikab Chan had to stop. Corban stood beside him; his gaze went to the knife, still in the big man's hand, and his fingers curled, wanting it.

Then Qikab Chan was giving the knife to someone else, someone Corban could not see. Even when he went away through the crowd, this person was invisible: only the parting and shifting of the people letting him be revealed, making a trail that led into the back of the tent. Corban looked where he was going, into the rear of the tent.

Here, on a raised place covered with mats, on a bench shaped like an animal, sat a man in a tall plumed helmet, or maybe a crown. Other people stood around him, slightly tilted toward him, eagerly attentive, and yet he sat at ease, his gaze stretched out across the tent at nothing and nobody, as if he were the only man there. As if nothing could happen without his word. Then the person who had taken Corban's knife got free of the crowd and came into sight, approaching the platform, and Corban saw he wasn't invisible after all, but only very short, hardly waist-high to most men.

Corban muttered something. Qikab Chan's hand tightened on his arm, a warning. Corban raised his eyes again to Tok Pakal.

He was older than Qikab Chan, Corban guessed, although the ages of the golden men were hard to guess. His face and arms were mottled with paint. The heavy rings that hung from his ears looked like real gold, not the bone in Qikab Chan's ears. Over his chest he wore a great fan-shaped collar, and Corban thought much of this was gold too.

Now the dwarf was giving him the knife. The dwarf, tiny, misshapen, was himself dressed much like Tok Pakal, with a little collar, a little plumed hat, even the same red-trimmed bands around his legs just below his knees.

Qikab Chan pushed on Corban's arm; they moved up to the very front of the crowd. Up there on the platform, Tok Pakal had the knife, and he drew it out of the sheath. Qikab Chan murmured under his breath and Corban saw he had not realized that the knife came out of the sheath, and laughed.

The hand tightened around his arm like jaws closing. He stiffened, resisting, his teeth clenched, determined not to give in. Pain shot up and down his arm; he thought the bone was about to break.

Up there, Tok Pakal turned toward him, and spoke in that other language.

The hand abruptly left his arm. The pain subsided. The people around him were all staring at him. Tok Pakal was staring at him from his high seat. Corban stood motionless, rigid, angry, unwilling to obey anybody now, and Tok Pakal, seeing him balk, thinking him perhaps stupid, turned and took a scrap of food from a dish beside his chair, and held it out and clicked his tongue, as if calling a dog.

Corban bridled up, furious, his head flung back. Behind him, Qikab Chan growled, "Go! Fool!" and shoved him, and he went one step forward under the shove and then stood his ground, out in front of everybody. All around the tent voices rose, a confused hubbub.

Tok Pakal's gaze remained on Corban all the while. His eyebrows rose. He tossed the food back on the plate, and said a word, and the babble abruptly hushed. He looked out in another direction, and shifted on his bench, one arm braced on the flat seat, his interest gone. Someone else came quickly up to him, speaking into his ear.

Corban looked around him, curious. Qikab Chan stood just behind him, and now reached for his arm, but the other man with him suddenly pushed Qikab Chan's hand aside. He said something in the other language, beckoning toward Tok Pakal, and then toward Corban, watching over his shoulder, and then gesturing up, and Corban saw as plainly as if he understood the words that he was telling Qikab Chan that he had given Corban to Tok Pakal now, and couldn't hold him. Qikab Chan's mouth curled down and his eyes glittered. Corban went quickly away through the crowd.

He glanced back toward Tok Pakal as he did, and saw his knife again, lying there on the broad bench. The flat animal head on the end of the bench looked a little like a cat. He circled toward the knife but while he was still far from the bench another man came and picked it up, holding it carefully in both hands, and took it away. Corban followed, moving through the crowd after the knife.

The people hushed and drew back as he went by, but nobody stopped him. They stared at him. He felt hot under his shirt, itchy, as if their looks raised a rash on his skin. Gladly he saw that his knife was leading him to the far side of the tent, where there were fewer people. There several mats had been laid down, as if marking a special place, and in the middle of the mats a man sat cross-legged. The man Corban had followed was just laying the knife down on the ground at the edge of the mats, he backed away with a reverent gesture.

Corban stopped; the people standing around him moved hastily away. Corban's attention anyway was fixed on the man sitting cross-legged, who had a long sheet of something on his knees, and a brush in his hand, and was drawing.

To see this carried him back through years, back to the island, to Benna sitting on the island, drawing the world around them. For an instant he hung in some timeless place, almost there. He came back to himself again; he saw the sheets beside the cross-legged man, and edged his way closer to see what was drawn on them.

He would know the Itzen, he thought, better than words, if he saw what they drew.

The sheets lay on the mats lengthwise; standing at the edge and tilting his head he could see them plainly. The heavy marks on them puzzled him at first, since they didn't appear to be drawings after all, not like Benna's anyway. He frowned, his gaze searching the dense blocks of lines, and then something else rose from his memory, blocks of lines marching across the flat face of the rune stone of Jelling, and he knew this was writing. This man was a scribe. These people made books.

He stepped back, gathering this in, looking around him. The strange pieces of cloth in the walls let in more sun than the hide, filling the tent softly with light. He looked toward Tok Pakal again, with his golden earrings, his golden collar, his animal bench, his calm arrogance.

I have seen this all before, he thought, and pushed the idea away, a trap, false knowledge. He had seen nothing before. His gaze strayed again to the strange patching of the walls, the leather overgrowing the cloth, a new thing eating an old one. Then, by his elbow, someone said, "What are you looking at, Animal-Head?"

Corban twitched, his gaze drawn down. At waist-level to him the dwarf's big lumpy face was tilted steeply up above the squashed body. Corban sank down on his hams, making himself the same height as the other. He said, "Don't call me that. Who are you, anyway?"

The dwarf grinned, showing gapped teeth like pegs. "My name is Erkan, although it was something else once. Don't be so quick to renounce what they call you. The Itzen love monsters."

He smiled contently, his lips wrapping around his face. "They take very good care of us."

Corban said, "That's nice to know." He glanced toward his knife again; the man with the brush was turning it over in his fingers.

"Where did you come from?" Erkan said. "Nobody has ever seen anything like you before."

"You're all idiots," Corban said shortly, bringing his gaze back to the dwarf 's face. "If I shaved off my beard you'd see I'm like you underneath, or mostly." There being few words for this in the local tongue he had run off into dansker and Irish, and Erkan blinked at him, and gave a little shake of his head; Corban expected him to make some sign against the evil eye. Corban snorted at him. "In my old country they threw people like you around for a game. Tell me about these men. Who is Tok Pakal?"

Erkan shrugged. "My own people hit me and kicked me. Then they took me to the Court of the Sun, and now I'm the happiest man in the world." He nodded toward the back of the tent, where Tok Pakal was. "He wants to see you."

"Is he their chief?"

Erkan waggled his head from side to side. "Well, he is chief of those here, for this trip, and he is high in the Great House at Cibala. But of all, no. In Cibala, Itza Balam holds the serpent wand." His face sucked hollow at the name, and now he did make a motion with his hand that Corban knew for a sign against evil. Then he was brisk again. "Come on, now, Tok Pakal is very subtle, very nice, and aren't you hungry? He'll see you're fed."

Corban said, "All right. Take me to him." He straightened up to his full height, gave one last glance at his knife, there on the scribe's mat, and went after the dwarf.

# CHAPTER SIXTEEN

Tok Pakal was talking to another of the Itzen, the older man with the nose ring whom Corban had seen before with Qikab Chan. The dwarf pushed in between the two big men with the comfortable familiarity of a child, or a dog.

He spoke, and Tok Pakal laid his hand on the dwarf's head, exactly like patting a dog. He sent the older man away, listened a moment to the dwarf's patter, and then turned toward Corban.

His look was full of welcome, his eyes brimming with curiosity, his mouth widely smiling. He said, in the local speech, accented heavily, "Well, I see you are a wise man, please, come join me."

Corban found himself moving forward even before he thought about it, drawn to this friendliness. Face to face with Tok Pakal, he said, "Wise I'm not, but I am a man."

The mild, intelligent face before him smiled broader. "I'm sorry if it seemed otherwise to me. What is your name?"

Corban told him. Tok Pakal's eyes searched over him, noting everything. He said, "I'm sorry to say it, but this name makes no sense to me. Where are you from?"

"From the east. Far to the east."

"There is nothing to the east but forest."

"No—if you go far enough, you come to a great water, and beyond it are other lands. That's where I come from."

Tok Pakal blinked at him, and one hand rose, tapping his fingertips to his lips. "I have heard of a great water to the north. Not to the east. This is to be remarked on." He nodded to Corban. "There are many men like you there?" With a word he reached his hand out, and the dwarf scampered away and came back with the knife. "What is this? Not the knife itself, of course, I see that."

Tok Pakal took the knife from its sheath, and touched the flat of the blade with his finger. "What is this it is made of?"

"It's called iron," Corban said, and struggled helplessly against the membrane of language. "Cooked rock."

"Aha. Your people made this? Because I have seen nothing like it anywhere in this country. The little people certainly have nothing like it."

"I brought it with me when I came here. Many of our tools are made of this."

"Aha," said Tok Pakal, and fell still. He raised his eyes to Corban, who suddenly had the strange feeling they looked at each other through a hole, like a window, between two worlds.

The golden man said, "Do you have books?" He used a word Corban had never heard before, but as he spoke, he gestured toward the scribe, and his writing.

"We have books," Corban said. "They're kept in special places, not for everybody."

"Wise," said Tok Pakal. "Our books also are kept safe." He nodded. "I am pleased to welcome you among us, Corban. I shall direct Erkan to feed you, and see you have a place to sleep, and tomorrow I would be pleased if you would ride with me."

"Ride," Corban said, startled. He had seen no horses anywhere. He said, "Thank you. I will." He resisted the urge to bow. Instead, he backed away, out of Tok Pakal's influence, and looked for Erkan, because he was hungry.

In the crowd around him, he saw Qikab Chan watching him with a scowl, and he remembered the big man's hand almost breaking his arm and turned away, half-angry. He had to be careful here. He had to watch out who was great and who was nothing, which was not what it seemed, obviously. But he was close to their city now. They would take him there, eventually. He thought of Epashti and Ahanton, now probably well on their way home; against his will his heart tugged after them. Suddenly, keenly, too late, he missed them. Erkan was coming up to him, his hand out, speaking importantly. Corban let the little man lead him away.

---

In the morning, the drums were beating a steady patter. Corban walked by the great line of them that stretched just behind the Itzen tents; the drummers, each wearing the short cloak of some rough tawny pelt over his left shoulder, pounded on the leather heads of the drums with clubs, held two to each hand. He stood to watch them. They wielded the clubs deftly, using one or the other, or two at once, by cocking their wrists as they struck. The flight of their hands back and forth held his eyes, the rise and fall and nimble twist of scores of arms in a row, like a dance.

All around, the camp was stirring, full of purpose. Corban realized the drums gave signals, told all these people what to do; he listened to the pounding, trying to distinguish the words of this language. An Itzen in feathered armbands sauntered along behind the drums, overseeing them, but all the drummers were ordinary people.

Little people, Tok Pakal had called them. And now the dwarf came bustling up to him. "Come along, Tok Pakal is waiting for you."

Corban followed him into the square in the middle of the Itzen tents. In the midst of swarms of people, two of the smaller tents were being struck; one sagged down suddenly, and the men around it whooped.

In front of Tok Pakal's tent there were no horses, in spite of what the chief had said, only the ungainly huge half-covered chair. The dwarf skipped on ahead of Corban and went nimbly up the side, into the seat where Tok Pakal was already sitting. The chief raised his hand to Corban. "Come sit with me, and ride with me, so that we can talk."

Corban looked around, and saw in the bustle and crowd of the square that there were three other chairs, two on the ground, but one being carried along; the chair rested on poles, and three men to a pole, front and back, bore it easily around. Corban hesitated, looking down at the front of Tok Pakal's chair, where now he saw the sockets for the poles, and the dwarf called, "Come, Animal-Head! Come with us!"

He climbed into the chair and settled himself carefully onto the seat beside Tok Pakal. Uneasy in the close quarters, he turned his gaze to the chair cover, painted inside with bright colors. Like the writing he had seen, the painting made close blocks of figures, but now he saw that these were drawings, people in fantastic headdresses, carrying snakes and birds.

Then suddenly the whole chair lurched. He twitched, grabbing with both hands for the frame, as the chair swung up into the air and started briskly forward.

The dwarf hooted. Corban caught himself sitting rigid, his body cocked forward, his hands clutching the side and the seat of the chair. He relaxed. The chair jounced along under him, the scene outside a blur. Closer, the backs of the men bearing the poles were already sleek with sweat. They wore pads of leather strapped on their shoulders, to cushion the heavy pole. Corban eased himself back into the seat beside Tok Pakal, letting go of the frame.

Tok Pakal put his hands up to his head, lifted off his feathered headdress, and handed it to Erkan, who stood on the seat of the chair to put the headdress reverently on the shelf above. The chieftain was watching Corban intently.

"You have no palanquins in your country?"

"No," Corban said. "We have . . . other ways of getting around." Borne in the chair, they were moving rapidly out of the camp, to the north, the men at the poles trotting along under their burden.

The regular pounding of the drums changed to a triplet beat. Corban glanced around the edge of the chair and saw the front of the army ranging along on either side, stretching away toward the hills on the left and the river on the right, and the other palanquins swaying and bobbing among them. The steady motion made the chair sway gently from side to side, and he began to feel a little sick to his stomach; he settled back into the depths of the chair.

Tok Pakal was watching him with mild amusement, Erkan with open glee. The dwarf clapped his hands.

"So you see! We have everything! We are the best people!"

Corban grunted at him, his temper heating. "Where I come from," he said, "we have beasts, like bison, only prettier, which we sit on the backs of, and they carry us around wherever we want to go."

Their faces went blank with disbelief. The dwarf gave a high-pitched snort of laughter. "He's lying. Isn't he, Tok Pakal Chan?"

Tok Pakal was staring at Corban, his lips pursed. He looked, down at the grinning dwarf, and laid one hand on his head. "We are always the best people, little man."

Corban turned his eyes away, out across the baking summer plain. He wanted to get down; the chair confined him, and he missed the steady work of walking. He could hear the drums beating another rhythm and he wanted to find out what they were saying, and inside the chair he could see very little.

He remembered riding a horse; he had never liked that, either.

Tok Pakal said, "Why did you come away from your own country?"

Corban turned his attention back to the other man. The dwarf had fallen asleep, his great head on the chieftain's knee. Tok Pakal lounged in the side of the seat, the shadow covering his face.

Corban said, "I never belonged there, either."

Tok Pakal seemed to accept that. He shifted his weight slightly, looking away out of the chair, toward the sun-beaten plain. "We left, also. We ran, after we lost a war." His voice was even, as if he recited this, an old story, boring but necessary. "Not I, my father's father. We lost the war and ran away, and then where we came to, where we tried to build a new city, that went bad also, and we ran from there. Up the big river, until we came to a place where there was already a mountain, so we knew we had come to the right place."

Corban said, "Cibala."

The big man gave a sort of laugh. "Yes, so they call it now. We named it Xibalba, for the place of exile and death, but the little people couldn't even get that right." He shrugged, the sunlight tinkling on the gold collar around his neck. The collar was made of green and gold beads in rays spreading away from a medallion, or plaque, some creature figured in the middle, claws and teeth and mottled skin in the tight folded style of the Itzen. Corban thought, I understand him as slightly as he does me, I don't even know what that animal is, but it must mean something great to him.

He said, to know something, anyway, "Where did he come from—Erkan?"

"Out somewhere to the west of here, on the plain. West of Cibala is endless plain. When I got him, he was just a tiny boy, and he was all bruised. They had beaten him, terrified and starved him." His voice went tight with indignation, and then softened to a silky murmur. "Now he is greater than any of them." His hand moved over the head of the sleeping dwarf. His gaze remained on Corban, his eyes full of considering.

Corban said, "In your stories, is there a tree?"

Tok Pakal frowned at him, puzzled, considering dispelled. "Yes, of course, the great tree at the center of the world. You see it figured in the sky, every night."

"And a serpent," Corban said.

"Yes, of course. You know our stories?"

Corban said, "No. Sometimes I wonder how well I know my own. What was the name of the place you left?"

"That was Mutul, the greatest city in the world. And the only right place for us. Someday we will go back." His hand cradled the dwarf's shaggy head. "Maybe not until the Fifth Age, but we'll go back."

Corban said, "I will never go back."

Tok Pakal laughed, his eyes crinkling. "Not now, anyway. But, you know, everything eventually returns where it was. The world is made so. Every night, in the sky, you see that confirmed." He gave the dwarf a little shake. "Up, my little friend—run and find us something to eat."

The dwarf got up, and skittered off. Corban settled back again, pulling this all into his mind.

He understood a lot more now, the tattered wall of the tent now, the bits of cloth, the patched chair he rode in; they had brought all this matter with them, from Mutul to the next place of exile, then somehow through the wilderness to Cibala, all the way losing pieces and trying to fix their gear, without the means to fix it properly. And in Cibala they had made something like what they had left, or at least, what they remembered of what they had left.

But like Corban, they were still looking for the sacred city.

He had thought he was almost there. Now he realized he should have known better, somehow, that something was wrong with his thinking.

How much farther will I have to go? She promised me. But now he wondered if he really understood what she had promised him, or even what he had asked of her. He tried to remember exactly what she had said, but the words escaped across the zones of language. She had told him he would find something, in the west. He blinked, drowsy, the end of the promise suddenly loose and flopping, unconnected in his mind; thinking was too hard, and the motion of the chair lulled him; soon he was asleep.

Near the height of the day, with the thunder rumbling in the distance, they stopped, and the other palanquins approached Tok Pakal's and formed a square, with an open area in the middle, the way they had set their camp up. Corban got gladly out of the chair, happy to stretch and move again.

Tok Pakal himself arose. Somebody brought his animal bench from the back of the palanquin and set it in the center of the open circle, and he sat down on it; somebody else came up with a big screen of feathers on a pole, and shaded him with it. Erkan came running up and stood by his knee, and the other Itzen gathered around him.

Corban recognized many of them now. The older man with the nose ring came up quickly to Tok Pakal and murmured to him, one hand on his chief's shoulder. Among the others was Qikab Chan, who caught Corban watching him and glared back. Corban kept his eyes on him, refusing to look away, and the big man started a step toward him, but then the others were pushing closer to Tok Pakal, and Qikab turned back among them.

They were talking in their own language, and Corban could not understand them. In their midst, Tok Pakal was the only one sitting, massive on his animal bench.

He was another man, here, than in the palanquin. He spoke in a loud, cold, important voice; he looked over their heads, distant and disdainful, although they bowed and put out their hands to him like beggars. He sent them this way and that way, and they went, bowing. Corban drifted off, before anybody commanded him again.

The palanquins were drawn up on a little rise in the plain, with the great army spread out around it. For a while he watched the Itzen laying out their camp. They began with a ceremony, in which everybody in a rapt silence watched Tok Pakal set three stones on the ground; then with whistles and yells gangs of little people rushed around throwing up the tents. The Itzen themselves all went off to a place just outside the camp, in the swale below the rise, where there was a tree. Corban went the other way.

The tents were going up like blossoms flowering into the air. Behind them, the drummers, in their shoulder capes, were dragging their oversized kettles into a single long line that curved around the outside edge of the Itzen square. This line seemed to mark the boundary between the Itzens and the rest of the army. Many of the drummers had gone somewhere, leaving their mallets behind, and all the Itzen were at their council. Corban stood by the end of the line of drums, looking out across the plain.

People filled it from the foot of the first hills to the bank of the river, people in endless rows, stirring and bustling and sending up a general unceasing clatter of voices all blending together into one featureless drone. Little campfires already studded their lines, sending up crinkles of smoke. They passed baskets up and down, and jugs of water. Even from here, he could see that many were women, and he saw children; he thought of Ahanton, and his chest hurt suddenly. He wondered who they were, this swarm of camp followers, if they were the families of the leather men.

These were the little people, he realized, with a gust of anger. They had no tents, no shelter, they were in the open, unprotected, with the thunder rolling closer, and the heavy clouds of a storm climbing higher into the western sky. His ears pricked up suddenly. More than thunder. He heard drums again. He wheeled around, toward the Itzen tents, as all around him the drummers came rushing back to their posts.

A crash of thunder sounded almost overhead. Two of the Itzen rushed by him, hurrying down toward the little people's camp. Corban twisted, watching them; as they ran the leather men gathered to meet them. The first rolls of the drums boomed in his ears, and under his feet the ground began to thrum. The drumbeat forced its way even through the march of the storm. The waves of the drumrolls carried across the camp, and from all sides leather men were running toward the south and west, gathering together as they ran.

Corban stood rooted where he was. The drums' clatter picked up his heartbeat and carried it on, harder, faster. Rain began to slam against him, pelting his head, his shoulders. More of the

Itzen ran past him, carrying spears and shields on their arms. He collected himself, excited; somebody was attacking them, he thought, under the cover of the storm, and he strode along the drum line, straining his eyes to see.

Under a gray boiling sky, in a rushing of the wind, Ahanton pressed her back to the rock behind her. She sat at the peak of this ridge, which ran like a long toe down away from her toward the river plain, and she could see all before her. Down the hillside, all the grass bent flat in the wind, Miska's long deep-dented back went farther and farther away from her. He had left her here; he would come back for her, when he was done.

The hill below her was steep, its flank buckled and creased into gulleys. Down where the land opened out onto the river plain, she could see the men moving in the gulleys, Wolves, and those others, Bears, people she didn't know. They knew her father. She watched Miska run down among them, going quickly from one group to the next, getting them ready. She saw the sticks of bows in their hands. She saw them crouching down in the brush, waiting.

Thunder rumbled. The wind caught hard at the red and blue cloak and she pulled it closer around her, in spite of the heat. He had tried to get her to leave it. "You can't run with this," he said. She refused. She clung to it, terrified of losing it, and he stopped insisting.

Now, down there, so small she only knew it was her father because she had never taken her eyes off him, Miska ran out onto the flat plain, four Wolves on his heels.

The sky overhead split open with a roar like all the monsters in the sky coming out; she winced down, her ears hurt, and the flash blinded her. When she blinked her eyes clear she couldn't see her father anymore, only the insweep of the storm, the darkening air rushing around her, fitful and damp, full of bits of leaves and dirt, all the grass and trees lashing.

She pressed her back to the rock. He had said, "Stay here. You will be safe here, you can hide for a while if you have to, and I'll come get you when we're done." She felt the rock slippery behind her, as if she were already falling. Out on the plain, where the black clouds boiled, a tree of lightning crackled down, branch on flickering branch. The thunder shocked her ears; the lightning struck again, this time so close her eyesight went to pure white, and she felt the fierce sharp fingers of the storm run over her hair and arms. The rain pounded on her like clubs. All around her was only darkness.

Under it, she heard another sound, a steady boom she had heard before, that stopped the breath in her throat and turned her rigid with fear.

Her body tensed to leap up. She had run from it once. She had hidden and escaped. This time she could not run, her father would come here, she would not leave her father. She reached her hands down and knotted her fingers in the grass at her feet, to hold her there, and waited.

The first rumble of the thunder sounded; Miska wanted to see if the thunder would cover the sound of the drums, and he trotted slowly toward the edge of the great camp on the plain, to let the storm come on a little. Ahead of him, the pounded dust of the plain stretched away to the first clogged rows of people, huddled on the ground before the storm, so that he could see all the huddled bodies beyond. The size again amazed him, the numbers; he wondered how they fed so many, how there simply were so many people.

Then at the edge of the camp somebody was running toward him, and another behind that, men carrying spears. He wheeled to a stop, glanced behind him, and waved the other Wolves on after him.

He had brought the four men of the lodges with him, his best fighters, but they were hanging back. Even Hasei and Faskata loitered out there, as far from him as he was from the spear-carriers. He waved at them to come on, and then he heard the drum begin.

He spun around again. The spearmen had gathered just outside the camp, between him and it. They had strange, misshapen bodies, and their heads were bald. One of them had a drum, and was beating out a song on it.

He yelled. The thunder crashed again but the drum beat on. Deeper in the camp, farther, he heard another drum pick up the rhythm, and from all around the vast camp, men were running this way.

Spearmen, and many of them. In a moment there would be too many. He lifted his war club and waved it at the little knot of spear-carriers closest to him, and shouted a string of insults. Then, with a stretching of his arms, as if he were only bored now, he turned and ambled back toward the hills.

The four Wolves waiting for him immediately sprinted off. He glanced over his shoulder, and saw the spearmen starting after him. First came the two or three who had been closest to him, but behind them, from all over, other men were running forward in a wave.

"Hai!" they shouted, back and forth, like the drums. "Hai!"

The air around him flickered, and then the thunder cracked out, ear-splitting, head-ringing; he broke into a dead run, following the others back toward the crease in the hills. He twisted his head around to see behind him. Like a pounding herd the spearmen rushed after him, the first three only a stone's throw away.

"Hai!" they roared at him, and steps from the green thickets where the ravine ended, he flung his arms straight up.

He wheeled around to watch. On the slope of the hill, in the ravines and on the high ground, all the Bears and Wolves stood up at once. They raised their bows at once, and fired, all at once.

The rain was driving down, darkening the air, and the arrows fell like hard rain down into the running stream of the longnoses. For an instant, the spearmen slowed, and shrank around, and Miska saw one or two of them fall.

The rest roared forward, shouting, "Hai! Hai! Hai!" headed at a dead run for the bowmen. Another wild shower of arrows pelted them, but none of them fell; as if the arrows could not kill them, they charged straight up the slope toward Miska's war band.

In one motion, Wolf and Bear, they turned and ran. Miska gave a bellow of rage, watching this—his fighters running like rabbits up the slope—and then in the great pack swarming up the hillside, three men veered off and started for him.

He set himself, his war club low in his hand. They were between him and Ahanton. Up on that hillside, Ahanton waited for him. They spread out, to come at him from all sides, and when the one directly ahead of him cocked back his spear to cast it he charged that man, with each stride ducking to one side or the other.

In a single breath they closed. His eyes took in the shiny hard chest, the round hard head, before the spear sliced toward him and all he cared about was that point. It jabbed at him and he coiled himself out of the way, struck at the taut muscled arm coming along with it, and hit the spearshaft instead. The spear broke. The longnose fighter shrank back, his arms up, and Miska lashed out sideways with his war club, aiming for the other man's ribs, a killing blow.

The blow only glanced off the spearman's shiny chest. The longnose went to one knee, his arms over his head, but his friends were howling at Miska's back, and instead of killing him, Miska leapt across him and raced up the hill toward Ahanton.

Here the slope was steep and he struggled to keep moving forward. The thunder rolled again and in the flash of the lightning he saw, up ahead of him, the rock where he had left Ahanton. He glanced over his shoulder and saw the two longnose spearmen coming after him, and he veered away from her, off back across the slope, running easier, anyway.

The rain pounded down, the ground under his feet already slippery, streaming; he raced down toward the thick close trees swaying and dripping in the cleft of the hills, and the two spearmen came doggedly after him. Men he could not kill. Running, he tried to remember their chests, their heads, what was strange about them, the shape—the shine—He leapt over a fresh windfallen branch and in the close wet sloping ground just beyond, he spun to face them.

One was many steps ahead of the other; he slid to a stop on the other side of the great leafy fallen branch and hoisted his spear. Miska gripped a mass of leaves and branches and lunged, pushing the branch up into the other man's face. The spearman dodged nimbly away from him, the branch in Miska's way as much as his, and sliced at him with his spear. The second man was crashing through the brush toward them. Miska plunged free of the branch, and struck with his club at the spearman's bare arm, and the longnose recoiled, whipped his spear around, and got the pole between Miska's legs.

Miska fell hard on his back. The two spears came jagged through the air toward him. His muscles tensed to meet the thrusts. Then, from overhead, something fell with a heavy crash, something with heavy red and blue fluttering wings, that flopped down over the two longnose spearmen and dragged them helpless to the ground.

Miska leapt up, howling. A few feet away his daughter was scrambling up out of the brush, her sodden hair all in her eyes; the red and blue cloak still shrouded the two spearmen. He gripped the strange hide and yanked it away, and then waded in, striking down hard, at arms and legs, whatever was bare, until the men only moaned, and didn't try to move.

"Come on." He grabbed hold of Ahanton's arm. "Hurry." He pushed her on ahead of him, up the slope, running; the rain was letting up, and the sky was suddenly lighter.

He thought, first, how badly the attack had failed; then he thought that maybe the Forest Woman had not deserted him after all. As he went along, he felt over his body; he had no wounds. It came to him that by this proof he could know if she had abandoned him. Ahanton walked beside him, and he took her hand, as if to lead her home.

# CHAPTER SEVENTEEN

The next day they did not move on. Before sunrise the drums woke them, and Epashti with the rest of the people around her stood up, waiting to be told what to do, but they went nowhere, only waited in their long lines, while the drums beat and something happened she could not see, up at the great lodges at the head of the camp.

When the sun had risen up above the distant trees, the drums fell still, and the food came around again. Slowly the people sat down, and the long lines dissolved gradually into little clumps, sitting together to talk and eat, to mend the scraps of their clothes and coddle their children. There was no other work. The leather men fed them. Slowly, by twos and threes, they made their way over to the ditch at the edge of the camp, and then back again to their places.

Epashti sat beside Leilee and some other women. None of them had known each other before. It was odd to sit among women and not even know their names. She wondered how to tell them who she was, when they wouldn't even recognize her lineage, much less the names of her mother and grandmother. They talked a little, fitful and wary.

Up ahead of them, she saw a leather man lead away some of the people down the line, in another group, and her belly tightened.

"What are they doing to us?"

Across from her sat a round woman with round red cheeks, whose name was Pila. She said, "Oh, it's not bad. You go to a big circle, and they give you new picked maz and you husk it and strip it. They did this before." She had two children with her; she made them sit by her, and gave them a bit of thong to play with. "After, they give you a garment." She plucked at the thin skirt she wore, plaited together of long blade-shaped leaves. She probed at Epashti with her eyes. "Didn't you say you were an herbwoman?"

Epashti stiffened, as if she had been caught doing something wrong. Wordless, she lifted her empty hands. The other woman pushed at her fingers. "Never mind. I'm not sick!" She laughed, harsh; one of the children pulled on her arm and she swatted at it. "Go play."

Epashti lowered her eyes. Pila seemed carefree about being here, gathered up with her children like deer started out of their home meadows and shunted toward some unforeseeable end. Different visions of that end paraded through her mind. A little icy thread of panic ran down her spine. She leaned toward Leilee and murmured, "We should try to escape."

Leilee's eyes flitted toward the nearest of the leather men, leaning on his spear near the end of their line. "They'll hurt us."

"Maybe they will hurt us if we stay. Maybe worse." Epashti put her hand up, shielding her mouth from the others. "I have to find my daughter." She wasted no worry on Corban; the Sky people took care of themselves, but Ahanton was somewhere alone, frightened, hungry, hurt.

Leilee said, "I want my baby back." Tears seeped from her eyes. With the heel of her hand she ground at her eyes, as if she could crush the tears before they came out. "Who will feed us if we run away?"

"Tonight, when it's dark," Epashti whispered. "Save what they bring us to eat then."

Leilee blinked rapidly. "I don't know. I can't."

"Ah," Epashti said, discouraged.

The thin girl reached out and gripped her arm. "Don't go. Please." Her face was slick with tears again; she had more tears than the maple tree in the story, that wept all winter long. Epashti sighed, lowering her gaze to the pounded ground; her heart ached.

She lay down where she was, trying to sleep; Leilee took her head in her lap. Even so, Epashti thought she would never sleep, in this place where nothing grew, where no one knew her. Then someone was shaking her awake, and she sat up, startled, into the afternoon sun.

"Are you the herbwoman?" A strange face leaned down toward her. "Please—we need an herbwoman. Someone said you are."

"I will come," she said. She gave a sideways look at Pila, now absorbed in mending her skirt. She stood, the dust sifting from her clothes.

The strange woman led her away along the line; the leather men turned, seeing them move, and watched, but did not stop them. The woman led Epashti through the scattered campfires to another group, where some mothers sat with their children.

They looked up at her as she came among them, their eyes shining, desperate. With a corner of her mind Epashti noticed they all wore the new skirts, given out for working. One of them pushed a little girl forward.

"A spirit has hold of her. She can't lift her arm. Please—"

Epashti sat down cross-legged in their midst, facing the child. The little girl put one hand over her face, trying to hide, but the other arm hung down, awkward, and Epashti saw she could not move it. Words rushed out of the mother beside her.

"It happened yesterday, the spirit took her, and tried to pull her out of my arms! But I held tight, only now—the spirit has her by the arm—I'm afraid to sleep—it will drag her away—" She stopped, her face crumpling.

Epashti took hold of the child's stricken arm. Relieved, she realized it was not dead, but warm and firm, and when she took hold of the wrist she could feel the little beat on the inside, the tap-tap of the life there. She put her thumb on the inside of the girl's elbow. The child was still, did not wince when Epashti touched her, only held her free hand over her face, pretending not to be there.

Under her thumb, on the inside of the girl's elbow, Epashti could feel a lump. She realized it was the end of the bone, which the spirit was pushing up out of the joint. She took the girl's elbow in one hand, and held her wrist with the other, and turned the wrist, pushing down the bone with her thumb. There was a little click, and the lump disappeared.

The little girl lowered the hand covering her eyes. "Hey," she said, and she bent the arm, and brought the hand up before her eyes. "Hey."

The women all cried out, and clapped, their faces raised like little suns around her. From every side they lurched toward Epashti and hugged her. The mother leapt to her feet and went around waving her hands and shaking her dress, singing something to drive away the spirit.

Epashti thought she should not do that; it was likely a kind spirit, trying to save this child from the leather men and their skirts and their thunder, and she hoped it stayed around them. She made a quick song to it, in her mind, and then sat back, soaking in the praises and strokes of the other women.

Her heart fed on their words and touches. Even here, where she had nothing and no one, and where nothing grew, yet something still remained of her; her heart was still good, she could still do good. The baby inside her gave her a solid thump on the ribs, as if agreeing. She lifted her head, and straightened herself, and went back to her own place, her head high.

---

Tok Pakal said, "In another place they would have been killed for doing this."

Corban gave him a startled look. They were sitting side by side in the palanquin, overlooking a broad stretch of ground by the river. A single tree grew out in the open here, and the Itzen had trimmed the tree's lower limbs back, so that only one branch stuck out. Now they were playing some game with a ball, centered on the tree.

Qikab Chan was one of the players. He wore a feathered helmet, a heavy pad on one arm, and bands around his knees; racing up and down the ground, he kicked at the heavy ball and tossed it up into the air, and then closed with it, hip first, knocking it higher. The other men shrieked and milled and leapt around him. The ball disappeared among them and they all rushed off down the field.

Tok Pakal said, "They don't know how to play it properly. They kick the ball, they even touch it with their hands, sometimes. That would have meant their deaths, in Mutul."

He put his hand out, and the dwarf gave him a cup to drink from. Corban's eyes followed the game, the players now churning back up the field, kicking the ball on ahead of them.

"Of course, in Mutul," Tok Pakal went on, discontented, "the ball court would have been made of stone, and the ball of sacred stuff that gave it life, and the crease would have been the very jaws of the serpent itself, the lord of time and death. All around we would have seen the greatest lords and warriors watching, instead of . . ." He waved his hand fretfully out to the air. "And it would have meant something then, it would have meant everything. But that was Mutul."

Erkan leaned on his knee, his eyes wide, with a little wrinkle between them. He glanced at Corban and caught his eye and winked. Then to Tok Pakal, he said, "The game's going to start, though, Tok Chan. Don't you want to wager?"

The chieftain reached out and stroked Erkan's hair. "Calling me to myself again, my little friend. Very well. Qikab will score first." He tapped the dwarf on the shoulder. "Two stones."

Erkan grinned at him, bright-eyed. "As you say, Tok Chan."

Corban wanted to find out about the fighting, the day before. His gaze strayed to the arrow the Itzen had brought back, laughing at it, an ash twig with a misshapen head of flint. The arrow now lay on the animal bench, beside the palanquin.

His knife was there, too, along with some sheets of bark or

whatever it was the Itzen wrote on, and some cups and a jug. He had to get his knife back. He glanced at Tok Pakal, keenly watching the game, which had started. First two of the players ran up and down the field, kicking the ball along, and then they all charged around fighting over the ball. Mostly they kicked and butted and knocked it around with their hips and thighs, but now and then they used their hands to bat it up into the air. All the while they slammed into each other, pushing and shoving.

Now the mass of bodies churned toward the tree, and the ball arched up suddenly, and fell across the outstretched branch.

There was a thunderous roar from all the men watching, and the players stopped and half stood around dejectedly and Qikab led the other half up and down the field, shouting and shaking their arms. Qikab jogged over before Tok Pakal. The young man's muscle-rounded body shone with sweat, and his face was bright with smiles. His gaze flitted toward Corban, and then he turned all his attention to his chief.

Tok Pakal said something in the Itzen language, and made some ceremonial moves with his hands. Qikab bowed down, and Tok Pakal touched the back of his neck. Then the young man strutted away, and a few moments later, the game started again.

Erkan turned to Tok Pakal and gave him two stones. Corban hitched himself around in his seat, seeing a possibility open up before him.

He said, "Are you—" and ran out of words he had in common with Tok Pakal. He pointed at the stones. "If something happens, you get stones, he gets stones."

Erkan giggled at him. "That's called gambling, Animal-Head." He nudged Tok Pakal with his arm, inviting him to join in the joke.

Tok Pakal made no joke of it, but said, "Yes, we're gambling. He has nothing, of course, so we use the stones for counters." He held up smooth round stones, pale blue-green, each marked with some sign. "Do you want to join us? Erkan, give him some stones."

"He won't know how," Erkan said sulkily. He took a pouch from under the seat and spilled out a handful of the stones for Corban.

"Then we'll both win more," said Tok Pakal, and laid his hand on the dwarf's arm. Erkan leered at Corban, comforted.

The game started again; Corban paid more attention. He watched Qikab and another man race down the playing ground, chasing the ball. Tok Pakal leaned toward him, saying, "They must take the ball two ends of the field before they can try to hit the crease." His large kindly eyes surveyed Corban. "You follow me? Erkan, two stones that Qikab takes the first end."

"Done," the dwarf said.

Corban's eyes followed the two men running. "They play against each other."

"Yes. On different teams. Whichever shoots the ball across the end gets that end." Tok Pakal lurched suddenly, watching the men run along, kicking at the ball and at each other, flailing at each other with their arms, the ball never more than a few feet ahead. "In Mutul," he said, "the balls were different. They were alive. I saw one once, years ago, when I was a boy. It bounced, it flew. Hah!" He jerked sideways, watching a move in the game, and Corban saw that in his mind he played as hard as the men on the field.

With a sudden sprint the man racing against Qikab bounded ahead, with one arm fending Qikab off, caught the ball with both hands, and dropped it and kicked it as it fell. The ball flew through the air in a high looping arc and dropped on the far side of a line of sticks at the end of the playing ground. Qikab stopped running; the other man dashed around with his arms over his head, bellowing. Down the field half the players screeched, ran to meet him, flinging their arms up, and the other half moaned and drooped.

"Hunh," Tok Pakal said.

Erkan held his hand out silently, and Tok Pakal gave him two stones. Tok Pakal said, "Kan Chak is getting to be a very good player. Qikab dare not let him win another."

"What?" Corban watched the two men coming back to the center of the field; Kan Chak, the winner, who was shorter, slimmer than Qikab, kicked the ball in short rolls in front of him.

"Never mind," Tok Pakal said. "There are some things you need not know. Here, are you hatching those stones? Make a bet."

Corban said, "Qikab will take the second end. Two stones."

Tok Pakal gave a burst of laughter, and turned to Erkan. "You see. He learns fast." He leaned back in the chair. "And well, and saves me. I can't very well bet against my own nephew, especially against a halfman, so you take the bet, Erkan."

Erkan shrugged. "I will." His eyebrows waggled up and down. "Corban," he said, "you can be too clever."

Corban turned his gaze toward the field. Kan Chak was facing against Qikab again across the ball, which lay on the ground below the lopped tree. Halfman, Corban thought. Shorter, slenderer, not even really the same color. Not a full-bred Itzen, a makeshift Itzen, cobbled together with local stuff like the coverings of the palanquins. He understood why Qikab had to beat him.

Qikab did beat him, this time, racing down the field a step ahead of Kan Chak and staying always between him and the ball, flinging his arms out sometimes to pen the other man behind him as they ran, and Erkan paid Corban two stones. While they brought the ball back up the field, he said, "Did something happen, yesterday?"

Tok Pakal grunted at him. "Much happened. What in particular?"

"During the storm," Corban said. "I heard the drums talking. Was there a fight? Where did that arrow come from?"

Erkan made a noise in his throat. Tok Pakal shook his head. "You don't need to know that, Corban. Don't ask." He waved his hand at the field, where Qikab and Kan Chak were facing each other over the ball. "They're starting. Bet with me."

Corban said, "Two stones that the halfman gets this end."

"Ah," said Tok Pakal, with a smile. "You learn very well, my friend. Taken."

Qikab won that end, and the next part of the game began, which looked to Corban like a constant knot of bodies churning around the ball, kicking and screaming. The ball arced up into the air and fell back, the men banging it high again with elbows and knees. Now and then one or two of the players would come out and sit down, panting, to get their breath. Corban tried to watch Kan Chak, at the center of things; he saw that each time Qikab sat down to rest, Kan Chak took himself out also, but never sat. His eyes always on the other man.

Corban saw also that the whole aim of the work now was to drive the ball up and over the limb of the tree again, and he turned to Tok Pakal and said, "Two stones that Kan Chak will—" He had forgotten the phrase; he held out his left arm and swung his right fist over it.

Tok Pakal laughed, reached out, and roughly palmed his shoulder. "Score first. Yes. Very good. The tree limb marks the crease. Watch." His eyes shone, following the game. "Ah!"

Down there Qikab suddenly broke free of the pack; with his hip he knocked the ball high, toward the tree, and rushed after it. Kan Chak was after him. The bigger man reached the ball a step ahead, and with both hands batted it up again, but it fell short of the tree, and Kan Chak rushed in and struck it away.

Corban said, "Double the bet."

Erkan muttered something in his throat, hunched down in the corner of the palanquin, in the shadow there. Tok Pakal's eyes shone, fixed on the game, his mouth drawn back in a forgotten grimace. "Done," he said, with a sharp nod.

The ball flew out of the pack, and Kan Chak followed it, Qikab on his heels. Their bodies gleamed; their feathered helmets and the knee pads and arm guards they wore gave them the look of great birds in a violent dance. Kan Chak reached the ball first, one hand out to push Qikab back, one foot planted, and the other swinging. The ball sailed up, a misshapen brown blob against the broad blue sky. It wobbled gracelessly in the air; it curved off to fall on the far side of the tree from the crease. All the men converged on it, grunting and shouting.

Beside Corban, Tok Pakal let out his breath in a whoosh. "Close."

Corban said, "Double the bet again."

"Aha." Tok Pakal clapped him on the back. "A gambler born, perhaps? Done!"

"This time for my knife," Corban said.

The smiling face before him froze a moment, startled, and then tightened into a frown; Tok Pakal's eyes glittered with the first heat of anger. Abruptly his face loosened, and a look of sly amusement came over him; his eyebrows went up and down. He smiled, and nodded.

"Very well. For the knife." He swung back toward the game.

The Itzen ballplayers battled back and forth for a while, neither team ahead; Corban saw that only Qikab and Kan Chak could kick for the crease and the score, but he could not see how the others played, except to shove and crash into each other, and slam into the ball. The ball came loose again, kicked in a long looping drive toward the palanquins, and Corban saw how lumpy it was now and when it hit the ground it stopped.

Tok Pakal growled in his throat. "This would not happen in Mutul." He called out suddenly, and stood up, and the game suddenly ceased. Corban sat back, alarmed, thinking if this were over, he would not get Tok Pakal to the point of betting the knife again.

But Tok Pakal was only ordering a change in the ball. He spoke and pointed, and somebody ran out and picked up the dead ball. From a box by the palanquins Qikab took another, this one considerably more round, its leather cover clean as a new calf. Tok Pakal sat down again.

Qikab ran forward, the ball in his hands, and made to kick it; all the men before him rushed back away from him, and he held the ball in his hands instead and ran half the way to the tree with it. Tok Pakal groaned, one hand over his eyes. A yell went up from the other players, who rushed at Qikab, and then Qikan did kick the ball, shooting for the tree limb.

Kan Chak leapt up out of the thronged players, his arm stretched up, and with his fingers knocked the ball up into the air. Wheeling under it he launched his body out to meet it as it fell. He seemed to hang in the air, his body taut, shining, and his legs swung, one back to balance and the other forth to strike, and with that thigh he smacked the ball up over the tree limb.

A yell went up from the watchers. "Great play," Tok Pakal murmured, on Corban's left. Out on the field, half the players were cheering and leaping around, beating each other on the shoulders. Qikab also roared; he spun toward Tok Pakal, brushed his hands together insistently, and shouted something. Tok Pakal hunched himself back into the shadows of the palanquin, his face twisted in distaste. Glancing at Corban, he said, in the low language they shared, "If he hadn't run with the ball to start with he could complain about use of hands."

"That's justice," Corban said. Kan Chak was jogging toward them, his cheering team behind him. Tok Pakal gave a short surprised laugh, still looking at Corban, and got up and went to greet the winner. Corban reached over to the table and took back his knife.

# CHAPTER EIGHTEEN

Ekkatsay leaned heavily against the rock. The heat of the day pressed down over him and he could smell the storm building in the air; his skin crawled. He felt utterly out of place. He was glad that Miska had pulled them up here into this shelter, deep in the hills and away from the plain and the terrible host there, but he itched to go back where he belonged.

It was the Sturgeon Moon, perhaps not here where nothing was the same, but certainly at home, and he had to get his people into winter quarters. But Miska would not leave here. Miska paced around the camp, crisscrossing the hollow among the rocks, walking and walking, his head down, and would listen to no one, and he would not lead them home.

The little girl Miska had somehow found out here sat on the other side of the hollow, wrapped in her raw-colored fur. Ekkatsay drew his gaze from her, and made a sign with his hand, under the cover of his other hand, knowing spirit work when he saw it.

There was a lot of spirit work going on here. He glanced at Hasei, standing next to him in the sun.

"They're not men. They're insects, or made of stone, or they have a spell that protects them. Our arrows can't hurt them. How can we fight them if we can't kill them?"

"Miska killed some," Hasei said.

Ekkatsay glanced around him; his own men were off into the west on a hunting party, trying to get some meat. Only Miska's Wolves were in this camp now. He slid his hands down his thighs. He knew Miska had kept him here so that the rest of the Bears wouldn't simply go home.

"He said he killed some. No one saw him. Or them."

Hasei stiffened. “I won’t listen to this.”

“If they can’t die—”

“I won’t listen.” Hasei went away from him; his course across the hollow intersected the course of Miska’s restless endless pacing and Hasei paused a step to let his sachem go by. Ekkatsay lowered his head. Miska was mad, he thought. They had to go home. He watched the Wolf sachem walk and walk across the hollow in the rocks.

Hasei went across the camp from Ekkatsay, wanting to get away from him, thinking if he stayed close to the Bear sachem the sense of what he had said might leak into him like poison. He knew Miska had no idea what to do.

The child Ahanton sat in the shade of a gray rock. He went over and sat next to her, feeling sorry for her; nobody knew what had happened to Epashti or Corban. He had some dried meat in his pouch, and he broke some off and held it out to her.

She gave him a shy look, and took the meat. Hasei studied her while she ate it. She would be beautiful someday, he thought. She was not of the lineages forbidden to him and so he could marry her when she was of age. The cloak around her drew his eyes, the strange web of the colors, and he began to think of words for this. Rainbow net was wrong, he cast that away, not a rainbow, although sky colors. The child sat still beside him, chewing. He put his hand out to the cloak, feeling the texture, not like hide, more like moss—the deep red faded at the edge to a sunset hue. Wandering in the words like a meadow he tried to find something in the blue, in the soft mossy touch on his fingertips.

She said suddenly, “I have dreamt of you.”

He started, jerked out of the dreamy wordflow. She turned her eyes on him, her eyes gray like Corban’s, like the Forest Woman’s, and he remembered suddenly where she had come from; he shrank back a little, as if he had come too near to the fire. He said, "What did you dream?"

"I dreamt of you in a tree. You were upside down in a tree."

She pulled the cloak around her and looked away from him, no longer interested in him. He sat rigidly wondering what that meant, that she had seen him in a tree; he climbed trees often, scouting for Miska, and one of his special emblems was the red maple tree. Now he could not find the warm dreamy word-river. Stunned back into the cold present he sat wondering what was going on, and what would happen next.

There was only one thing to do: follow Miska. He fastened himself to that, and let it lead him.

In the afternoon there was no ball game. The drums beat a steady slow thrum. The Itzen gathered around the palanquins, Qikab with great show taking his place in the one next to Tok Pakal's. Kan Chak stood outside the palanquin, nearby.

Corban stood with Erkan beside Tok Pakal's palanquin, and watched a little huddle of men come into the camp, stooping as they came and scraping the ground with their hands. An old man led them, leaning on a stick, and seeing him Corban stiffened with recognition. These were the Kisko hunters from across the river, who had taken Epashti and Ahanton prisoner.

The Kisko carried heavy baskets, so large each basket needed two men to haul it along; they set them down in a row before Tok Pakal, and then they lay down before him, their faces in the dirt. Corban turned his eyes away, unwilling to see this.

Afterward, he went off past the drum line, to make water, and the dwarf came after him. Erkan said, "You can be too clever, Corban." He snapped his finger at Corban's knife. "That made him angry."

Corban said, "It's my knife. Who is Kan Chak?"

"You shouldn't pay attention to any of that." Erkan rubbed his nose. "Well, maybe you should. Kan Chak is Itza Balam's son, like Qikab Chan, but his mother was a low woman."

"Itza Balam."

Erkan made a sign with his fingers, lowered his voice, whispered. "The Lord of the Serpent Wand. The master of Cibala. Tok Pakal's, and my and your master, now. You could see a lot more of him than you'd like, when we go back to Cibala." He gave Corban a deep, significant nod.

"When will that be?"

"Soon. They're done here."

"Done," Corban said. "With what?" He stopped, near the drums; the sun was going down behind the tree-covered ridges to the west. A low mutter of thunder sounded, but the sky was clear, spread with light from the setting sun, the wind still and the air soft.

Erkan said, "They've taken plenty of captives now, and talking like that today to those river people, that settles things with them for a while. And we took plenty of maz, they've been saying how much it is, a very great harvest this year. We can go back to Cibala in glory. Itza Balam will be well pleased. He'll see that Tok Pakal deserves to command four palanquins, he'll give him more, next time." Erkan gave Corban a sly look. "He'll find you very interesting too, I think."

Corban was still caught in the first rush of understanding. He said, "What are they going to do with all these captives, then?"

"Take them back to Cibala, to learn to work." Erkan turned briskly, rubbing his hands together. "Let's go find something to eat and get under a roof, I don't like being outside when the moon rises." He hurried off in his rolling short-legged trot, back toward Tok Pakal.

Corban turned his back on the Itzen camp, and looked out over the drum line, onto the broad plain now in the gathering gloom of the night sparkling with hundreds of little campfires like a field of embers. He felt as if Erkan had hit him over the head. For the first time he realized that these people were all slaves, that this was a slave raid. He had been a complete fool not to see, blinded by the glories of the Itzen, by his own little dreams, not to see what was going on in front of him. He remembered thinking all these people were wives and children, following the army; he remembered knowing they were miserable, out in the rain and the wind, and yet he had not understood.

He knew he was a slave, now, too. That was what Tok Pakal had meant, that time, agreeing Corban would never go back—what that sly look had meant, also, over the knife, since even if Corban took back the knife, Tok Pakal still owned Corban. Tok Pakal with his kindness, his pats and orders, would make of Corban something like the dwarf, that he could talk to and relax with, because he meant nothing.

Or give him to another Itzen lord, another collector, as Erkan kept hinting, perhaps his brother, the evil Itza Balam.

"Animal-Head."

"Hah." He whirled, startled, every hair turning.

Behind him, in the last light, stood Temuscah, the leather man who had first captured him. The soldier leaned on his spear, somber. He said, "I hear you are side by side with Tok Pakal Chan himself now. Lucky you."

Corban said, "It all depends on how you look at it. Did Qikab ever reward you for bringing me to him?"

Temuscah coughed a short, humorless laugh. "No, are you joking? The mighty Qikab Chan remember a mere slogger? I just wear the leather." He rapped his armored chest, which bonged softly, like a hollow tree, a little drum.

Corban said, "Well, keep watch, and soon maybe you'll be repaid."

Temuscah sneered at him. "Yes, one of those devils in the hills will kill me. Good keeping, Animal-Head. I'm sorry I let them have you." He went off along the drum line, his spear on his shoulder.

Corban turned toward the campfires again. Now that he was seeing what was really there, he thought about Epashti, and his spirit sank.

He had left her in the path of the Itzen only hours before they moved. She had certainly been taken. She and Ahanton were out there, somewhere, in the sprawling camp that glittered like the plains of hell. She and Ahanton would be carried off into slavery, like all these other people.

His heart contracted, sore. This was his fault. He had not done justice to Epashti. He remembered how she had fought to save the burned child; abruptly he understood how she had fought to save him, too, as she saw it, coming with him, trying to help him. And he had abandoned her in the middle of enemies, given her up for a selfish dream.

His sister had said he would find what he was looking for, if he went into the west. He remembered now thinking he was asking the wrong question. At last his eyes opened and he saw. This was the city he had been searching for, this swarm of wretched people, this was the city of the just.

He had never known what it would look like and now he understood why. He had always thought he was different from other people, that he at least saw what was wrong, and that was why he was so out of place. But he was no different from everybody else, he was just as willfully stupid and cruel as everybody else. He belonged where he was, and if he wanted justice he had to make it himself.

She was there, Ahanton was there, out in the night country before him, lost like stars in the dark. He had brought them here and he had to rescue them. He couldn't go looking for them. If Tok Pakal found out about his family, he would use them to keep Corban always on his chain.

His gaze roamed over the patternless fire-strewn plain, every little flame a captive. Slowly it came to him that to save Epashti and Ahanton, he had to free them all.

The thunder rumbled in the distance, the sky laughing at him, a little man who knew nothing. But his mind calmed. He began to see a way before him. His hand going to his knife, he imagined himself on.

---

Epashti woke in the morning, and took an empty skin bag and went down to the river. All along the bank the heavy stony ground had been pounded down into the river; the brush and water plants were all trampled into the muck. The water was brown and thick and dozens of people were already crowding the shallows, some of the bigger children splashing out in the deep water. Epashti went off upstream a few steps, to where the current ran in close to the shore, and the bank curved inward. In that shelter she relieved herself, and wading out to her knees in the flow of the water she washed her face and hands.

The river burbled and sang around her, heedless of what lay beyond its banks. She stooped and laid her hands on the surface, and sang a few words to it, but it only banged against her hands and went on.

She straightened, her gaze going off across the wide swift-moving current. Across the way the trees grew down close over the bank, their tumbling leaves bright in the new sunlight. If she could get across the water, into that wildness, they would never catch her.

She went back to the bank for the skin bag. From where she stood, she could see a lot of people, and she made a show of starting to fill the bag and deciding the water was bad. She watched around her as she did this and nobody seemed to be heeding her. The shrieks of the playing children kept most of these people turned that way. With the skin bag in her hand she went up the stream, watching for a way to get across the river.

Before she had gone more than a few steps a leather man stood up before her, his spear out. He said nothing. She held up the water skin, and pointed to the river. "I'm getting water."

Another leather man came up from the shore of the river, his spear on his shoulder. "What's this?"

"I'm getting—" She started to explain, holding out the skin bag, but then the second man was coming at her, and she saw what was in his eyes. She whirled and ran.

One of them shouted. A hand caught her arm; she jerked around, lashing out with the bag, and struck the man behind her across the head. He staggered back and she fled away down the riverbank, back toward the muddied water and the shrieks of the children.

She loitered there a while, the baby in her belly rolling like a stone, her mouth tasting bad. After a while she took the bag and went south along the riverbank, watching for a way to cross the flood; here the water of course was bad to drink, filthy from all the people in it upstream, so she had no excuse. Anyhow the bank ahead of her began to rise into a steep slope, and she saw a leather man on the height, and she turned at once and went back.

She had no heart to fill the skin; she went back toward her place in the camp. Now, trudging up from the river onto the sun-beaten plain, she realized that the whole camp smelled bad. She walked along, looking for something familiar. The camp stretched on all sides of her, endless rows of strangers. For a moment she could not see where she belonged, and her belly fluttered in panic. Then across two rows of indiscriminate bodies she saw Pila, the fat woman, and went quickly toward her.

Leilee was sleeping still, curled up like a baby. Epashti sat next to her and laid down the empty skin. Pila reached out and took the skin and shook it.

"Where is the water? Are you witless?" Her voice rose sharply, her cheeks red.

Epashti said, "The water is foul. People are stirring it all up, the leather men won't let me go anywhere else." She pushed her hand back with her hair. Without good water they could not stay here longer. She said, "Has the maz come by yet?"

Pila waggled her finger at her. "Maz only comes for those who do the work! Where is our water?"

"I'll get it." Another of the women rose up, took the skin, and went off down the row.

Epashti sat still, her hands in her lap. Pila's words rankled her. She thought of the leather men on the riverbank and now Pila here in the camp, ordering her around; she thought again of escaping. Her belly hurt with hunger, and now she was thirsty.

She couldn't stay here, where the water smelled so foul. Tired already, she rested her hand on her stomach, above the baby. She had to have some food to take. When the maz came, she would try to save some, and hide it. She wished she had her carrying pouch; she had nowhere to hide much.

Pila was still staring at her, frowning. "Just because you are the healer doesn't mean you shouldn't work. Are you proud? Do you think we should work for you?"

Two or three other women, sitting beside her, murmured in agreement and stared reproachingly at Epashti. Epashti turned away; she needed someone to help her, and she put one hand on Leilee, shaking her awake. The thin girl stirred, rising, her hair in her eyes. "I don't feel good," she said. She got up and walked away, stooped, her arms dangling.

Epashti sank down, her shoulders rounded, abandoned. Pila had stood up, and was looking around the camp; she said, "Here comes the maz, and plenty of it!" She turned toward Epashti. "Which you may have your fill of, no matter how little you do."

Epashti said nothing. When the baskets came, she took two cakes and hid one in her dress.

Pila said, "They are so good to us. They treat us very well, I think. I will be happy to see Cibala."

"Cibala," Epashti said. "Where is that? Is that where they are taking us?"

"I hope so," Pila said. "Cibala is the most wonderful place in the world. All the lodges are of stone, and very great, and there is plenty to eat, even in the worst winters."

Epashti swallowed, her hand on her belly again, thinking of the baby. Leilee came back, with the woman who had gone for water, and sat down heavily and lay down again, her head on her bent arm.

Pila said, "Everybody has to work. Is your sister a healer too?" She made it sound as if being a healer was only an excuse to sleep.

Epashti flushed. "She feels bad."

"Heal her, then," Pila said, with a snigger.

One of the other women murmured, "We should tell the leather men they are not working."

Epashti recoiled from them, whose names she hardly knew, whose lineages and signs she could not know, whispering against her. A tingle went down her back. She lowered her eyes, afraid, her throat dry with thirst. Pila was talking about the wonders of Cibala again. Epashti lay down and tried to sleep.

In the morning, before dawn, all the Itzen gathered in the center of their tents and watched Tok Pakal, in a long cloak made of feathers, stretch his arm out toward the east, pronounce words, and slowly move his arm up and over his head until it pointed west. After that they went to their own places, and the sun rose, and everybody ate.

Corban and Erkan sat side by side with Tok Pakal, but they were not given food; they would not eat until the chieftain was done. Corban watched the people who served them—all little people, as the Itzen called them. They worked quietly, quickly, their eyes down, their bodies bent; they were easy not to notice.

Slaves, he thought. Like me.

He turned to Tok Pakal. "Will your men play the game again today?"

Tok Pakal glanced at him. He had taken off the headdress he wore for the ceremony; a slave held it behind him, a bird's head, with staring eyes. Tok Pakal still wore the cloak, which smelled musty, the feathers at the edges bedraggled. Still, under the dust, the feathers glinted green and gold.

"Yes," Tok Pakal said. "You like the game, I see? I'm glad."

"I like to gamble," Corban said. "But it's true, the game is very exciting." He saw Erkan turn and frown at him. "I wish I could play it."

Tok Pakal gave a harumph of laughter, and didn't even bother replying to that. He stroked one hand over the feathered cloak.

Corban said, "I can't, of course. But I'd like to try myself against your men. I think I could beat them in a race, for instance."

Tok Pakal's eyes flew open, and he gave a bellow of mirth. All around them people swung around to stare. The chieftain reached out and palmed Corban's shoulder. "You do, do you? What an impudent little upstart you are. Qikab and Kan Chak wll leap at that, I'll tell you now." His face softened, kindly. "Don't do it, Corban. It will only make you feel badly."

Corban said, "Perhaps. But I want to try. If I am so much beneath them, I would like to know it."

Tok Pakal snorted at him. "I'll put it to them. They'll accept, all of them, everybody is very curious about you. We'll see if you grow bison feet." He chuckled again. "Once up and down the ball court, how does that sound?"

"Well," Corban said, "they'd certainly beat me on the ball court. Won't you give me a chance? Let's race from here to the hills and back." He waved his hand toward the low foothills in the west. "There are trees. Everybody could pick a twig to bring back, to show he'd made it that far."

Tok Pakal was wagging his head back and forth, the smile

broad on his face, his eyes twinkling. "A handful of twigs. Very likely." He raised one hand, holding somebody else off: one of the older men, standing deferentially off to one side. Tok Pakal nodded to Corban.

"We'll do it as you wish. You'll see, it will make no difference. Go on, both of you, go get yourselves something to eat. I have boring work to do."

Erkan clamored out of the palanquin; Corban was already starting away. The Itzen went by them, going to Tok Pakal's side. Corban walked off across the pounded dirt of the ball field, looking down toward the foothills; he judged them two miles away, maybe three miles.

A sharp tug on his sleeve brought him back. Erkan had hold of him, and was staring hard at him. "What are you doing?"

"Stay out of this," Corban said.

The dwarf studied him, his face mournfully long. "They will never let you beat them. Even if you could."

Corban lengthened his stride. His stomach was rolling, his nerves tightening; what he had started was out of his hands now, and he was beginning to see all sorts of problems with it. The dwarf didn't try to keep up with him; he walked on alone, through the Itzen camp. Many of them turned to stare at him: He wondered if the news of the race had already gotten around. Likely they were all laughing at him, as Tok Pakal had laughed. He went on grimly toward the fire pits, to get some food—maz, made by slaves like him. But he was hungry, and he had to eat.

# CHAPTER NINETEEN

The palanquins were all different, Corban noticed; he was walking up from the drum line toward the ball court, where the four chairs sat side by side on the swell of land opposite the tree, looking with their tall hoods and outstretched arms like huge old giants squatting on the ground. Two were bigger than the others, and one of them was wider than all the rest: that was Tok Pakal's, of course. The colors and patterns were different, although Tok Pakal's in particular was so patched it was hard to make out any pattern at all.

In among the patches he saw eyes looking out of the swirls and lines, eyes and faces, with the beaks of birds. People stood in rows, their heads down, their penises drooping. He put his hand down to his crotch, a witness.

He went up between Tok Pakal's and the next, where often the older counsellor sat, whose name was Sak Nik. Everything was ready for the race. They would start from the poor lopped tree and a crowd of young Itzens already stirred and laughed and shouted around it. The sun was well up into the sky; it would be a hot, windless day. He had gotten some water in a skin bag, and he stopped now to hang it on his shoulder, under his shirt, where it would keep cool.

He went around the palanquin, to Tok Pakal, who was sitting there as always with his cup and the dwarf at his knee. Corban was uneasy about this next part, not knowing how to manage it, but Tok Pakal greeted him with a broad grin.

"Ready? Why aren't you down there? They'll start without you!"

Corban said, "We haven't settled on a wager." He leaned on the side of the palanquin. Tok Pakal's smile slipped a little, suspicious.

"I thought your knife again."

"If I win," Corban said, "I want to win something important. I want—" he fixed his eyes on Tok Pakal "—if I win, I want all the people that you've taken to be set free."

Tok Pakal's jaw dropped. Behind him the dwarf shrank back into the dark corner of the palanquin and glowered at Corban. The Itzen chief's lips curled, and his thick brows heavy in a frown; he leaned forward a little, intense.

He said, "Now I see what's going on here. Who's been talking to you? Whoever they are, they're wrong. We are doing only good for these people. We brought them the maz, which keeps them alive—"

"You take it from them," Corban said. "You take their people away."

"We take only enough to keep us." Tok Pakal turned suddenly, snatched something off the bench beside him. "See this?" He shook a little soft pouch at Corban. He was in a rage, shaking, his voice edged like glass. "We will give this to the Kisko, in exchange for what we take. This will let them grow more and better maz. They will never miss what we take. These other people will go back to Cibala with us where we will teach them the arts of life, and eventually they will come back here and raise their people up."

He paused a moment, his eyes blazing. But he was convincing himself. He calmed himself. He sat up straighter, his chin out, proud. "Without us, these people would be mere animals, starving in the woods—slaves, if you will, to their wicked superstitions and their savage rites. We have come to save them."

Corban stirred, a little, hearing in this some uneasy echo of words he had said once to his sister. His gaze went to the pouch, wondering what was in it. He thought of the winters in the Wolf village, the hunger month, when he spent days catching one skinny rabbit to divide among thirty people.

He thought of his sister, and what she had promised him. He lifted his eyes to Tok Pakal's.

"Will you make the bet?"

"You're impudent," Tok Pakal said. "Choose something else."

Corban's gut tightened. Slowly, he said, "I will not race for anything else. Everybody knows now about the race. Are you afraid I'll win?"

He was watching Tok Pakal's face; he saw the golden man's eyes widen at the challenge, dark with temper. Corban said, to give him something, "If I lose, I will submit to you. I will go with you, wherever you take me."

Tok Pakal's broad face settled a little. "You will already." He bit that off; his eyebrows jacked up and down. "Very well, Corban. You need to learn. You will learn, now, why we are the masters. Go. Race." He waved his hand. Corban turned, and went down toward the tree.

They were to start the race when the shadow of the lopped branch crossed a line drawn in the dirt at the foot of the tree. He went up to the edge of the mass of men waiting for this to happen. At first nobody noticed him; he was smaller than any of them, and they were chattering in their own language, boasting and laughing, and making bets between themselves. Then Kan Chak, the halfman prince, glanced down and saw him.

He gave a chuckle, and they all turned, and they all began to laugh. Corban went up toward the tree, his ears itching, feeling hot all over. Beneath the tree, he lifted his eyes toward the hills in the distance, wondering what he had gotten into.

The sun sailed along in the sky, and the shadow of the limb crept toward the line; now it was nearly touching the dent in the sandy ground. The laughter of the other men faded away, everybody watching the line; only Corban stood aside a little, his gaze on the Itzen. Then all at once, like startled horses, they whirled around, and raced off toward the hills.

He saw at once that they were all trying to outrace each other, as he had hoped, and certainly they were all running as if the end of the race were fifty strides on. He started off at a walk after them. He could hear people laughing behind him, and knew they were laughing at him. He felt like a fool; he was going to lose. Already the Itzen were far ahead of him. He had seen them before this, sitting around the camp, fighting for the chance to ride in palanquins and dropping out of their games to rest, and he had misjudged them: they were better than he was.

He couldn't quit now. He began to trot.

Epashti could not endure to sit long on the ground and do nothing. Leilee cried or slept, and the other women, under Pila's spell, would have nothing to do with her. In the heat of the day at last she got up, and went down to the river, and splashed in the filthy water to cool down.

Many of the women had brought their children down to play in the shallows and their shrieks and screams made the place loud. She went off a little upstream, looking for someplace to rest, out of the sun, quiet.

A leather man came along the bank toward her. She stopped, alarmed, looked around. The crowd at the riverbank was in plain sight, but he was coming straight at her. She moved, starting back toward the camp, and another one strode up in front of her.

She stopped. She said, "Leave me alone."

They came up so close to her she could smell the raw sweat of their bodies. One said, "We hear you're a troublemaker, woman."

She fixed her eyes on the broad leather-covered chest in front of her. The leather was shiny and hard, like a beetle's back. He braced himself on his long spear, as she had seen many of them do. A spurt of anger stiffened her; she knew where this was coming from.

She said, "Pila is lying. Let me go."

The man behind her said, "Just so you know. We're allowed any woman we find outside the camp." His voice was smooth, and suddenly a hand was stroking down her back, feeling her skin through her dress. "Got that?"

She put her hand over her belly, her breath small in her throat. She said, "I am not outside the camp now." It would help nothing to let them frighten her. She lifted her eyes from the armor to the face of the man inside it. "Does that hurt?" She touched her own neck, on the side, where on his neck the armor had worn the skin raw.

"It's nothing," he said, angry.

"I am a healer," she said. "I can help you if you're hurt." She turned and looked at the man behind her. "Any of you."

That one laughed, but he stepped back, away from her; his armor clicked together at the sides, where it was laced up. "None of us is hurt," he said, loudly. "We can't be hurt. Tok Pakal keeps us under his protection."

"Then you don't need me," she said, and walked out from between them, going back to the camp.

They let her go. She kept her pace slow, her head up, each step farther from them. Then suddenly they were after her again.

She stopped, tingling all over, knowing it would do no good to run. They surrounded her. But now it was different, now they were begging.

"Come with us. Please." The man with the sore on his neck made a prayerful gesture with his hands. "We won't hurt you. Please."

She followed them down the riverbank to the south, past the edge of the camp. There some green trees still grew, and some grass was left, and these few leather men had a camp there—a fire pit, a scatter of clothes and sleeping mats.

On one mat, a wounded man.

He was lying on his back under a little tree, in the shade, one knee drawn up. She sat beside, him, and put one hand out to touch the hole in his side, blue and sunken in around the edges.

"Where is the arrow?"

"We took it out," said the man with the sore on his neck. "It didn't seem so bad, it glanced off his armor, it didn't go in very deep. Now—"

The wounded man moaned, his eyelids fluttering; his skin was hot and dry under Epashti's hand. She stroked his face a moment, trying to soothe him. He coughed, a hollow burst out of his chest, and she smelled poison in his breath.

"Bring me the arrow."

The leather man jerked his head, and somebody else ran. The man before her gave her a pleading look. "Will he die? He's my brother."

"When did this happen?"

"Two days ago."

She put her hand to the wound again, feeling the heat in him. "Does he eat?" Someone else came back, with an arrow in his hand.

"No."

She took the arrow, a slender ash twig, like every other arrow she had ever seen. The feathers were broken and the head was fouled with blood. She sniffed at it, and smelled poison again, like a greenness in the air.

She turned back to the wounded man, and laid both hands on him, one on either side of the wound. He groaned at her touch, and his head turned toward her, and his eyes opened, sleek and dark with pain.

"Be still," she said. "Drink water—here, you, bring me water. Don't eat. But drink water." She pressed her hands around the wound, so that the hole gaped. Only a thin trickle of yellowish blood came out. She stroked the edges of the hole together, whispering charms under her breath.

They brought water, and she helped the wounded man sit enough to drink. The other leather men were gathered around her, and one said suddenly, "He's better. She healed him."

"No," she said. She let the sick man down again, and poured

water over his wound. "There was poison on the arrow. But he's strong. If he lives two more days he will get all well." She turned to his brother, beside her. "Make him drink. I'm going now. But come get me if he gets worse."

She turned and walked away, going along the riverbank again, toward the camp. The brother came after her, and walked beside her.

He said, "We aren't allowed—if they find out one of us is hurt, it's bad."

She said, "I want to escape. Will you help me escape?"

He turned toward her, his eyes shocked. "No. Don't be a fool. I've seen what they do." He raised his hands, palms up, begging her again. "Thank you. You helped him. He's all I have, nobody's left to me but him. But don't try to escape." He shook his head at her, his mouth grim, and turned and went back, and she trudged on alone toward the camp.

---

"Ekkatsay," Miska said. "If you want to leave, go. The Wolves will stay with me. They're all I need."

Ekkatsay knew this was true. He had become friends with Hasei, Yoto, Faskata, the other Wolves, he knew their valor, had seen them, again and again, fight like more than men for Miska. He licked his lips. Stubbornly, he said, "It's almost Harvest Moon, Miska-ka. We're a long way from home. I don't know what's going on here, why all these people are here, but I know no way we can fight them and hope to win, especially since we can't kill them."

Miska shrugged. "Certainly not the way you fight."

Ekkatsay ground his teeth together. "We can't fight men we can't kill, who can kill us!"

Miska gave him a sideways look. "Get them close, you could have fought them. Like a bear fights, hah? Chest to chest?" He snorted, disdainful, and turned his head, staring away to the east, as if he could see through the hillsides between them and the great hosting on the river plain.

Like bison, Ekkatsay thought. His shoulders slumped. He was toying with the notion all these people were spirits of the bison, called out by some charm.

He felt Miska's scorn even when the Wolf shaman wasn't talking. He hung his head down.

His gaze drifted toward the little girl, who was certainly under some charm. She sat motionless, the strange hide around her. He had heard weird stories about her. Then his eye caught on something moving, coming toward them.

Up the little hollow of the camp, past the men sleeping in the shade of the boulders, ran Lopi, the skinny young Wolf who never stopped moving. He trotted up to Miska, his face bright with sweat and excitement.

"Something's happening. You said I should tell you."

Miska swung toward him. "What? Some kind of signal?"

Lopi swayed from side to side. "No—but they're all doing something. Or a lot of them are, anyway—running toward the hill, over there. A lot of them."

"Longnoses?" Miska said.

"I think so. They're coming from the place of lodges."

Miska rubbed his hand over his nose; his eyes turned toward Ekkatsay, but he spoke to Lopi.

"All right," he said. "Let's go down there. Get everybody moving."

Lopi went off; Ekkatsay frowned at Miska. "What signal are you waiting for?"

Miska said, "I don't know." He swung his head around toward Ekkatsay, his eyes glittering. "Something will happen, soon. When it does, Ekkatsay, you had better remember how to fight like a bear." He banged Ekkatsay's chest with his fist and strode off, headed toward the little girl. Ekkatsay turned to summon his men, to follow. He thought, After this, though, whatever it is, I am going home.

Corban passed the hindmost of the Itzen runners only halfway to the hills; this last man walked along, his head down, grimly moving forward, but after Corban jogged by him, he sagged down on the ground and sat still. Corban stretched his legs, going faster. He unslung his skin of water and drank as he ran.

A little while later he passed two more of the Itzen, both sitting down, and then several walking slowly along in a crowd, who as he came up tried to match him. Many of them did keep up with him for several strides, but these soon dropped behind him too.

Then he met Kan Chak, coming the other way, a twig clutched in his hand, moving at a steady jog. Breathing hard, his face streaming sweat, his gaze fixed on the distance, the Itzen never saw Corban. Corban could see the little bent trees at the foot of the hills, now, and he ran hard toward the nearest one.

A hundred strides from it, Qikab was sitting on the ground, his head sunk down between his shoulders. He watched Corban go by, his head turning; Corban went on to the tree, broke off a bit of a green stem, took another drink, and started back. When he passed Qikab, the Itzen prince got to his feet and followed him.

Corban began to run faster now, thinking of Epashti, of Ahanton; one of his knees began to throb. He swung the water skin around in front where he could reach it easily. Out of the side of his eye he could see Qikab falling behind him again. He passed the other Itzen sitting along the side of the track, but Kan Chak was still ahead of him, and Corban leaned into each stride, his arms pumping, running as fast as he could.

Kan Chak was ahead, but his lead was shrinking, and Corban saw that the halfman was down to walking. He pushed himself on.

His knee buckled once and he caught himself; a surge of pain went up his thigh. He clenched the knee tight with every stride to stay upright.

Kan Chak saw him coming and began to run again, and when Corban caught up with him, with the palanquins ahead of them looking down, the dark mass of watching people shimmering in the sun around the finish line, Kan Chak groaned and pumped his arms and drove himself back into the race. They went stride for stride along the pounded grass, the tree looming up before them, the shrieks of the onlookers insect-small in the distance. Their shadows ran side by side. Corban's lungs were burning, and with each step his knee wobbled.

Kan Chak staggered. His shadow slowly slid down behind Corban's, and he slipped back, and Corban ran on alone. He gave a yell. He flung his arms up. Driving his legs to a last furious burst of speed he raced in under the tree and in among the watching Itzen.

He slumped down, his hands on his knees, his head hanging. His breath sawed in and out of him. Around him the Itzen stood stonily, not cheering, not even looking at him, but somewhere, in the distance, there was cheering. He straightened, his whole body trembling, and his knee like a fiery stone.

On either side of the Itzen camp, along the low rise, were gathered masses of the little people, slaves and leather men, and they were leaping up and down, yelling. He straightened up, startled, and their cheers doubled, ringing in the silence of the Itzen. Qikab and Kan Chak were walking in under the tree, the other Itzen runners strung out along the track behind them; nobody cheered them at all. Corban went quickly through the glares of the Itzen, to the great palanquin.

Tok Pakal sat there, his arms folded over his chest, and his face set in a scowl. The old counsellor sat in the shadows beside him. The chief spoke in his harsh public voice. "You don't know your place yet, Corban. That will come. Meanwhile, stand there, and be silent."

Corban raked his hands over his sweat-soaked hair; he was still too tired to talk much, and he thought there would be more to this anyway. His water skin was empty and he tossed it away. Tok Pakal stood up in the palanquin.

Qikab and Kan Chak moved up toward him, and the other Itzen runners, panting and sleek with sweat, trudged up to crowd around; Corban stepped back to the side, intending to inch his way out entirely—expecting not to understand what Tok Pakal was going to say. But then the chieftain began to shout, and he was using the low language. Corban straightened, realizing he was intended to hear this, and looking around he met Tok Pakal's eyes on him, staring at him over the heads of the Itzen surrounding the palanquin.

"This is not over! Nothing has been proven yet. Certainly a bison could outrun a man. But a man has many arts! We'll let you rest a while. Then we'll see how well the animal-headed one can throw a spear."

Then Qikab, standing directly before the chieftain, flung his arms up, bellowing.

"The ball! Make him throw the ball!"

Beside him the halfman prince Kan Chak lunged urgently toward Tok Pakal. "The ball is sacred. We can't let a creature from the woods touch it."

The other Itzen stood listening, silent, their heads hanging. They glanced continually toward Corban, but never for long, and none looked at him from the center of his face.

Qikab said, "It's a piece of stuffed leather. But we can all throw it farther than he can. Make him throw that."

Tok Pakal's face looked suddenly hollow, his eyes dull, as if he saw inward. Corban remembered him saying the ball game was once sacred—the ball sacred. How nobody knew what it meant anymore. Then the chief was scowling at him again, dark, angry, pouring all his anger down on Corban.

"Throw the ball, then, Animal-Head. And I will accept your

offer, that your life is mine. In olden times, the loser of the game died. We will honor this place with your blood, when you lose."

Corban swallowed, his guts in a knot. Now, told what to think of him, they all turned to look directly at him, distant looks, as if they saw him far away. Already dead.

He turned and walked off, away by himself, his palms clammy. They would give him tests until he failed; he could not win.

He stopped thinking about that, and fixed his mind instead on the ball. He knew why Qikab thought he would not be able to throw it far: it was heavy, and too big for him to hold in one hand. Without ever picking it up he could not tell how heavy. He went off near the drum line, deserted as usual, and sat down and with his knife cut several long strips from the bottom of his deerskin shirt. Then he untied the sling from his belt, and doubled the length of the lines.

# CHAPTER TWENTY

The camp stank like rot and burning dung. Coming back from the river, Epashti felt her belly turning sick just walking through it, and she fought down the panicky will to run, heedless and witless, just to get away. She laid her hand on her swelling body, and deep inside felt a strong push back. Then, ahead of her, someone screamed her name.

It was Leilee, on her feet, shouting, happy for once, jumping and waving her arms. Epashti went toward her, startled at her exuberance, and then saw Pila and her little crowd of followers, slumped on the ground scowling.

Leilee danced toward her. "They said you were gone—they said you were never coming back! I have food for you—they said you wouldn't come back—" Tears squirted from her eyes. She caught Epashti's hand in both of hers.

Epashti hugged her, looking over her shoulder at Pila. "I am back, of course. Why do you listen to her?" She went by Leilee into their place, and sat down, staring at Pila.

"Woman, hear me. I know you are a liar. I know you are one with the leather men, and you are trying to do their work here. Stay away from me, keep your mouth shut, don't try to harm me again, or I will see to you."

Pila's cheeks blazed red; her eyes glistened. She could say nothing. The women on either side of her drew away from her, their eyes round, and their mouths ajar. Slowly they turned to each other, and began to whisper. Pila hunched her shoulders up, her mouth sinking at the corners. Epashti settled herself, shaking her dress out, and began to eat the maz cakes Leilee had saved for her.

Tok Pakal had another line drawn in the dirt of the ball court, and a stick put into the ground by it, and announced that when the shadow of the stick crossed the line, then the throwing contest would start. Corban went by there to see and the shadow was still a hand's breadth away, and anyway they would go one at a time. Then the dwarf stood in front of him.

"Corban." Erkan gave him a wild look from the sides of his eyes. "You are in a lot of trouble now."

"I'm always in trouble," Corban said. "I bring it with me. They do not call me Loosestrife for nothing."

"Tok Pakal will forgive you if you beg him for it. But you must not take part in this, not even try."

Corban glanced around, to see who was listening. "Did he send you?"

"Yes, of course! He likes you. He needs someone to talk to—" The dwarf's face fretted. "Smarter than me." The little man put out his short-fingered, possum hand. "I want you to stay too."

Corban squatted down on his heels, so that they were face to face. "Then go back to him, and remind him what he wagered with me."

The dwarf's eyes flashed, liquid. "You're mad. You can't win. You don't know what you're passing up. In Cibala you'll be like a lord. No work, the best of the food, of the women. Everything."

"In Cibala I'll be like a slave," Corban said. Then behind him, at the Itzen ball court, a yell rose, many-voiced.

"It's starting," the dwarf said, his head to one side, and his eyes mournful. "Give it up. Come with me."

Corban reached into his sleeve, and pulled out the coiled sling. "Erkan," he said, "I'll free you, too." He turned to go to the line, where the Itzen were massing for the throw.

The dwarf called after him, "I don't want to be free!" Corban ignored him, and went to take his place by the line. He didn't look in the direction of the palanquins.

Kan Chak went first, his face vivid with intensity; he palmed the ball, swung his arm behind him, took three steps and with his whole body behind his swinging arm hurled the ball out and up. The onlooking crowd gave a yell. The ball looped into the sky and fell, far down the ball court, and a slave ran down to mark the place with a stone.

Some others of the Itzen threw, none reaching as far as Kan Chak's. Corban walked up and down the side of the ball court, unable to keep still, his knee twanging with each step. Nobody pointed and laughed at him now; they avoided him with their eyes.

Qikab came to the line, throwing out his broad chest, and when a yell went up from the onlookers he turned around, his arms above his head, drawing the cheers. He took the ball in his hands, and turned and gave a deep look at the great palanquin, on the rise above the ball court.

He held the ball easily in one hand, his arm straight; he ran toward the line, and planting one foot hurled the ball up, his body coiling around, his topknot flying. The crowd yelled, seeing a good throw, and the ball sailed across the sky and dropped down and hit the ground well past Kan Chak's stone.

Qikab roared, flung his arms out, and spun to face the crowd, gathering in the cheers. Corban walked back toward the line through the wash of noise. There was no one left to throw; it was his turn now. As he went in among them, the Itzens' voices stilled. He felt them all watching him now. He looked at no one; he went to the ball, which a slave had brought back, and picked it up.

It was heavier even than he had expected. Throwing it as the Itzen had he could have moved it scarcely half Qikab's distance. He took the sling from his belt. A little murmur went through the Itzen, uncertain, alarmed. The socket of the sling was barely wide enough to keep the ball in place and he gripped the strings up close to the ball to hold it.

Then he went to the line. They hushed again, everybody watching him. He took hold of the strings, let the ball hang, and began to turn, one foot over the other. As he turned, the ball sailed out in the sling, flying around him, nearly pulling him off his feet. He spun around again, the ball hurtling around him, sailing out at the end of the sling, so heavy he had to lean against it to stay on his feet, and he whirled a third time and as he came around again forward to the line he let the lead string go.

The crowd gave a single sharp gasp. The ball soared up, making a rainbow arch down the ball court, hanging in the air for what seemed long breaths of time, and fell.

It disappeared; far beyond Qikab's stone, beyond even the end of the court, the ball vanished into the grass. There was a stunned silence among the Itzen, and Qikab sprang forward, his face dark with rage.

"You cheat! You cheat, you little monster!" With clubbed fists he leapt at Corban.

Corban bounded away, dropping the sling; Qikab struck him a broad-swinging blow on the shoulder and knocked him sprawling. He rolled up onto his feet; Qikab was stalking toward him, furious, his huge fists clenched up before him. Corban remembered another big man he had fought, long ago, and launched himself headfirst, staying low, to drive his shoulder into Qikab's knees.

The Itzen swayed, his legs buckling; sprawling on his belly on the ground, Corban gripped him by both ankles and yanked him down. With a thud and a howl the big man fell flat on his back. All around them the other Itzen were screaming in their own language. Corban scrambled up; Qikab pushed himself onto his hands and knees and Corban jumped with both feet on his back and slammed him flat again. With both hands he gripped Qikab's left wrist and twisted his arm up, and planted his foot in the small of Qikab's back.

The screaming of the onlookers abruptly cut off. Corban swung his gaze around them, at the wall of shocked Itzen faces, and brought his eyes to Tok Pakal, standing stone-faced in the front of the great palanquin.

"Give me what I have won! Three times now I've beaten you, give me what you promised me!"

With one last wrench on Qikab's arm, he let go and stepped back, leaving the Itzen groaning in the dirt. The other men were goggling at him. Then Kan Chak strode forward, his face set rigid with anger, but not to challenge Corban.

He went at Tok Pakal, shouting in his own language. In the back of the great palanquin the old man Sak Nik stood up, his gaze on the chieftain. The other Itzen pressed forward. They ignored Corban; they were all shouting at Tok Pakal in their own language, and they were getting steadily more angry.

Corban moved back, out of their way. Qikab's servants had come to bring the prince water and to help him up. Corban turned and went off, toward the drum line, his mind churning.

He had done nothing. He had been an idiot to think he could hold Tok Pakal to the wager. His belly knotted in a raw fury, at himself, at the Itzen, at the perverse and unjust world. Behind him the shouting suddenly died into an ominous silence. In a moment they would come to kill him.

He had reached the drum line. Beyond, the camp stretched out into the distance, open under the sky. The afternoon's thunderstorm was building on the horizon, towers of clouds, like another world floating above this one.

He had not saved a single slave. He turned, edgy, looking for something else to do. The drum line was the voice of their power; he could at least cut their throats. He drew his knife and plunged the blade into the stretched-skin head of the first drum.

It sang, when the blade hit, and then ripped from edge to

edge. Pleased with this, he went down the line, slashing the drum heads. Behind him, at the great palanquin, the Itzen gave one single many-throated yell.

He could yell, too. He stopped at the next drum he came to; the mallets that played it were lying on the ground, and he took them up and began to beat on it. At first he could make only a little sound, until he remembered how the drummers swung their arms, and raised the sticks high and banged them down.

Boom, the drum said. Boom boom.

He knew nothing of the language. He wanted only to confuse people. He played with the sticks, going fast and then slow; there were places along the edge, also, that sounded different. After a while his arms started to ache. He put the sticks down, slashed this drum also and went on down the line, cutting with his knife.

Epashti thought at first it was only thunder, the faint little boom at the edge of her hearing, but she lifted her head, and listened, and realized it was one of the drums.

A thrill ran along her nerves. Only one drum. Something about this was odd. She stood up, to see what the leather men were doing.

The camp stretched out around her in the midday heat, the air thick and moist with the coming storm. Most of the people lay flat on the ground as if blown there by a great wind. Here and there a leather man stood, and they were all facing the distant sound of the single drum.

They were doing nothing. Two rows from her one soldier leaned on his spear, listening to the drum; when she rose his eyes followed her, but he did not move. Then he turned away from her, and called out, "What does that mean?"

Down the line, another of the leather men lifted his shoulders in a shrug. All around the camp, they stood, caught in some spell, enchanted by the distant, solitary drum.

Epashti's heart began to gallop. She thought, I can go now. They won't know what to do. She stooped, and shook Leilee.

"Come," she said. "We are escaping." Leilee sat up, dazed; beyond her, Pila suddenly lifted her head.

"What? What is it?"

Epashti reached for Leilee's hand. "Follow me."

Pila sat up where she was, throwing a sleepy child off her lap. "Where are you going?" She reached out and caught hold of Epashti's dress.

Epashti said, "Let go of me, woman, now."

Pila clung to her dress, turned her head, and screamed, "Help me! She's trying to escape."

Epashti reached down and gripped Pila's wrist and twisted, and her dress came free of the woman's fingers. Nearby one of the leather men had swiveled his head around toward Pila, frowning, but the drum called him back, turned him forward again, telling him something he had to obey but did not understand. Epashti glared down at Pila.

"Stay here, you fool, if you want. We are leaving." She turned toward the river, and began to walk.

She did not look back, and she kept her steps slow, lest anything disturb the spell on the leather men. She kept her eyes on the river. Her heart was banging in her chest. She passed a leather man who stood, gaping, his brow furrowed, staring up at the drums; he paid no heed to her. Through the corners of her eyes, she saw other people walking, like her, streams of them, moving away. The faint little drum beat on. She matched her footsteps to it.

---

Miska squatted, and put his hand to the pounded dirt before him. They had come this way, the longnoses, run up here across the plain to the foot of this hill, to this particular tree, and then run back again. They had broken branches off the tree. He straightened, puzzled.

The hill rose behind him, sun-blasted. Before him, the Wolves had drifted out toward the plain, looking toward the camp. Over to his left, under the trees, the Bears were standing in a clump, looking ready to run at the first danger. Ekkatsay, in their midst, said, "What's going on?"

Miska shrugged. "I don't know. I—" His head turned. "What's that?"

The Wolves were stirring, uneasy, pacing back and forth; Hasei shifted his bow from his back to his left hand. Miska went up toward the camp a few steps. In among the Bears, Ekkatsay put his hand to his ear, turning his head, trying to hear something, and Hasei said, "A drum. From the camp, there."

Miska straightened. "Is it talking about us?" His ears strained, listening for more drums, yet only this one sounded, a thump at the edge of his hearing.

Ahanton came up through the midst of the men, small in the red and blue cloak, her gaze fastened on Miska. She said, "It's Corban."

Hasei said, "It's stopped."

Ekkatsay said, "It doesn't sound like anything to me," and Miska reached out and silenced him with a wave, stretching one hand out to Ahanton. "What?"

"It's Corban," she said. Her eyes shone, enormous, gray as frost. "I know it. I can hear his voice in it. It's Corban."

"The signal." Miska flung his arms up, drawing all eyes to him. They gawked at him, startled. He shouted, "It's the signal. Now we will surely beat them—Follow me! Run!" Without waiting to see if any of them actually did, he waved his war club up over his head and let out a howl, and raced out onto the plain, headed for the longnose camp.

---

Corban slashed the drums all down the line. This took him around behind the end of the Itzen tents, well away from the ball court.

They had stopped shouting down there, but he could still hear single voices, ringing out. He wondered if they had heard his drumming. If anybody had heard his drumming. At the last drum in the line, he picked up the sticks, and turned to look over the camp of the little people.

His heart jumped. The camp was moving, not orderly as it had before, but seething with people going in all directions—all except one. No one came this way. They were walking away from him. They all were leaving.

He gripped the sticks, joyous, and began to bang on the drum again, swinging his arms hard. In the west the thunderstorm was building, packed layers of cloud, and the muttering of the thunder lay over the drum, but still he pounded. Out on the plain, as the sun slid behind the edges of the advancing clouds, and the light began to fail, he saw now, even some of the leather men were moving away. Far out there a walking figure suddenly peeled off its chest armor and cast it down, and went on walking.

A hoarse yell behind him brought him whirling around. Qikab was striding toward him, a spear in his hand.

"So that is you, doing this. You think it will make any difference, monster—"

Corban flung the mallets aside, and drew his knife. The thin blade looked like a sliver of grass against the ribbon edge of the spear. Qakib thrust at him, and he dodged back, his knee not answering right; he nearly fell.

The Itzen crowed at him, and lunged at him again with the spear. "I'm telling you now, monster, you're lost! Tok Pakal is thrown down. Soon there will be a new man in the great palanquin, and I promise you it will be me!"

At that, he strode forward, the spear in both hands, the black needle head stabbing and jabbing, driving Corban back one staggering step at a time, never within reach of Corban's knife. Corban could not take his eyes from the tip of the spear, which poked at him like a snake, glass-tongued. He thought of the sling on his belt—if he could get away—find a stone—

He wrenched out of the path of the thrusting spear, and his knee collapsed. He went down hard. Qikab bounded at him, and the spear struck down. Corban rolled, but not fast enough; he felt the spear hit him in the side, slice through his skin and into the ground, and then he was pinned there, facedown.

He writhed around, trying to reach the shaft behind him with his hand, and the pain knifed through his side, freezing him with a gasp. He braced himself up on one arm, groaning. Qikab stood over him, a broad smile on his face, and kicked him in the hip.

"Now," he said. "This time, you lose." He reached to his belt to draw his knife.

Corban could not move; awkward, helpless, he gaped up at the Itzen prince, and Qikab smiled down at him. Cocked his arm with the knife. Corban stiffened, ready to lunge out when he struck, to fight somehow.

A strange look came over Qikab's face, and he straightened. He lifted the knife, almost lazily, like an afterthought, and then slowly he pitched down flat to the ground. Out of his back a skinny little arrow stuck.

Corban twisted, trying to reach the spear. Over his head, against the slate-gray sky, arrows in flights passed like geese. People were rushing toward him, up the plain. Then, under the patter of thunder, he heard the howling of the Wolves.

His hair prickled up. He gathered himself against the pain, and curled his arm carefully behind him and got hold of the spear. He wrenched on it. A wash of pain nearly sent him under, but when he got his head to stop whirling, he was lying flat, and the spear lay flat beside him.

He had sense enough not to stand. He could hear them running by him, all around, feel the pounding of their feet in the ground under him; they would kill anything in their path. Their arrows laced the sky again above him. Their howls rose even above the thunder. They swooped by like the wild hunt, like the army of the storm, and fell on the Itzen camp.

In the little silence they left behind them, Corban pushed himself to his knees. His whole side was slick with blood. When he moved everything hurt. He picked his knife off the ground and put it into its sheath on his belt, and forced himself up onto his feet.

He was facing the Itzen camp. Screams and yells erupted from it, half-drowned in the thunder. Through the spaces between the tents, he could see people rushing back and forth in the square, arms raised with weapons; he saw people stagger and fall. He couldn't tell who was winning.

The rain hadn't started, but the wind was picking up, plucking at the peaks of the tents, and now abruptly through the cloth patching of the nearest tent he saw the glow of a fire.

He staggered off along the drum line, his hand pressed to his bleeding side. As he came near the tent, the flames caught on the wall and roared up, and the wind lifted the flames into the darkening sky like a giant torch, spraying embers and bits of burning cloth. In the baleful light Corban saw into the square in the middle of the tents, into the wild thrash of the men there fighting.

He could see the Itzen, taller than the others, with their topknots. He stood rooted where he was, watching through the flames like a sheet of wrinkling red-gold water, as one by one these tall men vanished down into the dark thrashing mass of their enemies.

He turned away, toward the dark, the camp below him; he had to find Epashti. He laid his hand to his side, throbbing with steady pain, the blood leaking through his fingers.

The great black ledge of the storm cloud was stretching out over the plain, its blurry ragged margin creeping over the sun. Corban walked through the line of the slashed drums; the plain before him was disappearing into the huge deep shadow of the storm. The wind like a hand against his back pushed him into that whirling center. The camp was almost empty. He went by a row of dead fires, the earth pounded to dust under his feet, and another row, bed on bed of cold coals, where nobody sat. The wind lifted the dust up into the air and swirled it off into the storm like a flag.

The air was turning coppery, and new shadows flowed on ahead of him, rippling, watery, bloody red. He looked back, and saw the Itzen tents going up, one by one, in towering flames.

He looked around. In the camp he saw no leather men at all anymore, but here and there, some people still sat on the ground, staring dazedly up at the Itzen camp. He went on, passed by a chunk of something like a big shell, a beetle shell, and realized it was a piece of leather armor.

"Epashti!"

He screamed into the wind, and the wind carried it off into nothing. The first huge raindrops struck his head. He turned around, looking back again toward the lurid flickering light from the blaze of the Itzen. The books, he thought. The pictures. The scraps of cloth and feathers, brought all the way from Mutul. Then he saw, through the rolling smoke and the sheets of falling rain, two of the palanquins, rushing toward him.

A dozen of the Itzen carried them, running at a good lope, the long poles on their shoulders. Nobody rode in them. Swaying and creaking they went by Corban as he stood there; the second was the great palanquin, three men on each pole. After it, crying, his little arms out reaching, ran the dwarf Erkan.

"Wait—Wait—"

Just beyond Corban, one of the Itzen let go of the carrying pole and whirled around to catch the little man by the arms, and running a few steps with him tossed him up into the chair. Corban, squinting, thought it was Kan Chak who did this. Then the palanquin was rocking and swaying away, hurrying off through the rain, fleeing back to Cibala.

Corban thought, Let Kan Chak tell them not to come this way again.

His gaze sharpened. Something small and lumpy had fallen

out of the palanquin and lay on the ground in the steady driving rain. He went over and picked it up, and it was the leather pouch Tok Pakal had shown him, that would make more and better maz.

He held it, wondering if he should even keep it, and behind him, someone called his name.

He spun around. At first all he saw was the red and blue flutter of his cloak rushing toward him through the gray of the rain. Then he saw it was Ahanton.

He gave a hoarse cry, and stooped, and she ran into his arms. He wrapped himself around her. She burrowed her face against his neck. "I thought you were gone." She was crying. "Then I heard the drum."

He laughed, stroked her hair, her weight light in his arms. "It's good. It's good." He wrapped the cloak around her against the rain, pulled the edge up over her head. He laid his face against her as she curled against his shoulder. His side throbbed but that would mend. "We have to find Epashti."

"There," she said, and lifted herself up, and pointed.

He looked where she was looking. Up across the deserted camp, through the driving rain and the wind and the crash of the thunder, a woman walked calmly toward them, walked as if on her home earth, in the sunshine, her head up, and her smile wide. She came up to them, and said, "So you are Ixewe, after all."

"Wife," he said, "I greet you more gladly than I can say." He reached out to her, and she embraced him and Ahanton, warm and sweet, and they all stood together in the rain, happy.

Ekkatsay laughed, unsteady, exhuberant. The fight was over but the excitement still coursed through him, the thrill of being still alive. The crashing rain was swiftly soaking down the fires all around him, and already some of the other men were poking into the smoldering ruins, looking for things to take home. There were bodies burning in the rubble, giving up a stink of charred flesh.

Ekkatsay hung his war club on his shoulder, stretching his hand, working the fingers. They had struck the unwary longnoses like a fall of boulders, he and Miska, and shattered them to nothing. For a moment he longed for another enemy to kill.

He had seen some of them go off, carrying a hut on their backs, but the others had fought to the death. There were no prisoners then to make the trip home more of a problem than it had to be. He laughed again, his blood cooling, remembering how he had smashed down one of the longnoses—a huge, shining man; fighting empty-handed, he had still knocked other Bears down, until Ekkatsay himself laid into him with his club, and toppled him.

The rain was suddenly slacking off. The clouds broke apart and a burst of brilliant sunlight flooded the camp. Their camp, now. Ekkatsay began looking around for something to eat—all these people, he hoped, had something to eat that had not burned. Then Miska was coming toward him, frowning.

Ekkatsay straightened to meet him. He said, "Some Bears died. And I have wounded men."

Miska nodded. "Some Wolves, also." He was stroking his hand down his ribs, his arm, idly fingering his body, as if looking for hurts. Ekkatsay saw no hurt on him; he remembered the stories and thought they were true, he could not be wounded. Miska was looking away down the plain.

"Where did they all go?" Ekkatsay said. He wanted Miska to remember how Ekkatsay had run across the plain, roaring, and struck his enemies, and killed them. He wanted Miska to admire him.

Miska shrugged. He seemed uninterested, his face a little sunken, as if he went inside himself. His eyes poked away down the plain again. Indifferent, he said, "They're gone now. We did what I came here to do. Now we have to get home." He looked steadily away down the plain, over the camp.

Ekkatsay turned to look where he was looking. Some people

were walking up the plain toward them. One, he saw at once, was the strange child, Miska's child, leaping and running, bright faced. After her came a woman, and a man with a great shaggy head, like a bison.

The Bear sachem started up with amazement; he turned toward Miska, now steadily watching these people approach, and said, "This is your shaman." So all the stories were true, he thought.

Miska's lips twisted. "He is nothing of mine," he said, his voice low, and harsh. His hand stroked slowly down his side, feeling for wounds. Ekkatsay stepped away, uneasy, wondering why the air felt cold here. He glanced over his shoulder at the animal-headed man and went back toward the camp, back into the company of his own.

# Wind Music

# CHAPTER TWENTY-ONE

Miska had lost, and he knew it. Nobody else knew it; they all believed him greater even than he had been before, now that he had won such a triumph over the Sun chief and gotten the Wolves their revenge. That only made it worse. All the way back from the Big River country, whenever they came on other people, those people had come offering belts of honor and loyalty, because he had beaten the longnoses. Whenever he came to a village the people rushed out to meet him and offered him everything they had, bowing and spreading leaves and branches on the ground before him, that he should not tread even the same dirt as other men. So he had come home to glory.

But he had lost his joy. He walked in the forest, and it was only the forest, empty and ordinary; the feeling was gone that he might at any moment see her, that she might come to him with her smile and her eyes and hands and lips, and warm him to a sunlight heat, and lead him into sacred places. She was gone, gone forever, she had left him behind. She had never loved him.

She had left Corban behind, too.

He could not have beaten the Sun chief without Corban. Nobody knew what Corban had actually done but everybody knew without it the Wolves would never have broken through the spells that protected their enemies. The other men had stopped hating him; all the long walk back home, when he was around, they had shown him an open respect. Miska had even once heard Hasei call him Corban-ka, which had made the sachem laugh.

Corban laughed also. They had looked at each other, and for a moment between them there had been only the joke.

But she had loved Corban, not him. In his heart, like a worm in a nut, the suspicion gnawed that for Corban, she was still here.

Corban almost never killed a deer, but he had been lucky this time, getting close enough to a young doe to hammer her behind the eye with a slung stone. He killed her almost half a day's walk from the village, and the deer far outweighed him. He built a drag out of poles, and began to haul the carcass along, not getting very far, even out in the open, with the dense woods between him and the river and home. He began to think of cutting the deer and carrying home only the best, and coming back later for whatever the wild things left him.

Then ahead of him, where the trees came down close to the yellow grass, two men appeared. He knew they were Wolves by their shaggy hair, but they were too far for him to make out which. They stood watching him for a while, and at last one of them went off, but the other trotted toward him across the dry grass.

It was Hasei, Miska's second hand. Corban relaxed, watching him jog up, a solid, square-faced man with lively eyes.

Hasei said, "I'll help you. We should carry it between us," and they slung the deer onto the drag poles and lifted the poles on their shoulders, the way the Itzen had carried their palanquins. Corban thought about this a while, going along. Carrying the deer was certainly much easier.

They went down through the thick woods along the river, where the winter already had laid its hands on everything, the leaves turning and falling, the deep thickets frostbitten back to masses of tangled rotten stalks, many of the creatures gone to bed. Twice floods of birds rushed by overhead, casting long flickering shadows over the sun; their hoarse calls trailed after them like ghosts.

The two men crossed the river at the broad ford, and on the far bank, without talking about it, they stopped. Hanging the deer between the forked branches of two little trees they sat down in the late sun to rest. Hasei took a pipe from his belt pouch; while he packed it with fragrant leaf, he glanced weightily at Corban. Corban took out his tinderbox. When the pipe was ready he lit it and they smoked in silence for a while. The tinderbox had gotten bent somehow and Corban used his thumb to push the metal sides straight again.

"Thank you," he said, tying the tinderbox back into the corner of his cloak. "I could never have brought all this meat back by myself."

"It's a good thing for everybody," Hasei said. "And Epashti, you know, we have the same mother."

Corban glanced sharply at him. "I didn't know that." He realized he should know this, but he had never lived much among the men. Certainly Hasei looked nothing like Epashti.

Hasei leaned comfortably against the rock behind them, looking up into the high tops of the trees along the riverbank. They smoked a little more, saying nothing. Corban sat enjoying the warmth of the sun, the sweet fragrances of the air around him. He noticed how Hasei's eyes moved, looking up at the trees, and that his lips moved also.

Corban said, "What are you thinking about?"

Hasei's gaze jerked toward him, wide-eyed, and he frowned; Corban saw he was unsure about talking, and wondered if he should have kept his own mouth shut. But the Wolf gave him a long look, and then gestured up toward the tops of the trees.

"See how they move in the wind?"

Corban looked up; the young trees were spindling and naked, and the wind swayed their tops like fish baskets in the air.

Hasei said, "That's like seeing the wind blow. You can't see the wind, ever, except like that. Like seeing the music from the drums, you only do that when people dance. It's like music, the wind. Except it never ends, and it's never the same."

Corban blinked at him, as startled as if Hasei had just peeled his skull back and shown Corban the inside of his head. Then the Wolf said, "When you came here, you couldn't talk. Don't the Sky people talk?"

Corban laughed. This was easier than dealing with the inside of Hasei's head. He said, "I'm not from the sky. I come from another place on the Turtle's back. And I could talk, but not in Wolf words."

Now it was Hasei who blinked at him, who saw, maybe, into Corban's head. He lowered his gaze to the pipe, and packed it again, and they lit it again and smoked.

Hasei said, "You mean, you have different words for things than we do."

Corban nodded. He had gone back to thinking about Hasei's wind music.

"Where do the words come from, then?" Hasei said. "If not from the things they mean."

Corban turned his head and stared at him. Finally, he said, "That's an interesting question. I never thought about it before, and I don't know."

Hasei smiled at him. "I don't know anything. It's safer that way."

Corban laughed, and Hasei laughed also. The Wolf reached out and palmed Corban's shoulder, brotherly. He busied himself over the pipe. Corban leaned back against the rock, content.

Old Eonta groaned in long breathy exhalations, as if Epashti's hands pushed the air out of her. Under Epashti's fingers the old woman's muscles felt stiff and knotted, and her joints were swollen, her knuckles like nuts beneath the skin, her elbows shapeless knobs. Epashti rubbed up and down her grandmother's back, making her sing.

"Oooowwwaaaaa," Eonta moaned. "Ah, Ehia does not have your hands, my child. Oooooooow."

Epashti was vaguely glad that while she was gone her apprentice had not pleased people very much. The girl knew the most important herbs but she had no touch, as her grandmother said. "I will teach her." There was no way to teach someone's hands.

They were in Eonta's compartment at the end of the longhouse, with the door open; no one else was around. The cold weather was coming but the lodge was snug, smelling warmly of past meals, of new hides and curing leaves, of fires kept alive for generations. Epashti, working with her fingers at her grandmother's knotted shoulder muscles, felt again how good this was, that she was here now, that she would be here the next day, no longer walking and walking, that she would never leave again.

Eonta said, "It wasn't easy while you were gone, you know. No spring fruit pickings. Especially with the men all away. I sighed for you often. Are you done? What a pity."

"I'll come tomorrow," Epashti said, smiling.

She helped the old woman roll over and sit up, her wispy hair tousled around her, and found a comb. Eonta's body hung around her in wrinkled sacks. Her skin looked thin and shiny. She turned sideways so that Epashti could comb her hair.

"Where did you go, anyway? Was it so important?"

"It was far away," Epashti said. It felt like a dream to her now. "The men all seemed very excited."

"You know that the Forest Woman has gone."

Epashti lowered her hands. "Really? How do you know?"

"They found something. I've heard, anyway, they found her body."

"How could that be?"

"Exactly," said Eonta. "It wasn't a real body, just a shape. Like a mask, but for her whole self. It had an outside but no inside, it was smooth inside, like a clay pot. So they say. I never saw it." She nodded gravely, her eyes sparkling. "She left it for us to find. To let us know she was gone."

Epashti wondered if Corban was aware of this. She said, "What does that mean?"

Eonta shrugged. "I don't know. Lasicka is worse, you should go see him. Sheanoy thinks she might have a baby in the summer." She turned her look pointedly away from Epashti, up into the top of the lodge, her lips pursed.

Epashti said, "I will keep this baby."

"You say so now. But when the time comes you will do what must be done."

"I did not walk halfway across the world and back again that I could leave a child out for the ants."

Eonta faced her. "You're a woman, and this is what happens. When a baby is born, it has only a little heart. But the heart grows and grows. In a man, it stops getting bigger, when he has his hair bound. But a woman's heart keeps growing, because of all the pain she must bear."

Epashti met her stare. "Then I shall bear the pain, and the child not."

Eonta's gray eyebrows folded down; she pursed her lips, and shook her head. "Such a sweet, gentle girl you were, when you went away." She touched Epashti's cheek. "I am glad you're back, but someone I don't know has come back in you, I think."

"One who loves you," Epashti said, and the old woman's face softened, surprised into tenderness.

"I love you too, girl. Go, now, you have many charges."

"I'll come tomorrow," Epashti said.

"When you do," her grandmother said, "bring me some more of the elderberry tea."

---

Epashti went around the village, seeing to everyone who needed her. When she reached her own little lodge again, Corban was there, sitting in the warmth of the doorway, turning something over in his hand. There was no sign of Ahanton, who had taken to staying in Miska's lodge. Epashti sat down next to Corban, her great belly resting on her thighs.

He put his hand out, to touch her belly, and she took his wrist and pushed his touch away; from the beginning she had kept him from the baby. She thought he understood why; he gave her a long look, but kept his hands away.

She said, "What is that?"

He held out the little sack he was holding. "I found this. Back—after the Itzen ran away."

He kept things from her, too, she thought; he had had this all that long way back, and never showed it to her before. She took the sack and opened it, and spilled out a few grains of the stuff onto her palm. They looked like teeth, yellow and spotty. When she sniffed them, her mouth watered.

"Maz," she said, excited.

He laid his hand against hers, tipped her palm so that the seeds rolled down, and caught them in the Itzen pouch. He said, "Maz. What should I do with it?"

"Give it to me," she said. "I will plant it."

"But—" His fist closed over the pouch. He faced her, intense. "It's not all good, the maz. Look what it brought to the Kisko, and those other people."

She sat back; she glanced over her shoulder at the village, seeing her sister Sheanoy, with a crowd of children down by the oak, and several men coming in through the gate, carrying strings of fish. They had been home only a few days and the village still made her heart glad just to see it. She could not think the maz would change it. She said, "Go speak to Mother Eonta."

He shrugged that off, putting the pouch away inside his shirt. "I'll ask Miska what he thinks about it."

She put her lips together, annoyed; she wondered why he asked her to talk if he would not hear what she said. She said, "Have you seen your sister, since we have been back?"

His shoulders hunched over; he lowered his eyes. He put his empty hands together, cupped, like a bowl. "She's gone," he said, and spread his hands apart.

"What do you mean?" She looked around the lodge, and saw he had brought meat, a thick roll of a deer's backstrap lying on her chopping plank, and she knelt down to get it ready to cook.

He said, "What else can I say? She's gone. I'm hungry. I'll light the fire."

---

Ahanton shuddered awake, gasping, coated in sweat. She sat upright, the cold dream clinging to her. For an instant, staring around her in the dim light, she did not know where she was. Then her gaze came to Miska, sitting beside her; she jumped, and gave him such a look of terror that he recoiled, his face falling open.

"Ahanton." He put out his hands to her. "What is it?"

She took hold of his hands, but she turned her face away; she dared not tell him, so she said, "I saw you take Tisconum." She had said this before; he loved to hear it.

"Ah," he said, perhaps not believing her.

He gathered her close to him, as he always did after a dream, and held her in the circle of his arm. Leaning her head against his chest, she could hear the drum-thump in there, the lifebeat. She fought off the last of the dream, stuffing it down into a hole in her mind.

"Was there anything else?" he said. "You looked at me so strangely."

"No," she said. "Only that."

She leaned against him, his arm around her, her father, who held up the world. She was falling asleep again, she willed herself not to dream, at least, not that dream. Miska laid her down again on her bed, and pulled the blanket over her, and she went to sleep.

When she woke, Corban was there.

At first, stiff with fear, she thought it was another part of the dream. She could not move. She lay on her side, facing the long empty lodge with its streamers of belts, its cold hearth, the light pale as birch through the bark walls. Her father and Corban stood face to face by the hearth. Corban had something in his hand, and they were talking about her mother.

Miska said, "Have you seen her? Since we came back from the Big River country?"

Corban said, "No. She's gone, Miska." He tried to sound indifferent but Ahanton could hear the sadness in his voice. Her mind settled; this was not a dream.

Miska half-turned away from him, his face shadowed, his hands crooked in the air. "You mean—" He broke off.

"Either she's gone," Corban said, "or she's somewhere we can't know her."

Miska wheeled back, sharp-edged again, cold. "So she is here, then. You have seen her."

Corban grunted at him. "What did I just say to you? She's gone!"

"You even said she might be here, somewhere." Miska stalked away from him. "There's been talk. Rumors. I can't get it straight. While we were gone, the women had a free run, you know how they make stories. Maybe she's gone, maybe she isn't. You said you had something to give me?"

Corban stared at him a moment, his eyes gleaming above the tangled mass of his beard. Finally he said, "Yes. Back, where we fought the Itzen, I found this. It belonged to the chief of them."

He held out something, a big lump; Ahanton could not see what it was at first.

Miska said, "What did you call them?" He took the lump, which, she saw now, was a sack of something. "Is this more of that shiny stuff?" He spilled some of the sack's contents onto his hand.

"No, it's—"

"These look like seeds!" Miska's voice rose in an irritated whine. "What do you bring these to me for? Do you take me for a woman?" He flung the sack off across the lodge, spraying a trail of bits through the air.

Corban reared back, his eyes blazing. "You idiot—that could be the saving of your people, maybe, if you do it right—not killing everybody and these stupid bead strings." He flailed one hand up at the nearest dangling string. He thrust his face at Miska; Ahanton remembered what they had called him, Animal-Head, shaggy and fierce, and he was shouting at Miska, fierce.

Miska sneered at him, stiff at the challenge. "Don't tell me what to do, rodent. If she's gone, Corban, remember, I don't have to put up with you anymore!"

Corban took a step toward Miska, face first, the words like stones from his sling. "That's all you want, though, isn't it? You don't really want to take care of your people, you just want to fight, and kill, and win."

Miska stood nose to nose with him, talking over him. "I'll fight you, and kill you, if you don't remember you are in my village!"

"You'll never stop, will you?" Corban shouted on. "There's still Tisconum, isn't there? Take him, there will be someone else. You'll go on fighting until there's nobody left, you'll eat the whole world up."

Half of what he said was in a mix of strange words, that only Ahanton and Epashti understood, and even as he yelled, Miska was roaring at him, their voices colliding: "That's the end, Corban—"

Corban fell still, and the sachem's voice rang out. "You're a rodent, you're a worm, you aren't a Wolf, you don't belong here. I'm giving you until sundown, for her sake, to get out of my village. After that, we will kill you where we find you."

Corban straightened, his head back, his face flushed with anger, and his fists clenched. Then he turned, and saw Ahanton watching; she saw him stiffen with surprise, and he swung back to her father.

"For her sake, I won't say anything more. And I'll go, for all their sakes. Only: you will rot, Miska, if you touch my family."

He turned and went. Miska watched him go, and then swung toward Ahanton, his face blank, rigid. He stared at her, and she stared back, for a long moment, and then he wheeled around. He plunged away, out of the lodge, going another way he had, a secret door in the back wall, and even before he was gone he was shouting to the other Wolves. Ahanton got up, her legs shaking. He never shouted like that. Even in the war he had not shouted.

The little leather pouch lay on the floor, and the bits from it were strewn around the whole lodge. The bits were square, dark chunks, and when she put one in her mouth, the taste flooded her memory, the river, the delicious golden cakes, and the drums, and the fear. She gathered them up, as many as she could find, and put them into the pouch.

Then she went out of her father's lodge, and through the village to Corban's little hut.

He was there with Epashti, who was crying. Corban, holding her in his arms, looked near to crying. He said, over and over, "I'll come back. Somehow."

"No," Ahanton said. She went into the back of the lodge, and gathered his red and blue cloak up, and took it to him. "Go. And never come back."

They both gaped at her, surprised. Corban said, "I thought you loved me now."

"Go," she said. "Go." And thrust the cloak at him.

Epashti began to cry louder. "Go," she said. "Before they kill you. Before they kill you in front of us."

He gave her one more look, and went around the lodge getting his things. Epashti sat with her hands twisting together, her body huge with the baby, crying. Ahanton went into the back of the lodge and sat down; her heart hammered in her chest. She could not speak. The little sack was in her hands and quietly she put it away against the wall of the lodge, to think about later. When he left, she could not bear to watch. She kept her eyes down, hearing his footsteps go, hearing Epashti sob and wail. Her chest hurt. Her mouth opened, a hollow with nothing in it, only the empty wanting to call him back.

She could not call him back. He had to go. She knew he had to go. Now she had dreamt, three times running, the same dream. She saw the village, and at the center of the village she saw the stake, and there was a man bound to the stake, and the man was Corban.

## CHAPTER TWENTY-TWO

Corban crossed the Wolf river and went east, through the low wooded hills, already winter-blackened, the nights still and cold and starry. He followed the next river southward, scrambling over the steep slopes of its gorge, fishing in the cold pools, and crossed where the rush of water spread out onto a boggy little plain among the hills, and kept on going east.

The death of the year lay on him like his own death, the light shrinking away, the sun's course lower and lower in the sky, and some mornings he lay shivering in his cloak and thought not to get up and go on. He had lost everything, again, and he saw no hope he would live through the winter; the thought of Epashti gnawed at him like a rat. He had abandoned her again, pregnant and with winter coming. Always in the back of his mind he saw Ahanton casting him out, her wide gray eyes remote, ruthless, Mav's eyes, telling him, finally, even her: Go.

Mav was gone, that was the root of it, she who had bound him to the world.

He got up, always, and plodded away toward the sunrise. One afternoon as he was groping along a creekside looking for something to eat, the air darkened, as if the meadows all around had suddenly slipped into twilight, and snow began to fall. There was no wind; white as stars, the flakes fell silently through the deep blue air, clustering together into crystalline bundles, vanishing into the dark ground. He stood like stone, watching, engulfed in this beauty, and a sense of peace came over him.

But he slept that night without eating, and the next day, starved, he ate carrion and was sick for a while. He trudged on, heading steadily east, his mind streaming with bad thoughts; he thought over and over of his father, who had cursed him to this aloneness.

He thought of the old man as he had last seen him, a stinking corpse, who had stayed where he was and died.

The shapes of land he knew began to appear—the slope of the hill there, a boulder. At last he walked out onto the shore of the great bay, where he had first come into this country.

He stood looking out at the islands strewn over the expanse of dark water. The sea lay just beyond and the fierce wind was raking the trees and lashing the bay to whitecaps. The first incoming drops of rain stung his cheeks. Along the shore the tall dry reeds were bending and singing, little waves lashing up through them onto the mud. The sun was going down. All around the bay, huge flocks of geese were settling down into the marshes on the shore and on the islands. Their hoarse croaking made a constant uproar, rising and falling, windblown, sounding on all sides, and the flocks came down in such masses they seemed like great dark banners of smoke across the fading sky. He went west along the shore until he could see his island, the biggest of them all, which here came so close to the shore that he and the boys had often made a game of trying to throw rocks across it.

The boys. Somewhere on the other side of the world, his boys lived their unknowable lives.

The tide was in. Dark was falling. He went to find something to eat, and a place to shelter for the night. In the morning, at slack tide, he swam across to his old home.

He waded up onto the shore where he had lived for fifteen years. The shape of the shore was different, beaten around in the winter storms, part of the bank crumpled down, a broad arm of rocks and driftwood and weeds raked out across the edge of the water. Drifted stumps lay like wooden sea monsters basking on the low strip of sand at the island's foot. On the slope above, the grass and brambles grew up high as his waist. He found the wall, which he thought Euan must have built, all fallen down now, stone from stone. The walls of the old house had worn down almost to ground level, and the thatch roof was gone entirely, blown down, rotted, carried off by birds.

He could still see it all, the roots of the walls where he had dug them down into the earth, and the hollows of the rooms, even, ghostly, the shape of his bed.

Above the house, on the hill, he found Benna's grave.

He was wet from the swim and cold, and he began to shiver and he pulled the red and blue cloak around himself, even over his head; he sat down on the ground and put his face in his hands. He thought over and over of Benna and his children and their life here, hard but good, too hard and too good to last.

He sat there the day and the next night, going away only to piss or find something to eat, and he sat there the day and night after that, and the day following, and on the third night, as he sat there, Benna rose up out of her grave and stood before him.

He called her name, glad. He put his hands out to her; she was so truly there, her pale heart-shaped face beneath the cap of black hair, the direct intensity of her look, as if she captured everything she saw. But when he tried to touch her, his hands went right through her.

She said, "Corban, why have you called me up here, where it's so cold and dark? I'm happy where I am, and I can't do anything for you."

He tried again to touch her, unable to stop himself, and felt only the cold air. He sat back, holding her with his gaze. "Benna, I've failed again. I have nothing here. The Wolves have driven me out. I'm alone, I don't want to be alone anymore. There must be somewhere I belong, and I know I belong with you, Benna. Take me with you."

She smiled, and his heart cracked at the beauty of this smile and every other she had given him, layer on layer of memory all wakened by her smile. She said, "Corban, you're alive. You have more to do here."

"Benna, please."

Her eyes gleamed suddenly with tears, the smile fixed. Her gaze roamed over his face, and her hands rose, as if she wanted to touch him too. Then, firmly, with a little shake of her head, she drew back. "Go away, Corban," she said. She turned back toward the grave.

"Ah, you can't tell me this," he cried. "Where did I call you from? Where are you going?"

She looked over her shoulder at him. She had not changed, he realized. She was no older than when he had seen her last. He touched his beard, where the black was grizzling.

She said, "I am here, before, when it was good, before Euan came."

"I want to go there too, Benna," he said, but his hand curled in his beard, he felt all the scars he had gained since she had died, and he groaned, the living years between them carrying him away like the current of a river.

"Corban," she said, and smiled at him. "You're already there." She slipped away into the grave again and was gone.

He groaned, sank down on his knees, hollowed out like an acorn shell. If he died, would he join her? He thought he would just go on, an old old man, knocking on the earth, trying to find the way in.

The night went on. She did not come back. He remembered what she had said, that he had more to do. That meant he was not going to die yet. He thought of Mav, who was likely here, somewhere, who had probably not gone after all. Passed beyond his sight. But here.

So, when the dawn came, he got up, and swam back to the mainland, and he went off to find Tisconum. He had promised Tisconum something, long ago, and now he thought it was time to deliver.

# CHAPTER TWENTY-THREE

The women were making a long strip of the lowland on the far side of the river ready for new gardens. To begin, the year before, they had cut away the bark from the trees. Now the trees were all dead, although still standing in the ground, and with the winter on them the boys were breaking them up for firewood.

Finn was one of them. Since his mother left at the beginning of the summer, he had done as he wished, his aunt Sheanoy bothering very little about him, and his uncles soon gone also. Now his mother had come back, but she was sick, and nobody kept after him about anything. With his brother Kalu and the rest of the younger boys from the village he was scrambling up and down the dead trees, breaking off branches, and looking also for grubs, bugs, worms, moss, anything he could put in his mouth. He was starving all the time now, and anything he found by himself he did not have to share with anybody.

He followed his brother Kalu up a dead tree the color of bone, climbing up above the snowy meadow. The trunk of the tree was smooth and gleaming. The sky blazed blue. He clung with both hands, panting, looking out over the snow, all tracked around with the boys' running, toward the river and the village on the other side. A pang went through him; he should help his mother.

A snowball smacked and burst against the tree trunk in front of him. Kalu, above him, gave a howl of indignation; the other boys were ringing the tree, pelting Finn and Kalu with snow.

"Come on!" Kalu dropped by him, swinging nimbly from branch to branch, the dry sticks cracking under his weight. Finn followed, almost missed the branch below, slipped and hung by both arms from the one below that, helpless in a hail of snowballs. Just below him, in the crotch of the tree, Kalu was throwing bits of wood down at the other boys, screaming insults and dodging snow. Finn flailed out with both legs, trying to get back up onto the branch, and it cracked and split, the lower half still attached to the trunk, so the branch swung down vertical.

With a yell, Finn slid down the branch into the snow. The other boys swung around and began pounding him at close range. He curled his arms over his head; something struck him on the ear hard enough to make him dizzy for an instant.

Then other boys were reeling back, and he was in the open again. From the edge of the trees a small girl was rushing down at them, screaming. She threw snowballs as she ran, but like all girls she couldn't throw; half of them she didn't even pack right, so they fell apart in the air.

Nonetheless the other boys shrank back, not from the snowballs. They turned, elaborately unconcerned, and jogged off. Ahanton trotted up to Finn, panting. Her face glowed from her rush through the cold air.

Kalu jumped down out of the tree and stood next to them. "Come on," he said. "Let's get all this wood before they come back." He flung a hard look down the meadow, toward the riverbank, where the other boys were loitering.

Ahanton said, "I have something else," and ran back up toward the trees. She ran in long-legged leaps, like a deer, her arms flying.

Kalu followed her with his eyes. Turning to Finn, he said, "Letting a girl save you, now."

Finn started picking up dead wood, glad Ahanton had come. The wood was shiny and smooth, good to touch. "She's not really just a girl." He carried a load of broken branches to the drag they had made. Ahanton was coming back, carrying a hemp bag over her shoulder.

"We should show you how to throw sometime," Kalu said. "You throw like a girl."

Ahanton hardly glanced at him. She set down her bag and began to pick up wood.

"What have you got?" Kalu asked. Ahanton was better than any of them at finding food.

"Nuts," she said, and glared at him. "Stay away from them, Kalu, they're for my mother."

"She's not your mother," Finn and Kalu said, together, since she truly was theirs. Ahanton ignored them. When they had loaded the drag high with wood, she hoisted her bag again, and walked with them back to the river. Finn kept glancing at her bag, so heavy it took her whole strength to carry it: the thought of the nuts made his mouth water.

Kalu said, "If you take them back to the lodge, you'll have to give them to everybody."

She said, "That's why I got so many, so my mother would have enough."

Finn saw Kalu's face work; the little boy knew his brother wanted to snatch away the nuts, but like them all, he was afraid of Ahanton. The other boys came silently up and helped them get the wood onto the float to carry it across the river.

On the far shore, the other boys drifted away again, leaving Finn, Kalu and Ahanton to unload the wood. Kalu's head turned, watching them go; Finn saw he waited until they were out of earshot before he turned to Ahanton.

"We'll go up to the lodge with you."

"Whatever you want," she said, and the boys followed.

---

"I'll have to send Raki to get more wood," Sheanoy said. She twisted, looking up the dim corridor of the lodge. Eonta was taking her afternoon nap, in the head compartment, and everybody else had left or shut their own doors, to give her quiet. "Where is that boy?"

"Shhh," Epashti said. She leaned against the wall of the compartment behind her, exhausted.

When Corban left, Epashti had moved back into Eonta's lodge, taking over her mother's old sleeping compartment and the one across the aisle from it and the hearth in between. That had been in the fall, when there was still food, and she had been strong and able. Now she sat by the hearth, barely able to hold her head up, and watched her sister Sheanoy feed chips of wood into the coals. The little boy Aengus, just starting to walk, sat by Sheanoy playing with sticks; Sheanoy, who had taken care of him while Epashti was gone, liked him much, and he hardly knew his mother anymore. Epashti had heard her sister call him by another name, too, a Wolf name.

Ehia came in, Epashti's student, with one of her sisters from Anapatha's lodge. With a murmur of welcome the two girls settled in by Epashti and Sheanoy, and offered a few scrapings of dried meat.

"It's not much," Ehia said, her gaze on Epashti. Down the corridor a door opened, and someone looked out, and then shut the door again: not enough to come out for.

"Everything helps," Sheanoy said. She took the meat and divided it, so that each of them got the same tiny sliver: the four women and Aenghus, with a bit for Eonta, too.

Ehia said, "Have you heard anything from the men?"

Sheanoy chuckled. "Someone particular, girl?" Gaunt as she was, she was strong and lively; her boys were good foragers. "They'll come back when the moon's full."

Ehia sighed. She had her eyes on Lopi, the leader of the older boys, who would be taken into a lodge in the spring, and so be able to marry. Unfortunately most of the other girls had their eyes on Lopi also. Epashti chewed on her sliver of meat, grinding the taste out of it, the delicious hint of blood. Then Ehia was looking at her.

"I heard they may have seen—him."

Sheanoy leaned back, her eyes sharp. "How can you have heard this? A bird told you? The wind? Why say something like that to her?"

Epashti lowered her eyes. She wondered what had happened to Corban, if he had gone back to the sky. She did not believe that the men would catch him. She did not believe she would ever see him again.

"Now, look," her sister said. "You've made her sad again."

Epashti did not remember being happy. Her belly was huge, but the rest of her was disappearing. Her arms were sticks and her hair was falling out and she had lost some of her teeth. The baby hardly kicked at all now, only sometimes she felt something rolling in there, as if it struggled sluggishly around.

What use, she thought. What use—if it died—

The door to the lodge burst open, letting in a cold blast of wind, and the slanted pale winter sunlight. Ahanton came panting in, Kalu and Finn just behind her.

"Shhh," Epashti said, her hands lifting, her heart rising in relief; Ahanton always brought her food.

Everybody knew this. From the other compartments, from Eonta's room, the other people came quickly out and gathered around the hearth. After a moment Eonta herself, leaning on a stick, tottered down the corridor on her crooked feet and sat down next to Epashti. Ahanton had laid the sack down by the fire; now the child spread out the mouth, exposing a mass of nuts.

Leaning forward, her thin gray braids dropping over her shoulders, Eonta peered into the sack. "What did you do, girl, rob the squirrels?"

Ahanton said, "I left some for them." She glanced at Epashti, her face worried. "I never take all."

Eonta laughed. Her hand went forward, and then every other hand went forward, the long work-knobby hands of the women, the little claws of the children. Ahanton sat by Epashti and cracked nuts for her. Epashti saw the child did not eat. Saw also that Ahanton, always skinny, was no skinnier than usual.

The others, eating, began to talk, as if the talk grew from the nuts. Eonta made some joke and they all laughed. Ehia teased her sister about a lascivious dream she had had, about a man she would not name, but everybody quickly understood was Miska. The pile of nuts was disappearing. Epashti chewed the delicious meats and drank water—Kalu, bustling with importance, brought her the water. He and Finn ate, taking one nut at a time, which was proper. Epashti saw Sheanoy pick up a nut between thumb and forefinger and deftly sneak another into her palm with her other fingers; that was how she stayed so strong and lively. Sheanoy was still nursing Aengus, but the baby in her belly was still small, did not sap everything out of her; she would bear it in the summer, in the bounty of the year.

Epashti swallowed sourness in her mouth. She thought of what was to come and her heart shrank into a little curling worm, all fear.

Ahanton fed her a hazelnut, sweet as summer. The nuts were clean and whole, not musty, worm-eaten, mixed half with broken and empty shells, like all the squirrel hoards Epashti had ever seen. Feeling stronger, warmer, happier, she glanced at Ahanton again and wondered.

Now the nuts were gone, though. Eonta leaned around Epashti, put her hands on Ahanton's head and drew her close, and spoke into her ear. Ahanton laughed. The other people were moving away, off to sleep again, or to work. Ahanton curled one arm around Epashti, and leaned her head on her, and then went out, to go to Miska's lodge.

Epashti turned to Kalu, still squatting beside her, Finn at his side. "Go find me some wood."

"I will," Kalu said. He touched the birchbark cup. "I brought you water, Mother."

"Yes, I know." She smiled at him, tired. Behind them, Sheanoy picked up Aengus, who had climbed into her lap, and hauled him off to her compartment. Epashti said, "Get wood."

He went off down the shadowy corridor. Finn came over and snuggled against her, his arms around her arm. She patted his head and he curled up comfortably. She could feel his ribs through his shirt, but he was clever and fed himself and she had no fear for him.

All her children were strong. Aengus would live too, with Sheanoy's help. Epashti put her hand on her belly and the black thoughts sailed down around her again like bats. The baby would be born within the month—in the full Hunger Moon. She wondered if it would still be alive then. If she would have milk. If she could keep it alive on squirrel hoardings and water until the spring came and the wealth of the year began. Without Ahanton she would have been dead already. The baby would kill her and then die.

Eonta remained beside her, solid, her hands out to the fire. Now she said, "Ahanton blesses us all. Where do you think she finds this food?"

Epashti leaned her head against the compartment wall. "She said it was a squirrel nest."

The old woman smiled. Her cheeks, always round in the summer, were pleated into creases, but her eyes sparkled bright as ever. "Maybe they look like squirrel's nests to her. I will not ask questions. She should have her green bough ceremony. Have you thought about that?"

Epashti said, "I have. But her lineage, her other emblems—how can we know these?" Miska, her father, gave Ahanton nothing but a name; all her proper connections came from her mother.

Eonta shrugged. "Ask her. Her mother will guide us."

"Her mother," Epashti said. Tears burst from her eyes. She ground them away with her hands. "We lost her mother. We lost them both, Corban and her."

Eonta took hold of her hand and drew it down. The old woman's smile deepened. "Then where does her daughter find us all these nuts? Take heart, child." She squeezed Epashti's hand, and turned it up. "Here." She put some nuts into Epashti's palm. "Save these for later." Patiently the old woman planted her horn-toed feet, took hold of the compartment door, and pulled herself upright. "Talk to Ahanton about the green bough time. She knows more than you think she does." She waddled slowly off toward her room; her clothes hung around her like old withered wings. Epashti watched her go, and opened her palm and fed the nuts to her baby, one by one.

Epashti bore the baby in the middle of the night. None of the others would come to her, except Ehia, who brought the moss and the water and herbs, and Ahanton, who sat with her as she groaned. The terrific pains grew stronger, wringing her body, squeezing the baby down.

In the cold and the dark, her body flagged, too tired to do the work. The baby struggled to come out but she could not summon herself to the task. Sagging in Ehia's arms, her head too heavy to lift, she said, "Push it out for me."

Ehia had her belly against Epashti's back, her arms around Epashti under her breasts, Epashti's knees cocked up wide apart. "Push," Epashti said, again, as the next powerful clenching began, and Ahanton leaned over her and with her hands flat on the top of Epashti's belly she pushed down.

The pain wound her around like a vine, drew her thin and limp as a vine; dazed, she felt it squeeze her to nothing. Slowly the terrific hurt subsided. She could not see anymore. Too tired to see. Here was another one already, oh—

This pain pried her jaws apart and she gave out a groan deep as her belly, as if yielding up something out that end would help getting something out the other. Her head wobbled on Ehia's shoulder. Her body hung useless. She felt Ahanton's hands on her belly. Ehia's arms around her below her breasts. The pain like something driven down between her legs.

Bursting. She sobbed. Some great warmth rushed over her,

like a dark sunrise. Ehia held her, whispering in her ear. Down between her feet, there was a whimper.

Alive, she thought, but she had no strength to speak. Her eyes shut. Alive. She began to fall, long, quiet, soft, deep, forever, falling.

Ehia got the moon-baby out, and tried to feed Epashti a potion of herbs, but she had no strength to swallow. They had been sitting in the dark compartment all night; now the light was seeping in, the day coming. The baby was a girl, tiny, every bone visible. It had stopped its tiny cry and lay limp in Ahanton's arms; she wanted to take it somewhere warm and stroke it alive again.

Under her eyes Epashti was going away. Ahanton began to cry. She could not leave, yet she could do nothing. They would both die.

She clutched the baby tight, leaning toward Ehia, pleading. "Do something. Hasn't she told you what to do?"

"I don't know how—I'm not sure—" Ehia wiped her face. "She said something once . . ."

"Do it," Ahanton said. "Please. Do it."

So Ehia took the herbs she had soaked for the drink and made a ball, and she put the wet ball of herbs up into Epashti's body. They wrapped Epashti up in blankets and put emblems of life around her—what they could find; there were no new leaves or new twigs, but even in the dead of winter Ahanton had collected fat buds of lilac and willow shoots, and these they laid by her. Ehia took the water from the herbs and dampened Epashti's lips. Epashti never moved, her eyes sunken, her skin clammy.

Ahanton wrapped the baby in her old white deerskin blanket. It came into her mind that Epashti had gathered all these herbs, talked to them, loved them: they would know her, they would save her. She and Ehia cleaned up the mess of the birth and then lay down, one on either side of Epashti, to keep her warm. She held the baby in her arms, against her skin.

She did not think she would sleep, with all that had happened, but then she was somewhere far away, and a thin little cry was calling her back. She woke in the full light of day. Ehia was gone. Epashti lay beside her, asleep, still alive, and the baby was crying in her arms.

Ahanton leaned over Epashti, thinking to put the baby to her breast, but Epashti would not waken. Her skin was cool. She breathed hard. Ahanton took the baby down the corridor to Sheanoy's compartment.

She had to bang and pluck at the willowwork door a long while before Sheanoy would open it. When she saw the baby, the woman's mouth fell open, and her eyes shone. "She's had it. Maybe now she can get better, the poor thing. Are you taking it out to the snow?"

Ahanton said, "I'm bringing her to you, because you have milk." She held the baby up toward Sheanoy. "Feed her."

Sheanoy shrank back, her face pale with shock. "Oh, no. You must take it out. Take it to the midden heap. It's a hunger baby, it's not even a real baby, it won't live."

Ahanton held the baby out, and said, "I fed you."

Epashti's sister licked her lips, and her eyes darted from side to side, up and down the lodge. Nobody was out in the open, but surely they were listening and watching from behind their doors. The baby let out her tiny peeping cry. It was so small Ahanton could not feel its weight in her hands. She said nothing, but her eyes held Sheanoy's.

Sheanoy pressed her lips together, and her eyelids drooped. She took the baby and put it to her breast, and let it nurse, but she plucked it away after only a few moments.

"I'm dry," she said, and pulled back into her compartment like a clam into its shell and shut the door.

Then Ahanton went on through the lodge, to the other women

with babies at the breast, and she went to Anapatha's lodge also, and to Merada's, and she got all the women who were nursing children to take Epashti's winter baby to their breasts. Gallara's lodge was only old women, and she did not go there. Day by day she took the baby around from one woman to another, and Epashti lived and got stronger, as the sun grew stronger, day by day. Then the men came back.

---

This was an up and down thing. The men had brought back fresh meat, but they had been in a fight to get it, and one of them was dead, Yoto, Hasei and Epashti's brother. They had scalps, which they flourished with the usual bravery, but no prisoners, so there was no one to suffer for Yoto's sake. The women gathered under the oak tree, and sang for Yoto, and his wife cut her hair off and gashed her cheeks, but they all felt the heavy loss, and there was nothing to fill the hole, and the strength of the Wolves was pouring away down that hole, into nothing.

With the meat to make her blood stronger Epashti sat up, and she put the baby to her breast; there was no milk but the baby sucked anyway, a good strong hurting suck. Wrapped tight in her blanket, the baby opened her eyes, startlingly blue. Epashti started, wondering: Is she blind?

"Another woman," Sheanoy said. She was stripping out long strings of hemp to make a basket, the stem across her lap. They were sitting outside, in the first warm sunshine; there were still cold nights and hungry days to come but the sun was brighter, for now their bellies were comfortable, and in a few days the full Worm Moon would rise. "I don't see what use that was, frankly, Epashti."

Epashti was remembering what Ahanton told her, that Sheanoy had nursed the newborn baby, and when the child pulled fretfully away from the nipple, and wailed, she said, "Well, she's hungry now, here." She held the baby out.

Sheanoy dropped her jaw. "I have nursed your son! How can you ask me another?"

Epashti lifted her eyebrows. "Am I less than Ahanton?"

Her sister gathered up her face again into a frown of annoyance. She did not look at Epashti, but stared stonily off over her shoulder, took the baby, and clapped her to her breast.

"I am too good," she said. "I do not look out enough for myself."

Epashti said, "I think you do well enough, Sheanoy." She took the sticks of hemp and began to shred where her sister had left off.

"And another girl. Who will she marry?" Sheanoy said, crossly. "If all our men die, who will any of us marry?"

Epashti said, "There are other men." Yoto's dying unnerved her; she wanted to cry again, thinking of him. Now there were only three men left, besides Miska, three men in two lodges, which was not enough, as her sister said. The Wolves were disappearing, like Michabo's hunters running into the flood.

Eonta had been down to the river, and now she came walking up toward them; she was gaunt as any of them but her summer bulk seemed to hang around her like a shadow. She had gone barefoot, in spite of the snow still lingering on the ground; her feet were lumpy, her toes tipped in curving yellow claws. Seeing her come, old Merada came over from her lodge, with her two daughters, and they all sat together in the sun.

Ehia trailed after Eonta with a bark bucket of water. The younger woman helped the older settle herself in the women's circle and set the water down.

Eonta saw the baby, and leaned over to peer at her. "So she's still alive. Her father's power is in her."

Epashti said nothing, her eyes on the little bundle in Sheanoy's arms. Eonta made herself comfortable, and with a flick of her hand sent Ehia off for something else.

Sheanoy turned toward her, sharp-eyed. "Ama-ki, we were just talking about the fact that there are no more men."

Eonta grunted at her. Merada, between her two daughters,

lifted her head, listening. Ehia came back with a shawl and some handwork and gave them to Eonta. Above Eonta's head she glanced at Epashti, and gave her a broad smile.

Eonta said, "There are no such men anywhere else as our Wolf men. We have the best men."

"Ama," said Sheanoy. "We did have them. There are only four of them now. Are we all to line up in front of Miska's lodge?"

Ehia twitched, and Eonta's head lashed around like a snake. "Keep your tongue clean, woman. You can lie down in Miska's lodge all you want, since you already do."

The women watching all laughed, and Sheanoy flushed, her brows lowering, angry. Eonta sat back, smoothing the shawl over her knees. "There are other men, in other villages, who will come here and make husbands for you, and their sons will be Wolves. Miska will see to it."

Sheanoy said, "Yes, Bear men. Or even Muskrats and Beaver men, from the Long Lakes."

Merada said, "Or we could do what Epashti did, and get one from the sky."

Epashti lifted her eyes for the first time from the baby. "Don't do that," she said, "because the sky will call him back, and your heart will turn to mud."

Then she gasped, looking down, feeling her breast draw, and she burst out laughing. The other women goggled at her, their faces full of wonder. Epashti reached out for her baby.

"Give her to me. I have milk. Give it to me."

Sheanoy gave her the baby, and she pulled open the front of her dress and laid the child to her breast. The child began to suckle in long deep swallows.

Eonta said, "Such a muddy heart as this I wish for all of us." Her eyebrows were raised up like lodge poles. "What will you name her? Since her father is not here to name her."

"Blessing," Epashti said, smiling down at the tiny child. "My blessing."

Before this, men from other villages had come to Miska asking to dwell among the Wolves, but Miska had sent them away, because they would fight for him anyway, and it made no difference to him where they lived. But Eonta talked to him one day, and this spring, when some young men from the Bear village appeared at the gate, he let them come in to the village.

He knew these men, who had gone with him on the long raid against the Sun people. He sat with them in his lodge and shared smoke. When the leader of them asked if they could live in the Wolf village, he said, "This goes well with me. You must make your own lodge, and we shall see how it goes from there."

"We have Bear ways of making lodges," the young man said. His name was Ako; he wore his hair up in a sideknot, like all Ekkatsay's people. He looked like Ekkatsay, big and strong and solid.

"Make your lodges in the Bear way," Miska said.

Another of the young men said, "We have no women."

Miska smiled. He drew hard on the pipe and sent it around again, trailing smoke, and they all smoked. Then he said, "You'll have it hard here, then. If you do not get on with the women who live inside my wall, then you will not stay in the village, no matter what I say."

Ako glanced at the young Bear who had spoken, and faced Miska again. "We will honor the Wolf women above all others, if they will accept us. Otherwise we can go back to our old village for wives. But we will follow you, in your war band."

Miska said, "I will lead you. I remember, last summer, how you fought against Tisconum and then in the long raid. The long raid, that took me from Tisconum for the while, but I have not forgotten him. What do you know about him?"

Ako sat back, his hands on his knees. "He's finished. You

broke him in the fight in the burnt tree pass. His people have left him, gone down to the Turtle villages near the salt."

Miska grunted. "Strong villages." No belts from the waterland villages hung in his lodge. If Tisconum had lost his sway over them, then beating him meant less.

Ako's eyes gleamed. "They have much wealth there. And they don't fight."

Miska took the pipe and laid it aside. In his mind, to think about later, he laid aside also the young man's ambition. He said, "Where is Tisconum now?" He faced Ako, his expression bland, knowing an enemy when he saw one.

"Up the long valley, there, east of here, by the Shad River. His band is—" Ako made a shrinking motion with his hands. "Only bad men nobody else will have and desperate people follow him."

Behind him, one of his friends spoke. "Tisconum has a great shaman with him, though, I have heard."

Miska slid his gaze over Ako's shoulder, at the man behind him. "Who?"

"I don't know anything, save he has fire in his fingertips."

Miska could not help but smile. "Aaah." He sat back, gathering himself. "Where is he?"

"They are wintering at the Froggy Bend of the Shad River."

"Aaah," said Miska.

# CHAPTER TWENTY-FOUR

From this hill, the waterland spread away toward the south, gilded under the late spring sun, the broad flat bay spangled with islands heavy with trees. On the water the slanting sunlight picked out the shimmering of currents. Smokes rose on the distant shore, trailing upward in the still afternoon. Corban could see only the shoulder of his island from here, and nothing of his old home. He looked as long as he could into the south, remembering how he had fished these waters, taught his boys to sail, come home every evening to his wife, a happy man.

Beside him, Tisconum groaned, caught in the same haze of memory. "I was chief all over this place once, remember?" Tall and gaunt, the Turtle sachem leaned on his stick and pointed toward the gleaming water. "Everywhere, I went in first, I spoke first, everywhere."

Corban said, "What matters is now. What we do now."

Tisconum said, between his teeth, "I have nothing now, because of Miska. I will not forget that. I told you, I want only to see him dead on the ground." His eyes glittered, he looked at Corban over his shoulder, his gaze slanted.

"He'll come here," Corban said. "It may take him some while but he'll come."

Tisconum turned straight again, looking toward the bay. Presently, he said, "There are whales."

Corban looked where he was pointing, and saw, in the open water past the first island, a tall divided spray like a flower hanging in the air. The warm air touched his face, smelling of the salt. In the channel between the shore and the island a fish suddenly jumped—a splash, a widening ripple. The marsh along this shore clamored with birds nesting in the reeds, and birds by the thousands swam and fed in the shallows.

Mav had loved this country; Benna had refused to let it go. Like a knot, he thought, thinking of the twined figures of his birthplace, the bay was a knot of water and land, an endless curve. He remembered the terror of the winter, when the wind howled and the snow swept down over everything, and how the hills blazed in the autumn when the trees let go their leaves; he thought the Turtle sachem was right, and this was the center of it all, where life welled up into the world.

Tisconum said, "They hate me here. I hear the stories they tell of me in the lodges."

"They'll hate Miska worse, when he comes at them." Corban nudged him; it unnerved him how Tisconum gnawed on himself like a dog on a bone. "Let's go, Ofra and those won't work long if we aren't there."

Tisconum hung still a moment, wound around his staff, staring at the bay. The foul mood twisted his face. "I'll see him dead on the ground," he said.

Corban started away down the trail. He had come to Tisconum too late. The last battle had left him a dry husk, and the people he had with him were worthless. Still, he had to start somewhere. Defying Miska satisfied him. Thinking of defying Miska, which so far had not come to any action.

He glanced over his shoulder and saw Tisconum coming after him, and stopped to let the sachem catch up. Tisconum had not wanted to come back here, a place he considered doomed; Corban had talked him into it only for a hunting trip. The Turtle sachem was bent on recapturing control of a pass in the northwest, which he had lost to Miska the summer before. This meant staying north on the Shad River all spring. He would go back as soon as Corban let him.

He trudged up past Corban now, each foot deliberate. "Have you done that girl yet?" Leaning on the stick, he paced on by Corban as if stopping would mean staying there forever.

Corban followed him. "I have a wife. Two wives."

"Everybody else has had her. You wouldn't be the first. Or the only."

Corban said nothing. The girl's attentions were a steady embarrassment. He imagined suddenly that Tisconum ahead of him walked under the great heavy shell of his grievance. They went through a forest bursting with the brilliant green of new spring leaves and thunderously loud with birds. A dragonfly buzzed past his head. Lumpy black deer shit littered the trail. He kept a watch out for sign of gobbler-birds, which he liked to hunt. Beyond a screen of thin saplings a big moss-coated maple tree reared up its massy leaves; deep new slashes marked its trunk, high over Corban's head, four furrows ripping down into raw new wood.

"There's a lot of game here," he said. They could camp in this area for the whole summer: he had seen no recent trace of other people. From his years here, he knew the smokes across the bay were other Turtle villages, whose ranges extended on down the coast. He followed Tisconum out onto the bench above the little river, where the village lay.

The ruins of the village, anyway. Where the houses had been there were now only grassy humps on the ground like little howes, overgrown with weeds and brambles. When Tisconum and Corban came in, the five men were standing around the center of the clearing, watching the two women scrape the ground clear and set up a hearth. The men looked up at the sachem's approach, but they didn't start working.

Tisconum walked up toward the hearth, which the women had built with a minimum of ceremony in the open ground in the midst of the old village. The lumpy mounds of the huts stood all around as if the old village still watched them. The women had scraped together some kindling, and Tisconum turned and beckoned to Corban.

"Come light this. My bones ache."

Corban said, "We need more wood." He glanced around, seeing nothing gathered. The women had begun to pull together a wall of branches and trash broken out of the old huts, to form a nest for them all around the fire.

One of the other men stepped forward suddenly, rubbing his palms together, his eyes going between Tisconum and Corban. "There's that dead tree over there, what about that?"

Corban stepped back. Tisconum waved his stick. "Do it, Ofra," and sank down by the half-laid fire. Ofra with a bellow took the other men toward the dead tree, which stuck up like a stubby pale tooth at the north end of the village.

"Light the twigs," Tisconum said to Corban. "I'm cold."

"There's no purpose in lighting it before we have wood to keep it going," Corban said mildly. The women, working steadily, had piled up enough brush and branches to shelter the sachem, who squatted down behind it. Corban stayed on his feet. He had already seen the strangers coming toward them, up along the creek.

Tisconum had not. "Nobody obeys me, not even you! How can you say—" He stopped, seeing Corban staring away toward the riverbank, and his head swivelled, craned up on his neck, aiming his gaze over the top of the wall. He exhaled a loud sigh. "What's this, now?"

"I told you we needed sentries," Corban said.

Tisconum sneered at him. "Would they do any better as sentries than they did gathering wood?"

Corban laughed at that, which was entirely true. The women had stopped working on their wall, and were standing in a little group on the far side of the unlit hearth, watching. Off by the dead tree, even Ofra and the men had seen the newcomers.

These were not enemies, it seemed, although there were more of them than Tisconum's band. Three were older men, and the rest looked like their followers. Their hair was knotted high on their heads, gummed together with colored clay, and stuck with feathers, and the first two of them wore breastplates of white and purple beads in fine designs. They carried staffs clubbed at the top with gobbler tail feathers. They walked up from the creek bank onto the open ground at the edge of the village, ranged themselves nicely in rows, and waited.

Tisconum, gripping his staff, struggled to his feet. He swept a hand up over his head, where his hair was falling out of its bonds, and pressed the same palm to his naked chest. His face twisted. He stalked forward out of the shelter of the low wall, toward the newcomers.

"So!" he shouted. "You recognize me still! I know you—" He began to volley names, and with each name one or another of the older men before him stirred a little, struck. "Masito! Eskanto! Meeksanum!"

"Enough." The first of the elders stepped forward, his hand out. Tall, and taller by the height of his feathered headgear, he spoke in a loud declaiming voice. "We know you know who we are, Tisconum. We know also who your enemies are. We've come to—"

Standing behind Tisconum and a little to one side, Corban crossed his arms over his chest. The motion instantly drew everybody's eyes, as if he had suddenly popped up out of the earth, and the thunderous voice broke off, the big man goggling at him a moment. Behind him, among his followers, a murmur ran.

Tisconum said, "He'll be your enemy soon enough, Masito. And then he'll be your sachem."

Masito straightened up, frowning, and sneered down his nose at Tisconum. "We'll see. You cannot come here. You lost your place here, when you gave this village up to begin with."

"Bah," said Tisconum. "Nobody else is here. Everybody who has ever died here was of my lineage, and their spirits are all around us here, I tell you that, I can feel them. The huts and the hearths were all raised by hands of my lineage. Who else can live here but me?"

"He can't stay," one of the men behind Masito called. "If he's here when Ekkatsay comes—"

Corban said, "Ekkatsay is coming here?"

Masito stared at him again, his jaw dropping open; the man

behind him who had just spoken clapped one hand over his mouth. Tisconum swung around to glare at Corban, and faced Masito again, bristling.

"You can't throw me out. Over there—" he flung one long skinny arm out, pointing "—my birth-mate is buried over there. I belong here. I will stay. Him—" His arm suddenly twitched toward Corban, and his head split into a cackling laugh. "Throw him out. Try. Hah."

Masito glared at Corban and then at Tisconum. "You are ever unwise, Tisconum. We shall be back." He turned, erect and proud, and walked away through the midst of his followers, off down the riverbank again. The other newcomers turned to follow, each one pausing a moment to stare angrily at Tisconum and give Corban a brief intense look of fearful curiosity. Then they were going.

Tisconum sank down behind the wall. "You see," he said to Corban. "We should never have come down here."

"Well," Corban said. "I don't know about that." He stood watching the last of the other villagers go. Tisconum's people were all still standing around, doing nothing, their gazes on him. Corban turned and gave them each a hard look and the women went back to building their wall and the men started breaking dead limbs off the tree again in a sudden enormous flurry of work.

Tisconum fell asleep. The nest finished, the wood gathered, the other people came in around the fire. The darkness crept in around them on all sides. The girl Arl sank down beside Corban, who was sitting on his red and blue cloak with his back to the wall, considering this matter of Ekkatsay. The girl reached out one hand to touch the cloak.

"Do you want something to eat, Corban-ka?"

"Leave me alone, Arl. I'm thinking."

She sat still, patient, unoffended, unrebuffed, still touching his cloak. He could feel her gaze on him. His temper rose; it was hard to think with her there, like a rock in his eye. He wrenched his mind back on course. Ekkatsay was certainly coming here on some business of Miska's. His mind kept turning back to Masito and the other Turtle chiefs, with their feathered staffs, their ceremonial approach, their expectation of being heard.

Tisconum's band had brought deer meat with them from the Shad River and the women cooked it over the fire. The smell wakened Tisconum, who demanded to be fed. The older woman brought him the first pieces. A few minutes later Arl brought back a flat piece of bark with strips of meat on it, and set it down before Corban; her gaze searched his face. He was hungry and he ate, saying nothing to her. She was little more than a child, much younger than Epashti, an orphan; and he had seen how the other men were with her.

Night had come, the wind sweeping in off the bay tingling with salt, owls calling in the forest. Under the trees the fireflies began to twinkle, rising in flocks of little lights up into the dark blue air. Most of the people huddled closer to the fire but Tisconum went off into the darkness. Corban watched him go, knowing where he went, the old man's nightly round, circling the camp, setting up snares and traps and alarms all around the edge of it.

He tapped Arl on the hand that clutched his cloak. "Go bring me Ofra." The girl leapt up, her face shining, and ran to fetch Tisconum's warrior.

Ofra was a solid, square man, past his youth, with a hard jowly face, pitted cheeks, and narrow eyes; his hair was always tied back at the nape of his neck, like a woman's. He wasn't a Turtle but Corban had never heard where he did come from. When Arl brought him he stood in front of Corban, smiling and bobbing his head.

"Tell me what I can do for you, Corban-ka."

Corban said, "Sit down, for one thing. You hurt my neck, looking up at you."

Ofra sank down on his heels. "Whatever you say. Anything I can do to make you happy, Corban-ka, just mention it."

Corban said, "Well, I'm glad to hear that." He sat still a moment; he wished suddenly for a pipe, and some smoke, but of course Tisconum's band which had no gardens had no smoke either. He said,

"That, before, with Masito and the other Turtles—" He paused, wondering how to talk of this, his words uncertain. "What did it mean, the feathered staff, and how they came up, and just stood there?"

Ofra's shoulders twitched. "That they're chiefs, wanting to talk. No weapons. You can't fight. Not until you put the staff down." He watched Corban steadily, his sharp shrewd look the real Ofra, peering through the oily deference like some kind of shield.

"I see," Corban said. "Thank you. How well do you know the land around here?"

"Like the back of my hand, Corban-ka. Like the insides of my eyelids."

Corban grunted, half-amused. "How would somebody come down to the waterland from the Bear country, then?"

"Aha." Ofra smiled at him. "Somebody like Ekkatsay?"

Corban shrugged. "I went once by a way that led west from there. I remember, for a good day's walk after we left the shore, there were ponds and swamps, it was hard to get through, the trail wasn't good, and the water stank. Then we turned north into a long winding valley, and there was an old, deep trail that went by some big rocks."

Ofra chewed on his lip. "Yes. Brother Rocks, they're called." His eyes narrowed, his eyebrows curling in the struggle to remember. "You go between them, to go north."

"What about somebody coming from Ekkatsay's village?"

Ofra's brow smoothed, and he nodded. "Yes. He would come down from the north also, between the Brothers."

"Good," Corban said, although he saw Ofra obviously knew little more about the ground than he did. He said, "Around there, at the Brothers, that's where somebody coming down would likely stop overnight, wouldn't he—he wouldn't want to overnight in the swamps."

Ofra made an indefinite noise in his throat. His eyes were sharp black points in the meaty square of his face.

Corban said, "I want you to go down there."

Ofra said, "And do what?" His voice was weighted with doubts.

"Watch for Ekkatsay. See where he camps."

"How am I to send you word, from way over there?"

"When you see him, come back up the trail, I'll meet you."

Ofra thought this over a moment; Corban could see he was looking for an excuse to refuse. At last, he said, "What about Tisconum? I'll follow you, you know, anywhere, Corban-ka, but Tisconum, frankly—" He twirled his finger beside his ear.

Corban smiled widely at him. "Frankly, Ofra-ka-ka, you talk too much."

Ofra's face slumped. He lowered his hand to his knee. Corban said, "Can you find the Brother Rocks?"

"Yes," Ofra said, clipped.

"Then go down there, and watch for Ekkatsay, and see where he camps." Corban had travelled back part of the way from the long raid with Ekkatsay, and had seen how the Bear sachem made his camps; he liked comfort. "Near the water somewhere. In the open. He'll likely be there in a few days."

"Yes," Ofra said.

"Good," Corban said. "Thank you. Go."

Ofra slunk away, his head between his shoulders. Corban watched him wander off through the tight little nest of the camp. Only such a man would follow Tisconum now. Without someone to harry him along, he did nothing. Corban hoped he would at least get down to the Brother Rocks. He settled down, his chin on his fists, to think out how to get Tisconum and the others down there also; in the morning, he meant to go out to hunt for gobblers.

Ekkatsay had at first thought this was a great honor, going to the Turtle villages in Miska's name, but now he was finding it an increasing annoyance. He had brought three men of his own lodge, good companions who had plenty of smoke and stories, but Miska had sent Ako along also, a troublemaker, a friend of Ekkatsay's nephew Taksa; after the long raid Ako had gone off to join the Wolves and Ekkatsay thought well gone, but now here he was again.

Also: this was too large a group to travel fast and it had taken them three days already to get down to the Brothers. They were out of food with the evils of the swamp still before them. The warmth of the spring had brought out fogs of biting insects. Ahead of him lay still the matter of how to speak to Masito and the other Turtle sachems, which Miska had left for him to decide.

Then, he had thought that an honor, too. He had brought along his finest collar and belt, had imagined himself standing up splendidly before the awed Turtle chiefs. Nonetheless he had no idea what to say to them, and he was beginning to wonder if Miska believed he would fail, and give the Wolves the excuse to attack.

He walked around his camp once. They had set up on the shelving meadow above the little river, where an old beaver dam had made a pond, with a line of trees just behind to shelter them from the wind. The two women were building the fires smoky, to drive off the bugs. They would have to stay here for a day or two at least and collect some food. Fortunately there was plentiful sign of deer. He considered putting out a sentry but saw no reason: he was on Miska's business, and Masito never attacked anybody.

The sun was going down, and the other Bears were gathering inside the circle of the camp. The women brought out a basket of acorn meal and spitted the last of the meat to cook over the fire. Ekkatsay went in toward the fire, in among his friends, who murmured friendly greetings and shifted to make room for him.

Ako was still on his feet, strutted, setting himself apart from them, as if he were really a Wolf. When finally he sank down by the fire and took meat with them, the other men jabbed at him.

"So, I see your hair's still tied, Ako. I thought all you Wolves wore it loose."

Ako ignored them. He gnawed on a bone, the side of his head toward Ekkatsay.

Ekkatsay said, "They do that because of Miska. He was never bound. One of the many peculiar things about him." He stretched his legs out, wishing he were in his own lodge, where he could call for more robes to cushion the ground. "It will take Ako a while to grow Wolf hair, I think."

Everybody laughed but Ako, who sat straight as a birch, frowning, saying nothing.

Ekkatsay said, "Maybe you should think twice anyway. The Wolves did not win their great victory over the Sun people by themselves. Without the Bears, what could they have done?"

The others spoke out; this was an old song, and they all knew the words. "We did it all, if you ask me." "There were more of us than them, after all." "Nobody ever gives us any thanks." They bubbled up with tales of their deeds; the long raid was already almost a longer story. The pipes came out, and the smoke rose.

Through it all Ekkatsay watched Ako through narrowed eyes; he guessed Ako would take what he heard back to the Wolf village, when this chore was done. It was good to let Miska know that the Bears didn't think as much of him as some other people did. Miska wouldn't have sent Ekkatsay on this trip, if he didn't need his help. Nonetheless when he thought of facing Masito and the others his belly tightened.

"Ho," Ako said sharply, and pointed down toward the river.

Ekkatsay looked, and saw a line of people walking across the shallows below the beaver dam. They wore long cloaks, and feathers in their hair, and the first of them carried a long staff, topped with bobbing gobbler tail feathers.

"What's this?" He thought suddenly that Masito had come out to meet him, and a deep breath swelled him: this was an honor, surely, a sign that all this would go well after all. He got to his feet, waving to the other men to stand also. The women went into the back of the camp, and the men walked out to the open meadow, stood in a line facing the oncoming strangers.

Not all strangers. He gulped, and behind him one of the other men whispered, "Animal-Head."

This was not Masito. Stunned, Ekkatsay could do nothing, only stand there and watch as the people before him ranged themselves in a line facing his, and the man with the feathered staff stepped forward, and it was Tisconum.

Ekkatsay said, "I will not speak to you." It was all he could think of to say. His war club was back in the camp—none of the other men would have a weapon. He thought suddenly if he could lay hands on Tisconum, and take him to Miska, that would solve everything.

Tisconum stood stiff and straight before him, the staff in one hand, his face hollow as a skull, and his eyes glaring. "I will speak to you, Ekkatsay! You stand where you are and listen to me!"

Ekkatsay had his hand behind his back, and was trying to signal the other men. "Why should I listen to you? You don't even have a village anymore!"

"Ekkatsay." From behind Tisconum another man came forward, shorter than Tisconum, stocky, and his head shaggy and rough as a beast's. "Listen to me, then."

In the utter silence he was the center of everybody's looks. Ekkatsay clenched his fist behind his back. He was remembering this Animal-Head shaman walking up out of the wreckage of the Sun chief's camp, which he had somehow single-handedly destroyed; a name suddenly came into his mind. He said, "I have no fight with you, ma-Corban-ka."

The shocking pale eyes never wavered from him. The slow alien voice went on, picking words up like stones, and putting them down again in lines, and they all listened, silent.

"What has Miska sent you here to do? To start a war. Who will fight the war, Ekkatsay? You will, and your people. Haven't you seen how many Wolves have died for him? Do you want all you Bears to die for him too?"

Ekkatsay said, "Die for him, or die against him, as Tisconum will, there, soon enough." His mind flew toward Ako, behind him, surely remembering everything that happened here for Miska's ears.

"How could he fight without you? Too many of the Wolves have died. He needs you." Animal-Head leaned forward, and one hand rose, palm up, offering him something. "Go to Masito, and say, not, give in to Miska, but, let us join together and stand Miska down."

Behind Ekkatsay somebody began to whisper, and another Bear hushed him at once. Ekkatsay said, "Then certainly we would die." He thought suddenly of Miska, and his throat clenched; he remembered Miska's club, striking down Taksa.

"He has no fighters without you," Animal-Head said. "At least you could force him to talk."

"Talk!" Ekkatsay slashed his hand down. "That's all this is. Nobody can stand against Miska. Nobody can beat him. He can't die."

"Well," Animal-Head said mildly, "he hasn't died yet," and then, behind him, Tisconum erupted.

"Enough of this! Ekkatsay, you are Miska's thing, only, not a man! Not a sachem!" He strode forward, the feathered staff in his hand, and his eyes blazing. "I owe you nothing, evil man! I fling the staff down!" He cast the staff aside, and reaching under his long cloak he pulled out a knife and leapt at Ekkatsay.

Animal-Head bellowed; Ekkatsay staggered back, his bare hands raised against the knife, and tripped and fell. On the ground, he heard fighting, screaming, all around him, and then Tisconum was on him, a knee on his chest, crushing him down, the knife raised.

Animal-Head loomed behind him, and caught Tisconum's upraised arm and held it. The shaman was screaming volleys of words, furious, incomprehensible words. Ekkatsay gagged, choking, Tisconum's hand on his throat, Tisconum's knees on his chest, and the knife raised to kill him.

The shaman yanked Tisconum away bodily. Ekkatsay rolled over, sucking air, his head whirling, and lunged onto his feet.

"You held the feathered staff! You can't attack me—"

He stopped, looking down the shaft of the spear aimed at his chest. The man holding the other end of it smiled at him, narrow-eyed. Ekkatsay glanced quickly around.

The Turtles stood all around him, all carrying weapons, even the two women. He saw only one of his own men, held as he was at the point of a spear. The other Bears were nowhere. As he looked he saw the two Bear women sprinting away from the camp through the grass. He clenched his teeth, humiliated.

Tisconum strutted up toward him, grinning, although he was covered with dust. Then Animal-Head strode up, and knocked the spear down.

"What are you doing?" he shouted up into Tisconum's face. "You think this will help anything? Who will ever trust you again?" He turned toward Ekkatsay. "Go."

Ekkatsay roared, "He might as well have shit on the feathered staff!"

"Just get out," the shaman said. He pushed Ekkatsay roughly in the chest.

Back in the camp, suddenly, somebody let out a whoop. Ekkatsay wheeled. They were going into his packs. He gave a cry, and started that way, to save his belt and collar.

The other Bear said, "Ekkatsay. Come on." The Turtles around him were standing back, their weapons lowered; he turned, without waiting for his sachem, and trotted away across the meadow, heading up the well-worn trail toward the craggy rocks of the Brothers. Ekkatsay stood breathing heavily.

He said, again, "You dirt-eater, Tisconum."

"Go tell Miska all about it," the shaman said.

Tisconum said, "Maybe I won't let him." The Turtle sachem raised his knife, and Ekkatsay dodged a few steps away. Tisconum laughed. Ekkatsay turned, and grimly started off after the other Bear, going north.

Corban turned toward Tisconum, who was putting his knife away on his belt. "You are the most worthless fool on either side of the big water."

Tisconum shrugged one bony shoulder. He cast off the long ornamented deerskin cloak and the older woman came to get it. "I think you're the fool, Corban. Look, here—" He pointed toward the camp, and crowed with laughter, delighted. "I have won a great victory over Ekkatsay, and I have his belts to prove it!"

Corban glanced over his shoulder. The Turtles were riffling through the Bear camp, and Ofra had stood up, holding an ornate bead collar up over his head like a trophy. Corban swung back toward Tisconum.

"A great victory. They were unarmed and outnumbered." He put his hand on Tisconum's chest and thrust hard, knocking the Turtle sachem backward. "Nobody will ever let you talk under the feathered staff again, do you realize that? It's getting dark, let's get out of here before they come back."

Tisconum said, "They won't dare come back."

Corban grunted at him. He had worn a deerskin cloak also, to look like a Turtle chief; it was hot and he shrugged it off and flopped it over his shoulder. He looked up at the sky, turning red with the sunset. "I am leaving, Tisconum. You can come or not." He started back toward the ford.

Arl was quickly there at his side, her face shining. "You're right," she said. "What you said."

Corban said, "You would say that no matter what I did."

"You won't leave, will you?" she said.

"I want to be where Miska strikes," Corban said. "I think Tisconum just made that a little more certain."

He glanced back, and saw the others filing after him, carrying bundles of the Bear camp goods. Tisconum still stood there; Ofra had brought him Ekkatsay's collar, and he was putting it on. Finally he stooped and picked up the feathered staff and started after

Corban, strutting and parading with the staff. They crossed the ford and went off into the marshy land beyond.

⁂

Ekkatsay caught up with the rest of the Bears, all except Ako, and they went along quietly a while, until they came to the foot of the eastern Brother. The sun had gone down and in the gloomy twilight they found a place where the rock loomed up sheer above them, and made a camp there. One of the women had brought away the last of their food with her, and so they had something to eat.

They sat there in the dark, and one of the Bears said, "The Animal-Head cast a spell on us."

Ekkatsay said, "Tisconum is a dirt-eating skunk."

"But they wouldn't have done that to us, except the shaman cast a spell on us."

"Where is Ako?"

Somebody laughed. "He ran first. I haven't seen him since then."

Ekkatsay remembered his collar and belt and groaned. There was no use now going on to the Turtle villages on the bay; no one there would listen to him, after what had just happened. He imagined facing Miska and his insides turned to ice. He wasn't sure he wanted even to go to his home village now.

"He was right, though," said the man next to him, under his breath. "Miska only wants us to fight."

The others murmured, agreeing. Ekkatsay hunched his shoulders. They had to go home. Ako would tell Miska whatever Miska needed to know. He began to shape this a little; he said, "The Turtles by the bay have never hurt us anyway. We should go home, and let Miska fight them by himself." If Miska needed him, he might be willing to forget this whole matter here.

One of the other men whispered, "Let him fight the Animal-Head."

# CHAPTER TWENTY-FIVE

The lodges were empty, since Yoto died, with only Hasei in one, and the brothers Faskata and Toma in the other. Most of the older Wolf boys had been hunting and fighting with the men of the lodges for a while, and had gone on the long raid. So it surprised nobody when, early in the spring, Miska decided to bind up the hair of all the eligible boys in a single big ceremony.

The boys made themselves ready. In the Full Worm Moon, they went into the forest and built their own lodge there, and hunted together. While they were there the older men came and ate with them, shared smoke with them, and decided which lodges they would belong to. In older days they would have taught the boys how to make war clubs, and instructed them in the ways of the war band, but the boys already knew that now.

Three days before the dark of the moon, the older men left, and the boys shut the doors of the lodge behind them. They stopped eating. They sat in the lodge and sang, and beat drums. On the third day all the people came out of the village, and surrounded the boys' lodge and called them out.

As they pushed the door out, the women gathered around the opening, and as each boy crawled out they flogged him with sticks and branches. The boys struggled through, running even before they stood, and the crowd of women beat them until they were out of reach.

All the men stood around and watched, cheering and yelling, urging the boys on through the rain of blows. The boys tried to keep silent; even so now and then one yelped. Striped and bruised, one by one they escaped the thrashing of the women. One by one they ran into the village to the old oak tree, and there sat down in a circle. The men went around behind them and tied their hair up, and doing so named each one into his lodge. Then they all gathered around under the oak tree and feasted and danced; it was the first bursting season of the year and there was plenty to eat.

After their hair was tied up all the boys pulled the thongs out and shook their hair loose, like Miska's hair, so they looked no different than they had before the ceremony. Epashti, watching this, wondered what the ceremony meant. Maybe, she thought, they had to have it because what they did was so far from what they said they did.

She thought this had always been so, but everybody was so used to it, nobody noticed.

The baby squirmed in her arms and yawned. She was tiny, pale, not strong, her arms and legs like twigs. Ephasti kept her wrapped in the white deerskin that had swaddled Ahanton; she fed the baby all she could, her milk coming in strongly now that the spring was here, and the woods full of eggs and sweet young green shoots. Reluctant to put the baby down, she had not taken part in the beating of the boys, much as she wanted to give some of them a few good whacks, like her sister's son Raki.

Led by Eonta and Anapatha, the women had laid their sticks heavily on the boys. They all showed welts and blackening bruises. Watching Lopi strut around, Epashti saw the stripes on his shoulders; Anapatha's prize, he had drawn as many blows as anybody, especially from the younger women. Quietly Epashti sat down between two knobby roots of the oak tree and laid the child to her breast. Her son Kalu, tallest and strongest of the boys left unbound, raced up and down through the gathering of the people, whooping and leaping, the littler boys trailing him.

Just before sundown, one of the Bears who had come to live with them came into the gathering, out of breath, and filthy from hard travel.

It was the young man Ako, whom Sheanoy had given more than a favoring glance. Miska had sent him off to do something, which nobody had paid much attention to. Epashti glanced at

Eonta, sitting in the next lap of the tree, and saw the old woman had noticed him, her brow furrowed, puzzled also. Ako staggered up through the crowd of happy people, drawing everybody's eyes, and as the whole group fell still, he dropped down on his knees in front of Miska and clasped his hands up over his bowed head.

"What are you doing back here?" Miska said. He was sitting on the big stump before the fire, his pipe on his knee. His face was painted in Wolf marks for the ceremony and his eyes glittered out of a black mask.

"Kill me if I lie, ni-Miska-ka," Ako said. "We were set on. Tisconum betrayed us, he brought weapons under the feathered staff."

At that everybody pushed closer to hear, so that before Miska spoke there was a packed wall of bodies around him and Ako both. Epashti went up to the front of the crowd, holding the baby tight. She thought this would come down some way to Corban.

Miska said, "Where is Ekkatsay? Did you even get to the Turtle villages on the bay?"

Ako lifted his hands. "There were too many of them! And they had the shaman with them—Animal-Head." He paused, seeing them all around him watching. "They may have killed Ekkatsay."

The crowd let out a harsh gasp. Epashti slid her hand protectively around the baby's head. Across the open space between them, Miska turned his gaze to her, and met her eyes.

"Tisconum is treacherous, I knew that already. For that reason I will hunt him down. What's this about Corban?"

"He was with them." Ako's eyes glittered, and his mouth worked fast. "Maybe he was why they could strike us down. Maybe he used his powers." His gaze was fixed on Miska.

Everybody else had turned to look at Epashti, and Corban's name ran back and forth. Epashti thought she should have gone the other way. Then she felt someone brush against her, and started, and looked; Ahanton had come up beside her, and slid one arm around her waist.

Miska lowered his eyes to the Bear before him. "Corban has no spells. He has no power. We all know him better than you, and we know he is nothing, Ako. How many men did Tisconum have? Why couldn't you fight back?"

"I'm telling you—the shaman—" Ako stammered a little, and then bit his mouth shut. The crowd murmured, and somebody laughed.

Miska's voice went on, quiet. "What Wolf would run away from a Turtle? Even a Bear ought to be able to defend himself against a Turtle."

Ako shouted, "He cast a spell on me! My legs wouldn't work!"

"Except to run," Miska said. "Anybody can run from a Turtle."

Now everybody watching was beginning to laugh, and Ako hung his head down. Epashti felt sorry for him; she thought he would never be able to live in the Wolf village after this.

Miska said, "Ekkatsay didn't come back with you."

Ako said, looking at the ground, "No."

"At least you run fast, Ako."

The laughter swelled again. In the center of the crowd, Ako stood with head bent, looking straight down at the ground; Miska moved a little to one side, so that his shadow lay on him.

He said, "Ekkatsay was probably running too. Go back to your village, Ako. You'll find him there."

Ako straightened up, his eyes wide. "Should I bring him back?"

Miska shook his head. "No. We won't need Ekkatsay. We'll go after Tisconum ourselves, when the moon turns full."

At that, all around, the Wolves gave up a howl of excitement, all the new bound men with their flowing hair. Epashti started at the yell. She saw Lopi and her nephew Raki leaping and shrieking, one on either side of her, and then, in front of her, Kalu was leaping up and down and screaming too, his hair streaming free like theirs.

"I want to go! I want to go!" He rushed toward Miska, with Finn on his heels. "I want to go!"

Epashti clutched the baby tight, her gaze following her son, running so far out of her reach. The drums began to beat, pounding out the measures of the dance, and the men wheeled toward the fires. Miska stood still facing Ako, his hands on his hips. He spoke; in the din Epashti could not make out what he said, only saw his lips move, but she guessed at it, when Ako lowered his head again, and went off toward the gate.

The rest of the men were gathering around the fire. The women were drawing back, gathering their children, turning for home. Around the fire the stamp and lunge and howling of the dance began. Anapatha, big-bellied grandmother of half the village, turned and padded off toward her lodge. Eonta collected herself; Ehia brought her shawl.

The drums thundered in Epashti's ears, reminding her of the other drums, in that other place; she caught at some connection, just out of reach. Ahanton pulled on her sleeve.

"Let's go. Let's go." The girl's strange pale eyes were shadowy with memory. Epashti held her baby close against her. These girls at least would stay hers. She took Ahanton by the hand and went away to the shelter of the lodge.

Two days after the ceremony, Epashti went across the river by the float, to go to her new garden.

She had chosen this place because of the plants that grew there already, which meant it was a strong place. In the previous autumn, when she got back from the long raid, she had burnt over the dead stalks and leaves to make sure the spirits of the plants remained. It was on a slight slope above the river, much of it facing south. When she reached it, she sat down there for a while, as she always did, and looked around and listened.

Once some oak trees had grown here, but the women had girdled them, and then the boys had stripped off all but the stumps to feed the winter fires. She could see straight away to the river and the village, and through the village, every lodge was under her eyes, all the way to the gate. She thought about Miska, who had surely meant what had happened to Ekkatsay—maybe not exactly that, but something—as an excuse to attack Tisconum again.

Not Tisconum. It was Corban he was after now.

She had decided already that if he wanted her to go on his raid as the medicine woman, she would agree. That way she would see what happened. But her heart sank at what she thought would happen.

She got up, after a while, and hung the sleeping baby from a tree and went around the patch clearing away rocks. She had been picking up rocks all along, setting them in a wall along the side of her garden, but new ones came up whenever it rained. Under her feet the soil yielded, warm and deep, chunky with rotted leaves. She marked where the sun shone, how the daylight moved over the slope. Ahanton came up from the river, and Epashti pulled up a handful of grass and showed her daughter the pink and purple worms squirming out of the moist dirt clumped around the roots.

They worked all the rest of the day, moving stones, and making hills for the beans. The next morning, before dawn, they came back to the garden and Epashti planted her seeds, kept all through the Hunger Moon in a sealed pot in Eonta's compartment. She showed Ahanton how deep to put the seeds, using her finger to make the hole, one knuckle, two knuckle, three knuckle. She put her beans where the sun would be, and the squash behind that; and in the very back, where there was some shade all day, she planted four holes of the smoking leaf plant.

She sang while she did this, happy for the first time since Corban left. She sat in the garden afterward and fed the baby; Ahanton went off into the trees. Epashti told herself if Miska had his intentions, so did Corban. They had been set on this from the beginning, and without the Forest Woman to stop them, they would go to the death.

She looked out over the river flowing brown between its banks, the long lines of the float crisscrossing it, the children splashing in the shallows on the far side, and the disorderly sunlit bustle of the village on the bank. It seemed never to change, any of it. Yet it was always changing, always turning into something else.

Maybe she turned into someone else with it. Something Eonta had said once nudged her mind. The sun was high in the sky now. She got up and tied Corban's child to her back, and set off into the forest to look for mushrooms and eggs.

Ahanton waited in the trees until Epashti was gone. Out of her sleeve she took the pouch of maz seeds that Corban had found among the Sun people. Seeds filled it still, because she had picked them up when her father had cast them away. Now she went along through Epashti's garden, and in every hole where Epashti had planted a bean seed, Ahanton planted maz.

"I was there," Tisconum said, pointing to a boulder on the side of the pass opposite the burnt tree. "They came up from there—" He pointed to the west, the far side of the pass. "And from there." Swinging his arm toward the bulging rock behind the tree. Tisconum walked on into the saddle of the pass, looking west. "We had no chance."

Corban looked around at the broad bowl of the pass; he wondered how Miska had gotten down the face of the rock, saw a thread of a trail down one side, and thought, A sentry on top. He turned slowly, looking also at the high slope opposite, deep in flowering brambles. It looked impossible too. A sentry there too, high. That, he saw, was the trouble with passes. Glancing to the east, he saw the older woman, climbing the last steep way to the pass, her bundle on her back, and Arl trudging after her.

There was water up here somewhere, Tisconum had said. Under the burnt tree the ground was blackened and scattered with charred stones; they would likely want to make a camp there. But they should not. Everything in him itched to get out of here. He turned back toward Tisconum, who was still morosely wandering around the old battlefield.

"This is where they killed Palla, beat his head in like a rotten squash." The sachem walked with his head down, his arms cocked out, his back round.

Ofra and the other men were coming into sight on the trail below the pass. Corban walked over toward Tisconum. "We shouldn't stay here. This is a trap. All he has to do is surround us."

Tisconum said, "This is where he will come to attack us. This is where we have to fight him. And I will be readier than I was last time."

"He will be readier, too, and he knows this ground."

"I know what to do now," Tisconum said. "I will take his hair, this time."

"He knows you are a Turtle, that you will fight by drawing into your shell, and so he can come whenever he wants and try to get into your shell from any way, and now that you are set in this place he will try every way there is."

Tisconum lifted his eyebrows. "Where? I will put men at the top of the rock."

"Think of this the way he sees it. Where else can he come at you?"

The sachem's eyes wavered slightly. "I can't think his way. His way is evil, even to allow it in will rot me." He turned, starting away, toward the women now gathering under the burnt tree with their bundles. The last of the men were finally reaching the pass. Some had brought a few sticks of firewood. Supplying them up here would be a constant problem. Corban said, pitching his voice after Tisconum, "He probably knows already where you are."

Tisconum stopped, turned, caught again. "We just came here. Is he so magic?"

"No, but he's powerful over everybody, and you aren't. A powerful man hears everything, a powerless man has nothing but enemies. He will come another way. We have to be watching every other way. Or go somewhere else."

Tisconum took a step toward him, angry suddenly. "I am the sachem. I will decide what we should do." He pumped up his chest, sticking his jaw out. "Like down by the Brothers. Masito and those, they probably think much differently about me now, don't they?"

Corban said, "Likely they do, yes." He folded his arms over his chest.

Tisconum sneered at him. "I'll show you I know best. I will make a camp here, but one also on top of the rock. Up here we can watch for a long way. It will cost them to come at us. Few can defend against many. We will stay here. I like it here. That's what I'm saying to you." He turned and walked off toward the burnt tree.

Corban stayed where he was, morose. He saw Arl watching him from by the fire and turned his back. He wondered how many days it would take Miska to attack them. There had to be some way out of this. Later, just before sundown, he saw Tisconum going off to walk around the outside of the camp, building his shell, layer on layer.

He went in under the tree, over to the vertical surface of the great bulging rock, and sat down with his back to it. The men were sitting around the fire talking and picking ticks and lice out of each other's hair. The two women were tending the fire and cooking acorn cakes. Watching them, their quiet purpose, reminded him of Epashti; he fell to worrying about her and the baby, and about his other children. His thoughts pushed further back, to his wife Benna, and their children, and wondered what had become of them, scattered over the world. When Arl came over and sat down beside him, and slyly stretched her fingers out to touch his cloak, he almost slapped her hand away.

She saw his mood; she drew her hand back, but she didn't leave. Her eyes searched over his face. "Are you hungry?" Her first offer, always, to feed him.

He said, "Leave me alone, Arl."

She sat still, not moving, not talking, leaving him alone, but not. He turned his face away. The sudden impulse swept through him to hurt her, to see what would make her cry, what would drive her away forever. He clenched his fists against his thighs, his mind roiling, until the feeling passed. Night was on them. He got up and went around the foot of the rock, until he found the thin trace of a track going up, and climbed up to the top of the rock, to keep watch.

Ahanton shared the green bough ceremony with three other girls her age, two from Anapatha's lodge and one from Merada's. They went together into the new gardens, where all the ground smelled ripe with growing things, and their mothers and aunts brought green branches from the woods and each of the four girls made a lodge.

This was harder than Ahanton had imagined; the boughs bent too easily and also would not stay bent, so her framework was constantly coming apart. She began to wish she had helped Epashti more, and learned how to do this. Glancing over her shoulder, she saw the other girls had already raised their lodges, neat little mounds of leafy green in their mothers' gardens, and gone inside.

Her lodge fell apart again. Looking down at the mound of twigs and leaves she wondered if she could just crawl under it. No one was allowed to help her. She picked up the long boughs again and began again to force them into a dome shape, either end in the ground, and all bound together in the middle, but as she tried to hold the first and second boughs together they slithered out of her grip and fell on the ground.

Ahanton wanted to cry. The sun was going down and soon the old women would come, to do the next part of the ceremony, and they would see that something was wrong with her, and she could not become a woman. She thought of Epashti, who did such things as this every day without any fuss at all, her hands so sure and knowing.

The wind stung her damp cheek. Into her mind leapt the memory of her real mother. She remembered the pine tree, where she had dreamed of the serpent and the frog, and the cold night air, and the stars. She took her green boughs, and she heaped them around in a circle on the ground. She made no door. She climbed over the pile and sat down in the middle. As soon as she did, a cool calm fell over her.

In the blue evening, the old women came. They went from lodge to lodge, speaking through the door of each. They came to Ahanton's circle and stood, their faces seamed with uncertainty.

She said, "I am Ahanton. My lineage is the Frog. My signs are the pine tree and the river. Epashti is my guardian but not my mother. Miska is my father but not my guardian. I have said this, in this place, and it is true."

The women faced her; two of them hung back, reached out to one another and held each other's hands tight, but the third, Eonta, came forward to the wall of Ahanton's circle.

Eonta, everybody's grandmother but hers. The old woman's round face was serene, as if she had expected all this strangeness. She held out both hands, palms up, nuts on one, an egg on the other, and recited.

"We feed you, Ahanton, because you are one of us. We bless you because you are one of us. We ask your blessing because you are one of us."

Ahanton's chest swelled; she felt some power flowing into her, something passing between Eonta to her, from Eonta and all those before her; she could not look away from the old woman's eyes. "I give my blessing, because I am one of you. I am grateful for your blessing, because I am one of you. I eat, because I am one of you."

She took the nuts and egg, and the women went away. Night fell over her. She wished suddenly for the red and blue cloak, gone now, gone with Corban, wherever he was. She felt the tug of sleep but was afraid, for fear of dreaming, again, of the stake.

Then, in the dark, she heard a whisper. She lifted her head, startled. Someone was speaking her name, just the other side of her wall.

"Ahanton!"

"Yes," she said, puzzled, recognizing the voice. It was one of the younger women from Eonta's lodge.

"Please, Ahanton, give me your blessing for a baby."

She was silent a moment, unknowing what to do. What it meant. No one had told her anything about this. Then she said, "I bless you."

"Thank you." That woman went away.

But a few moments later there was another.

"Ahanton! Ahanton!"

"Yes."

"I want your blessing to get the man I want!"

She put her hand to her mouth to stop the laugh. She knew this woman too, of course, and longed to know what man she wanted. But she held her tongue. "I bless you."

So it went, on through the night, people creeping up to beg her blessing; she got very tired of it, and wanted to sleep, but at least she did not dream.

In the morning, Epashti came, and Ahanton made a way for her through the circle. Epashti had a smooth stick with her. "Do you know about this part?" she said.

Ahanton nodded, but she was afraid.

"Lie down, then, and spread open your legs."

Ahanton lay down; her thighs wanted to clench together, but she made them open. Epashti said, "From now on, you may go with a man. But you should be careful. Don't let in a man who is not clean and strong and upright." Cool and bony, her hand slipped between Ahanton's knees. "Don't let in a man who has no reverence for you, who wants only to use you." Ahanton shut her eyes, rigid, feeling the stick at her body's edge, almost in. "Don't let in a man whose babies you don't want."

The hand moved, sharp; she felt the stick glide into her and then a hard bright pain. The stick withdrew. Epashti sat back on her heels.

"Good." She wiped blood off the stick.

Ahanton sat up, with one hand brushing her hair back. "Is it over now?"

"Yes." Epashti threw one arm around her neck and hugged her. "Whatever you said last night, it was very strange. Merada has not stopped moaning. But Eonta is very pleased with you."

"Hunh," Ahanton said, surprised. She went to help Epashti work in her garden, where the first green shoots were appearing. That night, she slept in Epashti's compartment, as usual, in Eonta's lodge, and she dreamt that Epashti had broken her open, and that a river ran out of her, which flowed on ahead of her, on into the distance, on forever.

And she looked back over her shoulder, and behind her sat Eonta, and behind her, Eonta, and behind them another and another Eonta, the river flowing through all of them, out of the infinite past.

# CHAPTER TWENTY-SIX

In spite of what he had said, Miska did not go after Tisconum at once. He took the war band up to the Long Lakes for the spring hunting, leaving the women to their fields and their gossip and their little female rituals. The spring was very hot and the hunting went well, and the men came back with meat and hides, bear teeth and wolf teeth and other, rarer things, shells, horns, clear stones like little eyes, bits of mysterious rock.

The whole village celebrated the turning of the year, which was the time also that other villages often sent gifts to Miska. Miska gave all these gifts away, as always—the soft deerskins decorated with beadwork, the baskets and pots he gave to the women, and the war clubs and the armbands and breastplates he gave to the men. The food he gave to everybody, in one endless feast through the long day and the short night and the long day after. Then he gathered the war band, and he went east, toward Tisconum, going slowly, as if he were only hunting. But he sent Hasei out ahead of him, to find a way around the burnt tree pass, a way that would bring him into the pass from the east.

---

The day's heat bore down like a blast from the sky. Hasei tried to stay under the trees; he was working his way up a long sloping valley, where a creek ran. The trees clustered along it gave him shade almost all the way, but here and there their high sprawling canopies opened up and the sun got in and struck him. He was tired, and moving too slowly, and not caring too much, even, what Miska thought of that.

He stopped to wash his face in the creek, and sat there a moment, squatting on the bank, watching the water clear.

The creek ran over pebbles, streaming green weed into the current; stick-legged striders scooted along near the bank, where the water was quieter. Their feet made little dents on the water, like puddles of air. On the surface the clouds in the sky appeared, past the dark reflections of leaves, so that he saw everything at once, the sky, the water, the land underneath.

He thought, I will never get up, I will stay here.

He felt pressed down into the ground, under a huge darkness over him like an invisible web. He could not keep from thinking about Yoto, his brother, dead without revenge in the last raid. He had never felt as alone as this before. There was no one beside him now, no one to share meat with, or a pipe, or a word, no one to shield him from an enemy or a north wind. Even the sun-yellowed forest around him seemed far away now, beyond a grim surrounding layer of cold and death.

He pushed himself up and went on. Miska expected him to do this work, and he was nearly there now, although he was a day past when he should have been going back—Miska would be impatient. He pushed on up the valley, toward the burnt tree pass.

His mind sank down again under the gray murk of his grief. Yoto had foretold his own death, and Hasei thought over and over of that, how his brother had said, "We're all going to die, he'll kill us all, like this."

It would not be this time. Tisconum was a weakling. He had only a few followers.

Hasei trudged up through the trees, wishing he could get away from the memory of his brother's voice. Off to one side the sun glowed on the meadow, and a bird flew up; he saw the sun flash on its wings, and his mind rose with it. Fire-dappled feathers, he thought, walking. Fire-spangled feathers—

His foot touched the ground; something grabbed his ankle and whipped around and up. His feet went out from under him and he flew up, upside down in the air, caught by the ankle, hanging from the top of a young tree swaying wildly back and forth above him, turning and swinging him until his dizzy head whirled. He doubled up, grabbing for his trapped foot—for the snare line above it. Caught the line, a braided thong of rawhide, and groped at his belt for his knife.

His fingertips met air where the haft should have been, then the edge of the empty sheath. He did not look down, to see the knife lying on the ground under him. Hanging folded up in the air, he clutched for the tree above the line and could not reach it, and held onto the line itself instead. He couldn't get his weight off the rope. He began to gasp for breath, his back muscles aching, his arms burning with effort. His fingers tore at the loop around his ankle. His breath harsh in his ears, swinging and swaying back and forth, he picked desperately at the noose and couldn't get even a grip on it.

He lost his hold, fell down straight again, bobbing and swinging back and forth in the air. He felt his strength running out of him like an upended bucket. With a great gulp of air, he doubled up again, drove his body upward toward his snared ankle, and struggled again uselessly with the thong, tightening and tightening steadily under his weight. His strength was giving out. His fingers slipped off the thong again, and he gave up, let himself fall, and dangled down.

From the height of the ridge, Corban saw the great burst of birds scatter up from the trees, in the valley below. He went down the steep grassy slope, sliding some of the way on his backside. Where the hill broke off in a sheer drop he crept down the side of the rock hand over hand and cut across a long sliding apron of smaller stones toward the valley floor, all the little stones and earth slipping away in showers under his feet, moving the hillside down.

He reached the swampy edge of the meadow and circled it to the dry land. The birds were still racketting up over the trees along the creek. He went out through the meadow, watching with half his attention for signs of deer. Before he even reached the line of trees, he saw something big was caught in one of Tisconum's snares. When he came in under the trees, he knew it was a man, and when he went up to the edge of the trail he realized it was Hasei.

His belly clenched. A ripple of fear went down his spine. He turned quickly and looked all around, backed up out of the trees to look away south down the valley, seeing nothing unsual, no signs of any big group of men coming toward him. Quickly he went back in to deal with Hasei.

The Wolf poet was hanging upside down from a sapling snare, caught by one leg, the other hanging off at an angle, bent at the knee. His eyes were closed and he was breathing hard. Corban drew his knife. He remembered that this was Epashti's brother; he thought of what Hasei had said that one time, about words.

If they came this way, he thought, that was bad, there would be no escape for Tisconum and his people. He had to kill Hasei, or they were all finished.

He went over to the sapling, found the end of the snare line, and cut it. The snare jerked loose, dumping Hasei facedown on the ground. Corban squatted down beside his head, his knife in his hand. Hasei was not moving, his ragged breathing catching in sobs and gasps, but his eyes opened, glistening in a mask of dust, looking at the knife blade inches from his face.

Corban said, "Is she alive?"

"She lives." Hasei's voice croaked like an old door.

"The—the baby?"

"The baby lives."

Corban groaned; he wiped his hand over his face. He stuck the knife into his belt sheath. He put one hand on Hasei's head and pushed him down again, to show he could, and stood up, and went away up through the trees.

---

He went to Tisconum, in the new camp in the pass, and said, "I found signs of Miska's scouts in the valley back east of here. Fresh signs. They're looking to circle around behind us."

The sachem was sitting under the burnt tree, half-asleep in the sun. He did not sit up. He smiled serenely at Corban under his drawn black brows. "I told you he would come here. You were wrong, you see."

Corban looked around the camp. As usual the women had laid it out very roughly, using stones and clumps of brushy branches to make a circle around the fire. Nobody else was there, not even Arl. He sank down on his heels, facing Tisconum. His red and blue cloak was tied around his waist, and he pulled up one corner to wipe the sweat off his face.

"Yes, but he knows we're here. Which is why he's coming. You're not as good a prophet as you think."

"We've only been here since midsummer," Tisconum said. "How does he know we're here?"

"Because he knows you," Corban said.

"Well, anyway, I know him, too. I'll be more ready this time." Tisconum straightened, swinging his gaze around the pass, remembering the old battle, Corban knew, figuring out how to have won that old battle. "I am sachem here. I have the men out hunting for meat for us, and the women looking for food on the ground, as they do. The spring is still running well here. We can stay here for a long while."

"Until we all die," Corban said.

Tisconum laughed, his face clear and bright as a sunny sky. "Or they do." He reached out and clapped Corban on the shoulder. "Will it be you who gets him, Corban-ka? What an honor that would be! People all over the world would talk of that around campfires until the last generations of men."

Corban said, "I hadn't thought of it that way."

"Here they come," Tisconum said. "See what Ofra says." He nodded down the western slope.

Ofra and the other men were climbing into the pass, carrying a deer slung on a pole, three struggling with the pole and Ofra pushing on the deer itself. They looked tired but as they came into the pass they began to sing and wave their arms. "We have meat!"

"Great hunter—" Ofra wasted no breath in extra words. "Meat! Meat!" He gave up trying to help and plodded along behind the others.

Tisconum flung his arms up. "Good. We'll eat."

The men hauled the carcass into the camp, and stood around bragging about how mightily they had killed it, the most ferocious deer ever, and them almost bare-handed. Corban went around toward Ofra, who was standing with one foot on the carcass declaiming louder than anybody else.

"I found signs of the Wolves, in the valley east of here," Corban said.

Aiming his words at everybody, Ofra shouted, "We struck him down! Down!" His voice wavered; he lowered his gaze to Corban. "Where?"

"In the valley down at the foot of the trail."

Ofra stepped back; the other men were gathering around the deer, to break it up. Ofra wiped one hand across his forehead, his mouth loose. He gave Corban a black look for bringing him this news.

"What does he say?" He jerked his head toward Tisconum.

"What he usually says. He's all ready to die, and the rest of us with him."

"I'm not ready to die yet," Ofra said.

"Maybe we won't have to," Corban said.

"We have to get out of here."

"I doubt we can move Tisconum. And here at least we know he's coming. We know where he's going to be. We turned things on him once before, maybe we can do it again."

Ofra gave him a suspicious look. "That was luck, and you know it. And that was Ekkatsay."

A hoarse yell jerked them both around toward the western side of the pass again, where the trail came up. The women were climbing the last steep slope there, bent down under baskets on their shoulders. As they walked, the first of them, the old woman who tended Tisconum, was shouting and pointing back behind them. Corban went out onto the broad saddle of the pass to see.

From here he looked out over the broad varied green of the trees on the lower slopes, into the next valley. At the far end of the valley, the late sunlight glinted on the water of a pond. From somewhere around there, near the pond, a thick stream of brown smoke was climbing into the air.

He grunted. Tisconum was beside him, one hand to shield his eyes from the slanting sun, staring toward the smoke. "What's that?"

"Announcing his presence," Corban said. "Are you listening to me yet?"

Ofra came up to join them, saw the smoke, and muttered something under his breath. "He does that to make us run," Tisconum said. "Like flushing deer."

Corban kicked savagely at the ground, scuffed and broken from people walking back and forth over it. He said, "He's giving you something to look at. Which means he's doing something somewhere else."

Ofra rubbed his hands together, squinting at the sun. "Maybe he is flushing deer. This deer thinks we have enough daylight left to get pretty far away."

Corban shook his head. "Only until the next time."

He looked into the camp; the men were sitting close around the fire, talking, their hands idle, and the women were cutting up the deer meat to cook. Their tiny fire made no smoke. The first aroma of cooking deer meat reached his nose. They could break this camp in a few moments and be gone before the meat was cool. Perversely he resented that, their lack of weight, as if Miska could blow them away with a puff of his breath.

He turned to Tisconum. "How did he beat you the last time?"

Tisconum blinked at him, his jaws working. "He won't do the same thing again."

"Why not?"

The Turtle sachem's eyes narrowed. Finally he turned and looked around the saddle of the pass.

"He came from there." He pointed up at the top of the rock. "If he comes that way again, I will be up there first." He chuckled. "Then I will be over him, and looking down."

Corban glanced at Ofra's heavy face, still gnawed with worry, and turned back to Tisconum. "How did he get up on the rock?"

"There must be some trail up from the back, somehow."

"Find this end of it," Corban said. "Make sure you watch it. Where else did he attack you from?"

"Up from the west, as you would expect, a big rush up into the pass. That kept us all looking that way, we never saw the ones coming over the rock." Tisconum waved one hand toward the broad rise into the pass from the west. "And—" He took a step forward suddenly, remembering, his eyes going to the far side of the pass. "There were men with bows. Up there. I don't know how." He jabbed with his chin toward the slope.

Corban twisted to look where he was pointing. In the late light the far slope looked sheer as a cliff. Thick brush shrouded the lower half; knee-high wiry trees grew from the rubble of collapsed rock at its foot.

He said, "I'll go there." He nodded in the other direction, up at the rock bulging above the burnt tree and their camp. "You should get there now."

Tisconum grunted at him, his hands on his hips. "Not yet.

He's not that close yet." He waved at the smoke in the valley. "See how far."

"He's not there," Corban said, clipped. "He's anywhere but there. Likely right now he's waiting down in that valley to the east, to pick off any of us who try to run from his smoke." Ofra twitched, his eyes white. Corban went on, speaking to Tisconum. "Go up on the rock. Take everybody else up there with you." He turned to Ofra. "You come with me."

Ofra's jaws moved, as if he were chewing. He said, "Where?"

"We're going to find a way up onto that slope."

"It's getting dark. We can do it in the morning. Smell the meat. I'm hungry." Ofra's head bobbed, his hands rising, pleading. "He won't come at night, will he?"

Corban said, "Go get some of the meat and some water and come after me. Hurry up." He walked toward the opposite slope, looking for a way to scale it.

As he crossed the saddle of the pass, he noticed the air around him turning pale and pink, like blood in water. He stopped and looked around. The sun was setting, flowing its long red light across the whole sky, soft ribbons of color that brightened before his eyes to a fierce orange, streaked with glistening gold, as if some baleful fire burned in the west, swelling unstoppably toward him. A shiver went through him, in spite of the heat.

The red light faded. He stood at the foot of the rocky slope, looking up, and saw no path. The twilight was creeping up out of the valley, a wind rising with it, warm and moist. He worked his way through the thick thorny brush along the foot of the slope, watching for any seam, any handhold he could use to climb. Through some wispy branches he saw a tilted ledge of rock over his head, and scrambled up over loose shale and brambles toward it, groping with his toes for footholds.

Ofra came grunting and moaning along after him, a hide sack slung over his shoulder. Corban squirmed up onto the ledge and stood, and worked his way along the sharply tilted rock. The ledge rose steadily higher, angling back across the face of the hill; when he looked down over his shoulder he saw only the thick tops of the trees between him and the camp. Brushy stems and grass sprouted from the slope beside him. Ofra still followed in spite of his grumbling.

The ledge narrowed until he could slide only the edges of his feet along it, leaning against the slope to stay on. Then through the soles of his shoes he felt the narrow rim of stone vanish entirely. Ahead, twenty feet away in the twilight, he could see a thick green patch of brush that seemed level, but between him and it was only a stretch of open slope so sheer nothing grew on it but a single wiry little shrub.

He looked up; the slope overhead bent out slightly over him, impossible. With one foot he groped forward along the ledge, feeling for the seam of it, a continuing thread. Peering through the gathering dark he thought he could see where it went on, like a stripe across the slope. He took a deep breath and went straight out along it, scrabbled and shambled along the steep pathless slope, grabbing with the edges of his feet, his toes, his hands, clawing at the brittle slippery stony earth. Sliding down, he lunged sideways, throwing his body onward, got hold of a thorny bramble with an outstretched arm, and heaved himself into the green clog.

His chest hit level ground. He crawled in through the brush onto a ledge that widened out like a shelf, tilting up at the far end but with space enough for several people inside the fringing brush. He stood, looking down over the whole pass, the path coming up from the east, the broad saddle below the rock, everything now within reach of his sling.

From the ledge where he stood, a trail went on, a dent across the upper slope, but this was good enough. He turned to see Ofra poised at the far side of the sheer slope, his face wiggling with doubt.

"Throw me the sack," Corban called. "Keep your head up."

Ofra pitched the sack toward him, and he caught it and set it down against the back wall of the ledge. Seeing a little coil in the dust he stooped and picked it up. It was a bowstring. The Wolves had been here first but he had found it too. Maybe they had even come down by the easier trail. He dusted his hands off, pleased.

Ofra came up beside him, panting. He said, "If I hadn't seen you do that I would never have done that." He lowered the pack to the ledge. Behind, in the half-dark, Arl stood on the far side of the gap in the trail, looking sadly at them across the sheer plunge.

Corban spread out his cloak and sat on it, his back to the warm rocky earth behind him, and opened the pack and found the round skin of water. Ofra was still on his feet, watching Arl. "Go back!" He waved his arms at her. "It's too dangerous."

Corban ate meat. In the deep sky overhead the stars were pricking through, raining down their unreadable messages. He licked his fingers. Then Ofra shouted, and there was a rattle of stones and dirt and suddenly a small, light, smelly body careened over the brush and landed on Corban.

"Yow," he said, and pushed her off. She laughed. He had never heard her laugh before. She settled down next to him, and her fingers stole toward the red and blue cloak. He gave her some meat, to keep her busy, and they all settled down to wait.

---

He dozed, comfortable, the others on either side of him, waking often. Halfway through the night he came awake as if for the rest of his life. The blue glory of the sky spread over him, all stars. Somewhere below him an owl hooted its soft, explosive call. He sat thinking of what was to come. He had to die sometime anyway, he thought, but he wanted to take Miska along. If he could take Miska, he would gladly die.

Off through the pass, he could just see the moon lipping up above the horizon, a bulbous yellow glob, its forerunning light blotting out the eastern stars. He listened for the owl to hoot again. Away to the west, a wolf howled, maybe far away enough and westerly enough to be a real wolf. The hot summery night wind grazed his cheek like a moist caress.

Arl and Ofra slumped against him, one on either side, sleeping like lumps. He edged out from between them and went around the ledge, gathering up stones for his sling.

The moon climbed across the sky, washing out the stars as it passed, its crooked shape filmy with stray light. Corban heard the owl again, moving through the trees in the eastern throat of the pass. Then toward dawn, he heard another owl hoot, this one the wrong kind.

He turned, stooping, and touched Ofra's shoulder. The other man came swiftly awake; Corban on all fours led him up toward the front of the ledge, pushing into the heavy thorny brush. Then somebody shrieked, across the way, and somewhere off at the top of the rock, in the trees beyond, people started to yell.

Ofra grabbed Corban's arm. They crouched in the brush, listening, and Ofra said, "We came up here for nothing."

He made to stand up, and Corban caught him by the shoulder and pushed him down. Ofra said, "They're fighting over there, way over there, we should—"

"Shhh," Corban said.

The shrieks and screams were all coming from the far side of the pass, but looking through the screen of brush in front of him he could see into the eastern slope of the pass, and something was moving down there. He pulled his sling free from his belt. "Here they come."

"What?"

Corban stood up, to his waist in low brush, fitting a stone to his sling. The trail up from the east lay open before him, bathed in the first watery light of day. Along it half a dozen men were running, two with bows in their hands, heading up the open ground just below the saddle of the pass.

They saw him as soon as he saw them; but he had the stone fitted and the sling whirling, and they were right below him. His first strike took the leader off his feet, and the others scattered back, looking for cover on the bare slope. Ofra bellowed. He started hurling rocks down, bounding around the ledge to find more, prying chunks out of the hillside.

Corban said, "Watch for arrows." He stepped back, looking for more shot, and found Arl at his elbow, her arms cradling a heap of stones. He fit another to the sling. Ofra shouted, "Watch out," and they all ducked down into the brush.

An arrow slithered past them. Corban straightened up, saw the bowman crouching behind a thin shield of grass, and slung a stone at him; another arrow sailed up from below, and he moved around, wading hip-deep in the brush, trying to fix where the other shooter was. Almost directly below, in the pass, the man he had struck first was staggering up onto his feet, his arm hanging useless. Corban saw it was the boy Lopi. He could still hear people screaming, off on the height above the pass, beyond the rock, in the trees back there. He fired a stone at Lopi, not to hit him, but to get him moving.

Then from the ridge beyond the rock there came a tremendous crash, like the hillside falling. The day was breaking, white sky spreading up out of the east in veils of milky light. Corban strained to see through the dusk. He thought the line of trees behind the rock had changed—he thought he saw a cloud of dust flying up, way over there. Then Ofra was yelling, "They're going! They're running!"

Corban straightened. Lopi, clutching his bad arm, had reached the other Wolves in the eastern shoulder of the pass; with him in their midst they were rushing off down the trail, out of sight into the trees below. Ofra whooped; he threw curses and insults after them, and Arl, beside him, cried out the same words in a higher voice. Corban turned toward the rock.

The light of the sun was streaming into the sky, flooding the high ground of the pass. Across the pass, Tisconum ran up onto the top of the great rock, his arms high, and began to dance.

His voice shrilled out, high and fierce. "I beat him! I have beaten Miska!" He kicked his feet up, and pumped his arms, his knees flying, his elbows out, and the rest of his band came up from the woods beyond the rock and danced with him.

Ofra yelled, "You couldn't have done it without us," and waved his arms. "Hey! Over here!" Nobody paid any attention. Corban rolled his sling around his belt again, and went back along the ledge, looking for an easier way down.

Corban went around the pass, looking for bodies, and found none. There was a slick of blood on the ground where Lopi had fallen, and in a stand of grass he found a broken bow. A yell brought him around to see Tisconum and the others, rushing down the thread of the trail along the side of the rock.

Whooping and leaping, they bounded down into the saddle of the pass. Tisconum broke into his dance again, his arms over his head.

"I have done it. I have beaten Miska."

Corban went toward him; the others were still rushing around, hugging each other and cheering. Tisconum swung toward Corban, broadly smiling.

"He was coming up the back path, and we cast them down! You should have seen how they looked! They fell backward, they ran like deer. Then we threw rocks, and we broke down trees, and piled them all down into the path, so nobody can ever get up there again."

Corban said, "How many did you kill? Did you kill Miska?"

The Turtle sachem shrugged. "Who knows? Better he's alive, and knows I beat him."

"You say you clogged the path—did you go down it? Did you see any bodies?"

"I threw trees down on him. I hope he's alive! I have beaten him, Corban-ka. With your help." Tisconum suddenly flung one arm around Corban's neck and kicked out in another little dance.

Corban gripped the other man's arm and flung it off. "What are you doing? Did you leave a sentry? Get somebody up there! Do you think a few trees will stop him?"

Tisconum whirled away, flapping his hands at him, dismissing him. Corban backed up quickly, looking up at the ragged upthrusting rock, jutting up against the sky like a forehead. He cast a quick look around, seeing the others still laughing and dancing, or by the fire looking for something to eat, or gone across the pass to make water.

His lungs swelled. He bellowed, "Get somebody up there now, Tisconum!" He started toward the way up the rock, and as he did, the first bowman appeared on the top of it.

He screamed, wheeling around. Out in the middle of everything, Tisconum kicked in his jig, and an arrow whined down and took him through the throat, in one side and out the other.

Corban yelled again, and ran. Ofra and Arl were under the burnt tree and he ran by them and caught her arm as he went and dragged her along. "Run! Run!" He hustled her along toward the western pass, where the brush was higher.

He twisted to look over his shoulder, running, and saw Tisconum's band behind him, scattering over the pass, and the arrows showering down on them. He pushed Arl ahead of him, into deep grass, and then under a thorny bush.

Ofra plunged in behind them. "They came back," he said, his eyes round.

"Miska never gives up," Corban said. Through the brush he looked back into the pass.

On top of the rock men were milling around, but not shooting anymore. In the pass no one moved. Corban's belly clenched. He gripped Arl's arm still, and he looked once into her face, her wide frightened eyes, her lips trembling, and turned to Ofra.

"Go. Take her and go. That way—" He pointed west. "Get as far as you can. Don't let them take you alive."

Ofra swallowed once, his meaty face grim, and without a word started off, crouching, fighting his way through the brush. Arl said, "What about you?"

"I'm going to kill Miska," Corban said. "Go." When she hesitated, he pushed her. "Go!" And she went.

He waited a moment hiding in the dense thicket. The Wolves were coming down into the pass now, moving around it, pulling arrows from bodies. He heard their voices rise, light, unconcerned, and he saw Miska.

The Wolf stood beneath the burnt tree, his back to Corban. His long hair shagged down his back; he had his war club in his hand. Corban unknotted his red and blue cloak, which would only get in the way, and left it behind.

He crept off through the thicket, trying to get as close to Miska as he could. The other Wolves were scattered off across the saddle of the pass, still recovering their arrows and taking trophies from the bodies. Miska shouted, and several people answered from different sides. They were looking for somebody and Corban guessed who it was. Crawling on his belly under the prickly brush, he got behind some rocks and moved in. He drew his knife out of his belt.

Miska called again; he turned slightly around, more toward Corban, his head down, his face smeared with black paint. Corban broke out of the brush and charged him.

He took three steps to reach him, and that was enough for Miska. The sachem whirled and stooped and got one arm up, and as the knife swept down Corban's forearm struck Miska's. The knife flew out of his hands. Corban plunged headlong into Miska, trying to get both hands on the Wolf 's neck.

They went down, thrashing and rolling, and then suddenly the other men surrounded them; hands gripped Corban from behind and dragged him up, and he coiled his body up and kicked out but someone else gripped his wrist and twisted his arm around.

Hasei shouted in his ear, "I have him! I have him!"

Corban stopped struggling; Hasei's arm was around his neck, half-choking him, and his left arm was crooked up tight behind his back. Miska rose up before him, covered with dust. The black paint made his face hideous. Through the dirt and the black his eyes glittered with satisfaction, and he smiled.

He said, "He didn't get away after all. Tie him up." He reached out with one hand and flicked his fingers at Corban's beard. "For your sister's sake, I would have let you go, Corban."

Corban said, "You liar. It's for my sister's sake you're going to kill me."

Miska's eyes narrowed, red-rimmed, angry. "Take him away before I do it here."

Corban let Hasei pull him off around the rock toward the burnt tree. The Wolf poet avoided his eyes and neither of them said anything. With a hand on his shoulder Hasei made him sit down and then tied his hands and his ankles, and tied the end of the rope to the tree trunk.

He went away; Corban sat staring away into the air, trying to collect himself. Abruptly Hasei was back. He had the red and blue cloak, and he stooped and laid it down around Corban, not over him, but around him, like a little wall. His gaze was steadily elsewhere. Corban said nothing to him, and Hasei went away with his head bowed.

Corban thought of the tinderbox; he thought maybe he could cut the rope with the hard edge of the fire box. He groped around with his hands, and felt around the cloak to the corner, where he kept the tinderbox tied in a knot.

It was gone. The knot was open, the creases still deep in the cloth. He sat back against the rock, frowning.

It had been an easy fight, with no deaths, and only a few wounds. The worst was Lopi's broken arm, which Epashti fit together again and plastered with wet knitbone leaves and tied that to a stick. The whole time she said nothing. The Wolves were gathered under the burnt tree, eating what was left of the Turtles' food, and laughing and talking over the fight, making fun of the Turtles, and building up big stories of their own deeds.

Miska, she saw, was exuberant; he walked up and down through the camp, basking in their shouts of praise, their howling of his name, over and over. This was his victory feast, she thought, This is what he wants.

When she had done everything for the Wolves, she went around to the side of the rock, where Corban was tied up.

He saw her, and his face brightened, like the sun coming out. She sat down next to him and tears squirted out of her eyes and she put her hands over her face.

"Don't cry," he said. "Don't cry, Epashti."

Lowering her hands, she turned to him; his face was bruised, and she washed him, and put salve on him, all the while crying. He watched her face steadily. He did not seem afraid.

He said, "Where is the baby?"

She swiped the back of her hand over her eyes. "At home. With Ahanton."

"Ahanton," he said, and looked away, and she knew it still hurt him that Ahanton had cast him out.

She said, "She's a girl. She has eyes like yours."

He faced her again. "Good. Name her Mav, for my sister."

"Corban—"

"And find my tinderbox. Somebody's taken it. I don't want Miska to have it."

"I'll look for it," she said.

She gave him water to drink, holding the gourd to his lips, and then sat there, her hands useless in her lap. "I can't do any more than this."

"I know," he said.

"Lopi is there, see. Watching us."

His gaze flickered past her and returned to her face. "I see him." He smiled again, caressing her face with his gaze. "I'm glad you came."

"If you escape they'll only hunt you down again."

"I know," he said. Then he said something in his own gibberish, of which she picked out only her name.

But she understood. She began to cry again. She laid her cheek against his, the rough hairy scarred animal face, and whispered, "I love you too, Corban."

---

She could not find the tinderbox. But when at twilight she went off along the side of the rock, to relieve herself in private, she found Corban's knife, lying under a dusty thornbush.

The blade was still warm from the sun. Impulsively she laid her cheek against it. Then she put it away in her clothes, out of sight of Miska.

## CHAPTER TWENTY-SEVEN

Ahanton was taking the baby Blessing to Sheanoy, as always, in the morning, to be suckled, when she heard shouting outside the longhouse. She turned around toward the noise; the door of Sheanoy's compartment burst open, and Epashti's sister came running out.

"Don't you hear that? The men are back!" Sheanoy ran nimble as a deer down the center of the lodge to the door.

Ahanton hauled the baby up against her shoulder, wanting to put her down. Blessing was getting bigger and heavier, and she squirmed more, harder to hold. Still, if the men were back, then her mother was back. The jubilant yelling grew steadily louder. She went out of the lodge into the morning sunlight.

All the women were rushing up through the village toward the gate. Old Lasicka, the cripple, hobbled along leaning on his stick, howling in a breathless voice. She followed him up to the gate, where the people were gathered so thick she could not make her way through them.

If Epashti came back, she would take the baby, of course, which Ahanton longed for. But there was much new that Epashti would see and thinking of that Ahanton swallowed down a little feathery apprehension. She wiggled in through the crowd of women around the gate, their bouyant voices crisscrossing over her head.

"Look! There they are—Miska! Ha-Tonga-Miska!" That was Sheanoy, waving one arm over her head. "Raki! Where is my Raki?"

Other voices. "I see Hasei!" "There is Faskata—" "There is Lopi!" "Lopi! But he's hurt!"

Then, someone said, "They have Corban."

Their shrill clamor of voices fell still. Abruptly there was space all around Ahanton, and at the center of a hole in the people, she felt them, all around her, turn and stare. For a moment she could not lift her gaze from the ground. Her ears heated. Her scalp itched. Finally she made herself look up, because the men were almost in the gate.

First came Miska, his war club in his hand, and his face Wolf-painted, walking all by himself, and ignoring the screams and cheers of the women. The sight of him made her happy; she took a step toward him, her father, the greatest man in the world, and he saw her and smiled.

In the gate the women were all cheering and screaming. On the path behind Miska the whole pack of the men bounded and leapt, shouting and howling and waving their arms. As the women called names, and the men answered, the cheers grew steadily louder, because all had come back.

In the midst of this celebration, the baby forgotten in her arms, Ahanton looked up at Miska's face and her whole heart went to him; she wanted to do anything he asked. But then she saw Corban.

He was walking alone in the middle of them, the red and blue cloak around his waist as always, his hands tied behind his back. She stepped back out of the way, out of Miska's reach, the baby heavy in her arms. They went on by her, through the gate, and she stood rigid, clutching the baby, watching him, until Epashti who had walked last of them all came to her, and took the baby, and freed her at last from the weight.

---

Finn said, "That's my—"

Beside him in the crush of people watching and cheering, Kalu thrust out his arm out, and clapped his hand over his little brother's mouth.

⸻

They took Corban down to the oak tree and tied him to the huge boll, among the knobby roots all worn from people sitting on them. The women came and built the fire, and made ready for the feast of welcoming the men back, which would start at sundown. At sundown, also, they would see about Corban.

⸻

Eonta said, "You must have come here as soon as you reached the village, even before you saw me."

Epashti had put the baby into a cradleboard, so she could carry her on her back; she was unused to the weight and her face was sweating, her hair sticky. She said, "I had to get out of there. If I stay there I will go and sit down by him, and they will have to stake me, too."

Eonta gave her a sharp look. "Then best you came here." She trudged the last few steps to the garden, and stood, breathing hard, and looking around.

On the level meadows beyond the river the first-year gardens were sprouting up in shoots and tufts of green, glowing in the sun. The two women had come across the river on the float, old Eonta moaning and complaining at the effort, Epashti insistent. "There is something you must see."

"You chose a good place," Eonta said. She stooped and pulled up a piece of grass sprouting in the dark soil of the garden and ate it, her eyes roving over the new plants.

Epashti waited for her grandmother to notice what was here. When she had gone off with the men the first sprouts had only just been rising up through the mounds of earth. Ahanton had tended them, and now the garden stood high and green in the broad sunlight, raising its leaves like the palms of hands up toward the sky.

Eonta said, "It seems very good. We had some good rain while you were gone, and she has turned up the ground around them well."

Then she frowned, straining her old eyes, and Epashti stood and waited patiently.

"She's let enemy plants take hold."

"Come here," Epashti said, and led her grandmother up through the mounds of bean plants, where already the tiny new buds were growing, the tips swelling into white flower. In the center of each mound, like a post, stood a tall stem that opened into two long narrow leaves, with another tight-curled leaf coming up from the center. She reached in across the beans, murmuring an apology, as she did, for getting into their sunlight, and picked off a bit of the stem-post leaf.

She tasted it; she held it out to Eonta. The taste made her mouth water. She thought of the warm sweet cakes of maz, that first surprising bite, how it satisfied her stomach. The plants were growing tall and strong; some already had two pairs of leaves, one above the other.

Eonta was gumming at the strand of leaf. She shook her head slightly. "It's too faint for me." She turned her gaze fretfully on the post-stem plant. "I don't believe it," she said.

Epashti swallowed the leaf. In the lingering flavor she felt the power of the plant, and she stepped away from it, shaking her dress as she did, to throw off anything that might cling to her.

She said, "I know what this is, Grandmother. This is a plant I saw in the west, which gives so much fruit, and the fruit is strong to eat and can be kept, I think, a long time." She paused, considering the way through this. "Corban had some seed with him. I thought he had taken it, when he left."

Eonta said, "Ahanton tended this field."

Epashti said, "Ahanton planted it. And she has green hands, look. But Corban brought it."

Eonta lifted her eyes, looking across the river, and her mouth pursed, her cheeks sucked hollow. Epashti spoke to the doubtful trouble on her face. "He came from the sky to help us. And we are going to kill him. Miska will make us kill him, for his sake, not ours."

The old woman's voice came up from some deep place, ragged. "What has he brought us? Are you sure this is good? Did this plant grow free, there, in the west?"

"No, the women cared for it like children. The seed came from somewhere else; the longnoses brought it." Epashti shook her head. "That's where it gets crooked. I'm not sure that it is good, for all the good it is. Corban thought it was a great danger. The longnoses brought it. Who knows what comes with it?"

Eonta was still looking across the river, her hands together before her, her face slumped in thought. She turned toward Epashti. "When do they gather the fruit?"

"While we were there," Epashti said, "in the Sturgeon Moon, they were gathering it in then." Her head bobbed with a sudden new rush of understanding. "That was why the longnoses came then. To steal the maz. They sowed the maz among the people, and then they reaped it from them, they were gardening the people, the way the people gardened the maz."

Eonta's mouth quirked. Her eyes were moist. Epashti knew she could hardly see the river, much less the village, and yet she had lived here most of her life, she had everything in her mind, more clearly than anybody else.

Her head bobbed. She had decided. She turned her filmy rheumy eyes back to Epashti.

Eonta said, "Here, we are the masters. Let it grow." She started off toward the river, groping carefully with her feet through Epashti's garden. "Now take me back home."

Ahanton went to her father, in his lodge. She went in through the big door, the one he used, which no one else was supposed to use.

Miska was sitting at the far end, doing something with his hands. She went up through the quiet and empty gloom. The rows of beaded belts hanging from the ceiling were like an upside-down forest. She wanted to put her hands up and stroke them as she passed. She went up before him and sat down.

Miska said, "Look at this," and held out his hand to her.

He had Corban's fire box. Her mouth went dry. She imagined it growing and growing in his hand, hot and fiery, until the whole world burst into flame.

She blinked, startled at her own thought. Cautiously she reached out and touched the little box. The sides were squashed in and she tried uselessly to straighten them. She said, "He pushes out the sides sometimes." He put something into it, too, she remembered, but she was unsure what.

"I can't make it work," Miska said, sounding angry, and put his thumb to the part on the side that moved, and moved it.

A spark leapt from it; in the dark of the lodge it seemed like a flying chip of the sun. But it made no lasting fire. Miska growled under his breath, and tossed the box aside.

"What, now?" he said to her, already angry.

She faced him, hard as he was. "You must not do this to him, Father-ka."

"Humph," he said, and slashed one hand across the space between them. "I don't want to hear it. You can't change my mind, Ahanton. You are my child, the heart of my heart, but this is between him and me."

"If you kill him, I have dreamed it, we will all die," she said. This was not so; she had not dreamt any such thing, but she thought he might believe her.

Miska only laughed at her. "Everybody will die, little one. And I have to kill Corban. This even you must see, this is from the beginning, not mine to change. He is Malsum, I am Kooska, I must kill him, or he will kill me."

She gulped, the whole thing twisting, the lie she had told him come back on her in the old story, twisted. His face was like stone to her. She dared not speak against the hard ready anger in his eyes. She turned around and walked out of the lodge, and this time, going, she went out the little door, which the ordinary people used.

Usually the Wolves' prisoners shared in the feast with them, but they had no stomach to share meat with Corban, and Miska would not have let them anyway. It was a quiet feast, not even much dancing. Then when the sun was going down they brought Corban to the stake.

Hasei brought him, and Faskata, one on either side of him. Miska went up before him. Everybody stood watching, not knowing what to do; Miska was changing the way this was done, as he changed everything, at his whim, to his own purposes. They were supposed to welcome Corban, and speak kindly to him, but Miska went up to him, and suddenly slapped him on the face.

Corban's head turned. He said, "You are brave, Miska. My hands are tied."

Miska ignored him. He tore at the red and blue cloak, unbound it from Corban's waist, and flung it into the fire, now a broad bed of coals close behind the stake. "Tie him."

The two men pulled Corban to the stake, tied his hands to it, and forced him down on his knees.

"There was no death," Epashti called. "Nobody died. We don't need a life."

Her voice rang loud in the quiet. Eonta gripped her arm and pulled her back. "Be still, girl. See how he is."

Miska turned, and glared at her; she felt the force of his gaze like a blow behind the eyes, like the heat off a fire greater than the coals. He swung toward Corban again and said, "Yoto died. We need a life for Yoto."

Kneeling on the ground, Corban had set himself, his jaw locked, and his body coiled tight. Faskata had stepped aside, but Hasei still stood beside the stake. Epashti was holding her breath; she put her hand to her belt, where she had Corban's knife sheathed, although she knew she could not use it.

Hasei said, "Yoto was my brother. I won't take Corban's life for his. Corban saved me once, I won't touch him."

A sigh went up from the people watching. Beside Epashti, Eonta lifted her head, looking all around.

Miska gave Hasei a stare that drove the other man back several steps, and lowered his gaze to Corban, looking back at him. Miska turned and glared at them all, his eyes yellow in the fireshine.

"He attacked me. He will attack me again, if I let him go on living. I have to kill him, or he will kill me."

Lopi stepped up out of the crowd, his arm still bound against his side; his face was flaming with rage. "He owes me something—" He lifted his long-bladed flint knife and slashed it down across Corban's arm.

Corban recoiled against the rope, his head flinging back; blood sprayed across the dust. Epashti felt, around her, the whole people move suddenly forward, drawn toward the blood, toward the stake and the pain and the death. She glanced at the fire, to see if anyone was picking up coals.

What she saw made her gasp, and she reached out and took Eonta's arm and pulled her. "Look."

Eonta blinked her filmy eyes at the fire. Corban's red and blue cloak lay in the fire bed, but it was not burning. All around it and above it and below it the flames leapt and the coals glowed red but the cloak lay at the center, untouched.

Epashti thought, She is too blind—she will not see. Eonta took a step forward, peering toward the fire, and around them, following her, again everybody moved in closer toward the stake. Still in front of everybody, Miska wheeled, his arms up.

"Ask him—Corban, you will try to kill me again, won't you?"

Inside the closing ring of the people, Corban had pulled himself up again, the blood sheeting down his arm. He shouted back, "Give me the chance, Miska, and I will."

The crowd exhaled a high, breathless gasp. Eonta gave one look into Corban's face, and turned to Epashti, who bit her lip, and wished he had no tongue. Without a word the old woman took Corban's knife from Epashti's belt. Shapeless in her long dress, her gray hair wisping from her head, she swung forward again, as Miska cried out again, "You hear him! We have to kill him!"

Eonta took two steps toward Miska, as he raised his arms up, calling to them all, and drove the knife in under his arm, into his side between his ribs, deep into his body.

Everybody saw. A cry of horror went up from the people, and then silence fell over them.

He had never taken a wound before; he would never take another. Eonta still stood beside him, her hands at her sides, offered unresisting to his rage, but he paid no heed to her. He laid his hand over the spurting hole in his side, the fury draining out of his face, so that he looked younger, and he began to sing his death song.

At that the others all wailed again, because they saw he would die, that even he would die. They closed in around him, sinking down on the ground around him, weeping and stretching their arms toward him, afraid to touch him.

After that first cry, they hushed, to hear him.

He sang how he had become sachem, how alone he had driven out Corban's people, when they gathered on the island in the salt. He told of all the other victories since then, how he had defeated everybody he had fought, Bears and Muskrats and Turtles, east and west, north and south. He sang of the long raid itself, when he had brought down the arrogance of the Sun chief and avenged the Wolves' ancient hurt. He sang how he had brought wealth to his people and made them great.

He swayed, and sank down on his knees in their midst, the

women crying, the men whispering oaths and pleading with him, creeping as close as they dared, reaching out to touch the dribbles of blood that ran down from him.

"Don't try to find another one like me," he said to them. "I am alone. I was a leader to you but I was also a scourge on you. I fed you but I ate you up. I did nothing for any of you, all I did was only for myself, to win the one I loved, and in the end, I lost her."

He sang of her, how she had touched him, and guided him, and in the end deserted him. Slumped down, the life all but gone, he said, "I would give everything to see her again. Just to see her again." All his people huddled around him, terrified, knowing he was not only dying but also abandoning them, and he lowered his head, his eyes shuttering.

Then he raised his eyes again, fixing on the air above him. He cried out. "Oh, but she comes. She comes! See—see where she comes—" His face shone, beautiful in the sun like the face of an untouched child, and he struggled his hand up, to reach into the empty air. He sagged down, and his eyes closed, and he was dead.

They sat around him a long while, no one daring to speak or move, stunned at what had happened. Even Eonta was still, her eyes shut, hardly breathing. Then Epashti rose up onto her feet. Her face glistened with tears, and in one hand she took a knife, and in the other she took a pot. She knelt down by him, and began to cut his body, to put it in the pot, and one by one, weeping, the other women came to help her, to keep all of him that they could.

# CHAPTER TWENTY-EIGHT

While the people were still pressed tight around Miska, Epashti unbound Corban from the stake; she could not rouse him, and the deep wound on his arm was still bleeding. Half-carrying him, half-pulling, she got him away from the oak tree and the fire and up the slope toward his own little lodge, near the gate.

Behind her she could hear the drumming begin. The deep throaty mournful howling of the men. The sound raised the hair on her head; she knew they would kill Corban if they found him. She was afraid also they would try to kill Eonta. The old woman was trudging up the slope past her, going to her lodge, and when she got there she went in and shut the door. The other women were disappearing behind their doors also, and the village was all but empty, except for the clamor around the oak tree.

The night had fallen when Epashti finally struggled him into his lodge. The wound in his arm hung open like a mouth. In the dark of the little round lodge she laid him down, plastered the wound shut and wrapped it in herbs. She worked by touch, whispering all the while, telling her hands what to do, asking for help, explaining what she did. She felt the pain in him like a stinging in her fingertips. The stinging slowly faded, and his body relaxed and he slept, still breathing hard. She laid her hand on his great shaggy head and tried to settle her mind, to fit everything that had happened into some sense. Then the door of the lodge pushed open.

She shrank back, getting between him and the door, groping around her for a weapon. In the dark she could see only the shape pushing in, and she said sharply, "Stop there!"

Sheanoy said, "It's me, sister. Eonta has sent me. The old women are holding council and they want you to come to her hearth."

"I can't leave him," Epashti said, her hands on Corban. "If they find him—"

"We will be only in Eonta's lodge, very close. You must come. No one will hurt him." Sheanoy, in the dark, was hunched like an elder, her voice deeper, softer than usual. "He is one of us now. He was staked, and he was brave, and so now he is one of us. Come to Eonta, she needs you."

Sheanoy crept back out of the doorway, leaving behind a faint pale circle in the gloom. Epashti smoothed her hand down Corban's shoulder and went after her.

Outside, in the clear night air, the howling and moaning of the men sounded louder, wilder, higher-pitched, keen-edged. From the oak tree came the jumpy glow of the fire, throwing shadows up through the village like glimpses of things running. All the women had drawn back into the homes, taking their children with them. Following Sheanoy, Epashti went the few steps over to Eonta's lodge, and went in.

Most of the people were hidden inside, behind their doors, but the hearths along the center of the lodge gave some light, and she picked her way down the whole lodge to Eonta's hearth, at the far end. Sheanoy went ahead of her most of the way, but coming to her own place, turned aside there. Epashti was surprised, she had expected her sister to be one of this council, and for a moment her steps lagged.

Ahead of her, at Eonta's hearth, Anapatha looked up. "Come along!" She waved her hand. Epashti quickened her steps.

She took her place at the foot of the fire circle, across from Eonta, at its head. Anapatha sat on her left, and old Merada on her right. Eonta had wrapped a soft deerskin over her, covering her head, so that only her eyes showed. She held the deerskin closed with one hand; Epashti saw that her hand now missed two of the fingers, up to the first joint, the new wounds burnt black to seal them. Eonta had done it herself; she had not asked for help, she would not ask for help now.

Epashti said, even so, "Grandmother, do you need me?"

Eonta lifted her head, and let the shawl open a little. Epashti caught her breath. The old woman's face was sunken down, her eyes watering, her lips loose, her skin pallid; she looked near to dying.

Eonta said, "I am beyond needing you, my dear one. I am going to the Old Wolf, wherever she is, and to whatever she wills for me, after I killed the greatest of her children. I am only one old woman, and the people need you."

She stopped to breathe, her mouth ajar, and Anapatha leaned forward to speak.

"We have asked you here, Epashti, to speak for us to the men. You are the medicine woman. They know you well, better than they know any of us. You've healed them and mended them. You went on the long raid. They'll heed you."

Outside, down by the oak tree, there was a great bellow, like the wind out of a cave, a hot gust rising. All the women turned their heads that way, to hear it.

Anapatha faced the fire again. She said, "They will tear the village to pieces. We have to have a sachem. But who? Miska had no nephew. He had no sisters. All his lineage died with him."

Merada said, "The men will choose."

There was a little silence, when Eonta should have spoken. All looked at her but she was silent under the shroud of the deerskin, and the trail of talk seemed to end.

"No," Epashti said suddenly, into the silence. "The men won't choose. They'll only follow whoever is strongest."

Now they all turned toward her, pushing on. "Who is strongest?" said Ahanton.

"Lopi," said Anapatha, and, "Hasei," said Epashti, and, "Faskata," said Merada, all at once.

Surprised, they looked at each other, their faces ruddy in the little light, and Epashti said, "Yes. That's the first trouble. There are many strong ones, and if they fight, what will become of us? We must get them out of the village before they start."

"Then what?" Anapatha said. "Are we to be a village without men?"

"We are a village without men half the year anyway," Epashti said. "We do well enough, better even, maybe, when they're gone. But we must have a leader, for all of us. We will choose the sachem. We will send them away, and once they are gone, we will decide."

"Why should they agree to that?" Anapatha frowned, the shadows over her face like Wolf paint, her eyes glittering. "They are stronger than we are, and they have their own ways. Why shouldn't they just do as they please?"

"They will agree," Epashti said, "because we must all agree, or there is no village."

Merada spoke suddenly. "If they leave the village now, they will consent later."

Epashti's gaze went from one to the other of them, Anapatha and Merada, and Eonta at last, sitting across the fire, covered in her shawl. Her grandmother said nothing, but she nodded. Her hand clutched at the shawl, the lopped fingers twitching. Epashti imagined her hurt, and longed to take her hurt away, and knew Eonta would not allow it.

There was this other thing first. She said, "Then I will go, and tell the men they must leave."

Anapatha looked at her, her eyebrows arched, and old Merada said, "You are brave, girl."

"Stay here," Epashti said. "Watch over Corban." Rising, she went out of the lodge.

Hasei sat before the fire, staring into the flames, his mind too stuffed with memories to let him think. Miska's face floated always before his eyes; he saw the Wolf in the crackling flames, he expected with every breath to hear him, giving orders, giving praises. Miska was there still, although now his bones lay in the empty pot; Hasei felt him watching, as if his looks were darts coming out of the empty air.

He glanced at the pot. Miska was inside him too. He put a hand on his chest, glorified, unworthy, shaken by the enormous burden of it, to bear Miska in his heart forever now.

He rocked back and forth, his arms around his knees. The other men leapt and danced around the fire, letting out howls and wails. Even Lopi, with his bad arm, bounded up and cried out and flung himself down on the ground. Faskata had gashed his chest with his knife, over and over, until his body was streaming blood. Other men were gashing their cheeks, their arms.

Miska would not have let this happen, what weakened them all. What they did for his sake meant that he was gone.

What else could they do? He remembered Miska's words: There will be no other like me. I am alone.

There was no one to follow him, no sister-son, no heir. Miska had always been apart, first set against them, outcast and despised, and then up above them, their master. Hasei gripped his hair in his hands, his head full of agonies.

He felt the rough hair under his hands, long and shaggy, as Miska had worn it. He gripped his hair back with both hands. He would bind his hair, from now on, if he could not follow Miska anymore. The best part of his life was gone. He shut his eyes, heartsore. The dancing and shouting around the fire smothered out the rest of the world. Lopi's voice rose above the others in a shrill shriek.

Lopi might be the new sachem, he thought, and that made him want to spit into the fire. He hated Lopi.

He wasn't sure why he hated Lopi, except that he thought Lopi hated him. He had not noticed it before but he was sure now. He reached out and touched his war club, lying on the ground next to him, glad to have it near him.

Faskata came up toward him, glittering with blood. He sank down on his heels next to Hasei. "What are we going to do?"

"Do you want to be sachem?" Hasei asked him.

"Me? Never." Absently Faskata wiped his bloody hand over his face, already shining with blood. "What about you?"

Hasei pulled his hair back again. "Tie up my hair for me."

The other man blinked at him, his mouth opening to argue. Then his head swiveled, looking off, and Hasei followed his gaze.

Down through the flickering shadowy darkness, Epashti was walking toward the fire.

Hasei stood up; he thought suddenly of Corban, and looked at the stake and for the first time realized he was gone. The other men were still dancing. He got into Epashti's way, so that she had to stop before she reached them.

"Don't come down here, my sister, you see how it goes."

"I have to speak to them," Epashti said.

"It was a woman who killed Miska."

"I have word of that, too," Epashti said; her eyes were steady, her face calm. He remembered her quietly closing up a wound in his leg, giving him something to drink for a headache, laying her hands on him, healing him. Respectful, he stepped back, out of her way.

Faskata shouted. The other men broke off the dance and turned around toward Epashti. In the abrupt silence she stood small before them. She spoke in a clear, little voice.

"I am come from your mothers, with this requirement. You have to go out into the forest. This is the women's place, not yours. You have to leave the village."

The men closed in around her, all shouting at once, leaderless. "Why should we go?" "Make us go!" "We won't go!" Lopi's voice rose suddenly. "Where is the old woman who murdered Miska-ka?"

Hasei stepped forward quickly, in between his sister and the men, and put his arms out to shield her. "Leave her alone! Are you all crazy?"

Lopi wheeled around in front of him, his broken arm crooked

against his chest. His face twisted. His eyes were red and swollen. "Why should we leave the village, when they killed him?" He swung his good hand up to push Hasei out of the way, and the other men let out a hoarse yell.

"Let the women repay us what they have stolen from us!"

Hasei stood fast, his arms spread, protecting his sister and all the other women. He spoke straight to Lopi. "You speak of repaying. Epashti healed you. Will you harm her in return? Is that how you repay?" He held Lopi's eyes with his gaze; something else came to him, a longer view. "Eonta struck, but the knife was from the sky. Miska brought this on himself. He brought it on all of us."

The younger man's face settled, still warped with his grief. His eyes shone with pain. The others had fallen still, listening.

Lopi swung back toward Hasei, angry. "Who are you to command me?"

Hasei grunted at him. "Keep your head. We have to talk, don't we?" He lifted his voice, speaking to them all now, making use of the quiet. "Miska said there would be no other of him, but we need a sachem. The women are right. We should take this out into the forest, get off by ourselves, and settle things."

Lopi still stood in front of him, his face grooved and old. "Who gave you the big feather?"

Faskata spoke up, just behind Hasei's shoulder. "You have a bad arm, boy, you should watch what fights you pick. Let's go, we don't want the women in the way anyhow."

All at once, the men began to move, trudging on up the slope toward the gate. Some started howling again, and singing of Miska. Hasei let them all go off without him, and when they had gone he turned to Epashti, behind him.

"Thank you," she said. "Mind you, Eonta is dying. She avenges herself on herself. She will follow Miska by the morning."

"Hunh," he said.

"Go find us a sachem," she said, "if you can," and turned, and went back to her lodge.

⁂

She went to the lodge only to see Corban, but when she came in, Ahanton was there.

Epashti opened her arms, and the child came into her embrace. Her face against Epashti's was sleek with tears. She said, "I have dreamt this, all along, that Mother Eonta would kill my father, but I never understood." She began to cry in slow terrible sobs. Epashti held her, but she said nothing; she knew no words to cast over this. Ahanton slept, and Epashti laid her down next to Corban.

He was fiery hot. When she put her hand on his face she gasped. She found a gourd of water, and washed his face; he lay under her touch like a corpse.

"Sister." It was Sheanoy, whispering at the door. "They want you again."

"I have to stay with him," she said, her back to the call.

"Sister," Sheanoy said, again, patient. "They need you."

She knew this was true. She laid her hands on Corban and felt no answer in him.

"Sister."

"I'm coming," she said. "I'm coming."

⁂

Ahanton dreamed, and it was her last dream.

She saw Corban beside her in the lodge, dying. His soul left his body and ran away, looking like him, only paler. He ran into the forest, and she followed. He ran into the center of the forest, and climbed the great tree there, and she climbed the tree after him.

The tree turned thinner and smaller, until it was only a slender stick with branches on either side, and she climbed up and up, after

Corban far ahead. She was running, her feet bounding from branch to branch, and looking down she saw the tree had become the serpent's back.

The back of the serpent, glittering like fire, like beds of vermillion embers, wound away from her across the blue-black night, and far ahead, she saw something bright. She ran toward it, following Corban, and ahead of her, she saw a woman made of sunlight.

It was her mother. She sat in the coil of the serpent's body, with its head above her, its glowing eyes like hot stones.

Ahanton ran hard to catch up with Corban before he reached her; she knew when he came to his sister that everything would be over. She ran hard, but she seemed to go nowhere. Her legs were mired. She dragged herself closer, and as she came closer she saw other people coming to her mother, other shadowy souls, and as each reached her Mav tore him to pieces and gave the pieces to the serpent.

Her father had just appeared before her, and Mav tore him like the others, as if he were nothing to her, and she gave what remained to the serpent.

Now Corban had reached her and stood by her shoulder. Ahanton gave a loud cry, and hurled herself forward to reach her mother before she tore him to bits.

Her mother lifted her gaze from the work of her hands. Her eyes were pools of stars.

"I want him back," Ahanton said. "I have lost my first father, let me not lose this one."

"Lucky the one who has two fathers." Mav said. "But I do not give Corban to the serpent. He goes with me into the sunrise."

Then Ahanton looked, and she saw the light all around her, boiling and blazing with the coming of the sun; the whole arc of the world was on fire with it. She turned and fixed her gaze on Corban, longing for him, afraid.

Corban smiled at her. "I will go back. I love them, and I haven't seen my baby yet. I will go back."

Her mother said, "I will give him back to you, Ahanton, but you must give me something in return."

Ahanton faced her mother. Everything in her seemed spinning and whirling, and yet she was as still as ice. Mav said, "What will you give me?"

Ahanton held still a moment, but she knew at once the only thing she had that was great enough to ransom him. She said, "I will give you my dreams. It's no use to know anyway."

"I accept," her mother said, and to Corban: "Go."

Corban turned and reached out his hand to Ahanton. The child blinked. Suddenly there was ordinary daylight around her, and she was lying on the floor of the lodge next to him, and he was lying beside her, smiling at her, his eyes open, shining, alive. She put her hand to his face.

"Were you there?" she said, stupidly.

"I'm here now," he said.

"I'll find Epashti," she said, and leapt up, and went out into the sunshine.

The women were all coming out of their lodges. Sheanoy passed her with the baby Blessing slung on her hip, and then Epashti, red-eyed and worn, her forehead fretted. Ahanton went up and caught her by the arm.

"Corban is alive. He's better."

Epashti looked toward the lodge and her face eased. She said, "Something good must happen, somehow, now and then. You will be an herbwoman someday, Ahanton."

"I gave up my dreams, though," Ahanton said.

Epashti touched her face. "You are greater than your dreams, daughter." But she did not go to the lodge, to see Corban; she went on after Sheanoy and the other women.

Ahanton went beside her. "What is it?"

"The men have called us to the gate." Epashti's voice was weary. "We have been talking all night. No one has slept. I have been everybody's enemy, and everybody's friend, at least once. Come with me."

Ahanton slipped her hand into Epashti's. "Have you thought of what to do?"

"I don't know," Epashti said. "I think it may only cause more trouble." She wiped her eyes, her mouth drooping. "But Corban is better?"

"Yes," Ahanton said. "He's awake and he talked to me." She leaned against Epashti, wanting to be comforted. They went by Miska's lodge, and she pulled her gaze away and her eyes began to burn and she scrubbed at them with her fist. Torn to nothing, all his glory; what had it meant, then? They went to the gate, where the rest of the village was crowded around, the women and children on the inside, and the men on the outside.

Hasei and Lopi stood side by side in front of the rest of the men, who were bunched together on the path. Ahanton squeezed in past Epashti, to see better. She thought Lopi looked older and not so handsome anymore. A little pang of loss bit her, as if his beauty had belonged to her also.

His bad arm was bound against his chest. He wore his hair long and down, as they all had done, while Miska led them. But now Hasei wore his hair bound in a tight knot at the nape of his neck, and so did many of the men behind him.

Anapatha, in the center of the gate, said, "What are you doing back here, when we sent you away?"

"This is our village," Hasei said. "We will come in if we want."

"Have you decided on a sachem for us?"

Lopi cast a quick hard look toward Hasei, and stepped forward. "No, we can't decide. You must choose. Me or Hasei. Make a choice, now, and we will come into the village and live here, as we are supposed to."

A growl went through the men, and their feet shifted. They

glared around at each other like fighters to the death. Anapatha turned around, her gaze sweeping the crowded women, and at the desperate look on her face Epashti stepped forward. When she appeared, all the other people hushed, their gazes on her.

Ahanton went along behind her, holding on to her skirt. Epashti looked tired, old, bent, and strong, like an old bent tree, that nothing could move.

She said, "We have decided already. We will have Hasei for our sachem."

Hasei stood motionless. Lopi bellowed, furious, and his good arm flexed. The little pack of men on the path behind him let out a single many-voiced yell. Half of them were rejoicing, their arms waving in the air; the other half stamped the ground in disgust. Half leapt to one side and half to the other, and they stood scowling at each other.

Epashti said, "And we will have Lopi for our war chief."

Before her, the young man straightened, and his fist drooped. He turned toward her, scowling. "What does that mean?"

"We will see what it means," Hasei said, "but I will agree to it anyway. And you, Lopi-ka, you agree to it also."

Lopi twitched; his good hand went to the arm bound against his side. Faskata stood behind him, between him and the waiting, watching men. Lopi's face smoothed out suddenly, as if he sucked all his feelings inside.

He said, "I agree. We shall see what it means."

"Now we'll go into the village," Hasei said, and the women stepped aside, to let them in the gate.

Ahanton got the baby from Sheanoy and took her back to the little round lodge. When she got there Corban was sitting in the sun in front of the lodge, his beard all tangled in with his hair, and his red and blue cloak spread under him.

She sat down next to him; she wondered if he knew of the dream. It seemed impossible he did not know. She watched him through the corner of her eye for signs of that.

He saw nothing save the baby. He reached out and took her, careful of his bad arm, lifting her into his lap. She gurgled at him. Still small, she was lively, sat up at once on his knees, and reached out with a soft intense bleat to take hold of his beard.

Ahanton said, "They have made Hasei the new sachem."

"Good," Corban said, and his head bobbed. "More poets should be kings." He laughed down at the baby's face, and she laughed back.

Ahanton said, "They have made Lopi something else, I did not understand it. Something about the war band."

Corban grunted. He put his hands out, and the baby took hold of them and tried to draw herself to her feet.

Ahanton said, "Is that good?"

"Good," Corban said. "What word is that? People made it. Nothing people make is all the way good." He shot her a quick look from under his brows. "If they make it what they all want, it will work. Not for long."

Ahanton said, "But how can we be sure of it, then? What will happen to us?"

Corban lowered his hands, the baby clinging to his fingers. "Why are you asking me this? How can I know what hasn't happened yet? Who is sure of anything, and also right? Would it make it so different if you knew what was to happen? Tell me what's important. What is her name? And where is Epashti?"

Ahanton said, "Her name is Blessing. Epashti is down by the oak tree, making sure the men don't fight."

"Aha." Corban bent over the baby. "That's very apt." He bent to the baby again, laughing. Ahanton sat back in the soft warmth of the sun and shut her eyes and slept.